Exhibit 'A'

The Kairos Clock

By

Arnie Exel.

Copyright © Arnie Exel 2024

Second Edition.   First published 2014

The author asserts the moral right under the Copyright, Designs and Patents Act 1988 to be identified as the author of this work.

All Rights reserved. No part of this publication may be reproduced, stored in a retrieval system or transmitted, in any form or by any means without the prior written consent of the author, nor be otherwise circulated in any form of binding or cover other than that which it is published and without a similar condition being imposed on the subsequent purchaser.

Dedication.

I dedicate this book to my lovely partner, Cher, for her amazing patience, her help, understanding, encouragement and extraordinary kind heart.

She is truly a very special woman.

To say, *'thank you,'* only serves to cheapen the gift.
But in the absence of a suitable alternative –

Thank you.

WARNING.

The contents of this book are fictional and contains printed words describing, amongst other things, acts of a **sexual nature, violence, graphic detail of human anatomy, suicides** and **exploratory forensic and medical procedures**. There are **spiritual references and humour** too. If any of these subjects may cause you concern, trauma, outrage or offence, it is suggested you read no further. The decision is totally yours.

You may not agree with the authors views, work, opinions, perceptions and comments; that is your right and freedom of choice in a democratic and free society. Likewise, it is the authors right to express and exercise their sovereign freedom of choice, speech and rights.

Should you decide to continue reading this material and feel offended, disturbed or otherwise adversely affected, then the issue lies solely with you; you have been warned. Any issues or problems you may have, are yours, not mine.

DISCLAIMER.

The author, agent, publisher and seller of this book accepts no responsibility for any adverse, upsetting or distressing effects upon anyone choosing to read it.
To read the contents of this book is an acceptance of the terms and conditions that the reader is wholly responsible for any resulting issues they may have.
What has society become?

For: -

18-Year-olds plus.

Common sense.

Society.

Sanity.

Justice.

Freedoms.

Unity.

Hope.

Democracy.

Entertainment.

Good.

God.

Common sense.

--.--

NOT FOR: -

Vulnerable people.

The Easily offended.

Sensitive people

Or

those seeking attention.

5

Chapter 1.

TIME PAST.

Built at the turn of the twentieth century, it was once an elegant Floral Hall. A structure made of glass and ornate ironwork, where back in the day, afternoon tea and cake could be taken amongst an abundance of colourful, sweet smelling flower displays. Its clientele surrounded by plush furnishings, crisp white table cloths and served by polite waitresses wearing a warm smile and immaculate French maids' uniforms; black stockings, black high-heels, black skirt, frilly white pinny and white blouse.

A smart, middle-aged string quartet or organist would entertain during the weekends and the holiday seasons, providing a pleasant, uplifting background musical ambiance.

It was a great place to meet with friends. It had remained that way for many decades since Victorian times.

It was an especially popular place to visit just after World War 2 when people were content with the resumption of a peaceful way of life after the power-mad politicians of the world had sent millions to their slaughter and caused global mass destruction, poverty and hunger in the name of their ideology and their deluded belief that they were right and could create a *'better'* world at the expense of the lives of others. Many who pushed for war, increased their wealth enormously, under the banner of righteousness and building a better world.

Better for whom though, is the question; the politicians themselves, their friends and cronies, the governments, the rich investors of the *industrial war machine complex* and the well-used excuse for increased government power afforded during such crisis?

Or was it better for the ordinary man and woman making up the population, those who lost their lives; their loved ones; their homes and all they had?

The question remains; better for whom?

Grateful, that they merely had life, if not much else, society wished only to be left alone so to enjoy the post war era. They had survived. Not much else mattered. Many of those they had known were no longer alive; their time on Earth was over; cut short due to the insanity and selfishness of political ambitions. Everyone was more than happy the war, for now, was over. Yet another war to end all wars, they said.

Peace is all the masses of ordinary folk, wanted.

Time moves on, the years pass. The world was now rebuilding and looking much rosier. It was in stark contrast with the recent harshness of the war years still fresh in people's minds.

Nothing stays the same. There was a new generation; one that had not experienced the hardships and trauma of war. They had more time, more money and a live-for-today attitude. Society quickly changed. Hippies, free love and flower-power of the 60s came and went in a flash. Sex, drugs and rock and roll was hot on its heels.

No-one wanted sedate afternoon tea at the Floral Hall anymore. Fun and wilder times is what the younger generation craved. Life was too short to be taken seriously and so the Floral Hall was abandoned.

But not for long. All the extensive windows of the once magnificent building were bricked up using grey concrete blocks. The glass roof replaced with metal industrial sheeting. No effort was made to hide the resulting industrial external façade produced. And no-one really cared.

A new era slowly dawned. Disco lights, sound systems and a drinks bar were installed.

It had a stage with dance floor in front. It became one massive room on two levels and now the place to be for the young and the not so young but young-at-heart crowds to meet, drink, dance and party and maybe find romance.

All traces of it once being something fine and of its time, had gone forever. It was now just an ugly, single story detached building overlooking the sea; Le Trokadera night club, as it was now called, had been born.

More years rolled by.

Life was good. It was fun. It was almost two in the morning. The *last song of the night* was about to be played, down at Le Trokadera; '*The North East's finest place, for a great night out*,' as it billed by the Tourism Board, twelve years earlier.

Hot, sweaty bodies packed the dance floor; it was uncomfortably warm and humid. It had been an unusually hot summer and was no cooler outside. Some of the nights were as warm as the days. It was too warm. Unusual for that hour of the night, up-north on the East coast.

Le Trokadera; all the locals of the Edwardian seaside resort affectionately knew it as, The Trok or Trok club.

It had somehow survived into those heady glam-rock days of the '70s night clubs and discotheques when everyone loved dancing to the music of such bands as Abba, T. Rex, The Sweet, The Bay City Rollers and Slade.

When Paisley patterned shirts, big collars, flared trousers, platform shoes and long hair and '*the great smell of Brut*' deodorant was the fashion for the boys. As were Bovver boots, skin-head haircuts and fighting.

The Bay City Rollers; Tartan scarves and half-mast Tartan pants were worn everywhere, male and female. Fashion influenced as ever by subtle persuasion stemming from clever marketing, popularity and wanting to be part of the in-crowd.

Most girls wore pretty dresses, looked feminine and were proud to be so. They behaved nicely, were gentle and smelled sweetly of perfume; Musk or Chanel.

They were proud and unashamed of their gender as were the boys. Some were not so much but no one really cared, it was a free world; their choice. Yes, there were Gays – so what? We all got along.

Many extremists, attention seekers, influencers, main stream media, politicians and Marxist ideologists were the ones stoking the flames of division through subtle discrimination and hatred. It's an age-old tactic to distract, divide and so conquer. Is it different today? No, somethings stay the same. It's the corrupted system. But who cared back then? They were too busy, too distracted.

Just as today, people just wanted to make the most of their lives and enjoy it whilst they could. But that's not good for government and big corporations if *the people* live happily in harmony. Government needs to be needed. They know that. They make it so. Their mantra is – create problem; to create reaction; create solution. It's a well-tried and tested formula. Problems often government contrived.

Anyway, it was a saner world back then when society was strong, cohesive, moral and caring. Caring for one another through mutual respect and understanding and so moderated societal behaviour through kind actions, honesty, rationale, reasoning, facts and challenging appropriately. No-one identified as such objects as a mythical Unicorn, a loaf of bread or lump of coal on a shovel or labelled themselves such as *a woman with a penis;* though born as a man, or calling themselves a *man with a vagina* even though born a woman. It mocks rational thought, biological science, logic, suppresses free speech and causes division and creates distraction. Control and closing down freedom of speech.

Has the world gone mad these days? The vast majority would say, *'yes, it has.'*

Back in the day, caring people would have kindly helped them with reality. Perhaps right now it's some kind of latest fashion; a phase, we are passing through? And yet a very small minority expect others to comply to their wishes and narrative of whatever they want to be identified as, even though it defies science, logic and truth and is an affront to one's very own conscience and sense of order and of what's right and real. We all have the right to free thought and free speech no matter where we are aligned.

For example, who would ever be fearful enough or weak enough or foolish enough to go along with the pretence that some human being is proclaiming they're really a mythical creature known as a unicorn because they say they are? The following day that very same person may decide they're a feline creature instead. Who are they kidding?

Some demand, through tactics such as threats, violence, demonisation, screaming and shouting and so-called cancellation, that others must support their fantasy without questioning the delusion and fantasy. Contradiction, not allowed. They are expecting others refusing to follow their narrative, to deny their own right and freedom of choice and thought and speech. Yet to do so and to surrender, would be merely humouring them and encouraging their fantasy perhaps at the expense of our own formulation of thoughts, opinions, reasoning and conscience, would it not? That applies to many subjects. Who has the monopoly on science, fact, free speech, sovereignty, the order of things; reality?

By all means, be whatever makes you happy but don't expect others to comply with the notion. Just do your own thing for yourself, not others. Let's all get along.

Anyway, fashions change, they come and go. They always do. Time moves on, nothing stays the same, except for Le Trokadera.

The place appeared magical with the lights down low but in the glare of brightness the spell was quickly broken when it was seen for what it was; a dated, worn, tired and run down space.

Plush seating, once new and bright crimson; now faded, heavily stained from spilled drinks week on week year on year, tacky and ripped. Threadbare carpet, sticky underfoot. To describe the place as shabby would have been complimentary. Fortunately, few noticed any of it through their bleary, drunken eyes with the lights down low. Anyway, no one cared.

The kitchen was next to the faulty overflowing toilets which had been that way for years. There was always a peculiar smell that hung in the air at that end of the club; ammonia mixed with the odour of greasy fried burgers, French-fries and *scampi in a basket*.

The whole place could be described as the pits. But no-one cared back then, it's just the way things were. It wasn't important. Besides, there was nowhere else to go and everyone was too busy looking for a great time.

The last song of the night to be played was always Rod Stewart's, '*I am sailing*', to let the punters know it was the end; time to leave, time to go home.

Everyone knew the words and joined in. They sang with passion. Hair ruffled, arms swaying just like Rod. It was a nostalgic tradition.

A tradition started at Le Trokadera when Britain was at war in 1982 with Argentina over the Falkland Islands.

'*I am Sailing,*' was played on the TV documentaries over footage of the Falkland's bound warships. It became imprinted in the country's psyche, the same way Rod's *last song of the night* had with the patrons of Le Trokadera night club; '*The North East's finest……*'

Memories; patriotic images of ships packed with heroic armed forces personnel sailing for a place no-one particularly knew of or had even bothered with for three hundred years; the Falklands. Memories kept alive every Saturday night down at The Trok. As though stuck in *a time;* a good and proud time. The place and its patrons clung onto the past.

The war, which lasted 74 days, claimed the lives of 255 British military personnel, the lives of 3 Falkland Islanders and the lives of 649 Argentinian military personnel. Lives cut short.

A high price for those no longer with us and for their loved ones; their families and friends they left behind. Forty years later and governments talk of handing back the Islands. Was this part of history for the Industrial war machine to make companies rich?

We are indebted to our courageous military and forever thank them for their service. May those Fallen, rest in peace.

There is nothing good in war; the banks and the rich get richer; the poor always get poorer.

As wars go, it's reported to have been an horrific close-combat struggle with high casualty rates.

Sadly, since the end of that war, about the same number of British armed service personnel who returned home have, over the years, taken their own lives perhaps now amounting to more in number than those killed in action there.

Meanwhile, politicians' revel in the reflected glory of so called *winning* and of those who sacrificed their lives for a cause that fades quickly with the passing of time.

'*I am Sailing.*' It was a nostalgic song, linked with that war; a war that had made the nation proud and gave them a feel-good factor.

Some punters of the Trok became Rod Stewart impressionists after a night on the lager at Le Trokadera. They mimicked Rod; they strutted and sang into invisible microphones whilst twirling invisible mic stands. It was the same, week in, week out.

Small groups of men, *the 2 o'clock shufflers,* knew it well. They'd stood all night hanging around the edge of the dance floor watching intently, drinking; fantasizing, drooling.
Their intended victims were unsuspecting groups of young women dancing around their handbags placed upon the floor. It's what they did in those days.
They wore heavy eye-shadow and curled their hair outwards; it was the fashion. They were out for a dance, a fun-time, a laugh - nothing serious.
Although the contraceptive Pill was freely available then, sex wasn't. It was different back then. Girls were different. One-night stands and casual sex was rare. People could have a good time without that. There was more self-respect. Sure, some girls were known as 'loose women' but they were the very minority.

Those *2 o'clock shufflers;* drooling, lecherous men, muttering; *'I'd like to give her one,'* their mates agreeing, or disagreeing. But it was irrelevant. They'd spent the whole night building up the courage to have a dance, then a little before closing time at *two o'clock in the morning,* they'd shuffle onto the dance floor. When they did, they didn't stand a chance.

Some were happy to admit they were a *2 o'clock shuffler.* They'd laugh about it. They were generally harmless enough, perhaps just a little shy.
Others were in denial; serious. They'd become encouraged and excited if a girl looked at them for more than a moment. They'd think it was *'the come-on.'* She'd probably be unaware of what she'd done. She'd have meant nothing by it.
They'd subtly stalk her around the club and become angry if some other guy muzzled in. *'Slag,'* they'd sneer to their *2 o'clock* shuffling mates. Then they'd target another. So, the pattern continued.
They were all too afraid to do anything about it. They remained in their *2 o'clock shufflers* groups. They'd spend the night drinking and leering then make their move onto the dance floor at 2 a.m. as soon as the guitar intro of Rod's, *'I am sailing,'* boomed from the speakers.
At 2 a.m. the floor would suddenly fill with these guys. Mimicking Rod wasn't their style. Instead, they'd grab a girl, pull her in close then shuffle around with her, whether that's what she wanted or not.
Saying nothing or using the same old sad chat-up lines that never worked; they were lucky if they got her name, let alone her phone number. But they felt good and brave and macho. At least they'd, *done it. They'd tried,* they thought.
They were there every week and usually walked home alone or with their mates. *'The one I got must have been frigid,'* one would say, *'or a lesbian.'* Their mates would agree but not really believing it. It made them all feel better about failure. But they lived in hope; *next week would be different, next week they might, 'score.'*

The last song of the night had finished, handbags were picked up and goodbyes were being said. It took several minutes for the last of the night-clubbers to leave. Amongst them that night was Michael James Petty and his mate, Colin Arthur Cross. They were a duo and the complete opposite of a *two o'clock shuffler.*

Lots of people knew them. They were usually referred to as just Petty and Cross. Petty had a nickname – Chopper due to a part of his anatomy. Cross was known as Rabbit Teeth or Bugsy as his front teeth were big, white and prominent. Yet not unattractive. Their names were always mentioned together as one, like Laurel and Hardy, Starsky and Hutch, notorious Burke and Hare or Fred and Rose West of similar infamy. Petty and Cross were always together.

Petty and Cross had grown up together. They were best mates together throughout school. They'd had fun times together, outrageous and extreme times too. Some serious times also but always together and always fun, no matter what.

'*Even got expelled from school together.*' They used to boast; '*they said it was serious but it was just a bit of fun. Besides, she wanted it. They couldn't pin it on us,*' they would laugh.

They thought it was funny, Cross and Petty, the allegation of twelve-year-old Lucy Carlos being raped; '*gang-banged.*' they said. '*They couldn't prove it,*' they said.

Indeed, it was never proved.

They thought it was funny. From beginning to end, they thought it was fun; a laugh.

Little Lucy Carlos; she'd been taking a short-cut across the local authority housing estate's, Westfield Park, on a sunny afternoon in early spring.

It was a fairly cold day. There were very few people about. The ground was still soft from the winter. She trod carefully and edged around the football pitch. She glanced at the same lot of older boys who played soccer there most weekends.

'Hi!' One shouted. 'Pretty girl. Come here, I want to talk to you. I've something for you.'

She was a quiet, polite girl. Out of courtesy she flashed him a slight smile. It meant nothing to her. She wasn't interested. She immediately looked down at the ground to break eye contact. It's then she noticed how muddy her shoes had become. She was a little upset as she liked to keep smart and clean. She'd clean them later, she thought.

She kept her meaningful pace; Granny was expecting her.

The soccer game played on, though not as intensely. There was a distraction. They all noticed the pretty little girl with the long blonde hair, pink cardigan over a lemon cotton dress, white ankle socks and black shoes.

The game slowed to a halt. They wolf-whistled, clapped and hollered.

She ignored them. She was more mindful of the muddy ground and getting to Granny's for tea the way she always did of a Sunday after church.

The excited boy's hollering continued. Pack-like, they drifted towards her.

She never noticed.

She was a lovely girl; any parent would have been proud of her. Small for her age, undeveloped, naïve and un-spoilt. Not yet reached puberty. Innocent. A loving daughter and the apple of her Granny's eye.

The wandering pack advanced. The jeering got louder.

It got her attention. She shot them nervous glance.

One of the players pulled his pants down and exposed himself, laughing as he did so. He was clearly excited and proud of what he had to show.

She was sweet and innocent. She blushed and looked away; she didn't understand. Sh kept her head down. Her pace increased; she didn't care about the mud on her shoes anymore. She wanted nothing to do with the rude boys.

It never stopped the team advancing. They were a group of eight and of an age where they could leave school forever if they wanted at the end of term. They regularly met in Westfield Park for a kick-about.

They were hot, sweaty and muddy. Some had acne and stale teenage body odour.

The locals knew who they were.

So did the police.

So did all the other kids who witnessed Lucy Carlos pinned down, naked and screaming; that cold, sunny day in early spring, just after church service.

Pinned down so tightly; she couldn't struggle. Defiled by every one of the eight, one after another, the afternoon she was on her way to Granny's.

They'd dragged her; ankles and wrists, out of the way to some bushes next to the play park railings. They grabbed at her clothes, stripped her naked and mauled her.

The younger kids playing on the swings, seesaws and slide, innocently watched on as the young men tore her apart, one after another.

They were strong and fast and hard and quick.

She screamed and cried and pleaded with them.

She pleaded with her onlookers.

The first three didn't take long but for her each one seemed a lifetime.

The fourth to have a go was, Chopper. He was a freak of nature, that's how he got his nickname. He was well built, tall for his age and enormous.

Looking into her eyes, he laughed.

She didn't understand but she understood what the pain was.

The remainder had their go after Chopper. Some missed their target in their excitement and reckless frenzy. They only realized that when she cried out louder. When she did, the hand over her mouth and nose that suffocated her would tighten, pressing harder.

It was nearly impossible for her to breathe.

Gasping for air she thrashed her head wildly, side to side, against the firmly placed hand that stayed clamped over her face.

They thought it funny and carried on.

Time after time she thrashed; thinking it would be her last breath; that her heart was going to burst. It couldn't beat any faster.

The hand kept tightening, pressing harder.

It became so hard for her to breathe. Everything around her was spinning. She thought she was going to die.

There were brief moments when no-one was on top of her little star-fished body. It's then she could see the deep blue sky, it was so bright but all around felt so dark. Figures moving close-by. The sounds and smells of teenage boys, words she'd never heard before, belt-buckles, zips, grunting, sounds of relief and laughter.

Staring skywards, she wished she could be up amongst the clouds or with grandad in heaven, anywhere but there. Anywhere but laid naked on the cold, wet, muddy ground.

The pain started over each time another stranger's face appeared above her.

Silenced by the suffocating hand, only her eyes could speak. They were wide, tearful and terrified; they pleaded with *them* to stop. They pleaded for someone, anyone, to help her; to save her; to stop the confusing pain. Her petrified eyes pleaded with the man walking the Alsatian dog who watched briefly, then walked-on by. The same dog walker who later told everyone, *'How terrible it was. What animals they were.'* And, *'That poor little girl,'* but never helped her and never came forward. *'He was scared to do anything then, there at the time,'* he said.

He was scared to do anything later. *'Besides,'* he said, *'it was nothing to do with me.'* He thanked God it wasn't his little girl. He asked others what the world was coming to; he said, *'it was dreadful, shocking! What was the world coming to?'*

The last one to have a go on her was the smallest of the group. He felt he had something to prove. He made it last as long as he could.

His best mate, Chopper, told him to *hurry it up.*

He carried on. He took his time. He sunk his big prominent white teeth into both sides of her neck.

When he was done, he spat in her face then got to his feet. *'Get over it bitch!'*

No-one on her, they had all finished, they'd had their fun. They stood circled around and studied her a moment.

She never noticed. She was pale and lifeless. Her eyes were fixed and hollow. She never moved. Her mind had left her.

Chopper scanned the gang looking on. He asked if anyone wanted *a second go.*

Some heads shook. There was a, *'no,'* here and there. Most were silent. They were all done.

'Let's go. We're all done,' one of them said.

When they were done, they ran away - laughing.
When they were done - the young children carried on playing.
When they were done - the world carried on.
When they were done - Lucy staggered, stumbled, naked, bleeding and in agony towards nearby Granny's. People stared but carried on by. *They didn't want to get involved.*

Granny went into a state of shock when she answered the door to see her beautiful Lucy standing there like a pathetic wretch; naked, covered in mud and clearly defiled. They were both hospitalized.

It made the front page of the local news. The whole city was quite rightly appalled and repulsed by the incident. It was on everyone's lips.

The police appealed for the public's help.

With anonymous information the gang was soon rounded up.

They'd told their lawyers the truth; *everything.*

Upon the advice of their lawyers, all of them except one, made *'no comment,'* replies when questioned by the police.

'It's for the police to prove.' The lawyers told their clients. *'Innocent until proved guilty. That's the law.'* They smugly proclaimed.

Lucy was assessed as being too traumatized to testify in the near future. So, the police had no *primary witness* to offer in any court proceedings. Giving court evidence and reliving the experience would have an adverse effect upon her, *they* said.

The *playground kids* who had watched on were witnesses but were too young to testify, *they* said. Besides, their parents didn't want them *to get involved.*

The man with the dogs was traced by the police. He walked his dog the same time every day, that's how they found him. He told them he'd not seen anything. They pressed him harder; they were certain he saw what happened. He said, *'he was sorry he couldn't help them; he was afraid to get involved. He had his own little girl to think about.'*

'He was a vital witness whose testimony could have put the gang behind bars but the police cannot force a witness to speak up,' his lawyer advised him.

No-one else came forward. They had to let the group go free.

Although there were ample quantities of semen recovered, there was no such thing as DNA testing back then. It could only be identified as semen of a certain blood type, that's all.

The police did their best. They wanted to nail the gang but there was insufficient evidence.

Several weeks past, the case had run out of steam. There were no new lines of inquiry.

They had an idea. They had nothing to lose. A bluff; a lie, was their hope of cracking the case and getting some justice for Lucy. Manipulation through a lie; with the excuse that *the end justifies the means.*

So, they pulled in one of the gang members. They told him the lie that one of the other gang members was thinking about giving evidence against them all to save himself. And if he did, it would mean them all going to court, except for the one giving evidence to save himself, that is. The police told him *they needed only one single gang member, not two, to confess and turn Queens evidence, to look after himself before he was beaten to it; to save himself.*

They said they were fed up waiting for a decision from his mate. They told him they now wanted to give *him* that chance, a chance not to go to court for what he'd done. They only needed one witness. *'One is all they needed, no more, just one,'* they said.

He felt pressured but wasn't impressed. He was having none of it. He trusted his gang.

'Your choice,' they casually told him.

Though it was bluff, they said there may also be some other evidence coming to light where they wouldn't need a gang witness at all. *'They wouldn't need him or his mate,'* they said. *'It was just only a matter of time.'* They asked him if he wanted to take that risk.

He started to feel more pressured. He didn't know the truth. He didn't know whether to believe the police. But he wasn't ready to crack.

'He would be throwing his one chance away unless he helped right there and then,' they told him.

They casually mentioned the man walking the Alsatian and the children playing nearby that day. They hinted they could be witnesses willing to make a stand against the gang. They told him they were giving him one chance to look after himself before one of his mates grassed him up. *'First come, first served. No more messing about. Last chance,'* they said.

He asked for his lawyer.

His lawyer told him not to disclose anything. He didn't believe the police. He knew the gang well. He'd successfully represented them many times during their short criminal lives. They were lucrative 'repeat clients' to have; the Legal Aid system was very generous. He always did all he could to protect them; he went the extra mile above and beyond his duty. They knew that; that's why they always asked for him to represent them.

The smart lawyer knew the gang would stick together; they wouldn't *grass* each other up. He resisted the police's offer. He wanted to know, in confidence, which member of the gang was thinking of becoming a witness so he could best advise his client.

They refused to tell him.

The lawyer said, '*In that case, there was no deal. Release my client.*' He demanded.

One old caring police officer present, gently asked to speak with the lawyer in private. He agreed.

They left the 'client' alone.

The caring officer knew that around 40% of men and women admitted in a survey that they had cheated at least once on their partners. There was a good chance the lawyer was one of the 40% cheaters.

He quietly asked the lawyer if he was still having a secret affair and did his wife trust him? It was a bluff of course. '*Just asking.*' He smirked then popped a piece of gum into his mouth and chewed slowly. He made it clear he would do everything to crack this case and how they both knew the *client* was guilty as hell. He told him. '*Theres more than one way to skin a cat.*'

The lawyer was now in the officer's territory and out of his comfort zone of clever words. His past *flings* flashed through his mind; two of his secretaries, his friend's wife and a few more. Then he panicked at the consequences of his wife finding out and divorcing him; missing his children, the cost and the loss of all he'd worked for. He wondered how the officer knew and which one he was referring to. He blustered; asked a few questions as to how he knew; what evidence did he have? He indignantly accused him of blackmail; said *he was faithful; clean as a whistle; a family man.* He was bluffing too.

The officer mentally noted he'd touched a nerve; took a long pause, said little in return. '*Just asked you a question, is all.*' He raised his eyebrows knowingly; slowly chewed some more. Sometimes, *less is more*, he used to think.

The lawyer couldn't take the risk. He panicked. It was either him or his client.

It was a short meeting.

The frustrated red-faced lawyer, full of guilt, rejoined his client. He was flustered and advised him to cooperate.

A deal was struck. He gave *evidence*; a written statement in return for the promise of immunity from prosecution.

He admitted his part in the rape.

For coming clean and dropping the rest in it, he would be spared a court appearance. Instead, he would become their witness against his gang. The police didn't tell him that they'd no other evidence apart from his testimony; that it was all a bluff and no one else was willing to cooperate and assist them; that they'd hit a brick wall.

He put them all there, every name; Petty and Cross; the lot. He detailed the whole event in chronological order; who did what and in what order. He was a good witness; it was a good and detailed statement.

Not good for young Petty, Cross and the team.

The gang were re-arrested. They continued to deny the accusations. They were charged on the strength of that one statement. But one against seven wasn't ideal. It would still be a difficult case.

The gang member, *turned witness*, was never re-arrested or charged like the others were. Since then, he'd been beaten-up, his parent's home had been torched and his dog had been stabbed to death in the front garden. His own life had been threatened; *unless he withdrew his testimony.* Petty gloated when he told him he was the one who killed his dog. He threated; *'he'd do the same to him as he'd done to his dog.'* He didn't care.

He withdrew as a witness. He was still covered by the immunity deal.

It was an horrific rape case, as rapes are. It never went to court; lack of evidence. It was marked NFA (No further action) and filed away in some dusty old police storeroom along with all the rest of the NFA's. Some had lain there more than forty years.

The boys, *the rapists*, had gotten away with it. They had been temporarily expelled from school whilst the case was investigated. Once it was over they were all allowed to return. Most of them had no intention of going back for another term. But they did. They had good reason to; their lawyer saw to that. The school was told they had acted too hastily; they should have waited for the outcome of the investigation, they were told. They gang shouldn't have been expelled. All eight were each given financial compensation for their hasty expulsion. It was a substantial sum.

They gang were happy. They were welcomed back to the school.

Lucy's parents objected. They didn't want them to be at the same school. They didn't want her in the same place as the eight.

She didn't want to be in the same place either. She never wanted to see them again, *'Ever!'*

Her parents fought their case with the school. They argued why their daughter shouldn't ever have to see the boys again.

'But the boys had rights,' they were told. *'They had not been convicted, so were innocent in the eyes of the law and of the school.'*

They asked that their daughter be allowed to start another school somewhere else. They didn't want her anywhere near the rapists.

'Sorry. Not possible. No grounds for that,' they sympathized. They were strongly advised not to refer to them as rapists.

'In that case,' they threatened, *'we'll keep her home, out of class,'* said the parents.

'Do that and you'll find yourselves in Court,' they were informed; promptly backed up by an official letter sent recorded delivery the same day. *'They had to uphold the Education law,'* said the warning letter.

So back to the same school it was to be for Lucy. She'd no choice.
'There were lots of positives,' she was told. *'She'd been a model pupil; all her teachers had said so. And all her friends were there too.'*

'She was very intelligent and so very well liked,' her caring and loving parents told her so, through strained voices. *'Now very brave, also,'* they said. *'She could go to school and still attend her twice weekly counselling sessions. She'd be fine. Ignore the other kids. Ignore your attackers.'*

She returned as soon as she'd physically healed. Her counsellor advised it. '*The mental scars would be with her until the day she died,*' her counsellor said. '*She'd have to accept that and live with it.*'

And so, she returned to school.

The *eight* were already back there. They were heroes amongst some of their warped peers.

She was taunted by some, but endured. The teachers and her friends were supportive of her.

By the time the summer holidays arrived she'd become seriously withdrawn.

She was relieved school term was over. Not because she looked forward to anything; she had no plans. It just meant she didn't have to see the gang each day and that was enough. They were a constant reminder of an horrific event she'd rather try to forget.

It was summer holidays. All the other kids had a great time. She rarely went outdoors; stayed mostly in her bedroom with the door closed. She felt safe closed inside her room. She wanted to close the world out. She tried.

She tried so hard. Her life was becoming impossible. She self-harmed by clawing her arms and cheeks. She cropped her own hair. She would spend hours sat on her bed, huddled in a ball, rocking back and forth whilst tears streamed freely down her cheeks. Her anguish was too much. She thought she had gone to hell.

She was given more-frequent counselling. '*Time is a great healer*,' she was told.

In deed it seemed to be. She seemed to pick up as the weeks went by. She was much improved as the autumn term approached. Her parents had renewed hope. '*She was much better, thank you,*' they told everyone politely, when asked.

She hanged herself on the day the autumn term commenced.

Her Dad found her that morning hanging behind her bedroom door by her school tie looped around her neck.

He'd gone to her bedroom with her breakfast cereal, as he always did. It puzzled him as to why the door was heavy and difficult to open that morning.

Her favourite brown smiling Teddy bear, Charlie, that had comforted her since she was a baby, sat on her pillow next to a note. It read: -

Goodbye Mummy.
Goodbye Daddy.
Goodbye Granny.
It's too much for me.
Please look after Charlie for me,
I'm going to join grandad.
Sorry.
Love you. X X X

Lucy Carlos………*her school neck-tie around her neck was fastened to a coat hook affixed to the rear of her bedroom door. She'd taken the weight off her legs, slipped quietly into unconsciousness and slowly asphyxiated to death;* The coroner's report recorded.

Tongue out, purple and swollen, blue lips, fixed bulging stare, head to one side. Her slight frame in school uniform hanging limply like some grotesque floppy rag doll. Her bodily fluids down her legs and on the carpet beneath her. That's the image her father's mind recorded the day his life was shattered, his heart broken.

Granny never spoke a word after Lucy's funeral. She lost the will to live and died of a broken heart that same year.

Now in their early twenties they were more than good mates, Petty and Cross. They'd done lots together. Some of their old mates had too. Some were already used to the penal system.

So far, the Petty and Cross duo had escaped custody for their wrong-doings. And there had been many. They shared many secrets; many horror stories of criminality, violence and a long list of people they'd made their victims. Their secrets and horror stories were often one and the same.

They'd been coming from the city to the Trok for a couple of years. They had a reputation. They were known as violently *hard men*. A good night to them was ten pints of beer, a fight and a Chinese takeaway. Tonight, was like any other night out.

It was 2 a.m. In the harsh light of the club, the DJ boomed out; *he thanked everyone, hoped they'd had a good time, safe journey home and would see them next week. Thank you Rod and thank you all....... aaaand..... gooooood....niiiighttt!*

No-one listened.

The last song of the night; *'I am Sailing,'* was finished. The end of another Saturday night at *The Trok*, as it was known locally.

Dave and Paul, the door bouncers; *good bouncers at that*, hit the fire doors metal release bars. They banged open over the revellers chatter. Stale air and staler bodies poured out into the night air. It was warm and balmy. They had a great relationship with most of the punters apart from a few; Petty and Cross being two of them. They knew not to mess with Dave and Paul. They were professional bouncers who could handle themselves. Paul was built like Goliath and until his size and strength was needed, was always a gentle giant. A nicer man you couldn't wish to meet. Dave was much smaller and an ex-semi-professional boxer and could have gone to the top but realised there were other priorities in life, so quit. They both preferred defusing confrontation with words rather than using the very capable physical skills they possessed. They were well liked and respected.

Petty and Cross behaved in their presence. Bullies are cowards and know when to behave so they don't get a taste of their own medicine. They choose their victims. Besides, they didn't want banning form the Trok.

Now, at shortly after 2 o'clock, The Trok club goers had spilled out into that small seaside town. It seemed as though half the population had been there. There was little else to do of a Saturday evening. Three TV channels, back then, did nothing to keep their audiences at home.

It was a safer world back then, when crash helmets could be left with the motorcycles that were lined up near the main doors of The Trok, waiting for their riders to return, knowing that no-one would steal or damage any of them.

There were shouts and laughter as the crowd dispersed. Some admired the bikes especially when Petty got on his noisy baffle-less Honda 500 twin, Cross on his Yammy 350 Power Valve, and fired them up together. Opening and closing the throttles, it was deafening. Heads turned as the noise broke into the night. It was like a mating call to some of the girls; they were attracted and went over.

The rest of the crowd carried on. They were mostly locals who all sort of knew one another. Many were couples. They headed to various places; mostly home. Some went to the beach or some other out of the way private place. Lots headed for the Chinese take-away.

John, his mate Jerry and a couple of girlfriends chatted outside the club for a while.

Suddenly, three bikes mysteriously crashed sideways onto the tarmac. No-one was near them, only Petty and Cross. They gave it full throttle, low gear, as they shaved dangerously past everyone on the footpath. It impressed some of the walkers, annoyed others.

Due to Petty being around six foot four tall and heavily built his bike looked small under him. His long blond hair flowed out from beneath his helmet. He wore thin, steel-rimmed glasses with thick lenses. He looked like an academic; he didn't look like a biker. He didn't look like a hard and violent man. But he was.

Cross was small; less than five foot seven, muscular build, tanned skin, exceptionally white prominent front teeth that didn't spoil his looks. It kind of enhanced them. His dark hair was longer than Petty's, it too blew in the wind. Due to his small stature, his machine looked bigger than it was when he rode it.

The bikes disappeared out of sight but they could be heard for quite some time on that quiet summer's night.

John and Jerry finished chatting and headed for home, it would take them past the Chinese. A few of the girls walked with them. They were all hungry and decided on a takeaway. It was about ten minutes to get there but twenty minutes after a night's drinking - one step back, two steps forward, pause for a chat; one step forward, one back; chat. They got there, eventually.

They'd been drinking heavily. John wasn't good at keeping it in. He said *he'd join them in a couple of minutes, he needed a pee.* Jerry and the girls went in and ordered four curries.

John was bursting. He searched around for somewhere to *go*. He was a cop so had to be especially careful where he went. He saw a dark alley leading to the rear of some houses. *A good out of the way place*, he thought, *no-one would see him.* He stopped a few paces in and unzipped against a wall.

A girl shouted, *'No.'* It came from farther down the alley.

Surprised, he quickly zipped up as he peered into the blackness. His eyes struggled to adjust to the lack of light.

He heard a man who sounded angry and demanding. He could just about make out some figures farther along, deeper in to the alley; *looked like a couple leaning against the wall.* She looked bare from the waist down; long pale legs. He thought he could see something white on the floor near to them. He couldn't be sure. '*Perhaps her panties,*'

Thinking it was a couple who didn't make it to the beach or elsewhere after the club, he turned to leave to find somewhere else. He smiled to himself.

'No. Please. Don't!' she sounded muffled.

Sounds like a girl who's changed her mind. He thought. He carried on walking. He took a left out of the alley, away from the Chinese. It wasn't easy finding somewhere to go. It took another forty yards to find a spot.

He felt much relieved as he headed back to meet his friends inside the Chinese. He was nearly there and knew his takeaway would be just about ready.

'No!' Screamed out from the alley he'd first planned on using. *'Help!'*

He couldn't believe they were still messing around down there. *Ah, drunken fun on a Saturday night. The effects of drink,* he thought. He recalled he'd had quite a lot to drink himself. He smiled and carried on. He was imagining what was happening in the alley but his tasty curry was more on his mind.

'Help me! Please!' a girl shouted.

He stopped in his tracks. She sounded serious; desperate. He wasn't sure. He listened some more. There was some screaming. It was muffled as though a hand kept covering the screamers mouth.

He waited. He listened.

Nothing.

But he couldn't help himself; he had to take a look.

He backtracked. Seconds later he was peering down the alley again. He could hear some noises. He squinted into the darkness. It seemed to take an age before his eyes started to adjust and see into the darkness.

The couple were no longer against the wall, he could see that. His eyes searched. There seemed to be a huddle of bodies on the ground near to where the couple had been earlier. *It didn't look right.* He thought. He peered harder; looked like one guy knelt over the girl's head with another guy laid on top of her, her legs thrashing either side of him. But he wasn't sure; he couldn't quite make it out. He didn't believe his eyes.

Instinctively, he called, 'Hello?' assessing the situation, not knowing his plan of action. Not knowing if he was doing the right thing.

The *head* guy jumped up and ran at him. He was just a dark figure in a dark alley until the last few strides when he came into the street light and transformed into a six foot four, long blond-haired, jam-jar bottoms wearing monster, known as Petty. Though John didn't know his name then. It had taken him around three seconds to cover the twenty-five yards to the point where he could square up to John.

He was huge and towered over him. Not in the same physical league as Paul the Trok bouncer, but huge. 'There's nothing doing here, mate. Push off, if you know what's good for ya,' he said.

'What's going on?' demanded John, wishing he had Paul or Dave by his side.

'They're just having some fun, mate.' He bent his arm to form a crook, elbow down, fist clenched. Slapped his other hand on top of the crook then flexed like some symbolic erect penis. 'You know,' he said, with a knowing smile. 'Whoaaaa! You know!' He paused. 'Ok, mate.'

Mate? They'd never met before, thought John. *And he definitely didn't feel like his mate.* He felt threatened.

The big guy glanced over his shoulder, 'Hurry it up Col. Finish off mate!'

The girl cried out, 'Help I'm......'

There was a silent moment.

She screamed, 'Help. I'm being......' it tapered into a muffled, '......raped! Somebody, help me!'

John's mind was dulled and fuzzy through drink. Processing information was slow. He didn't react.

'Help me! Please, help me!' she screamed some more.

Silence.

John looked through the monsters' jam-jar bottoms. The magnified eyes behind them were shifty and full of guilt. Something was definitely wrong.

'Someone, help me!' echoed from the darkness of the alley.

John sidestepped to see passed the big guy. His shirt was grabbed instantly and held.

He looked back up into the jam-jar bottoms. 'I'm a police officer. Get out my way! Get off me! Let go of my shirt!' He banged the big guy's forearms with his fist to release his grip.

He was strong. He kept hold.

'Now!' He banged again, hard as he could.

He never let go. He was too strong.

There was a ripping sound as John pushed him aside and sprinted towards the bodies on the ground.

The guy was up on his feet before he got there. A dark figure, smaller than John, smiled. His bright buck teeth glowed in the dark as he fastened his jeans.

The girl was up just as quickly. She was in bits, shaking, lines of mascara down her face. Her neck was marked and bitten.

'What's going on?' yelled John.

In tears, she sobbed loudly, *'He tried to rape me! That's what's going on.'* She felt her crotch. *'In fact,......'* she hesitated, *'he has raped me.'* She returned her hand to her crotch for dignity then went nose to nose with the buck toothed man. He was still smiling. She took a deep breath. *'Bastard!'* she screamed into his face. *'You bastard!'*

He turned, looked sideways at her, laughed, turned back then spat into her face. 'Bitch!' he yelled venomously. He took his fist back to punch her.

John immediately pushed him in his chest, one handed. It caught him off balance. He lost his smile as he staggered backwards into the wall. It knocked the wind out of him with a grunt. He held his hands up in surrender. 'Ok, ok. What's your problem? he snarled. 'We were just having some fun.' Cross was the cowardliest of a bully and was weighing up if he could make John a victim or whether he would become the victim in trying to do so. He seemed to sense something about John that concerned him.

'You bastard!' She cried uncontrollably, over and over hysterically, 'You bastard!'

He stepped away from the wall and laughed, 'Psycho bitch.' He shouted. 'Get over it!'

John angrily pushed him backwards harder using both hands.

Fists made, he stepped towards John aggressively. He glared at his stony face and thought better of it. He lowered his fists.

The girl, now sobbing, stepped in front of her attacker again.

There was a moment.

He ignored her and looked over her shoulder towards his mate at the end of the alley. 'Wait up, Mike,' he shouted, 'I'm coming.' He laughed.

He laughed again as he pushed passed her. She turned and watched as he strolled away to became a silhouette against the street lights at the end of the alley.

She screamed at the sky, long and hard, like a wolf baying at the moon, 'Bastard...! Bastard...! Bastard...!' as though it would somehow change what had just happened if she shouted long enough and hard enough. Anger and frustration gave way to more sobbing.

John wasn't functioning well, at all. He regretted drinking so much. He felt bewildered.

She started searching the ground for her things; skirt, panties, top and high-heels. They were all scattered, along with the contents of her handbag. He noticed her back and buttocks were grazed and looked sore from the rough gravelly ground.

John felt unsure about the incident. In the absence of knowing what quite to do he searched around also but he was useless. His eyes still not fully acclimatized, his mind clouded and elsewhere, he was still trying to assess the situation. The drink wasn't helping, his thinking was fuzzy. He looked at the man walking towards his mate. *He was getting away; they were getting away,* he thought. *He couldn't allow that, even though he had the victim to consider. And even though he'd had too much to drink, he had to do something.* 'Do you know these blokes?' he asked.

Sobbing, she yelled indignantly, 'No. I don't!'

'Ok. Sorry.' He coughed nervously. 'What happened?'

She didn't answer immediately. They both carried on searching; it seemed the right thing to do.

'I just came down here for a pee,' she sobbed. 'I'd just squat down. When I looked up, he suddenly appeared.' She paused. 'The bastard!' She broke into floods of uncontrollable tears. 'I was scared.'

He tried to calm her. It didn't work.

'He slapped me to the ground straight away then pulled my pants off. I couldn't stop him. I tried.'

She cried some more.

He waited.

'I managed to get up when he was unfastening his jeans. Then he pushed me against the wall.'

She fought back her tears.

'Then his mate came and grabbed me as well. He pinned me down.'

Her crying overwhelmed her for a moment.

'Ok. Sorry.' He allowed her to cry even though he felt he wanted to comfort her, to put his arms around her, to make it all better. He didn't know whether to or not. His police training advised not to touch a rape victim. Probably the last thing a rape victim wanted was for a man to touch her. He decided not. Instead, he thought about the definition of rape. He'd never dealt with one before. *The slightest penetration of a woman's vagina by a man's penis, without her consent,* he recalled.

He wondered how to ask her, delicately. He knew what the answer would be but he had to check; he had to be certain. Regardless of what she'd been screaming about, he had to know if he'd *penetrated* her and if so, *was it against her will?* He had to be sure.

He asked, timidly, 'Did he enter you?'

She cursed. 'Enter me? 'Course he entered me!' She cursed again, frustrated by his question. 'Yes. He entered me!'

She returned her hand to her crotch then stooped further in the pursuit of her belongings.

She found her white panties, skirt and top. She bundled them up with one hand. The bundle replaced her crotch-hand.

As much as she'd wanted to find her clothing, what she really wanted to find was her dignity again. But that was lost forever.

John gathered up her high-heels. He offered them to her just as a shoe shop assistant would.

Still in tears she snatched them from him and placed them on the ground. Trembling, she held onto his forearm for stability. She forced them on, let go of him, wobbled; almost fell over. He caught her. She grabbed him.

They kept hold of one another as they instinctively started a few steps towards the street. She soon stopped to tease her panties from the bundle held at her crotch. They were so twisted; they were unrecognizable as panties. Using her forearm to keep the bundle in place she freed her crotch-hand then awkwardly unravelled the tangled garment she'd had so frantically yanked off. She persevered. It was important to her. With a shake, they suddenly resembled panties again. John innocently watched on. She noticed and shot him a hateful glare.

He guessed what she was about to do and so obliged; he looked away and carried on searching, though it wasn't a priority. It was an excuse to look away and allow her some dignity.

She tried one-handed. She got one leg in but caught the other on her shoe. She cursed.

He swung round to see why she'd cursed.

She kept trying but she couldn't get them on. They caught on her heel each time. She glared at him again. She was angry at him; she was angry at him for being a man. She was angry at the world.

That anger would be with her the rest of her days. John knew that.

He turned his back to her to save her embarrassment.

More struggling and cursing followed.

He found her handbag. He was pleased and looked back at her. She was still naked, still struggling. He saw the problem; she was unsteady. He supported her elbow.

For a moment she became rigid and scowled. Then she relaxed. She was no longer bothered by him seeing her naked. She dropped the bundle and used both hands. It made no difference. She still couldn't get them on. She cursed again, screwed up the panties and threw them into the darkness.

'*Evidence!*' he thought; it was his training. But they wouldn't be going far, he knew the crime scene would be cordoned off by his colleagues and examined at first light for forensics and corroboration of the crime.

She was more successful with her wrap-around rah-rah skirt.

He held out her handbag.

She snatched it and probed inside; a pack of tissues.

He scooped up some of the bag's items and offered them to her in his cupped hands. They were full.

She took a few items at a time and stuffed them angrily into the bag. She missed with some; they fell back to the floor. She didn't care. She kicked them away in temper.

No more items, she hooked the bag over her shoulder out of the way to free her hands.

He focused on the two at the end of the alley. He needed to act or they'd get away.

He'd made his mind up that at least one of the duo wouldn't be going home that night. Whatever it took!

She cried out as the tissues joined the panties.

John looked and glimpsed the white ball disappearing into the darkness.

'Evidence!' But that wasn't his major priority right then. Neither was the fact the assailants were getting away. He now saw three figures at the end of the alley; one was his mate, Jerry, balancing a tray of curry in each hand.

Jerry was a great guy, well-liked by everyone; a gentle soul, a man of peace with a misplaced belief that everyone else was of a similar nature; passive, reasonable, none-violent. He and John had gone through school together and had remained best pals. He was tall; over six foot two, he feared nothing. But he wasn't a fighter, he wasn't built for it, he was the nearest thing to a human equivalent of a Stick Insect. He was more of a rational talker and a good one at that. Although painfully thin and clearly lacked muscle, he made up for it in many others ways; he had belief, courage and conviction. He believed in right and wrong. He particularly believed in *right* and certainly had the courage of his convictions, whatever it took. If push turned to shove; Jerry would shove back, best he could.

He'd heard something of the commotion when he'd left the Chinese takeaway with the girls. He presumed John was down the alley having a pee when he saw the duo. He knew something didn't seem right. He opened his mouth before thinking and asked them what they were up to. He had a tone that sounded like a headmaster questioning errant boys caught in mischief. The duo took exception to being confronted; besides, to them it wasn't a good night if they'd not beaten someone up before the end of it.

John saw them squaring up to his pal. Next; two curries trays were knocked to the ground. They splattered across the pavement.

'Do you mind? What do you think you're doing? I bought those to be eaten, not spread over the pavement,' said Jerry in his forthright headmaster-like tone.

His righteous voice could be clearly heard and he was right. Unfortunately, it was making the duo very, very unhappy and very, very angry. And unfortunately, he didn't know when to shut up. He paused and peered down the alley. He saw John and the girl. 'You alright, John? he shouted. 'We were wondering where you were, me and the girls. I did have your curry for you.' He looked at the mess on the ground then looked back. 'I don't anymore,' he chuckled. That was Jerry; laid back, always saw the funny side to everything.

The body language told John that his pal was about to be annihilated. The small guy had him by his lapels, his head tensed back like a cobra ready to strike.

Jerry was oblivious to the impending attack; he was still chuckling.

He left the girl and legged it towards them.

Before he got there the small guy launched a vicious head-butt as Jerry turned back to face him. There was a sickening thud of forehead on face. Jerry's head jolted back as his nose collapsed and burst. The big guy followed that by throwing in a fast uppercut that landed on his jaw sending his head spinning through ninety degrees.

Jerry didn't know what had hit him.

The small guy immediately stuck the nut on him a second time. It split open his cheek and crushed the bone beneath. His body went limp.

The small passing crowd that had gathered, gasped as one.

He let go of his lapels.

Jerry staggered backwards, dazed and sinking towards the deck.

The small guy stepped after him, kicking him full force in the face.

His head snapped back.

The crowd watched on; another gasp in unison.

He hit the deck. He was on his back but refused to stay down. He sat straight back up, not knowing what day it was. His blood appeared black in the amber street lights; his face was covered in it.

He lined him up for another kick.

Onlookers intervened, they shouted at the small guy to stop.

They were immediately threatened by the big guy's boxing stance and cursing. He shadow-boxed out at a few until he turned his attention to John who'd now placed himself between Jerry and his attacker.

John, adrenalin flowing, breathing heavily; 'Hold it!' He gasped. 'Stop there!' He paused for breath. 'Police!' he yelled. He was pumped, in cop mode but more in survival mode. He was aware that he was slow and uncoordinated. He'd been taught that *action is faster than reaction;* his streetwise police colleagues had told him that. *The one who pre-empts an attack has a definite advantage.*

The small guy stepped forward; wide-eyed, hyped, fists clenched and ready to go. He hesitated a small moment; he knew a threat when he saw one. Suddenly, unsure, he looked over his shoulder for his huge mate. He was there; reassurance.

The big guy, fists clenched and raised, closed in on John with purposeful strides. 'Leave 'em to it, mate,' he growled. He adopted a static fighting pose. 'Or else!'

John was already lining up the small guy so as to defend Jerry. He went into *defensive stance just like he'd been taught.* Right foot back, hands held low. 'Get back!' he yelled.

Something else he'd been taught by his more experienced police colleagues was in more simple terms, *'Get the first one in,'* - the first strike, part of the *action is faster than reaction* theory.'

The small guy feeling brave with his mate behind him, pulled back to swing but it was too late, John had already launched a fast, pre-emptive strike; he'd *got the first one in*. His fist had more than 90kg of body weight behind it and was headed the small guy's way.

It caught him, centre of target with the kind of sound that said, *good strike;* hard, effective; damaging. The small guys' body visibly relaxed instantly as though his off switch had been flicked. Black poured from his nose instantly. He reeled backwards.

Jerry was up on his feet, dazed and now heading for his attacker. He followed after him, flailing for all he was worth. The crowd cheered.

Then, for John, things suddenly went black, very black and very quiet. The big guy had ploughed in, dropped him with a blind-sider then stamped his size twelve doc Martins all over his head until he was motionless.

His senses slowly resumed a short while later. An unknown time later. He felt he was coming out of a deep sleep. He became aware that he was laid face down on the cold, hard footpath and that he couldn't move. His world remained dark, peaceful.

Sound slowly returned as one of his five senses. He heard concerned voices asking if he was ok. He didn't know the answer, he was unable to respond. He wanted to but he couldn't. He'd lost that ability. Things; sounds and noises, seemed distant at first then became clearer and louder. He felt, *sort of ok*, he thought, *a little confused perhaps, otherwise, sort of ok*. His recollection started to return. Then he didn't feel, *so ok*.

It took some time before he remembered where he was and what he was supposed to be doing. His fingertips felt a slimy substance on the ground. His cheek was in it too. It smelled familiar, he thought. He recalled what it was; the splattered curry that was knocked out of his pal's hands. His memory was coming back up to speed; it was all coming back to him. Within seconds he remembered, in disjointed flashes, exactly what had happened apart from how he ended up face down in the curry.

He opened his eyes. Things were blurred; there was a transmission problem from eyes to brain. That was for sure.

Locals helped him to his feet, pulling at him, instructing him, asking if he was ok; being careful not to get covered in the curry sauce that was all over him. Once back on his feet, they moved away like a fighter's seconds getting out of the ring to go back to their corner.

Looking like a fighter getting off the canvass on the count of nine and three quarters, he looked around to get orientated. The crowd whooped with encouragement; the fight was not over yet.

He blinked, he squinted, he shook his head and tried to get his eyes into focus. He saw that he was surrounded by a semi-circle of concerned faces, maybe twenty or so, and he was in the middle. He was puzzled by their concern.

He tried smiling at them. It hurt. There was a shocked gasp and murmuring. Some winced and held their own mouths in a fearful sort of way. He wondered why. He wondered what he looked like. He thought the crowd was maybe like a mirror that reflected in noise rather than image.

Then his knees trembled, he felt weak to the core. His brain hurt like it was being squeezed dry. There was a metallic taste he recognized as blood. His ears rang.

The ground below his feet felt like it was a moving cakewalk. He counterbalanced it by staggering. But the ground kept on moving. It came up and hit him. He rested on it, one knee and two hands. It stopped. He summonsed all his strength and thrust vertically. Though wobbly, he was back upright on two feet. The crowd cheered. It made him feel like smiling again; he thought better of it. It hurt too much last time.

He looked around, focused hard then even harder. Lots of onlookers were in a neat semicircle; in the gap, the big guy. His eyes were locked onto John. He stepped out from the audience towards him then shuffled like a boxer in a ring past the audience.

John predicted what his immediate future had in store. He had to do something about it. He felt wobbly and couldn't shake off the feeling. Trying hard to regain his balance and get his legs to work, he concentrated on resuming his *defensive stance. Right foot back; right fist tucked in against right hip, ready to strike. Left fist held out in front, elbow slightly bent,* he said to himself as he got ready. A year of Karate lessons had taught him that. Although a little embarrassed to adopt such a martial arts stance in front of the crowd, he was sufficiently self-disciplined. He believed in his own ability. Besides that, he believed a karate strike was his only effective option. He also considered how much more embarrassed he would feel if it didn't work. *But what had he got to lose?* he thought. *Trying to slug it out with this guy was never going to work in his favour.* All these thoughts flashed through his mind in a single second.

Little did he know then that the same stance, years from then, would be used with lethal consequences. But with a slight adaptation.

He pivoted on his back foot still focusing hard. He kept in line with his opponent who kept bouncing around, changing direction; right then left, forward and back just like heavy weight, Mohamed Ali. He was confident and energetic. *The guy definitely looked like a heavy weight boxer.*

John kept his posture. He saw some of the incoming haymakers and felt them before he had chance to react. His head was snapped back several times. He could always soak up a good punch but not too many more. He knew he had one chance to land *a good one*. He was going to throw a *fast, snappy punch when the time was right.* He rehearsed it in his brain. Meanwhile, he kept pivoting. Meanwhile, the big guy kept jabbing at him.

Rehearsing, visualizing, psyching himself up, he could hear his old karate instructor's voice in his head; *snappy, straight punch from the hip. Connect and follow through. Imagine the contact site is actually six inches further back than it is. Strike beyond the target! Strike beyond the target!* he used to call out as the trainees practiced in rows up and down the gym. He'd never tried it for real.

Several more haymakers connected whilst he was thinking about it. Waiting for his chance he jabbed a few lefts in return just to keep him back. Waiting for his chance. Waiting some more.

The left jabs and seeing John's stance had made him wary, but not for too long. He circled once more and moved in for a final attack. He was going for it. He did his Ali shuffle as he approached.

Waiting some more was no longer an option. He had his target in his sights. *It was time; all or nothing.* He stepped forward, launched a snappy straight punch with his right, at the same time followed through with every kilo that he had.

Strike! His head jolted back. His jam jar bottoms were destroyed and fell away, mangled.

The crowd cheered and *whooped!*

Time stood still for a second whilst the crowd *oohh'd* and *ahhrr'd* and cheered and clapped.

John was as shocked as the crowd He felt relieved. *At last, it was over,* he thought.

But no, he kept on coming.

John's heart sank. He felt like all he'd done was anger a wasp's nest. He'd no choice than to carry on the fight. He cocked his fist back against his hip; back in the breach, ready to launch again.

The big guy was back in range. John launched his fist. Smack! Another *strike* to his face. He never saw it coming.

He backed off and glanced around his feet for his jam-jar bottoms. He needed his glasses to function properly. He couldn't see them. He was distracted. John's fist launched again, it slammed into his mouth. It angered and re-focused him. He gave up on the glasses. He came forward again, furiously swinging wildly and out of control, no longer looking like a boxer. He got close.

John was too slow to step back. He instinctively reverted to street brawling and landed another one. It was sloppy but it had an effect.

The big guy was shocked.

John was on a roll. He hit him again and again then again and once more. The crowd loved it. Then a quick three steps back followed by a charging leap forward into the air and some kind of messy flying kick. It looked more like a footballer trying to put a volley in the back of the net than a karate technique. He'd aimed high but got him much lower at the bottom of his breastbone just below his solar plexus. A lucky place to hit. The big guy's breath was knocked out with a sudden, painful, 'Ughhh.' It folded him. Holding the impact site, he sucked hard to get his wind. The big guy still had his forward momentum; he was on his way down. It was like a re-enactment of the biblical, David and Goliath; small goodness triumphing over the greater force of evil.

John was as much surprised and impressed as the crowd was. He sidestepped the giant bulk of a man as he stumbled passed, eventually crashing clumsily onto his hands and knees. But not for long, he was soon on his way up. He swung around as John moved in. He caught John another one in the face; a glancing blow. He hit back then went around behind him. Reaching up around his neck he wrestled him backwards to the ground in a twisting head-lock. Both men hit the deck. Somehow the big guy ended up laid face-down with John forcing his arm up his back. Both men gasping for air, their fight was all but over. It had been messy; not like the street fights in the movies, at all.

He was a big strong guy. It was a struggle to keep him. John relaxed his full weight on top of him whilst forcing his arm up his back as far as possible to near breaking point. It gave him a chance for a breather; to assess the situation. His heart pounded, his nose throbbed and his lips were numb. He could taste more blood. His tongue felt sharp, broken teeth. His head hurt like it was about to explode, his ears ached and were ringing.

He heard noises above and to the left. He looked across. Jerry and the small guy were running all over and still slugging it out. Each attacking the other; advancing, retreating, kicking out, punching, dodging, hitting and missing. A small group, mainly girls, swarmed around them like flies around something tasty. They were all on Jerry's side, cheering when he landed a hit and booing when the other guy did. They were enjoying the entertainment. Jerry enjoyed the encouragement and admiration; no way was he giving up. He was giving a good account of himself, though he was in a bad way. It was painful to watch.

They both looked exhausted. Their enthusiasm faded. They'd both had enough. They stood looking at one another. There was a stale-mate. It was over.

John watched on. He was relieved his pal was ok. He looked down at the guy he was laid on and gave an extra push on the arm, 'You had enough?' he snarled.

A strained, *'Yeah,'* was the answer.

John cautiously got up off the guy. Some onlookers helped him get up.

The big guy stayed face-down; his arm stayed limp up his back. The nerves had been deadened.

John went over to tend his pal, Jerry. He looked a mess; they all looked a mess.

Both sides quietly retreated unnoticed. The crowd dispersed.

The police arrived moments later; two of them.

Good timing on their part, thought John, *now it's all over.* Feeling somewhat disgruntled he introduced himself; said he was also a cop and that Jerry wasn't. He told them of the rape and that the girl had disappeared.

The cops appeared mildly interested.

The two pals were given a ride in the patrol car to search for their attackers. The cops knew where they'd be heading, they said.

Half a mile up the road they came to a rowdy group of about ten, making their way back to the holiday camp. Amongst them were the assailants, Petty and Cross, pushing their machines.

Though their names were not known at that time, the patrol car's passengers positively I.D'd (identified) them; they were pretty distinctive. They weren't going to forget them in a hurry.

The patrol car pulled over about ten yards back, then radioed in. The cops turned around to their rear seat passengers and firmly told them to stay in the patrol car; *they didn't want any more trouble.*

They went over to the group and checked them out. They matched the descriptions; they could see their battle scars.

The two pals watched from the patrol car.

The group was hostile and noisy at first. It was clear they had no respect for the cops and saw them as no threat. It was equally clear from the cop's body language that the group won the nonverbal communications war in dominance. The cops seemed to be caught on the back-foot. They seemed to be the submissive ones whilst the group were the ones who appeared confident and sure of themselves. The pecking order established, the posturing and testing settled down and became less interesting for John and Jerry. They tended their wounds instead, then watched some more.

There was nothing much to see.

They tended their wounds again. They put the interior light on. They looked at one another. Jerry looked like he'd been hit by a truck. John wasn't any better to look at. They noticed their torn clothes and scuffed shoes. *Ruined,* they grumbled, then laughed at the situation and the state they were in. It hurt to laugh, they tried not to, that made them laugh even more.

They turned the light out and watched from the darkness. A lot of talking was being done. The crowd, cops and crooks laughed and made hand gestures. It looked friendly. The bikes were casually checked over. Cigarettes were being handed around for a second time. Notebooks were out; details were taken.

Cigarettes finished. Butts discarded. Goodbyes shouted. The group walked on.

The cops returned, alone.

They dropped into their seats, belted-up, started the engine the same time the cig lighter was pushed in. Click, click, vroom, click. No other noises.

Nothing was said.

John leaned forward between the front seats. 'Well? What's happening? 'He asked, hopefully.

The driver coughed his throat clear, 'Hospital for you two.'

'I mean, what's happening with them two? Who are they? Why aren't you locking them up?'

The driver looked at his colleague. 'Well, you've all had a bit to drink, all of you.' His tone changed. 'Six of one, half a dozen of the other, we reckon.'

'Well, you reckon wrong!'

'You're young in service, son. The job doesn't like this kind of thing. If you insist on pursuing it you might find yourself in the unemployment queue. My colleague here will back me up on that.' He sly nodded a wink at his mate in the passenger seat. 'Isn't that right?'

He acknowledged, 'That's right.' He kept facing forward and raised his voice for the benefit of the rear passengers. 'You're a new larker, aren't you? How long you been in the job, a year? You're a probationer. They can get rid of you just like that. No questions asked. No reasons. Half the probationers are gone within their first two years. You don't want to join them, do ya?' He paused. 'And your mate here might get done for assault and disturbing the peace too if he makes a formal complaint. Only needs them to make a counter-allegation, the other two lads, Petty and Cross.' He smiled. 'But you both know all that, right?'

They didn't reply.

He spun round to the two in the back, 'Right?'

It was one of the few times Jerry kept quiet.

John shook his head in disbelief and grimaced through shattered, bloody teeth.

The cop winced. He felt some sympathy. 'Bloody hell. You're pearly-whites are a mess. That was one hell of a fight you got into.' He looked across at Jerry and winced again. 'The bruises are really coming out now.' He looked some more. Another wince, 'Was it worth it?'

They felt angered by his stupid remarks. *It was definitely worth it,* flashed across their faces; *they'd had no choice.*

It registered. The officer backed off. His conscience pricked. 'Look, come down the station in the morning, when you're sober.'

'We are sober,' said John. 'Sober enough. We had no choice about what happened tonight. And I would have locked them two up if I was in your position.'

'Ok. If you still want to report it then….' He hesitated and glanced back at the driver for approval. Nothing. He paused for his reaction. There wasn't one. He didn't finish his sentence. He looked back at John. Embarrassed, he quickly turned to face front then gave a fleeting glance to his oppo in the driving seat.

He was aware of it. He returned a look then craned over his shoulder at the two. He said nothing then faced forward again.

The rowdy group was much farther away by now.

They all sat in silence and watched them disappear into the distance.

'What about the victim, that girl?' It hurt John to speak. His lips were scabby and twice their normal size.

The driver shuffled uncomfortably. He cleared his throat. 'No-one's made a complaint yet.' *Pop,* went the cigarette lighter. That was his cue to take a cigarette pack laid on the dash, select one and slide it between his puckered lips. He casually chucked the pack to where it had been, pulled out the lighter and poked his cigarette into it. The end glowed bright and crackled as he took a long suck. He replaced the lighter then rolled his window down. He breathed deeply. His words floated out on clouds of smoke; 'She'll come in tomorrow if she wants to cry rape.'

Feeling exasperated, 'Cry Rape?' said John. 'She was raped.'

There was a moment. No-one spoke.

He took another drag, flicked ash outside over the top of the window, pursed his lips then blew out more smoke. 'She probably had a few too many lagers, probably changed her mind at the last minute.' Another drag, more words in clouds of smoke, 'You know what they're like, these young women.' His eyes grinned in the rear-view mirror, waiting for agreement.

They were greeted by a scowl from the two in the rear seats.

The grin was lost. 'You're in the job. You know what they're like.' He asserted. 'We'll spend half a day taking a complainant statement from her, then a few days later she'll come in and ask to withdraw it. They're all the same. She was probably gagging for it.' He looked sideways at his oppo for support. 'We see it all the time. Right?'

'That's right.' He squirmed. 'All the time.' He didn't sound so convincing. He was a weak, 'yes man'.

'What about the scene?' John asked. 'Her panties and things will still be there.'

'Leave that to us son.' He sighed. 'And I'm a bit long in the tooth to have the likes of you telling me how to do my job.' He snapped. 'Thank you very much.......'

John struggled to contain his boiling anger.

There was a long silence.

The arrogant cop stubbed his cig in the ashtray as soon as he'd finished his last drag, selected the gear, dropped the parking brake and did an angry U-turn.

No-one spoke.

They were soon at the local A & E.

It was a small hospital built in Victorian times. It stood in its own grounds. It looked more like a modest stately home than a hospital. It had one main front door and double ones around the rear for stretcher cases.

They pulled up at the main door. The cops stayed buckled up.

'There you go lads. The hospital staff will answer the door if you buzz them. Sorry we can't stay.' He kept the engine running and looked at his mate for support.

He took the hint. 'Yeah, that's right lads. Sorry. We gotta go; late for supper and a game of pool back at the station.' He joked.

'You know how it is.' He revved. 'You know what it's like, John.' Twisted around in his seat he gave the injured a final look-over then winked, clicked the side of his tongue against his back teeth then turned back. He revved again and selected a gear. 'Leave it with ya kid.' He said cheerfully.

'I'm not a kid, I'm a police officer. What about that girl?' Snarled John. 'What about the scene?'

Jerry growled, 'What about us?'

He replied by tapping the throttle again, revving the engine louder.

The wounded looked at one another, they took the hint. They knew that was their cue to get out. There was no more to be said.

They both got out and slammed the car doors in protest.

Jerry went up the few steps which led to the reception door. He pressed the buzzer for attention whilst John watched the cops drive away, pondering not for the first time his disillusionment in the police, in justice, in punishment, in everything. Instead, his belief in the rationale of revenge started to fill his mind, not for the first time. He wondered about the girl and the rape scene; about Petty and Cross, the behaviour of the cops and their reluctance to do anything. He felt let down. He felt angry. Right then he felt especially angry and especially revengeful. The car went out of view. He breathed in a deep lungful of fresh morning air then joined Jerry on the steps. Below the buzzer a notice read, RING ONCE ONLY. John immediately pressed the button impatiently.

Several more seconds passed. No-one came.

Jerry, pressed again.

After what seemed like several minutes, a sleepy Matron gingery pulled the net curtain aside at one of the large sash windows and cautiously peeked out. She didn't look pleased. She was more used to reading a novel or getting a good night's sleep on the night shift. It was rare to have callers at that hour of the night, it was clearly an inconvenience. She dropped the curtain back and headed for the main entrance.

The injured pair heard several clunks as she unbolted the door. It half opened. They were greeted by the figure of a stout, large bosomed, middle-aged Matron. She wasn't an unattractive woman, especially to two young men who'd been drinking and in need of some comfort. In fact, she appeared quite attractive to them in her nurse's uniform.

She looked down at the injured standing on the lower steps like two naughty boys. One at a time, she looked them up and down, said nothing, stepped back then invitingly pulled the door open wide.

The boys remained; waiting to be told what to do next by Matron.

She beckoned them inside with a business-like, matter-of-fact inflection in her voice that could easily have been interpreted as an exasperated order.

She made it clear they were on her territory and she was in charge. 'I'm Matron! Do I need to ask what's happened to you two?' She didn't expect an answer. She had seen it all before, many times over.

She was a matron through and through, even resembled the stereotypical image of one; well-built, large rounded bosoms, wide beam, hair in a bun. She closed the heavy door and barked an order at a skinny young nurse waiting in the background who jumped to attention then ran off somewhere else.

She led the boys along a corridor into the inner sanctum. They followed in her wake, single file. She left a faint trail of an odour; cheap perfume laced with antiseptic. They entered a small room that contained old pastel coloured wall cabinets, several dark wooden chairs and surgical-type lighting on top of a stand with wheels. She allowed them in then closed the door firmly behind them.

They stood and waited for instructions.

'*Sit.*' she commanded crisply as she nodded at the chairs, she wanted them to use. They did so quickly, quietly and without hesitation. She snapped on some thick latex gloves whilst she ran a beady eye over both of them. They were meek and intimidated but strangely comforted and reassured. *Just what they needed.*

They sat next to one another. She stepped up close. Their little faces looked up at her.

She looked down at them. Expressionless, she studied the face of one, sidestepped to the second, then examined that one too. Then back again to the first. Her eyes narrowed, she wrinkled her face in disapproval and looked at both in turn. She certainly wasn't happy about the young men before her all battered and bruised, covered in blood and curry sauce, through fighting. The boy's half expected her to take them by their ears and lead them to a hot bath for a good scrubbing. Or was that fantasy? Just then, the door banged open. A stainless-steel trolley loaded with sterile dressings and a bowl of hot water came through, followed by Nurse, a moment later.

Matron and Nurse got busy cleaning away some of the blood and curry sauce with hot, wet cotton-wool. The boys were soon feeling much better. Their little upturned faces staring at the ceiling all the while. Nurse was very careful, Matron not so much, *'She'd no sympathy,'* she told them, *'Even though they looked in a fairly bad way.'*

The boys tried to explain what had happened. She ummned, ahhrred and tutted at their story. She listened but wasn't really interested. Eventually she said, *it was more than she could deal with. She wasn't happy with their injuries.* 'The on-call doctor would have to be called-out and he wouldn't be happy either,' she told them. She sent nurse to make the call. '*He wouldn't be long.*' Matron told them. *'And he won't be very happy.'* she repeated.

She was right on both counts. He *wasn't long*, he arrived within couple of minutes and *he wasn't happy* - right on both counts.

He was an old, overweight guy who must have lived nearby to get there so quickly. Matron fawned over him, she called him *doctor* every other word, it seemed.

He examined the pals. He concluded; two *concussions, two fractured noses, one displaced septum. One suspected fractured cheek bone, four black eyes, several broken teeth and two dislocated knuckles, numerous cuts, abrasions and contusions to faces, hands, elbows and knees.* 'He wasn't happy,' he said.

He'd seen those types of injuries more times than he cared to remember. 'But not so many shared between just two people,' he said. 'But you'll live,' he told them. 'Can't do anything tonight. Take pain killers. Come back tomorrow if you like,' he said abruptly before pausing, 'Won't be able to do much for you then either. But come back if you like.'

'Ok doctor. Thank you,' they both said respectfully.

'I'll leave it with you to finish off, Matron.' He smiled and was out of there. He must have been home and back in his bed within 20 minutes of leaving it.

Matron finished up, led them to the exit, reminded them to call back later then bolted the door behind them.

It was nearly daylight; the dawn chorus was in full flow. The early morning air was fresh but neither of them were able to fully appreciate it through swollen noses.

They were both groggy and arranged to meet later. They sombrely walked off their separate ways.

They met up just after midday. They looked each other up and down. They wore their wrecked shoes and the same ripped, bloodstained clothing as the night before; the police had asked them to for photographic purposes, if they decided to report it.

Jerry's left eye was completely shut and unrecognizable as *an eye*. He peeped out from the right one. It was in there somewhere; it was almost the same as his left. His nose was normally quite small, narrow and straight. It was handsome. It wasn't now. It was spread across his face and to a side. It hurt to speak; scabs had formed on his lips. He tried not to move them. When he did, he sounded like an amateur ventriloquist, 'Waste of time going back to the hospital,' he said.

They tried not to laugh at the strange voice but it was impossible not to.

John's laughter faded to a broken toothed smile that resembled some cartoon character's teeth that had been hit with a toffee hammer by a mischievous mouse. *Shattered porcelain* came to Jerry's mind. He asked, 'What about the police?'

'We've gotta report it,' he carefully replied through tight lips. His tongue reminded him of his broken teeth. 'And look at the state of your eyes, Jerry. We can't let them get away with it. We have to report it.'

'How can I?'

'We'll go together. Don't worry.'

'No.' He tried not to smile. He fought it, 'No. I…...' The smile was winning. His lips were hurting.

John puzzled.

'I meant, how can I?' His shoulders shook as he contained his laughter.

John joined in, though he didn't know why. He couldn't help himself. 'How can you what?' He chuckled.

Pointing to his own face, 'I meant, how can I look at my eyes? I can hardly see out of them.'

They both tried not to laugh. It hurt.

They made their way to the police station. It was small; built in the last century with frosted windows; tall and arched, like church ones. A square blue lamp with the word POLICE written on it hung over the entrance. The heavy wooden door beneath led into the public's reception area.

They went straight in. Reception was basic; worn, brown linoleum floor tiles met turquoise gloss painted brickwork. Its ceiling had been lowered and covered in polystyrene tiles. A brass shop-bell was chained to the pale-blue melamine counter. An engraved piece of Teak with the word, *Reception,* hung above it on chain.

It looked like it was stuck in another time, Victorian with 1960s updates and add-ons, like it didn't quite know which era to belong. Overall, it could have been described as a quaint place.

They could hear officers talking in the back office over a transistor radio's cricket commentary. It was clear they were listening to it, judging by their comments.

They must have heard them come through the door, they thought. They waited patiently expecting someone to attend them.

Nothing.

John shouted, 'Hello?' respectfully. It was a rural station and they did things differently to the city station where he worked. They were a close-knit lot, out in the *sticks*. He knew they weren't too friendly towards the city cops even though they were all on the same side. They saw the city cops as brash, impatient, unfriendly, even aggressive.

He could have walked straight into their station and gone into the office but he didn't. He tried to show respect through his behaviour. He didn't want to cause any resentment by presuming anything. Being humble and unassuming was his normal tack.

There wasn't an immediate reply as expected. The officers finished what they were saying first. Someone shouted dismissively, 'Ok. Won't be a moment,' then carried on chatting.

They waited some more.

Nothing.

The officers carried on listening to the radio and discussing the match.

He'd been patient; his normal tack changed. The top of the brass bell had a white button labelled *Press*. He banged it once with the palm of his hand. It was strident; effective. 'Hello?' he said again through tight lips. He was now in no mood to be messed around.

An officer popped his head around the office door. He saw the two standing there. He was clearly a little shocked at their dishevelled appearance. He hesitated. 'Won't be a minute.' he said in a friendly, fatherly tone, then popped back out of view.

It calmed them a little, besides there was no point in setting off on the wrong foot with them. They'd wait. They looked around to fill time. There were various posters on the walls. Some of the larger ones stood out. An A3 size one warned of the danger to potato crops from the Colorado beetle and to catch and report any that were seen. It had an enlarged picture of a beetle with black stripes on its back. A bit like the equivalent caricature of an insect criminal, if there were such a thing. *It looked fairly innocent,* they remarked.

Another caricature poster showed a cameo of a man wearing an eye mask, black striped top, running with a sack slung over his shoulder. The sack had *'Swag'* written on it. He was inside a black circle with a diagonal line through him, like a prohibited sign. It read: *Watch-out. There's a thief about. Report anything suspicious.* The pals quietly expressed their indignity at the condescending poster and discussed the insult to their intelligence but it was more for the want of something to talk about rather than any offence taken. Conversation dried up. They stared around for a topic for conversation.

Still no sign of life; only the sound of the radio.

They started on the smaller notices: the new fees for pig-movement licenses; shotgun license fees and reminders to renew them; the next parish council meeting and a hand written note about a lost tabby with owners' address for any sightings or if found. No name, no phone number. Few people had phones back then. People were poor.

John looked at Jerry. He banged the bell and twice more.

'Ok. Ok. We know you're there!' A scruffy cop with his jacket undone drifted around from behind the partition, mug in one hand, tabloid in the other. He was reluctant to venture out much farther than the doorway. His eyes narrowed when he saw the injuries. 'Ummnn.' He said thoughtfully, 'What can I do for you gents?'

They said nothing. John pointed at his face. He tried to smile.

'Ahhh.' The cop paused. He looked at John, 'You must be the young man who stuck his nose into someone else's business last night.'

He tried to scowl, but nothing worked like it used to.

There was a moment.

Then he tried to make a smile; he'd remembered he wanted him on his side. That didn't work either.

The cop took his time, sipped his drink and looked over at Jerry. 'And you must be his mate.'

The two wounded nodded.

'The lad who should be dealing with it isn't on duty until six tonight. You'll have to come back then. He's not dumping this one on me.' He said uncaringly.

Jerry glared. 'Not happy.' He said through ventriloquist lips.

The officer necked his head back. 'What?'

'I'm not happy.' He repeated.

John took over. 'I'm in the job. I'm not happy either. He should have locked them two up last night and dealt with it properly.'

'You're probably right, son. I won't argue with that. But it's nowt to do with me. Come back later.'

'What about the girl?' asked John.

'What girl?' Then he recalled. 'Oh. Her who's cried rape?' He laughed, then turned serious, stepped forward a pace, chin up, 'What about her?'

'Did you find her? Has she been in? Has she reported it?'

'First thing this morning. Never even had time for a brew or bacon banjo.' His mood lightened, 'Nice enough girl.' He reflected. 'She looked like she'd been through a hedge backwards; looked like she'd not been to bed. Mascara all down her face. Said she'd had a bath though.' He paused. 'You know.' He cringed. 'Washed everything.' He paused. 'Nice enough girl though.'

'Oh well. At least we know who she is, that's something. Even if she has washed, you'll get something from the scene. We might get them to court with what we have,' said John, hopefully.

'Doubt it.'

John cocked his head, painfully, 'Well, her panties and stuff were left there. Evidence; corroboration.'

'I'm sure it's been taken care of. It won't make any difference though.'

'Why? Why not?'

'Changed her mind, didn't she. She doesn't want to complain now.'

No-one had a chance to say anything before another equally scruffy cop appeared and stood alongside his oppo, one fist wrapped around a large chocolate bar, the other around a white tin mug; over-sized - just like it's owners' gut. No jacket, braces hanging down to his knees. He shook his head as he inspected the two punch balls that used to be faces then stepped up to the counter and right in front of John leaned over into his personal space. He examined his face like he was some kind of expert, a doctor maybe. 'Wouldn't let anyone do that to me,' said the cop, in a slow, country drawl. 'You need to toughen up sun-shine if you want to make it in this job. Grow some balls.'

John's contempt suddenly raged. 'When was the last time you found your balls? And I don't mean the ones hidden under your fat gut.' He blurted out.

He stepped back in shock and coloured up; faltered and stuttered, 'For, for your information, it was me, me who spoke to the girl. I know her mum. She was a slapper too, in her day.' His hand trembled as he slurped from his mug. It gave him time to think and recompose. 'I caught her down back alleys with fellas a few times in her younger days.' He looked to his colleague, 'Like mother, like daughter, eh?' He slurped another mouthful.

The other cop did nothing.

He turned back to John. He paused. 'You've, you've a lot to, to learn sonny. Ok?' His patronizing tone with his stammering wasn't convincing. He frowned as he looked at the injuries again. 'Any, anyway I saved her and us a lot of tru, trub, trouble.' He sipped. 'Advised her how she'd be medically and intimately examined by the police surgeon, cru, crus, crusty old Wal, Wallis and in the box too.' He sniggered at his own juvenile double on tundra. He repeated, 'In the box too.' And snorted. His mate supported him. They broke into a short schoolboy giggle.

No-one else was laughing. Jerry looked puzzled.

'Very funny,' said John, sarcastically. *Pathetic*, he thought. He was not amused. He kept his stare on the cop. He felt embarrassed in front of Jerry. 'Box. The witness box in court is what he means, Jerry.'

The cop pulled himself together. 'In the box,' he said in all seriousness, trying to recover the situation and any maturity he possessed. He suppressed a snigger. 'In the box if it went as far as court. Anyway, I said how old Wallis would have to fiddle about with her bits, take photos and samples and that a policewoman would be watching. She wasn't keen on that. I knew she wouldn't be.' He smiled proudly. 'I reckon I've done her and everyone a favour.'

He waited for some agreement.

There wasn't any.

He continued. 'If she'd been raped, she'd have wanted to go ahead with it all. Experience, see?' He paused. 'You're still wet behind the ears son.' He looked at his oppo, 'Leave it with ya.' Officer, Braces down, turned and wandered off into the back office.

There was a moment.

'As I say, come back after six this evening if you like,' said the remaining cop.

Braces down shouted from the office, 'You want to be careful you don't lose your job with an, an attitude lu, lu, like, like that.' He paused then muttered, 'Impudent yu, young bu, bug, bugger.' He stammered.

John was incapable of shouting back through his swollen lips. He looked angrily at the remaining cop who shook his head and said softly, 'Just leave it, son,' Eyes narrowed, he gave a fatherly nod.

John whispered through gritted teeth, 'He's a coward. He should come out here and say it to my face.'

The cop looked over his injuries again, closed his eyes a moment in disbelief and shook his head. He glanced over his shoulder to where officer Braces Down had escaped. Turning back, he leaned into John and whispered, 'Just leave it. He can be a real back-stabber if you upset him. You don't need that as a rookie probationer cop.' He gave a friendly wink, straightened up, then resumed normal volume. 'I'll let the lad know you've been in when he comes in at six. Ok?'

The wounded were resigned. 'Ok. Thanks.' They said despondently.

They left the station and agreed to meet back later to report it. John headed for the alley.

There was more rubbish in it than he'd seen in the darkness. The panties were gone but two balls of tissue were still there along with lip-gloss, eyeliner and a comb. He recovered them all and dropped them off at the station. The officers weren't interested so he bagged them up in evidence bags himself to preserve any forensic evidence.

A long and painful day, passed.

The two friends later regrouped.

They were made to wait forty minutes at the station after the six o'clock-shift man booked on.

That cop from the night before made no apology for the delay and said he knew who the aggressors were. 'They were in the town most weeks,' he said, 'looking for fanny or a fight,' he laughed. 'They stay on the holiday camp.' He knew who they were from the descriptions and where they'd be heading, he admitted.

The injured made statements and waited over two and a half hours to be photographed by the police scenes of crime officer.

Three weeks passed. The rural cops did nothing to bring the case to a conclusion. Petty and Cross remained free; at large.

One of the locals, a friend of Jerry's who witnessed the fight, saw the duo in the Chinese takeaway one evening. He knew they were wanted, so called the police.

They were arrested and charged. They appeared before the Courts nearly six months later. Their lawyer plea bargained; it was a routine part of the judicial system. It was accepted practice and catered for.

They pleaded guilty in return for a lesser charge; a quick hearing and a minimal sentence. It was like a ransom; a quick court hearing in return for lesser consequences for the defendants. Consideration was always given to the offenders but not so much the victims.

John sat quietly in the courtroom as a member of the public. He watched the two defendants in the dock as he slowly ran his tongue over his front teeth. They were now fixed; no longer splintered, sharp and painful. Now they were nice and smooth and perfect. Perfect, except they weren't real. They were now on a pallet. Acrylic.

Mr Wilson, the dentist, had told him they were so badly broken they were beyond treatment. They had to come out.

John had disagreed.

Mr Wilson, the dentist, insisted. He told him it would be better if they were out; health reasons. He could whip them out there and then. 'It would save the others from being pulled at a later date,' he said. He was in a hurry, he had other patients waiting, he was agitated – time was money and John's appointment time was running out. Other customers/patients, were waiting. John couldn't decide on such an important and irreversible matter so he was given another appointment and told to decide what he wanted to do before then.

John spent several weeks agonizing over the decision before he returned. The dentist was the expert, thought John. He thought he ought to trust him to do what's best; after all he had a lifetime of dental practice behind him. John had been conditioned, like everyone else, to trust anyone who was an expert in anything such as doctors, dentists, teachers, government, lawyers and so on. Mr Wilson was a well-educated man with qualifications, letters after his name and spoke with a posh refined accent like he knew what he was doing and was superior.

He made a decision. And so, he found himself back in the dentist's chair. He argued last minute, he panicked, he didn't think they were that bad and didn't need pulling.

The dentist was impatient, overbearing, not interested and dismissive and quickly convinced him otherwise.

John relented.

The dentist was pleased. His mood lifted.

And so, it was to be. He wasted no time. He numbed his mouth and took out the broken teeth along with some other perfectly good ones.

John wasn't aware some good teeth would be pulled too. That was never mentioned, if it had been he would not have consented to it. He would have made a different decision. He was shocked. The young dental nurse present had tears in her eyes. She appeared as shocked as he was. John noticed.

Mr. Wilson abruptly dashed from the room to go into another so to start on the next waiting patient, leaving the nurse to clean up his mess. Hurrying from one patient to the next was his way; clearly - time's money.

She apologised and comforted John; saying she didn't know he would pull so many perfectly good teeth when only a few were broken. She too was upset.

Sometime later, he found that they needn't have been pulled. They could all have been treated and saved. He felt angry in the extremist; he had been maimed for life so that Mr. Wilson, the greedy, selfish dentist, could receive extra payment. But it was all too late for John, he couldn't change what had been done; he couldn't turn the clock back.

He developed a habit of running his tongue over his new teeth. It was a reassurance and a subconscious reminder, especially when there was imminent physical conflict.

The dentist was nearing early retirement and got paid for the treatments he carried out. Straight forward check-ups with nothing to do, paid little. He needed all the money he could earn so that he could enjoy a retirement in good financial comfort. He drilled and yanked his patient's teeth like they were going out of fashion. That was Mr. Wilson; he'd done it for years. He was ruthless and cared not of the lifelong consequences for his patients; his victims. As a Mister, as a dentist, a man with letters after his name; meant most people were in awe of him and never questioned his practices. He was held in higher esteem than doctors in those days. He was a greedy and immoral man whose goal in life was to make money at the expense and misery of those who trusted him. He had no conscience. He maimed many individuals for a lifetime.

There were a lot of ruthless dentists back then. There were lots of people fitted up with fillings, missing teeth and dentures, who shouldn't have been. This fact was evidenced in later years. Lots of dentists worked their businesses this way to become wealthy. Some were held to account but that meant very little. Most were excused by the establishment.

Little did Mr Wilson know it, but his clock was running for sure. Mister Wilson's unscrupulous ways would one day catch up with him. It was just a matter of time.

The court case of Petty and Cross unfolded in the small Edwardian seaside resort. It didn't reflect the events of that violent night at all, as court case presentations often don't. It was hurried and brief; a summary of events. The lawyers and magistrates didn't want to spend longer than needs be in the courtroom, they all had better things to do and the sooner they concluded business, the better.
The cop in the case flowered the report to say he'd recognized the offenders from brief descriptions given by John and Jerry. There was no mention that he'd spoken to them on the same night or that he'd taken their details, checked their bikes and even knew them. Or that their arrest was the result of it being called in by the local who'd seen them in the takeaway. The informant never got a mention. Instead, the cop claimed he'd spotted them in the Chinese takeaway by chance whilst out on routine patrol. That he'd recognized them from the 'vague' descriptions given on the night of the incident. He was in fact lying of course. He was doing it to impress and looking to take undue credit; making out he was a good, conscientious, vigilant, hardworking cop. It would look good on his police CV.
The court was shown the photographs of John and Jerry with their injuries. They were passed around with mildly passing interest. No-one realized that John sitting in the court was one of those in the pictures, he was unrecognizable in them.
The hearing droned on.
The accused were represented by a lawyer at public cost. Tax payers' money.
Except to give their names and their plea, the defendants never had to speak; their lawyer spoke on their behalf. He gave an unending list of reasons why it wasn't totally his clients' fault. Numerous lies and excuses were made; '…. if anything, they could be the victims in all of this, the defence lawyer told the court: -
'High spirits; young men having a good time…...One young man's word against another….'
'The demon effects of drink. We've all been there as young men….' He smiled.
'The case wasn't as serious as the police or victims were alleging…...'
'The witnesses were fully recovered and, in any case, they'd probably gilded the Lilly, as they say…,' said their lawyer. And so, it went. He was a charmer. He laughed as he came up with the excuses; as though it was all so trivial and light-hearted, as though it wasn't a real event that had happened. He slyly checked from time to time to judge the Magistrates reaction to what he was spinning them; to see if they were falling for it.
They were. Their bemused expressions and fawning showed they were being taken in and hoodwinked by the lawyer's charming web of deceit.

He continued, '…. how it was six months on and everyone involved is now ok and perhaps better people for the experience. How his clients had learned from their mistakes and how their lives were much more stable now. How selflessly they had pleaded guilty to save the courts time and the witnesses,' trouble and distress….'

He repeatedly told them he didn't believe they'd re-offend and how sorry they were for the events of that night, now just a distant memory in everyone's mind.

He told the court; 'they were extremely remorseful; they had bright futures and any punishment to fit the crime would adversely affect their lives.'

He finished by adding; he'd stake his reputation on saying that the courts would not see the two young men in the dock, ever again. They'd learned their lesson, he claimed. He'd told the courts that claim, many times; anything to win the case.

It was a serious matter with serious criminal offences being heard before the court. Lengthy custodial sentences could be given. The magistrates retired in private to consider the punishment options available. They returned with a decision a few minutes later.

Michael James Petty and Colin Arthur Cross were smart, wore smart suits and laughed on the way out after a severe, 'wrist-slapping,' – a punishment that was of the lightest order and hardly worth giving.

John was seething; there was no justice that day. He'd seen little justice in the two years he'd been a cop. The rationale of revenge filled his head once more. He ran his tongue over his teeth. It had developed into a habit. A bad habit that was a constant reminder of the past; like his occasional lisp and the half pack of gum he went through daily.

They walked straight passed him, within inches, on the way out of the courtroom. They didn't recognize him.

He joined them outside in the corridor and watched them from a distance. He envied Cross's natural, white bucked-teeth.

Their clever lawyer joined his clients. As he approached, he laughed triumphantly and punched the air victoriously before shaking the hands of the duo. He was ecstatic.

In return they patted their sleazy Brief on his back, thanked him for doing a great job and said, 'they'd definitely use him again!'

He thanked them and handed them his business card. 'Please do,' said the slimy lawyer.

They shook hands again then headed their separate ways; the Brief for a private side room, the duo for the exit.

John couldn't believe what he saw. Revenge! He couldn't contain himself, 'Clock's ticking!' he said loudly with a lisp. It echoed around the corridor.

They both spun around indignantly with attitude. 'You talking to us?' asked the taller one, he now knew as, Petty.

John flashed his teeth at them through an awkward smile and then chewed hard.

'What do you mean?' asked Petty, aggressively.

Suddenly, John himself wasn't sure why he'd said that. *Perhaps for want of something smart to say,* he thought. *Or was it the thoughts of revenge that filled his head? Or was it just an expression of his anger?* He didn't know. The only words he could come up with again in response were, 'Clock's ticking, that's all.'

He took a step towards John, shoulders back, chest out, fists clenched, 'What's your problem?'

He made no reply. He felt certain, strong; fearless. He searched again as to why he'd called out that remark. *He didn't know what he meant right then*, is all he could come up with. He'd just got an urge to shout it. Clock's ticking; he didn't know where it had come from, he just knew he had to say it. He felt lost. He smiled contemptuously and shrugged. He felt strangely calm under the circumstances.

The duo frowned at the stranger standing eight meters away with the odd smile.

'Who is he, mate?' the blond one asked.

His buck-toothed mate made no reply. He wasn't quite sure who John was, though he looked familiar.

'Ignore him.' They turned away.

'Petty. Cross. There'll be a day of reckoning for you two.' Johns' words stopped them in their tracks. His words were spoken with menacing confidence. Somehow, they all knew something was waiting sometime in the future for them.

Cross broke the moment, he turned to Petty, 'D'ya fancy a beer, mate?' They laughed and continued out. The laugh was false. John knew that.

John looked at the old court wall clock. Both hands were on the twelve; midday.

At that time, none of them knew their paths would ever cross again. The Kairos clock did. It was set. A time was marked somewhere in the future. Nothing could change it -

For Michael James Petty: Nine years, three months, two weeks, four days.

For Colin Arthur Cross: Eleven years, two months, one day.

Their clocks were running; for sure.

The case was briefly reported in the newspaper later that day. It was a serious assault in the small town. The offenders were given small fines and had to pay compensation for the torn shirts. There was no mention of the rape and the real reason for the fight.

John kept the newspaper article folded in his wallet. He felt there had been a significant moment in time. A piece of history had been captured and frozen somehow, not in time as he knew it then but in some other way. He somehow knew it wasn't the end of the matter. He somehow knew the future was set; as though it had happened before and was like history trapped in a continuous circle, to be repeated evermore.

The officer in the case got a commendation from the court for his hard work, attention to duty, dedication and powers of observation. The Chief of Police gave him a pat on the back too. Although false, it was indeed good for his CV.

He was promoted to Superintendent within fourteen years of service. Such speedy promotion was rare. He knew how to work the system; he was a clever man; Officer Mayhew Lomax was going places.

Officer Lomax and officer Braces Down also concocted a damning report about John, the young, beaten-up cop with attitude who poked his nose where it didn't belong, according to them. He was put on reports for six months and came close to losing his job; just as they had subtly threatened.

No-one knew it then but their clocks were also running.

For the eighteen-year-old girl, the victim of that night in the alley, her clock had stopped months ago; well before the court case.

Regardless of the negative dispersions placed upon her reputation by the officers, she was a moral character and virgin before that night, a romantic too. She was, 'saving herself,' for that special man she would one day meet and marry. She dreamed of a wonderful church wedding, a loving husband, a modern semi and three kids.

Her mother was proud of her. She so loved her daughter. She came home from work late one evening and discovered her laid on her back, stretched out on the kitchen table, naked from the waist down, knees apart, ghastly pale and stone-cold. It looked like a butcher's slab with the small beginnings of a foetus and some afterbirth lain amongst the congealing blood; the floor was covered in it. She had been dead for some time. Her apparent do-it-yourself abortion had gone wrong, horribly wrong or so it appeared.

The police were called and made inquiries surrounding the tragic death. They took the usual statements; knocked on a few neighbours' doors and asked a few questions; routine.

Photographs were taken. The suspected abortion instrument fashioned from coat-hanger wire was recovered as evidence. A presumption as to how and why she had died was hastily made there and then.

The sad scene appeared to say it all. No-one had any reason to believe a third party was involved.

A Yammy 350 Power Valve motorcycle had been seen outside on the road that day. It was dismissed as, 'of no consequence; probably irrelevant, a mystery but insignificant; not worthy of pursuing.' No-one made a connection.

Very little was discovered out of the ordinary surrounding the sudden and tragic death that day.

The police collated the information and presented it to the coroner. He recorded an open verdict. He wasn't satisfied that the girl could have reached the site of the punctured birth sac without assistance; the coat hanger wire shaped as it was. He believed it possible that someone used a far greater force than she was capable of. The wire had been pushed so far and so hard that it had ruptured an artery. Not only that, the dead infant also had several puncture wounds which indicated that the wire had been used to hook and drag it out of the womb. He felt unable to give a definitive verdict and criticized the police for their poor investigation. The police response from the criticism was that, *they'd learnt lessons from it*. Who cared, it was just another job another statistic? Who cares?

John cared. He cared very much.

It was reported in the same newspaper as Petty and Cross's court hearing. There was some time between both events. No-one linked the two.

John did. He linked more than that. He kept his own counsel.

CHAPTER 2.

NIGHT TIME.

Man has but a short time to live, so it is said.
It's true; the years measured in Chronos time pass quickly. Kairos time is different and not comparable.
Time passing is relentless, regardless of how it's measured. It waits for no living thing.

Like water flowing under a bridge; moments had been and gone.
Many years had passed since that night at The Trok and the resulting court case. In fact, more than nine years, three months, two weeks and four days, had passed.

It was a little after eight thirty on an unusually warm, late September's evening.
Petty was home with his wife. She was the third he'd had. They had children. None were is.
Her and her children feared him.
She was a single mum with children when she met him. Times were hard being alone and single with three children to raise. *No man would want her*, she thought, *not with kids; baggage.* She was desperate and vulnerable. Petty recognized this and capitalized.
There were many times she regretted ever meeting him. She felt trapped and couldn't see a way out; not with three children and the kind of man he was. At least they had a roof over their heads, even though it was on a Local Authority housing estate and wasn't the best of places to live. He provided for them, of sorts.

A patrol car swung into a quiet cul-de-sac a little over a quarter of a mile away. All but a couple of the street lights had been smashed and were out. The ones intact were white single bulb, low wattage; ineffective.
The patrol car tyres crunched broken glass and other debris as headlights lit-up the abandoned houses as it went slowly by them at walking pace. They were plunged back into darkness as the vehicle drove on by. The driver, with chevrons on each arm denoting he was a sergeant and with medal ribbons above his breast pocket, scanned methodically side to side; robot-like. Scanning. He passed them all until he reached the turning circle at the end, then braked. Two rusty wrecks, bumper to bumper, no wheels, rested on their chassis'. They'd been there ages. He knew that.

They filled the circle and made turning difficult.

He knew that.

He pulled the gear lever into reverse before twisting around to look out the rear window and slowly reversed before depressing the brake pedal. A figure bathed in the red of his brake lights suddenly legged it across the road, passenger side to drivers' side. He hadn't expected that. He had to do a quick opposite twist to track the figure before it disappeared between the buildings on the other side.

He froze in thought, a moment. Then chewed and faced forward, blankly staring through the windscreen at nothing in particular.

Another moment passed.

Into first gear he slowly carried on. The road was narrow. It was tight; a five-point turn was needed.

He headed on back towards the main drag then parked half way along; away from any light. He switched off his engine and lights, unfastened his seatbelt.

He sat. He waited. He chewed.

He listened to his radio frequency. He filtered out most of the chatter and listened for the word, Sarge. His real name was John. He insisted they used, 'Sarge,' Sarge; short for sergeant rather than his real name, John. His correct radio call-sign; Romeo Hotel five zero; was too impersonal, he told them. He preferred the old ways, the old days; names rather than phonetics and numbers.

They all knew him as Sarge and so that's how they addressed him, even when they met him off duty, which was rare. Not that he was rarely off duty; it was just that he preferred not to socialize with colleagues. He had many associates but few true friends, he would profess. He liked it that way; he kept it that way. He kept his distance. He was something of 'a loner' but not in that sense of the word, not like the kind of misfit society tends to shun. He saw himself more as an island, regardless of the saying; no man is an island; well, he was. He preferred it that way. That way he could stay focused; friendships, relationships and emotions didn't get in his way.

He sometimes questioned whether he was psychotic. If he was, he was ok with that. It wasn't such a bad thing in his line of work not to feel or show emotions; not to have feelings and a conscience that would get in the way. To lack compassion or to make strong relationship attachments didn't hold him back. Though he admired individuals who could show their feelings and bond with others and make close, long-lasting friendships. It just wasn't for him. He believed it made for vulnerability. It just wasn't for him. He'd been hurt and betrayed too many times. His expectations dashed. Sometimes he wished he could be like others. It didn't last for long. He found human nature deceitful, insincere, manipulative, self-serving, false and unkind.

John was a sergeant through and through. He'd been born to be a police officer. The police force had been made for him or was it him that had been made for the police force? He thought he had been made for it. He wasn't the perfect officer by any means. No-one was. In fact, he believed there were many officers far better than him. He knew that. Everyone has their strengths and weaknesses. He knew his; he knew himself.

Without The Police Force, he would have had little purposeful meaning in life. He just wasn't cut out to be an office, nine to five, slippers and TV man. Never cut out to know what he'd be doing tomorrow, next week or twenty years from now or even what he'd be doing in the next hour. Routine, normality and predictability was never going to satisfy him. He always felt he was put on Earth for a purpose. The Force was the part of the Establishment which allowed him help victims and to do battle with the bad guys. It made things legal; he had 'right' on his side, even if sometimes the law wasn't. His sense of justice and upholding law and order was immense. As was his sense of being a Protector.

He used to say that if they sliced him open that he'd have, *Sarge,* written through the full length of his body *like a stick of seaside rock candy*. His ex-father in-law would have agreed, though he actually referred to him as *a legalized thug* rather than an officer of the law. He had his reasons. Sarge didn't mind. He understood police were not everyone's cup of tea.

He sat. He waited. He listened some more.

He watched impassively. A car would pass the end of the street now and then; a flash of headlights and taillights. Seemed like every other one was a boy-racer with a dustbin for an exhaust. Noisy. All illegal. They'd give out more decibels than any sports motorcycle with a race-can. He heard them coming ten seconds before they passed. The boom echoed down the empty street. Ten seconds later it was quiet again.

Meanwhile, Petty was laid back in a comfy chair, the only one in his living room. He sat in the dark, his lanky legs sprawled out. Mobile in one hand, remotes in the other. The fifty-inch flat-screen flickered blue around the room as he scrolled through the channels. There was nothing worth watching. He wasn't bothered; he was only waiting, passing time.

He wore expensive designer gear; tinted Cartierm custom-made spectacles with thick lens due to poor sight. Gucci jeans, white Christian Audigier tee shirt. Top of the range Nikes completed his ensemble. His long blond hair flowed from beneath a cheap, grubby NY baseball cap which always perched on his head. He was proud of his cap; '*You can take the boy out of the estate, but you can't take to estate out of the boy,*' he used to joke.

His wardrobes looked very healthy. They were packed with the best money could buy. Most of it couldn't be sourced locally and was bought in London. '*What I wear on my back costs more than what this lot around here gets in a month,*' he'd say.

He had expensive tastes in lots of things. Like the apartment in Kensington. London; his *retreat* and the place for his main hoard of cash. He had millions. Storing it was a problem; he would get *flagged up* if he put it into a bank account. He needed to remain anonymous. His apartment was secure, so that's where he stashed it. He boasted he had enough stashed there to live the good life for at least ten years. He told no-one the address.

No address.

He never took anyone there and so no-one believed him. He'd worked that one out. He knew he shouldn't have told anyone of his London Pad but being an estate boy, he had to tell someone, he had to show he'd '*made good.*' It was the *estate* in him.

The police knew where it was. Well, one police officer in particular knew, one with a very keen personal interest. He knew the address. He knew it wasn't registered to him at the official Land Registry office either. But he knew it was his.

In fact, it had never been registered since 1971when the previous owner; a politician, was more than happy to hand over the Deeds in exchange for a sack full of U.S dollars. U.S dollars that came from Irish well-wishers based in New York and Boston sent via Dublin, Ireland; no questions asked. No Customs and Excise; no Inland Revenue.

No questions asked.

Petty had also done a cash deal in return for the Deeds. The previous owner with an Irish accent and the Red-hand of Ulster tattoo on his forearm fled the country well before The Good Friday Agreement, never to return. He'd seen it coming. He had a new life and new identity awaiting in the U.S.

Out there he'd had to diversify his business slightly by not using the three paramilitary initials he'd hidden behind for thirty years as an excuse for terrorism, murder, drug dealing, robbery and the great lifestyle he'd enjoyed in the Capital of a country and government he'd claimed to despise. Idealist sympathizers had financially supported his expensive tastes especially U.S citizens of Irish ancestry.

He was older and more honest now, a citizen of the U.S himself; now just another out-of-the-closet drug-trafficking gangster, not shielded by some paramilitary organization with three initials pretending to be for the good of its country, liberation, its people and its supporters.

Some of his closest Irish friends and colleagues also did well; extremely well. They became respectable politicians overnight. Each taking half a million a year from tax payers' money from a nation they'd despised; the very people they'd hated, bombed, killed, maimed, terrorized and fought intently with for more than three decades.

He'd been a *major player*, a commander in fact. But the writing was on the wall long before the Anglo-Irish agreement was in the public domain. He would be an embarrassing skeleton in the cupboard that they could do without. He'd been given lots of tax payers money, courtesy of his politician friends, to keep his mouth shut and stay on the other side of The Pond.

He'd enjoyed living on U.S dollars in Kensington, London. He may have stayed where he was if he'd known that one day, he and all of his colleagues, even those in prison for murder and other crimes committed under the flag of republicanism, would have their atrocities virtually pardoned and be set free. None of his organization could believe the great deal they were given by the Mainland Government to stop their acts of terrorism. They achieved far more than they'd ever expected. But surrendering to the Government's generous offer meant that future *crimes*; drug dealing, robbery and extortion would merely be just that*; crimes.* Crimes without justification and support; not carried out under the umbrella of a political movement. They'd lost their legitimacy to break the law but at least the leaders on both sides got what they wanted.

Pardons and freedom for past crimes is a powerful tool when it comes to negotiation. Some called it persuasion and bribery. Some called it giving in to blackmail and terrorism. The Government of the day said it was '*a victory for peace.*'

Those who'd suffered and who'd lost innocent loved ones in *the troubles* said it was '*an abomination.*'

Money is a powerful tool. The top of the organization's pecking order was financially looked after, courtesy of a generous Government salary. Some say they sold out their true believers in *the cause;* the foot soldiers and campaigners, for their own ends; cash, respectability and of course, political status.

Petty kept links with the tattooed Irishman who was now a U.S resident living a new life. He did a little business dealing with him and his old organization from time to time; the ones with the three initials signifying a banned political terrorist movement.

He also liked the thought of breaking free, not to the U.S like his Irish mate, but to the big city and away from the North East. He dreamed of one day becoming a full-time Londoner.

He used to go there alone by train at least once a month. At those times he was relaxed, not looking over his shoulder. *He let the train take the strain,* he'd joke. He'd stay over a few days. That's when he did his clothes shopping too; *well, you can't take it with ya,* he'd joke. He could never stay there too long; *commitments.*

He was smart, always one step ahead. He had a P.O box number with the Raphael Street post office, SW7. He'd send parcels there from his hometown then collect them on the way to his *'retreat',* as he called it. He called it *his 'Drum' or 'Pad' when he was down there because that's what they, the locals, all called their homes,* he boasted. He liked to blend in with other city dwellers when he was there.

He enjoyed the walk from Kings Cross train station to get there, nipping into the post office on the way. His post office box number was registered in someone else's name who had died years ago. That way the PO Box wouldn't be connected to him should anything go wrong. He *inherited* their identity after the deceased's relatives carelessly threw out his personal belongings and documents. Petty was smart.

His apartment was smart. It allowed him to meet with his millionaire neighbours. He could see that some of them used his illicit products. He could have made customers of them, but he didn't. He kept business separate from there. No-one knew what he did; how he earned his fortune. Some were curious but he never told them. He enjoyed his exclusive apartment when he could.

He was followed there after a tip-off. It took months to do it. One experienced cop, good at his job, managed it. There were no legal grounds, solid evidence or reason to raid his *Drum* but at least his secret address had been discovered and was no longer secret to one particular police officer.

Petty was unaware of the discovery. He kept a fancy key on a fob with his other keys. He boasted it was for the seven-lever lock to his Drum, *Excellent security. He didn't want any thieving bastards breaking in,* he used to joke.

Friday night was usually a busy night for Petty back in his home city. Most of the people in his area had been paid that day one way or another, mainly social security benefits. Though lots were earning a living and from the better side of town. They all used him, all walks of life. He was a major player. They all knew who he was.

So too did the police but catching him was another matter. It was a difficult and potentially dangerous task requiring precious resources and great effort, so they left him alone. They had also found success rates for turning over suspected drug dealers had plummeted in more recent times. Targeting easier offenders, such as motorists, now seemed the preferred option. That was the public's perception which of course included the *Dealers* too. But it wasn't as simple as that; drug dealers had gotten wise. The one's that managed to stay out of the courts didn't keep their *supply* at home anymore. They didn't have callers. They didn't turn their homes into fortresses that attract attention. They didn't worry about a visit from the cops.

A mobile phone with an unregistered pay-as-you-go sim and a *Dead Drop* was the answer. Drugs were now hidden away from the dealers' homes, usually within walking distance, and in a place no-one would look; a place known as a Dead Drop, a place with no connection to the dealer. Some Dead Drops were changed regularly. Others weren't.

Petty's *dead drop* was less than five minutes' walk from his home. It was under a loose slab inside a disused garage. He kept his cash separately from his supply and in ten-grand bundles at various other *dead drop* locations. Ten-grand was a manageable size. Spread out in those amounts meant he'd only loose a relatively small sum if one was discovered.

His phone lit up then buzzed as he sat in his living room flicking through the channels of his big-screen TV. He put the remotes on the chair arm, drew in his legs and sat to attention all in one movement. He'd done it thousands of times. He reached down to the floor for a worn notebook. At the same time, he flipped his phone over, screen up. He checked; *193 Dave,* lit up on the screen. He pressed *talk.* 'Yes, mate?'

He listened to the jumpy voice on the other end and waited for it to finish. He repeated back to the caller, 'One nine three. Dave. One, three, five, three. One pack.' Then said, 'Ok. Hang on, mate.'

He put the phone on the chair arm and the book on his lap. He thumbed the pages. Each one had a column of numbers and names. Next to each number was a name followed by a string of individually crossed-out numbers that led to one that hadn't been crossed out; the last one in the line.

He found the page he was looking for then ran his finger down over the column of numbers on the far left. He stopped just below, *193*. He then ran his finger sideways under, *Dave,* then the string of crossed-out numbers that followed. He stopped - *1353*. The last number in the line. He read the line, *193 Dave, (crossed out numbers), 1353*. It checked out. It matched the caller. It was ok.

The full line above that one, *192 Debbie*, had been crossed-out. The letters, OD, written at the end. OD; (Over Dosed). There was no other number. It was the end of the line for her, in more ways than one.

The fourth line above that one; *188 Sue*, was crossed out the same but had the letter 'P' at the end. P; (Prison). But after the P, was the number 1173, not crossed-out. Not the end of the line for her, in more ways than one. That line had more crossed-out numbers than most. She'd been a busy client, a good customer.

Every line on the pages told a story.

He dwelt on, *188 Sue,* awhile. She'd been very profitable. Often buying in quantity, *cutting* it further and *dealing* herself. It funded her habit. She was a heavy user. Petty knew this. He could see from the line too.

He knew she had a four-year-old daughter. What he didn't know was that the estranged father to her little girl was a cop who was unwittingly funding her *habit* instead of the child fully benefiting from his alimony payments. But that wouldn't have concerned Petty unduly.

He also knew she had sex for money with his old mate, Col, and that she had a hundred other guys who paid her. He knew that.

Even though she was trapped in a harsh and addictive world, she'd saved up quite a pot for her daughter's future. She wanted to break out of her seedy world. She wanted the best for her daughter too. She was motivated. She wanted a better future for her little girl.

Petty didn't know that.

He knew that Col was the one who asked him not to give her a *bad deal* after he found out she'd helped grass him up. But that didn't stop him.

He gave her a *deal* that was *cut* more *pure* than normal; known as a *concentrated purity*.

She didn't know that.

It was the same strong batch as used by *192 Debbie*, OD. His best mate, Col, helped him with 192s fate.

The concentrated purity, knocked *192* off her perch but it was only just enough to put *188* Sue into Intensive Care. Her body had become more tolerant to the mind-warping substances than *192s*.

She was released after ten days. Her friend, *192 Debbie*, had already been cremated by then and her kids taken into care. One had run away.

It was a reality check for *188 Sue*.

They told her she'd done irreparable damage to her internal organs; heart, liver and kidneys. Her life expectancy would be greatly reduced.

She was determined to change her ways. She realized she had a lot to live for; that life was precious, just like the daughter she loved so very much. She'd dreamed of seeing her grow up differently to how she had. She dreamed of seeing her educated, with a good job, a husband and kids; happy. Innocent until she was old enough to deal with an adult relationship and all that goes with it. To know what love really means.

That's all Sue had wanted for herself. But being raped from aged ten by mum's boyfriend, Uncle Billy, changed everything. Forever.

Uncle Billy's fat, sweaty body, mounting her once a week for two years whilst mum was at the bingo, turned her into a drug-dependent whore who interpreted sex and abuse as love and affection; normality.

It wasn't her fault. And it really wasn't.

But fat Uncle Billy told her it *was* her fault; that she was a willing participant and that she was the instigator. That her mum would hate her and throw her out if ever she found out what she did with him.

He blamed the little girl for all that took place between them. She believed him. After all, she was the child, he was the adult. He knew best. But that confused and jarred with her self-belief.

She felt dirty, confused and guilty. She was made to keep *their secret*.

She knew no better. She was innocent; vulnerable.

She self-harmed and attempted suicide twice before going to the police about Uncle Billy.

Her mum didn't believe her. Thankfully the police and the medical examiner did.

Uncle Billy was arrested and eventually stood trial at court.

Her mum couldn't believe it. He claimed he was innocent. She stood by him.

She believed him, testified and vouched for him. It wasn't her fault; he was a manipulative character. She was weak, she knew no better. She loved him.

The young girl victim made a good witness, as did all the other witnesses in the case. The evidence and corroboration were excellent.

It was a lengthy trial, as was the defence lawyers' summing up. He had taken up most of the previous day to deliver it. It was quite a speech. He used every trick in the book to bore and bamboozle the jurors and cast doubt upon the prosecution's case. He made Uncle Billy appear to be a wrongly accused man, a man in the wrong place at the wrong time, a poor victim himself. And that his accuser was a liar with mental issues, jealous and who resented uncle Billy, her mother's latest boyfriend. He relentlessly pleaded Uncle Billy's innocence. He had a vivid imagination which he used to the full to dream up alternative scenarios to the facts presented. His imagination was in overdrive. The jury was a captive audience with no choice than to listen. Under the court rules, the prosecution was prevented from challenging the defence lawyer's drivel.

And so, it went. It wasn't about truth or justice. It was about a clever lawyer trained in the art of using words to distort facts and so confuse. He was a clever lawyer trained in the art of winning, regardless. The jurors felt relieved when he'd finished his performance.

The court was adjourned.

The jury of twelve good men, strong and true, went to deliberate in a private room adjoining the body of the court.

Everyone believed the outcome was inevitable; Guilty. It was a foregone conclusion.

It took almost a full day for the jury to decide. Finally, they were ready to give their verdict.

The court was reassembled. Uncle Billy was led back into the dock. He was sweating profusely. He was a worried man. There was an air of anticipation amongst the public gallery. Emotions ran high, some called out insults and obscenities at Uncle Billy. The court officer called Order and asked the jury for their verdict.

The jurors' spokesman stood up. 'Not Guilty, on all counts!' he forthrightly announced. That was the verdict.

A gasp rippled through the court. There was mutterings and widespread disbelief.

Uncle Billy had got off with it. He couldn't believe it. He had a shocked, O.J. Simpson reaction the very moment, *'Not Guilty...,'* passed over the juror's lips. He momentarily cried with relief then quickly regained composure. He grinned and punched the air with delight. His ordeal was over, he thought.

But it wasn't. His Kairos clock was running and running fast, the moment the jury decided upon, *Not Guilty.*

Not Guilty! The police couldn't believe it.

Not Guilty! The girl couldn't believe it. He was free to live back with her and her mum in the same house.

The girl made another suicide attempt that same night. She wasn't expected to live. But thankfully she did.

She lived with the scars on her wrists. She lived with the ones in her mind.
Uncle Billy didn't……
…….live, that is. His clock was stopped at 11.12 p.m. the same day the trial ended when he answered someone knocking at his door.

Petty had prematurely crossed out the *188 Sue,* line. He'd awaited confirmation before putting a code mark at the end.

He was surprised she pulled through. But that was ok. He grassed her up the next time she walked away with a large *deal* he'd supplied. His best mate, Col, helped him.

Six months in Holloway Prison, London, hurt her. Being separated from her daughter, unable to protect her, hurt her far worse than her time in prison. She knew Petty was responsible for her being caught with a stash. She would never forgive what he did. He had no idea what was in store for him.

He was pleased with the result. He felt good that she suffered in prison. He taunted her about her having to live in London the first time he met back up with her over a *deal*. His jibes didn't affect her outwardly. She handled it well. She never said anything in response; just smiled.

Her mind was on something else. She had plans for him.

Another line on the same page had R.I.P written at the end. Another had a question mark. All the pages were dotted with his codes, marks and crossings out. He liked to keep his client records updated. Most were regulars. He knew lots of them but couldn't remember them all. But they all knew him as a ruthless hard man, not just a dealer. No-one crossed him. He wasn't going to get caught again, he'd promised himself that much, he'd make sure of that.

They depended upon him. He held their lives in his hands. They trusted him to supply, '*good stuff; the right cut*.' The '*right cut*' was mixed with something quite innocuous; sugar or talc. *Good stuff*. They could handle a mix of about 4% purity. That's what their bodies were used to.

More than 15% and they'd be having OD written after their names. If that happened, the only column their name would be appearing in is the obituary one of *the local newspapers*. There was usually one druggy every few months off the estate named in it.

They had to trust him.

192 Debbie had trusted him even though she and her girlfriend, 188 Sue, grassed him up to the cops.

And he knew it.

Neither would be crossing him again. He'd make sure of that.

He kept another book for milder substances like cannabis, ecstasy, amphet's; prescription pills; junk. He didn't much bother with that stuff anymore. The money was in Heroine and Coke.

But there were so many on his *books* now. He'd had to devise a system so that he was never trapped by the police again. And that's what he'd come up with. It had evolved over time.

His system made sure he knew who was calling and who he was going to sell to. Only the caller and he, thanks to his book, knew the new number. Simple.

The lists were in numerical order. Their first number made it easier for him to find their name in his book. It made for easy reference. Their name was a double reference; to be sure. A double check when they called.

He'd find their name next to the number then read along the entry for the last number he'd issued them, the last time he'd dealt with them. That number was the one to be used the next time they wanted a deal. Like a reference number; authorization. A code.

He checked the number in his book with the last number they gave him over the phone. That way he knew who it was for sure. Like a password or PIN number; security, that it wasn't a set-up; a trap. That it wasn't the cops on the other end or some cop's informant or some other dealer about to bring him bad news.

The druggie knew that if ever their name and number was used to set him up, that they were as good as dead. He would know who it was using his system; who had grassed him up.

He ignored unknown callers. They had to be introduced by his hard-core, loyal users.

He crossed out the old number when they called but only after they'd confirmed who they were by using the last number he'd given them, the last time they'd dealt.

He checked the number in the back of his book where he'd recorded the last one to be issued.

He wrote the new one after it. He then wrote that new number next to the one he'd just crossed out. Simple.

He'd done 40 deals since *193 Dave 1153*.

The next new number to be issued from the back of his book was now 1194.

1194 minus 1153 equals 41.

It was his 41st deal-to-be, since 1153, he worked that out as he wrote *1194* on the sixth sheet down of a yellow pad of *Post Its*. The top sheet had *1189* on it.

He tore off the top six before standing up and stuffing them into his back pocket.

They could remember the numbers with their names they'd been given but he didn't trust them to remember their new numbers. *Most of them didn't know what day it was half the time,* he used to joke. He couldn't trust them; *they were a waste of space* he used to say. So, he gave them *Post Its* with their new number when they collected their *deal*, so they wouldn't forget it the next time they called.

The waiting cop wearing chevrons a quarter of a mile away, sat in his patrol car. He ran his tongue over his front teeth before popping in a piece of gum. He chewed a little uneasily.

He pulled out a small khaki nap-sack secreted under his seat. He placed it on his lap and looked in; stainless steel flask and plastic lunch box is all that could be seen. He lifted out the box and pulled off the lid; Mars bar, hard unripe apple that he'd struggle to eat; pack of sandwiches; bottle of water.

He peered back into the nap-sack. A couple of Jiffy bags, one medium, one small, lay at the bottom. They were postage stamped with type printed addresses and ready to go. They just needed to have their contents placed inside.

The small one had a piece of paper tucked inside with a typed address and note: -

Have a good life.
Go. Never come back.
Might see you sometime, who knows?
Tick-tock! XXX.

There was a hand-drawn smiley face at the bottom and three chevrons like the ones on his sleeves.

He placed the nap-sack on the passenger seat.

He'd used the same bag to carry his meal in for years. It was faded, worn and frayed at the edges. Others identified him with it. He liked familiarity. For him to change it wasn't an option. He tried it once for a week but everyone asked him about it as though it was a pet dog he no longer had or like a child who always carried their favourite Teddy bear around with them, then suddenly they don't. They all asked about it in one way or another. Cops were like that; curious, observers by their nature. They noticed the unusual from the usual.

He listened to the air traffic coming over his radio that fed into his ear through a personal earphone. He'd wait another twenty more minutes before calling-in to let them know he was taking his supper so they'd leave him alone. He chewed.

And waited.

He chewed some more

Chewing was a habit he had. It often reflected his mood. It was rarely open-mouthed and arrogant; he never chewed for that purpose - posing or image. No, for him, he was just pleased he still had the ability to chew, things could have been worse. Chewing often bought him time before he spoke. When he was younger, he was known for having a short temper and speaking out before thinking first. He saw it as being open and honest; others often interpreted it as hot-headed, fiery and not what they wanted to hear. He always learned from his experiences. He'd take time to reflect on all he did.

Reflective practice is how the training staff interpreted *remembering, learning* and *improving* from past experiences.

Sarge was a good *reflective practitioner*. No matter how many times he'd done something, he always analysed and explored ways to improve. Learning from past experiences was his forte. He was a quick learner who strove for perfection but never achieved it. Well not by his own perception anyway. He was hard on himself and at times it took its toll. But through his efforts he had proved himself to be adaptable and a good officer. It had given him the keys to many police departments such as the *Criminal Investigation Department*; CID.

He used to be the sergeant in the CID and had lots of experience but now he was back on the beat. He liked being on the beat; anything to get back at the bad guys. It was more hands-on, more challenging, varied and physical than the CID.

He'd worked on the Vice and Robbery squads, Surveillance Team, Pro-active Unit, Firearms and the Tactical Support Group (TSG) and others.

He'd done the lot but he couldn't hack the Child Protection Unit and transferred out after a year. He couldn't handle all the paedophiles that he knew were guilty but got off scot-free. It was worse when they went back home to live with the child victim again.

He was a protector by nature. Injustice got to him; he couldn't cope with it. Justitia Et Fides he used to quote; Latin, meaning Justice and Fidelity. He believed in it.

There was a particularly ugly case where he knew for sure the 'uncle' had done what the girl had reported to him. But he later got off at court.

It was a case that was one failure too many for Sarge. He was furious at the *not guilty* verdict given by the jurors; the Court. He was more furious when he watched the defending barrister laughing as he gave his client a triumphant high-five in the court corridor afterwards. He brought back echoes of the past. He recalled the barrister doing the same thing as a young lawyer many years previously. It was a flashback to an earlier memory involving Petty and Cross.

The offender was a horrible fat man with a police record that showed it wasn't the first time he'd gotten away with abusing little children. He'd targeted two other women in recent times that had children. They all alleged sex abuse. There was lots of corroboration but he never went to court; lack of evidence. The victims were too young and vulnerable. It was their word against his. He won, they lost; lots.

He was furious alright, Sarge told his colleagues, '*Someone ought to go round with a baseball bat and cave-in that fat bastard's head! Do the world a favour,*' he said, the day fat Uncle Billy walked out of court a free man and gave his lawyer a *high five.*

The other officers didn't seem to take it too personally. They mildly agreed with Sarge then shrugged it off; got on with their day. Sarge couldn't, he took it personally. It was his protective nature and belief in justice, retribution, punishment, right and wrong - Justice.

He'd calmed down before the end of his working day that finished at eleven that evening. He was due back at eight the next morning so he left on the dot and headed for home. Nine hours between shifts; *quick turn around* with a thirty-five-to-forty-minute drive home.

He had a reasonable night's sleep and was back at the station by 7.38 a.m. He looked a little more ragged than usual for an early-turn shift with a quick turn-around and little sleep. He felt a little pricklier than usual. He was conscious of it. He fought it. He said a few cheery, '*good mornings,*' to the cleaners, got a coffee from the vending machine and took it up to his office to read the *overnight occurrence* sheet (situation report; sitrep.) that would be waiting on his desk.

It was the usual stuff, stolen cars, assaults, burglaries, suspicious persons; things like that. He skipped over them. He looked for the interesting stuff. He was looking for something in particular.

Two items caught his eye: The first included the name of the girl in his child abuse court case the previous day. *She was in the hospital Infirmary after a suicide attempt and wasn't expected to live,* it said. It went on to say that a preliminary examination suggested she had also been violently buggered and suffered serious internal bleeding. The suspect was, '*Uncle Billy,*' *it said.* The *footnote* congratulated the night-shift officers who attended her home, gave her first aid then rushed her across the city rather than wait for the medics. It said she may have died had it not been for the officer's response.

Those footnotes were always added for the officers so they didn't feel so bad if the person didn't make it afterwards, he thought. *It was a kind, supportive thing. A good thing.* He was pleased.

He thought about it awhile.

Then he felt anger.

Then his anger turned into mixed feeling. He chewed hard. He glanced around nervously.

He'd felt angry at the offender, it was his fault she was so screwed up and now at the Infirmary.

He'd felt angry at *the system* that had so gravely let her down.

He'd felt angry at all the girl's reasons of wanting to end it all.

He'd felt angry that she'd given up.

Most of all he'd felt angry at himself for thinking that if she died it may be a blessing in disguise; he'd seen the consequences for the abused victims and it wasn't pretty. Their lives rarely resumed to normal, the majority were sexualized and became involved in the sex trade; prostitution; porn, alcohol & drug addiction; the inability to maintain a normal relationship; fact.

But it was a life and a precious life, as life is, he thought. His mixed feelings were, *wishing she died or wishing she recovered.* His mind flitted between the two possible outcomes. He didn't know. *To die*; would give her eternal peace. *To live*; would give her a life of hell and torment. Never to be normal.

He sipped his coffee a moment.

The second item was a murder. *Uncle Billy's head had been stoved-in 'by a person or persons unknown, a little after 11.00 p.m.'*

The report read, '*Initial inquiries and examination of the scene suggested he was pole-axed the second he opened his door.*

He blew his coffee and sipped some more.

He visualized the scene, he'd been to plenty; fat Uncle Billy would be in a heap in the doorway, festering in a pool of his own blood. He'd be drenched in it. It would be splattered up the walls and everywhere. Brain-matter would probably be hanging out where bony skull used to be.

He read on: *A wooden baseball bat was found at the scene.*

He thought; *Half the homes on the estate had a baseball bat behind their front door. Everyone had one. Hell, even the police property store had so many seized ones they could personally issue every cop in the station with one and still have enough left over to open a shop. With so many in circulation; they'd no chance of finding, 'the person or persons unknown.'* Though it was looking bad for him, he thought, as he recalled what he'd mentioned in anger to his colleagues the day before. *He would be a prime suspect, especially as the scene was close to his route home. On the positive side, at least the little girl wouldn't have seen the mess at the door; she was upstairs trying to end her life. Her mum would have been on her way home from bingo.* He wondered who'd have found him. He imagined the mess they'd have been met with, whoever it was that found him.

In his mind's eye he saw Uncle Billy at home as usual that evening whilst his missus was out on her *bingo night.* The weekly fear within the little girl left home alone with him, her mother not there to protect her. The dread of his fat sweaty body crushing her, hurting her, squeezing out her last drops of innocence.

He angrily sipped some more.

He recalled the girl's account in her complainant statement to the police; He visualized Uncle Billy peeling off his bulging tee shirt that was so tight it looked like a second skin, his white flab spilling out as he did so. He'd make her watch. Next, he'd pull his blue nylon tracksuit bottoms that he always wore, down over his enormous white arse. Then the massive soiled Y fronts would be dropped to expose everything to the little girl sitting naked upon her pink bedding, trembling and numb with dread.

He'd conditioned her to strip when told and to help with the precautions. He'd make her do it. He got off on it. He'd help her, then force her backwards by pushing on her shoulders. She'd stare at the ceiling, elsewhere in her mind as he rolled on top. So heavy she could hardly breathe. That's the way her statements described his actions. He had a routine. It conditioned her.

He looked back at the sitrep. He had obviously buggered the little girl sometime during the evening, thought Sarge. He'd read of cases where some paedophiles used it as a form of punishment and control over their victims. Sometimes they did it out of anger. Sometimes they also used an object to do it with; to inflict pain, humiliation, fear. He presumed Uncle Billy must have used something for such serious injuries. He must have been so confident he could get away with it now the Courts had decided he was not guilty. Seems like he was going to make sure she would never dare report him again.

Sarge's mind drifted back to the girls account and what may have occurred the previous night. His mind's eye could see fat Uncle Billy grunting, sweating and having his sick fun. He'd suddenly finish; his face red as a beetroot. He'd lay motionless a moment then slides off to get dressed. He always wiped his armpits with his tee shirt before putting it on.

She, laid there, quiet, still, eyes staring and fixed on the ceiling, tears running down her cheeks. Wishing and waiting for him to leave her.

Acting all normal, he'd go down the stairs and wait, ready for her mother to return. The little girl would stay in her room; hurting, feeling guilty, sobbing into her pillow, arm wrapped around Pooh Bear. Terrified, confused.

He sipped his coffee again.

His imagination disturbed him. He sniffed a quick short sniff. He had a habit of doing that when he gathered his thoughts and something disturbed him.

He sipped his coffee again.

He thought some more; *Last night could have been pretty much as it always had been*, he thought. *Except Uncle Billy would have heard a knock at the door and would wonder who it would be at that time of night. Then he'd guess it was the bingo-girl returning but then think, she'd no need to knock, she has her own key. Ah well, she must have left it*, he'd think. *He probably looked at the time and see she was due home - a double check. A little early*, he'd think. *He'd prize himself up out of his armchair and waddle his bulk to the door, pretending everything was fine and nothing had gone on whilst she was away. He may be a little sweaty. He was the sweaty type anyway so she wouldn't really notice. Other than that, everything would appear fine.*

He'd open the door, pulled it right back expecting to see her, expecting her to walk in. He'd be confused to see no-one there. He'd wonder who'd knocked. He'd take one cautious step then stop half a yard short of the doorstep. He'd lean forward; his plump head and wide eyes would crane around the door-frame to look up the street one way. Empty; no-one there.

He'd swivel his head around to look in the other direction and see some guy standing there just a yard away, arms raised like a church bell-ringer holding a baseball bat for a rope. Confused, he'd freeze.

No time to be afraid or react, the bat would crash into his skull. The sickening sound of wood on bone would ring out like leather on willow. He'd have known nothing about it. He'd have hit the deck like a great-big-fat-bulging-bag-of-shit, twitching, eyes rolling, blood and snot all over.

The stranger may have put in a couple more swings, just to make sure. Then he'd be off back into the night; all over in no time; Crash, bang, wallop - job done. Bye! One less menace for society to deal with. Justice dealt; one child and countless others protected. He thought a moment longer. He sniffed. He allowed himself a slight wry smile. *The day was looking brighter already,* he thought.

He sipped some more and was pleased that the little girl was hanging-in and that Uncle Billy had bit the dust.

The police service; *the Job*, had been good to Sarge. They'd trained him well and sent him on lots of training courses. He was trained and qualified as a *child protection and vulnerable* person's officer.

He'd even satisfied his fascination in the workings of the human body and got a degree in Anatomy and physiology. He was given time off work to do it all and they helped him with the fees.

He was a qualified Martial Arts coach, courtesy of *the job,* and taught officers such skills as *defensive techniques against knife attac*ks. It was a valuable skill for them to have. As part of it, he'd studied and researched real-life incidents of fatal stabbings along with the world-renowned knife-fighting techniques used by the Cuban, Korean and Japanese street-fighters.

The job had even sponsored him to visit the USA to help with his study, where fatalities from knife attacks were more common. There were many case-studies. He learned that a punctured artery could render a victim unconscious within three seconds and they'd bleed to death within thirty. That a stabbing weapon much less than seven inches in length and even as short as one and a half inches was sufficiently long enough to reach the heart through the chest wall.

He found some gangs in the US and Asia made their victims suffer a prolonged death by targeting an individual's lungs or lower intestines. They would die for sure without urgent medical attention but it would be a slow, traumatic and difficult death. The victim would be aware of their impending fate.

He also spoke to the survivors of stabbings. It had a profound psychological effect on them. They said when the weapon was plunged into them it was as though their bodies were being violated. It was a foreign object inside of them; something entering them. Some likened it to a feeling of being powerless; raped.

Stabbings and knife crime was on the up in his country. It had become a culture in some areas, a status symbol. Yet more victims were being stabbed in spare of the moment incidents with screw-drivers, than with knives. More and more officers were confronting head-bangers with knives and some were getting stabbed.
    Violence and knife crime were escalating for sure. Officers were issued stab proof jackets; they shared two amongst the whole of the city's police divisions. Only two jackets; 'Cost,' *they said*. Cash before cops!

    They'd also trained him as a police diver and a motorcyclist. He'd been given the chance to do so many things. He had many strings to his bow. *The job* had been good to him. He'd been good to *the job*.

    And now here he was back where he started, a uniformed beat officer sat in his patrol car working a busy area.
    He scanned the street contemplating all manner of things then started on his lunch box.
    At the same time, Petty passed through the bare kitchen where his wife and her three children sat at a dining table watching a small portable TV. She looked at him and subconsciously touched her swollen cheekbone. She glowered. Hate was in her eyes. The kids glanced at him then fearfully glanced away.
    He didn't look at any of them.
    Nothing was said. They knew where he was going.
    He paused before opening the rear door. He checked his mobile and patted his pocket, making sure something else was there inside. It was. It was habit, a kind of reassurance.
    He went outside into the rear yard secured by high fencing and razor wire. A gravel path led to the gate. It was bolted. He kept it that way. He quietly slid the bolts back then carefully opened it. He peeped out both ways up and down the dark alley. It was wide enough for vehicular access but no-one used it for that. *No-one about, nothing out of the ordinary,* he thought. *It looked safe*. He closed the gate then took a left. He walked thirty or so yards, then stopped.
    He looked, he listened. Nothing.
    He doubled back. It was part of his routine heading for his *dead drop*. After another fifty meters he crossed a road and dodged into another alley. It was his way of making sure he was safe, that he wasn't being followed.
    He zigzagged his way across the maze of alleyways on the estate before emerging into the bright lights of the main street where he waited a moment. He lit a cigarette, looked around and behind, listened; *all clear*. He crossed over into the alley opposite. Twenty seconds later he was at his *dead drop*. It was an insecure garage away from everything. It had the usual rubbish inside and it was dark but he knew his way around. He lifted the slab in the floor that hid his dead drop. Dozens of little packets nestled in the hollow below. They had been weighed and sealed. He slipped on latex gloves; *fingerprints,* then felt inside. He counted a half dozen out then dragged the slab back over to cover his stash. He kept the gloves on.
    He had at least ten other dead drop places that he used within four hundred yards of his main stash. They were just ordinary out of the way places that were fairly permanent; a phone box, a fire hydrant, behind a street bin; near a post box, behind a telegraph pole;

places like that. Quiet, out the way places not overlooked. Plenty of escape routes, places he could tell his customers where to meet to go collect their *stuff* after they'd paid him. Where he could emerge close by, then disappear.

He was smart. All the dead drops were near alleys. He could get around most of them within minutes without having to cross any substantial roads or be in any bright lights. He was usually out of sight. *The cops would never see him, they would never catch him.* That was his reasoning. He was right too; he'd gotten away with it for years.

He carried the packets in a black *dog-poo* bag in his gloved hand, ready to be dumped if he felt nervous - suspected something was wrong. No prints; no connection. They'd never be able to connect *the gear* to him. The case would be NFA'd. Besides, no-one bothers with dumped dog-poo bags, not even the cops.

It was the second visit to his *stash* that night. He sneaked along the unlit alleyways and stopped forty yards from one of his dead drops. He knew that if ever he was going to get *set up* or caught, it would be close to a dead drop. He thought the cops would be capable of covering a small area like that. He didn't worry unduly; he knew they were too busy chasing traffic offenders and other minor misdemeanours. Those cops who weren't busy chasing their tails were without imagination or were too lazy to be pro-active to come looking for the likes of him. He knew that. He was fairly confident that he was safe to go about his work, *dealing*, but he never let his guard down. He was just another dealer, one of many that the cops couldn't catch. It was like an unspoken acceptance that he and the others were left alone. There were too many of them. The problem was far too great to conquer. The police had tried and failed so many times. It was a problem they realized they couldn't win. Drugs were rife, they were now a part of society. Some cops believed that if the Government could have taxed the illegal substances, then they'd have made it all legal, just like the alcohol and tobacco trade. But the problem was so underground and widespread that it would be impossible for the tax collectors and Customs to police it effectively. To keep it all illegal also meant that it was another way for the Old Establishment to exercise power and control over the masses. There were of course genuine reasons and concerns for its prohibition based on health grounds. But anyone awake knows the government don't genuinely care about the electorate's health. Its illusion and deception. An old game.

He took one bag out and placed the remainder on the ground hidden out the way under a shrub, an instant temporary dead-drop. That way, if he were to get caught, they'd only find one packet. *They* wouldn't be able to prove he was a dealer. At worst, they'd only find a total of six. His main stash would remain safe.

He carried on. He took a couple of more lefts then right, scaled a wall, another right another left, through a garden and then a final right before he was there. It was a trashed phone box in a trashed street. He was three meters from the disused box. He kept in the shadows, waited, listened and watched. All clear. He threw the single packet towards the *drop* from the safety of the alley. He stepped back farther into the blackness then accessed his mobile's *'last numbers received'* list. Apart from *193 Dave* on the list there were five other callers logged as *received calls* and others as, *missed*. He called the earliest one on his list. It had been around half an hour.

The druggie at the other end answered instantly; they'd have been waiting desperately for his call; their body craving *a fix*. They all knew he dealt roughly every few minutes or so. The anticipation heightened their need, their nervous system reacted; cold sweats, unfocused, confused, shaky. Petty had no concern for the state they were in, he was running a business. He was cold and harsh. He told him he had less than five minutes to turn up with the cash in the usual place near to, *that phone box*. Then cut off.

The guy turned up in time, shaky; on edge, money clutched tightly in his hand.

Petty stayed in the shadows. He took the money. In return he told him he could go pick up his deal, *but not until he was gone*. Often nothing was said, the druggie knew where to find his deal without being told. They knew the routine. It was always the same, safe routine. If the cops were to somehow manage to bust him at those times all they'd get was him taking money and maybe find some drugs nearby with no connection to him.

Money in hand he disappeared back into the safety of the maze of alleyways.

The druggie knew where to look, found his wrap and was away.

Petty retraced his steps towards his temporary dead drop and *speed dialled* the next one on his list. *'The fire hydrant. Five minutes.'* He was there well within two. He tossed the packet from the shadows. It landed within a yard of the target.

The guy turned up; same condition as the last.

He took his money.

And so, the system went. One at a time he'd tell them to meet him near one of his dead drops. He named the place and was there well before them. The *deal* was in place before they turned up. He scuttled around like a rat in a rat-run, dead drop to dead drop. He knew every inch of the area; every dog that sniffed under a gate as he passed, the dogs that told their owners someone was passing, even the same predictable time a dog's taken for a walk. He knew every rubbish bin and prowling cat; security lights that triggered, gates that were never left open and ones that were not, the houses where stormy couples argued most nights but still tried to live together; the ones that lived lovingly and harmoniously as couples. He peeped in on some. The empty homes and the full ones; he knew. His senses were heightened and on the alert. He knew the abnormal from the normal, the usual from the *something's wrong*. Like a sixth sense.   He'd worked the area for years; he knew it well.

Not far away, the cop had finished his sandwiches; soft cheese, no crust, butter wiped on then wiped off. He tried to avoid fats - arteries to think of. He'd sliced the Mars bar up into bite size chunks, couldn't manage the apple and finished off the water. Acrylic scraped on tooth; his tongue searching his mouth, looking for bits. At the same time, he pressed the backlight button on his wrist watch; 21.03, *three minutes past nine,* he thought, *one hour fifty-seven minutes before end of duty.* His tongue kept searching.

Just then, twenty meters away, a figure stepped out purposefully from between the empty houses, three steps, before freezing and bobbing back in. They'd spotted the patrol car for sure.

The cop noticed. But did nothing.

Less than ten seconds later the same figure ran across the road behind the patrol car from passenger side to driver's side.

The cop saw it in his rear-view mirror. He'd anticipated it. But did nothing.

He sat and watched and waited.

The figure peeped from the darkness a moment, then vanished.

Petty was busy. One punter never showed. All the rest had. He pulled down angrily on the peak of his NY cap. He didn't tolerate *no-shows*. He tolerated nothing.

He had one packet left and a yellow *Post It* that read, 1173. He knew who it was; 188 Sue. He knew her well. He'd known her for years.

He held his mobile near to his face and lit up his contact list, selected and tried her again. It rang out unanswered then clicked onto voice-mail. He pressed *cancel* in temper, and cursed. *Where was she? He'd had enough of her,* he thought. *He wished he'd done a better job on her. She should have been dispatched the same time as her mate, Debbie.*

He paced a yard circle like a caged animal, kicked the wall then headed back to where he started.

He looked up to the stars with gritted teeth. Red and green lights flashed high overhead before disappearing. He thought little of it. It was a familiar sight over the estate - the police helicopter. His chest heaved as he cursed again. *Where was she? He'd give her one more minute!*

He tried again – *redial*.

Nothing; just the patronizing recording; *this mobile is switched off. Please try again later.* He pressed the *End* button hard and growled with more anger and frustration before stuffing his mobile into his pocket.

He left the wrap on the ground near the bin. He wasn't going to risk recovering it. He was feeling edgy. It could be a trap. His paranoia was kicking in. *And what was the helicopter doing?* He wondered - paranoia. He listened and searched for the lights in the sky again. *Was it looking for him?* All he saw were stars and wispy clouds. All he heard was the city noise and a barking dog in the distance. His mind wondered what the dog would be barking at but chose to ignore the question. He relaxed a little. He recalled how his *no-show* had him trapped before. *She was lucky he let her live,* he thought. *Bitch!*

'Bitch!' He muttered aloud. He folded the *Post It* twice, tore it, put the bits together and tore again before throwing the strips into the air. They scattered in the breeze. He cursed and turned for home.

The patrol car hadn't moved. Sarge got out. He stood near the open driver's door; vigilant.

His jacket and trousers were well pressed and had sharp creases exactly where they should be. He looked smart, like a man who was self-disciplined and respected his uniform and all that it stood for.

He scanned the street. A long moment passed.

Everything seemed ok, he thought.

It was a warm night; he took off his jacket. Holding it by the collar he waited another moment; vigilant – looking and listening. It was safe. He folded it over his left forearm then stooped into the vehicle. He ran his hand along the side of the driver's seat to the catch that released the backrest. He yanked it. It immediately sprang forward with a loud clunk, allowing easy access to the rear seats. It seemed especially noisy in such a quiet place. He quickly straightened up and listened, looked right and looked left. *Seemed ok.* He folded the jacket once more, leaned back in and carefully placed it on the rear seat. He backed out and slowly pushed the backrest upright so that it made less noise. He closed the door to within a few inches then leaned on it to complete the action. The mechanism engaged softly and with little noise. He didn't lock it. He slowly swept a three sixty. Nothing but lifeless buildings quietly hiding in the dark; watching with blackness separating them; the dark alleys they had created.

He paid extra attention on the blackness where he'd seen the figure disappear earlier. *It seemed ok.*

He set off back along the street, randomly shining his Mag-lite here and there, looking right, looking left, paying special attention to the blackness and the shadows.

The houses looked sad and betrayed. He danced his beam over some of them. All the doors and ground floor windows boarded, first floor ones not; no unbroken panes in any of them. Grey gravel-rendered walls, some prefabricated concrete, some with brown hanging tiles covering the upper half; cheap constructions that once formed someone's home. They would soon be nothing more than a pile of rubble then a blank empty space like they'd never existed. But for now, they echoed the past. John fleetingly recalled some of the incidents he'd attended. He walked on.

Before he knew it, he was over at the turning area where the wrecks were resting. They weren't far from his vehicle. He stopped. He did another three sixty before covering the final ten steps to reach them. He circled around and paused at the front of one. Always alert, he scanned a three sixty, one more time. Clear.

He exchanged his Mag-lite for a pair of black leather gloves he pulled from his pocket. He scanned the area again, *it seemed ok*, before he pulled them on.

He ran his fingers under the bonnet to the catch, he knew where it was. It popped up; *Thud.* He carefully lifted it using the same hand in one movement. He held it up and peered in. A small sports bag was tucked in the engine compartment. He glanced a little nervously over his shoulders before yanking it out. He looked around furtively then quietly lowered the bonnet. He took what seemed a long walk back to his vehicle with the bag, looking left and looking right all the time. He reached his vehicle and checked around before climbing back in. The bag was placed in the front passenger foot well. He sat upright in the driver's seat and watched through the windshield awhile. He saw nothing but passing traffic at the end of the street.

The back-door suddenly banged open. Mrs. Petty's peace was broken, her children startled. The ruffled dealer had returned. They all looked at him.

He glared back.

They could see he was in a bad mood. They guessed someone had failed to show. He took disobedience badly. He used fear to condition others not to cross him. He made sure he punished those who dare. The last one who made a no-show spent a night in the Infirmary soon after. Petty made sure of that. They needed plastic surgery to their nose and fifteen stitches to a slashed cheek. Maimed for life.

He had a wad of cash in his gloved hand. He threw it at Mrs. Petty.

Held together by an elastic band, it deflected off her head and rolled across the floor.

She ignored it. The kids ignored it.
They feared him; they hated him.
They all got back to watching the TV, her and the kids.
He waited by the stainless-steel pedal bin near the door and snorted through his nostrils for attention.
They ignored him.
He snapped off the latex and dumped them in the bin; habit. He took two steps, bent over and snatched up the wad. Just then his mobile lit up and buzzed inside his pocket. He pulled it out. *102 Sammy.* He automatically looked at the time on the display: *9.06pm.* He shot an angry glance at his wife and her children. They weren't looking. They dare not.
He stormed through into his living room and flopped onto his chair, pressed the talk button, *'Yes mate,'* he snapped. Then picked up his book,
It wasn't long before six more *smack-heads* were waiting for a call back. 188 Sue was one of them. She'd convinced him that she was with a *punter* earlier and turning a *quick trick* when he'd called and so couldn't answer; *she couldn't speak with her mouth full,* she laughed. *It wouldn't have been polite.*
He laughed too, but he wasn't happy.
She apologized and asked for a ten-wrap deal and perhaps she'd need another five later. *She'd make it worth his while!* She said suggestively.
He knew she'd do him no favours but couldn't resist selling, so he agreed. She was a valuable customer and bought more than most. He wrote her the new *Post It.* 1173. It wasn't too long before he set off on his rounds, six *Post Its'* in hand.

Red and green flashing lights slid across the black back-drop of the night sky and came into Sarge's view directly ahead and three hundred yards up. *Probably two clicks away. India Delta Nine Zero,* he thought. He frowned and chewed hard.

India Delta Nine Zero was the call sign for the police helicopter. Sometimes called India Delta or Nine Zero for short. It used its own radio frequency with the Command Centre except for when they wanted to direct *ground troops* and then it would switch to their frequency so they could talk directly to them.

He watched it bank left, circle slowly a couple of times then rear up and hover. He wondered what task it was doing. *He'd not heard it mentioned over his radio,* he thought. *That was unusual. If it was on a task, it would be talking to the ground troops over his channel frequency.* But it wasn't. He stopped chewing, leaned forward onto the steering wheel and thought some more. *What was it doing? Nothing had come over the radio.* He puzzled.

He watched the coloured lights in the sky with its white flashing strobe, for several minutes. It was a long way off. He knew even at that distance, and in the dark, that their night vision camera could pick him up clear as day. They'd even be able to read his registration plate never mind the large black *unit number* stencilled on his roof. *But their video tape didn't role unless they were gathering evidence,* he thought.

Judging by their position he guessed they were above the dedicated cycle track that crisscrossed the city. It was well used, especially by the burglars and motorcycle thieves to go undetected after committing their crimes. It wasn't wide enough to get a car down so once a crook was on there, they had the advantage over the police.

He stared at India Delta nine zero adjusting its position as he recalled one night chasing a motor cycle along the track. It was *two up* and they both were wearing ski masks and coveralls. They had just pulled an armed robbery using a shotgun at a filling station. He just happened to be passing as it sped off the forecourt right in front of his patrol car. He chased after it, blue lights and two tones, as far as the track then ran after it on foot. He called in other units. They moved in up ahead to ambush them. He made his way after the robbers. If they turned back, he'd be waiting, baton drawn.

He'd brought many criminals off their motorcycles merely by holding out his baton for them to run into with their forearms. It always brought them off, sometimes with a broken arm at the very least where the baton struck. *The job* didn't like it; injured criminals, *too aggressive* they used to tell Sarge even though the law was on his side. It made no difference to him except he learned to word his arrest reports a little differently - he could be as economical with the truth as any politician. Well not quite. Sarge was of the old school and tried to make the system work to the advantage of the public he was dedicated to protecting. Bending the rules sometimes was necessary for justice. He told himself; *The ends justify the means.* There were many cops of his generation who felt the same. It's the way it was. They bent the rules to make the system work.

As he made his way up the track that night, he recalled how he came across a small fire about half a yard across just to one side. He never paid it too much thought; it was that kind of place.

The robbers were eventually caught by the officers up ahead but without their masks and coveralls. It would have been damning evidence but the mask and coveralls were gone. They later admitted using a can of lighter fuel to destroy them leaving no evidence at all, just a pile of ashes with metal zip teeth in it; no forensics. They'd thrown the gun away. Sarge then realized what the fire had been about that he'd passed. *Ingenious*, he thought. They'd planned well and had done a good job of dumping and destroying any evidence that would compromise or incriminate them. All too often it's something like clothing or a weapon that gets the offender convicted; evidence - corroboration. It's difficult to convict without hard evidence such as a weapon or other corroborative evidence, Sarge knew that. Circumstantial evidence alone is poor. The armed robbers were found hiding in an allotment shed, motorcycle abandoned nearby and no explanation. Sarge asked others officers to remain outside the shed whilst he had *a quiet word* with the suspects inside. They were soon willing to admit their wrong-doings and explain how they'd done it – corroboration and admission. Strong evidence. With many previous offences to their names, they got two and a half years a piece. Their planning was good for that class of offender but they'd not planned on Sarge being part of it all; a cop who'd bend the rules for justice.

India Delta Nine Zero, crept forward, paused and rotated. Its observers would be working hard, scanning the city below through camera screens and the aircrafts windows. It crept some more. It put more distance between it and the sarge and then paused.

Even at that distance it was still over the estate. It was the third largest in Europe. Those aboard Nine Zero would see sweeping lines of white and amber street lights below with boxes scattered between them; they were actually homes that looked randomly placed as though the local authority's planning department had taken handfuls of tiny model buildings and thrown them like dice over a table to come up with the layout. It had created narrow footpaths, alleyways and ten foots. They were dark, unlit and like rat-runs. Every hundred yards had the equivalent number of hiding places. Routes fed off in all directions. Lines of full terrace's; some made up with only as many as blocks of six. Some were two storeys, some were three. Lots of semis; some apartments, some were single storey. They were open-plan at the front with small yards at the rear, some were without either. Few had vehicular access. Some formed large courts with one way in, one way out; no-go areas in their day. There was a dozen high-rise, thirty storeys high and clustered together. Parallel rows of garages were in areas away from homes; break-ins went unseen. Most had doors missing and were deserted.

Underpasses ran under main roads. Fleeing robbers, burglars, thieves and 'twocers' (**t**ake **w**ith**o**ut **c**onsent – temporary theft of a vehicle), had an unlimited choice of escape routes.

It was a burglar's paradise, crime was rife. Social income benefits, single mums, stolen goods, violence, drugs and drug dealing was all a way of life. And no-one really cared about the hundred thousand people that were stuck there except for the local MP who promised them so much. He made a life-long career out of false hope and failed promises. Most residents were conditioned by family and the Old Establishment/ Main Stream Media, to vote for a particular political party no matter what. It was in reality all an illusion, a game played by both sides of the political divide. The MP got very rich on the back of his constituents and Government pay and from the lobby groups he supported. For all the sleaze and scandals that surrounded him over the decades, he was made a Lord. Reward for playing the Establishment system so very well.

The estate was near top of the national league in most crimes and a huge problem to the Establishment. It was an enormous drain on finances and resources. Their solution was to sweep it under the carpet and try to keep a lid on it.

The second generation there knew no other way. Most were decent people, most never managed to get away from the estate. Its very name alone had a stigma attached to it. It was all declared a social-housing disaster. As always, no one from government was held responsible.

India Delta banked left, increased speed and dropped height as it tracked north before disappearing behind a roof-line to Sarge's left. *It hadn't stayed there long, maybe ten minutes or so,* he thought. *Four miles north out of the city was its hangar, they'd be there in less than two minutes. Either the job was cancelled or it was running low on fuel. Or maybe they'd headed to base for their supper.*

He relaxed, looked back and carried on chewing. *They'd be back in time for when the bars and night clubs chucked out and things racked up a notch. Drunks, assaults, car thefts, burglaries, suspicious persons; police requiring their assistance.*

Ten more minutes passed. He leaned sideways in order to pull his wallet from his back pocket. He flipped it open and looked at a photo behind the clear plastic. It was of a young child looking back at him. He sighed and blinked a couple of times to clear teary eyes before moving on.

Stuck to the leather on the other side was a *Post It*. His eyes drifted over to it. There were two numbers written. One was three digits; the other was single. He recalled where it had come from. When 188 Sue was doing her prison *time,* she'd asked for police to visit and got one. She had something to tell. She wanted some things doing but needed help. The cop who saw her was good. He didn't follow the beaten track; it's just what she needed. He was her kind of cop, dedicated, experienced, cunning, cynical and bitter. He was *'an outside of the box,'* thinker; a veteran of *the system; a* survivor.

He chewed a lot. That she could do without. It irritated her but no so much. He got on well with her, a friendship built. She gave him lots of information. He liked what she told him. She was unsure what to call him. He said she could call him whatever she wanted, *just keep the information coming.*

They both agreed never to speak about a man they both knew when she was younger, she called him Uncle Billy.

Sarge liked her and understood her problems.

She liked him and understood his. They had a bond.

In some ways they were from similar backgrounds.

She was intelligent, basically decent and above all a survivor. She was of great help to him.

She trusted him.

He trusted no-one.

She trusted him to protect her and her daughter.

He trusted himself to do just that. He was a man of his word.

She had presented him with quite a problem but he was a seasoned problem solver who enjoyed a challenge. He was an *'outside of the box,'* thinker, he told her. He had few social barriers, always considered all options even extreme ones in everything he did.

He visited her several times over the months and chatted regularly with her when she was back home, having done her time. She'd paid her debt to society.

She was a reformed character. *She had seen the light,* she told him, *it had been a life-changing experience inside jail. She'd also found God. Or He'd found her, she wasn't sure which way around it was.* All she knew is that God had come into her life and that her life had changed dramatically. She told him that, *it was as though she had meaning to her life for the first time. That she no longer felt alone in the world. Things were clearer and for the first time in her life she felt a love she'd never felt before, a protection stronger than anything she'd known and a path she knew would lead her meaningfully through life. She didn't know what God was or what God looked like, she said that wasn't so important.* 'Living a life that God wanted her to lead is what mattered,' she said.

He listened intently and chewed hard. He wasn't sure about any God. He knew there was *something*, something greater than what was physically around but he didn't know about a God. He'd seen enough horrors in life to think there may be no such thing. The Devil; maybe. But he believed in *something,* he didn't know what. He'd seen evil for sure, and so if there was evil perhaps there was possibly something of quite the opposite, *Good perhaps.* But a God? No, he wasn't sure about that.

She'd read the bible twice-over whilst waiting to be released. She shared parts of the

Good Book with him though he didn't much care for it. But he listened, he could be good at that. He always kept an open mind. '*A wise man is a quiet, receptive man,*' he told her when she questioned whether he was really listening to her.

She had her *up days* and her *down days*. It was her way. Today was an *up day*, the day when they'd met over coffee at a Costa, she was particularly excited about the *Good Book*. He was used to her ways.

For all she'd had a tough life she still looked healthy, young and sexy and turned heads. It made Sarge feel good when he was the guy she was with, even though they were little more than friends.

She carefully picked up her oversized cup, the size of a soup bowl, full of exotic coffee. She shook her long brown hair out of the way before taking a delicate sip then placed it back on the bar. 'D'ya know, Sarge, I've discovered there's more than one kind of time?'

'Really?' he smiled, 'Well you should know.' Raising his eyebrows at her, he sipped his drink.

She frowned. 'What d'ya mean?'

'There's time and then there's, *time*. The kind you've just done these past six months.' he said matter of fact. 'Your *time* served in prison.'

She laughed sarcastically then stopped abruptly. 'No. There's the time we all know. The time that's measured and divided into parts; hours, minutes, seconds. Days, weeks, months. There's another time. A time......'

He casually interrupted, 'I know, the *time* you did inside.' He took another sip. 'I presume it goes a lot slower in there.' He snorted.

She tutted, 'Very funny.'

'Sorry. So go on. I haven't got that much, '*time,*' today.' He laughed at his own quip. She didn't, she ignored it.

He noticed she was serious, 'Only joking. Ok. So, tell me, what's this other time?'

'Well, it's not that kind of time we know. It's not a measurement, not as in segments anyway. It's more a thing or lots of things. It's something I know you'll be interested in.'

She looked to where he was looking. She saw he was distracted by a pretty young woman across the café as he drank his espresso. It was a bad habit of his - people watching, especially pretty women.

'Are you listening?' she snapped.

He turned back to his friend on the stool next to him. 'Of course, Susan but if this is building into one of your bible-bashing lectures, I'm not interested, you know that. If it's something else, then that's fine.'

'Well, it is...,' she hesitated, '......and it isn't. You see there's a *time clock* and there's what I call a *Kairos clock*.' She gathered her thoughts.

He immediately filled the quiet space. 'Kairos clock? Sounds Greek to me. I didn't know they made clocks.'

'Stop messing!' She thought a moment. 'Well actually it is Greek in a way, well the word is. They called the time that we all know, Chronos time, as in tick-tock time, chronology - measured in minute's etcetera. Chronos, as in chronology but Kairos time is....,' she paused. 'Hold on. I need help.' She dived into her backpack laid on the bar next to her elbow. She pulled out a notepad, found the page then read excitedly, picking up where she'd left off...... 'Here we are, Kairos. Kairos time is heightened time, a significant time, a fulfilled time, time bursting forth with meaning, it is a moment, pregnant with possibilities, a unique moment in time…....'

He jumped in. 'Slow down. There's a lot for an old cop's brain like mine to take in.'

She looked up at him, took a deep breath and deliberately slowed. She read on, 'A special time of harvest, a definite period or season.' She paused. 'It's a kind of God given time of opportunity, a season, a fitting time, a time to act. That last sentence was off the top of my head. Hold on.' She searched the pages for more.

It was a long moment.

He thought about what she'd said. Then moved on, discreetly eyeballing the pretty girl a couple more times.

There remained a silent, empty space.

He filled that space. 'How's the little one? Still doing well?'

She never looked up. 'Ummn…, she's fine. yeah, she's fine.' She replied dismissively. She was more interested in the writing. 'How are things with you?'

He ran his tongue over his teeth and considered her question.

Not waiting for the answer, 'Here we are,' she continued. 'It could be described as a God-given moment of destiny not to be shied away from but seized with decisiveness; the floodtide of opportunity.' She paused and looked up at him to make sure she had his full attention. She had. She carried on. 'You'll be interested in this next part,' she said with bright eyes and a smile. She'd lost her place, backtracked and found it, '…...the floodtide of opportunity and demand in which the unseen waters of the future surge down the present. It's the alignment of natural and supernatural forces creating an environment for an opening to occur; a time when heaven and Earth align with one another in a spiritual sense; a time when heaven touches Earth in a way that will never be forgotten.' She reached for her coffee. Looking for a response she kept her eyes on him whilst she drank. He was listening. She put her cup down and smiled. 'What d'ya think?' she asked.

'I'm not sure. It sounds good and I like the way you've written it. I presume it's for that bible-study thing you've taken up, is it?'

'No. I wrote it for me.' She smiled sweetly at him, 'Well, and for you. You know, for what we've been talking about. Do you understand it?'

He considered the question as he drained his espresso then placed his cup in the saucer. He peered into her cup to see if she was ready for another. He registered that she wasn't. She watched him expectantly.

He felt *on the spot,* a little uneasy. He sniffed. 'Well, kind of.' He said hesitantly. 'What you're saying is that this *Kairos time* isn't about the time we all know but time created by *moments* in life that have a knock-on effect for the future and that some ordinary moment in time has the capability to forever change the outcome of time itself. Something about heaven having a hand in it too, though I'm not sure about that part of it. You know; heaven and the God thing?' He winced. 'I'm not into that.'

She was pleased and couldn't contain herself, 'That's right. Well done! It's the moment of decision, the moment of action, the moment of change. It can be a moment or entire season of moments. The intervention or assistance of heaven too.'

'Not so sure I know what you mean about the seasons bit, and that.' He sipped his dregs.

'But you see that one event, a moment in time, can affect the future and in so many ways we are responsible for what the future holds. Some things we can change and some things are changed for us.'

'Like Karma?' he asked.

'Ummmn…Not quite. I don't see it like that. Though I believe in, *do good; get good back….*'

'Do bad things, get bad in return…...? What goes around comes around, as the old cop who showed me around used to say. God rest his soul.' He paused. 'Look, you got me at it now. He used to say, *get the first one in,* as well. He didn't mean coffee either.' He fisted his palm to show her what he meant. He laughed. She didn't, she was busy pulling another book from her pack, a small hardback. She offered it to him.

'Here. Read it. It may help you understand.'

'No thanks. Not interested in your God. I got my own. It's black, made of titanium, twenty-one inches long when extended and it's what violent men understand. I call him Mr. Baton. One strategic whack with that on anyone and it brings them to their knees. That's the God that I believe in and that's what saves me,' he laughed. 'Or my CS gas.'

She remained serious and wouldn't take no for an answer. She poked the book at him.

He took it and looked at it a short moment.

'So, Chronos time, as in chronological, is divided into parts, hours etcetera as a measurement,' she said. 'Kairos time is time measured by events. Something significant, that's Kairos time. Get it?'

'Just about. Two clocks recording time but in different ways. Does the Kairos clock, tick?' He smiled.

She frowned dismissively. 'I'll ignore your stupid remark, I'm being serious. Some believe that Kairos time has already been; it's already history, that a Kairos event is what makes the future. So, if you do something against God's plan, you'll be later punished in Kairos time. That's as I read it. I could be wrong. Others say it's all God's time and God's plan and that whatever He has in store will happen, regardless.'

'Not the God stuff again, please. You're starting to sound like a Religious Education teacher. By the way, you ever thought of becoming one? You're bright enough.'

She frowned and shook her head.

'Seriously!'

'Thought about it when I was younger. That or a nurse,' she said thoughtfully.

'There's still time.' He cringed slightly.

'Is there?' She looked sad; resigned.

'Sorry. I wasn't thinking. So, you look so healthy these days. You really do.'

'Well life doesn't always work out or run smooth but I think that sometimes we have to suffer to help us with the bigger picture and to make us who we are. I'm not sure about the events in my life. I don't know why I had to go through what I have. Maybe one day I'll find the answer. Anyway, we all have to die, Sarge. And that holds no fear for me anymore.' She crossed herself then took a moment. 'I know I'll be going to heaven. God forgives all those who truly repent their sins.'

He further regretted what he'd said. 'Sorry. You look so healthy. I forget.'

She smiled forgivingly and squeezed his forearm reassuringly.

He took a deep breath. 'Sorry,' he paused. 'Getting back to the subject, so it sounds like this Kairos thing is like fate, in a way?' He still felt awkward from his remark. He peeped into her cup again, he nodded at it. 'I'm having another. D'ya fancy one?'

Her mobile rang just as she declined his offer.

He put the book down on the bar and went and ordered. He looked around as he waited. The pretty woman was still there. She caught his eye and they gave each other a warm smile. He thought of it as a little Kairos moment; *may lead somewhere, it may not.* He saw his friend still on the phone, slipping her backpack over her shoulder. She mouthed across the room, 'Gotta go. See ya Sarge,' then gave a cute little wave.

He mouthed back and gave a smile and a *thumbs up*. 'Ok,' he mimed.

She looked over at the girl he'd been smiling to then back at him. She smiled and slightly shook her head at him in fun disapproval.

He raised his eyebrows and shrugged boyishly. He mouthed, 'Everything ok?'

She nodded and left with the phone still to her ear.

He returned to his seat and the book she'd left. He sipped his coffee then glanced around a moment later. The pretty girl had gone. He took another sip. Wrapped up in his own thoughts he stared into space, he was miles away.

Someone dropped a fork. The crash of metal on ceramic tile brought his mind back into the café. He gazed around blankly. He checked his phone for something to do then randomly opened the book left on the bar in front of him. A *Post It* sheet with numbers on marked the page. He peeled it off and laid it in his wallet. He read for something to do: -

Almost every living soul has moments of Kairos - instances where a person is so dramatically overwhelmed with life events that time stands still and is no longer relevant. When the things of common, normal life cease, and a person's focus is directed on one defining, specific, notable and special moment that has deep significance to him, as life itself is put on hold, and the drama of Kairos unfolds.

Kairos is an ancient Greek word meaning the 'right or opportune moment.' It is used to define a specific time that exists in between regular time ("Chronos"); a moment of undetermined period of time in which something unique and special happens. A watershed moment that affects every aspect, forever more, of the person's life, and is measured with the nature of time that is defined by quality rather than quantity.

He paused momentarily to sip.

He continued; *it's the experience of time that occurs between the clicking seconds and moving hands; time stand still as life unfolds and takes eternal significance. When our loved ones die, it happens. When we are faced with a truth that is so horrific that our normal minds can hardly grasp, it happens. When we are faced with a life change beyond our control, when our souls are overwhelmed with sadness and lostness, when change abruptly comes to us unawares, the time of Kairos transcends the defined time of man.*

'Wow.' He said quietly out loud. A little embarrassed he looked around to see if anyone had noticed. No-one had. He lifted his espresso without looking and carried on reading. *What if our newest understandings of time were applied to the ways of our Lord God?*

What if the aspect of Kairos was the movement of God Himself, as the defining moments in life are without the restriction of time?

What if His Will is moved and offered to those in the time of Kairos, and the decisions to accept His way forever joined to Him through time eternal?

He turned the page. A tatty, passport-size photograph fell out onto the floor from somewhere else between the pages. He slid off his stool and picked it up. It was of a young girl. He studied it for a while and gently caressed it with his thumb before carefully slipping it in to his wallet. He sat back down and carried on reading, *what if it was Him that stopped time for our souls, to allow us to face the horrific, confusing, difficult, trying, emotional, life-changing events to give us an opportunity to reflect, analyse and respond with clear mind and intent? The Word of God speaks of times of Kairos.*

There were suddenly too many *what ifs* and *God* words for his liking, though he was fascinated with the concept of Kairos. He reflected upon one such moment many years ago. The thought entered his head without effort. He thought back to the time in the court corridor when he'd shouted, *'Clock's* ticking,' to Petty and Cross. He remembered it as a defining moment somehow. He didn't know why he shouted it or where it came from or what it was supposed to mean, perhaps it was a warning or even a threat. It was as though it was an involuntary reaction, as though someone spoke through him. He pondered a moment.

He was uncomfortable in his mind and shuffled on his stool, he sniffed then gazed out of the window, deeply in thought. He was oblivious to the hordes outside going about their daily business. Instead, he was thinking of the Kairos time, similar to a ticking clock but rather measuring life in segments of moments rather than measurements of time as on a clock face. He liked the idea and believed that's the way he'd been living his life for some time. It was a realization; *Perhaps God had been in his life all along and maybe He was with everyone all their lives.* He pondered some more; *Perhaps we are all instruments of God's Will and it's that which makes God's plans successful, a kind of divine intervention through mere mortals. Perhaps,* he thought, *he ought to listen to what God wants him to do rather than making his own plans.* Then he thought, *what the hell am I thinking about? It's time to stop this way of thinking!*

He closed the book and looked at its cover. It had a picture of a clock face with black handled commando daggers as hands set at the eleventh hour; eleven o'clock. It was entitled, **The Kairos Clock**. It prompted him to look at his wristwatch; it too showed, *11.00.* His heart missed a beat. He wondered of the significance. *'Coincidence.'* he thought. *'Time; what's it all about? Two different kinds but somehow linked perhaps.'*

He finished off his drink and headed out. He left the hushed sanctuary and surroundings of the Costa and was hit by the hustle and bustle of the noisy city street. It brought him back to the here and now. He had a one-minute walk back to the station.

He stared back at the book he was carrying and thought of the dagger his father had left him. It was very much like the ones on the book cover. It took his memory back to when his father had died a couple of years ago. He missed his father; he'd been his rock. He left him a few things upon his demise; the usual household contents of an eighty-year-old; decades-old worn-out furniture, dusty carpets and old-fashioned curtains.

A wardrobe full of clothes from an era past. Cardboard boxes containing memorabilia that meant little to anyone except to their owner.

Cards from his kids; Christmas and birthdays stretching back over thirty years. Faded photos piled in a biscuit tin with letters from someone he'd never heard of.

Personal papers; Certificates of achievement, birth, marriage and divorce. Receipts and *yet to be paid* utility bills, things like that; the usual stuff. He had the task of sorting through it all.

It was a difficult moment for Sarge; going through his father's possessions as it is for anyone in that situation. Not easy.

He binned the lot except for two things: -
One; a red oblong presentation box about 30cm long with a red velvet lining
Two; an unlined tobacco tin that had seen better days. The word **Crap** was felt-tipped on the lid in large scrawl. It held four medals from the Second World War. The discs of nonprecious metal, ribbon attached, rattled unceremoniously within and seemed to have had little value to its former owner; his father, who'd been one of the Marines that stormed Sword Beach on D-Day - June 6th 1944 when 150,000 allied military personnel stormed the beaches of Normandy, France. It was a pivotal moment in the battle against the invading German army of World War 2.

At fifteen his father, Mike, lied about his age to join the Marine corps, so ended up there on that most significant, bloodiest and cruel date in recent history. He was not even eighteen years of age on D Day.

More than half his troop never made it to see sunrise the following morning. He occasionally mentioned some of the events and personal conflicts of that moment in history but never spoke of how he'd won the four symbols of recognition; discs of metal with ribbons attached stored in the nondescript tobacco tin discarded at the back of a drawer. It was as though he'd rather forget.

Sarge recalled when, as a child, seeing his father cherishing the red box. It was home to the commando dagger that had saved his life during the Sword beach assault. *When sand rendered his weapon useless his twelve-inch length of tempered steel had saved his skin more times than he could remember,* he used to say. Although Sarge at the time was a very young boy when he heard the story, he used to let him handle the dagger and was told, '*It was very special, it was blessed.*' He believed him; after all, he was his father. He was also a young boy of an impressionable age but knew he could trust his father's word. '*It had it blessed by the local vicar before he'd been shipped out. That it had possessed God's strength and guidance. It was sacred instrument of righteousness. It had protective powers and he should always keep it even when he'd passed on,*' he told his son. '*It was made to destroy evil. He was sure it would one day be righteously used again sometime in the future.*' His fathers' words had been burned into Sarge's memory.

The weapon did indeed seem special somehow. It had been made to protect and save and yet in order to protect and save, it had to destroy. Its design was simple, its purpose clear.

It was designed as a stabbing weapon as opposed to a slashing knife. Its reliability had been proven, times over.

Black in colour, made from one piece of around 250grams of tempered steel with a handle that sat well in any fist; it looked lethal even when laid in its box.

The business end was seven inches long; enough to reach any man's vital organs. The handle five inches in length, it was overall, from tip to top, twelve inches (30cm) in length.

It was a shade over an inch at its widest point that tapered down to nothing. A two-inch guard separated the blade from the handle to prevent the hand slipping forward upon impact or resistance. Even moderate pressure applied to the tip could produce the equivalent of several tons per square inch pressure giving it great penetrating abilities.

Even though it was a stabbing instrument as opposed to a slashing one, its edges were fine. It was capable of piercing any living thing. It could enter a body quickly and be easily withdrawn. It needed little training to be proficient in its deadly use.

It had no moving parts to jam or go wrong. It would never run out of ammo or misfire. It needed no maintenance. Cleaning was nothing. Its length not too long to be unwieldy; short enough to be fast, manoeuvrable, effective; lethal.

Some would view it as an ugly destructive instrument, purely a killing weapon.

Sarge saw it as a thing of beauty that saved his father's life.

And if it had not been for that piece of sharp steel he wouldn't have existed, for he was born not long after the war. *He had that inanimate object to thank for his very being,* he thought. *He would always keep it*. He'd keep it for many reasons, not only because his father had told him to; it had sentimental value and his father's words concerning it remained forever fresh in his memory. It was a link with the past. He somehow believed in his father's spiritual belief and the mystique foretelling of the knife's future use.

Seeing the *Post-It* in his wallet had triggered so many memories in an instant yet was over in a flash. But he was now returned to the here and now. Leaning forward onto the steering wheel he looked back up at the sky for Nine Zero, he wasn't exactly sure why. It was all clear. All that was up there was the amber glow of the city lights and the brightest stars shining through. Some patchy cloud lingered at an altitude of about five hundred yards. *Only a cloud base of less than two hundred yards would probably ground the twin engine, MD 902 Explorer helicopter. It had a maximum flying ceiling of around three hundred yards,* he recalled. He enjoyed retaining certain facts and data; it's the way his thought processes worked.

He had a good knowledge of the aircraft; he'd dabbled with the idea of joining the aircraft unit and read up on it in preparation. It's something he'd wanted to do with a passion but an adverse report lodged in his personal record from some years previous, prevented him. The senior officer of the aircraft unit also had a dislike of him. Sarge was well qualified for the job but was black-balled before he had a chance. *It was the force's loss,* he used to think, *not his.*

He took out the *Post It.* In a slight trance he touched the photo momentarily with deep affection, *snapped out of it* and stuffed the wallet back into his pocket. His mind drifted, he imagined the aircraft just coming into land back at base, its noise increasing to ninety decibels as its fibre woven composite quills braked its descent until the skids felt the tarmac; it's one-hundred-and-ninety-gallon fuel tank, almost dry.

It would have been in the air maybe three hours, burning fuel at a rate of fifty gallons per hour, increasing to more than seventy gallons at full throttle when rushing to its next task at over 150 m.p.h.

The crew would be ready for a stretch and a break, he thought. *It would be a chance for a brew and ablutions whilst it refuelled and had its Integrated Instrumentation Display System thoroughly checked whilst on the ground. IIDS, as it was known, provided both digital and analogue read-outs for clarity.* He recalled.

He knew it would be refuelled and ready to scramble at a moment's notice. He'd researched well for the Nine Zero interview that never happened. He enjoyed technical data and was fascinated with how things worked. That's the way he thought. That was him. And if he was going to do something; he was going to do it well: Pride. He liked to be well prepared. *Fail to prepare; prepare to fail*, was one of his motto's. His officers had it ringing in their ears many times after a cock-up where they had failed to prepare. But he usually covered their backs; as they covered his. *Everyone had their strengths and weaknesses.*

He looked at his wrist watch. It was getting on for 21.30. He waited for a gap in the radio traffic and called in *'code three'* along with his badge number; *officer taking refreshments*. One of the few times he used his number. He never took more than thirty minutes and usually a lot less. He couldn't see the point of wasting time after he'd eaten; there were bad guys to catch out there.

He was often lucky to get a break at all, never mind thirty minutes. He worked a busy station and its officers got little let-up during their shift. He was more fortunate, he could more or less pick and choose the incidents he attended. The Command Centre would direct him to some incidents; serious assaults, robberies, difficult or unusual tasks, things like that. To supervise, take responsibility, delegate, organize and assist officers at the scene. Draw on other resources and generally make sure the job was done correctly. The rest he would choose himself. The rank of sergeant had some privileges and pulled some weight.

He popped in gum, chewed. He thought about The Kairos Clock book. He wondered whether everything that was to be in the future had already taken place. Whether anyone really had any control over events that would form people's lives; their *Kairos moments*.

His understanding of Kairos time was that if a significant event occurs then it has consequences to all that happens in the future. That mankind was just some sort of chess pawns in a complex game - a Matrix of sorts.

He realized he was thinking too deeply, so stopped.

Time to get down to business, he thought. And so, he rehearsed in his mind the next Kairos moment he was going to experience. He stared blankly, straight ahead.

A long moment passed.

Then a small figure, holding four Rottweilers, two pulling either side, came into view. They grew bigger as they got closer and further from the main drag until they were with Sarge.

The dog walker remained a short guy. His dogs were all muscle and huge.

He stopped and looked in at the sarge sat in the darkness of his patrol car. The dogs wanted to carry on.

He noticed the guy stopped. He watched him out of the corner of his eye. He looked familiar. Thick white hair stuck out both sides of a craggy face with a long, bent nose. He was distinctive with a face that would be hard to forget. He had dark, kind eyes.

Sarge didn't move, hoping against hope that he'd not been noticed or that he'd get the message he didn't want to engage with him and his dogs. He hoped the man and his canine friends would go about their business whilst he got on with his. This was not in his plans.

The little man remained; seemed like he wasn't going to go away.

Sarge stopped chewing. He slowly turned his head and looked sideways at him and his big dogs. *Little man syndrome,* he thought. *If you can't fight, get a big dog. Or if you can't fight wear a big hat,* as in '*a police helmet.*' That was the saying given to some officers who were bullies and cowards and hid behind their uniforms. He smiled to himself at the police term and visualized some of the ones he was thinking of.

The man smiled back. 'Evening officer,' he shouted with a cheery smile. His dogs barked. A command was made. They were instantly quiet.

Sarge accepted he'd been seen and nodded in acknowledgment. He raised his hand then looked forward, hoping the man would get the message and walk on.

He waited a moment.

They left his peripheral vision. Expecting to see the man and his dogs behind his vehicle, he twisted around to check. He was surprised to see him standing near to the rear passenger side window. *Doesn't look like he's going away; better get out and scare him off.* He quickly jumped out of the vehicle and stood in the open driver's door as though ready for business, one hand on top of the door and one on the roof. 'Can I help you?' he said abruptly. He tried to sound unfriendly, officious.

'Hello officer,' the man replied with a happy, foreign accent. 'No thank you, I'm ok. I just walking my dogs.' He reined them in. It took all his strength.

Accent; *Eastern European maybe. Perhaps Polish,* thought Sarge.

He introduced his dogs as though Sarge would like to meet and get to know them all individually. With a nod to each one as he proudly said their names, 'This Pliny, this Plutarch, this Socrates and this is Puppy. They, my babies. They look after me.'

Pliny, Plutarch and Socrates, Greek names. Maybe he's a Greek then? Thought Sarge.

He couldn't see them too well from where he was. He left the safety of the door and met him on the pavement, keeping a distance between himself and the four jaws with dogs attached.

'Well-behaved dogs you got there,' his tone more friendly, a subtle hint to keep control of the hounds. He moved closer.

The dogs wagged, they sniffed, they pulled and barked. Their sounds amplified in the quiet night air.

Sarge stopped in his tracks, tried to look unconcerned, but couldn't.

They were excited, protective and aggressive. Each one, the potential to be a brutal killing machine. A pack like that could become an uncontrollable force of instinctive wild behaviour. Powerful, unpredictable; unstoppable. That thought flashed through his mind in a second.

Necks extended; snarling rows of sharp white teeth flashed in gaping mouths wrapped in muscular jaws that could crush bones.

Unsure, afraid, Sarge retreated back a pace - casually, to save face. He lifted his hands up to his chest, out of the way. His stare locked onto the dogs.

Each dog would have weighed as much as their owner and was far stronger. Without training and discipline, just one dog would have been more than capable of pulling the man along wherever it chose. And to do whatever it wanted. Yet they were trained, very well trained in deed. And disciplined. They were basically raw savagery, sheathed in black and tan fur over lean muscular frames.

The thin, craggy faced man yanked their leads, barked each name one by one and followed it by a word of command. Each one responded in turn and immediately became obedient, still and quiet except for their panting; as though turned off onto standby mode. The control was impressive. Four lethal weapons on hairspring triggers, all controlled by their owner's simple voice commands.

Sarge tried to regain psychological ground. *It wouldn't do for the police to appear afraid.* 'So, what you up to?'

The man ignored the question. He sensed the fear. 'You can stroke if you like. They won't bite,' He smiled mischievously, 'unless I tell them to.'

Sarge looked on, unsure. *Could he trust this man? Statistics show cops get caught out every year, some get maimed even killed,* he thought. *He didn't want to become one of this year's statistics.* His eyes flitted between the dogs and the man's face.

'Go on, stroke. It's ok.' He encouraged. 'They get to know you. You become friend. They remember you. Then they not bite. I instruct them to remember you.'

He moved slowly forward, chewed hard and paused. He looked into the man's eyes for more reassurance.

He nodded and smiled. 'Friend, friend. Good.' The canines were programmed.

Reassured, he warily reached out and bravely rubbed the nearest one's head. In return it sniffed and licked his hand. He stroked each one in turn then used both hands on the one nearest, casually, like he'd never been afraid.

'Used to live down here, officer.' The man interrupted. 'Sixteen years. Me and my wife. Kids grew up here.' He paused. He appeared distressed, he searched for words.

Sarge waited patiently.

'Wife was killed, you know.' He turned away and nodded, 'Just over there.' His voice broke, 'Only last year.'

There was a solemn moment.

Sarge knew. He recalled reading about the incident reported in the sitrep. He was tempted to ask about his wife, he knew he ought to, but didn't. He resisted. It would be a whole new can of worms. '*Time,*' he thought.

'It used to be nice place to live at one time.' He turned back and smiled through sad, watery eyes, 'Kids playing here around neighbourhood. Nice people. Many proud gardens.' He looked up and down the street remembering how it used to be; a street bathed in brilliant sunshine, a happy place with white painted fences, the scent of summer and flowers, neighbours chatting, the sound of children's laughter. Sarge's eyes and imagination joined him, he saw it too.

An uneasy silence settled.

Sarge felt his pain.

The man took a deep sigh. 'All clean and tidy back then. We knew all neighbours. This street was nice street.' He discreetly wiped away a tear. 'Until all the blooming druggies took over, that is. Scum! They mug me one night. So, I tell police. They arrest them. Then scum come to my home later and stab my dog many times. He in garden. Poor thing screamed. He in so much pain. Then they stab him through heart. Me, kids and neighbours, we all see it. We couldn't stop it happening. He was the big druggie man, the boss. He come into my garden, broad daylight. He killed my old dog Plato. He a lovely dog. Druggie – he bad man. Everyone knows man but afraid of him. He bastard! Bastard. So, no-one gets involved. Police say, *sorry, can't help.*' As usual.'

Lost for words, Sarge nodded thoughtfully. Besides, no words would be enough. He knew that. Not really wishing to engage in a lengthy conversation either, 'Yes. It's a shame,' was the best he could offer, *Time was running out.* He thought. He had things to take care of.

'I know what I'd do with them!' The dogs rippled; they sensed his anger.

He sniffed. 'You and me both, sir!' then chewed. *One of those individuals who probably says the same thing every day to everyone, a damaged soul. He felt for him, he was an ok guy after all. First impressions can be wrong,* he thought.

A moment of restlessness rippled through the dogs again. One sharp word made them freeze. 'Friend.'

'What good dogs you have, sir,' he said, changing the subject. He wished he had more time to talk to the man, but he didn't. 'They're a credit to you, sir.' He glanced down at them. He happened to notice his own boots were dull and dusty. Instinctively he stood on one leg and rubbed them lightly on the calf of his trousers. Shiny again, he felt like a smart cop.

The man watched. His dogs, never off guard, shuffled tensely at the action. Another word of command and 'Friend', they relaxed.

'You now have shiny boots, yes?' He smiled. 'Smart.'

'I like to keep them that way. Spit and polish. Habit.' He sniffed. 'Standards. Smart, yes.' He smiled. *But maybe not that smart tonight*, he thought.

'Like soldier in army. Yes?'

He smiled, said nothing.

'It's a changing world, officer, I don't like the way it's going. This country used to be wonderful place to live. No more. Sad, very sad. It all change.' He looked along the street. He stared.

Sarge joined him. As though they were both back in a time, a better moment that was now history.

It was a long moment.

Cold, soulless buildings huddled shoulder to shoulder, stared back. Abandoned. A testament to a flawed vision, of arrogant incompetence and weak Local Authority. A weak Authority made from a judicial system geared up to make lawyers rich regardless of morals, truth or justice. Regardless of upholding the law and protecting those who were the victims. The true meaning of Justice had become lost many years before. The rights of criminals had become key and overshadowed common sense and the strength to stand up and be counted. To uphold the fundamental ethos of democracy.

His strong accent, a little difficult to understand at times, 'They'll all be flattened in next couple of weeks.' He said, 'Private development. I just taking last look. I walk this route most nights.' He paused. 'The scum of the Earth is taking over officer and spoiling it for rest of us. Smart lawyers and Government see to that. All they care about is themselves and making lots of money at our expense. They don't live like we have to.'

'I wouldn't say that. I think it needs redeveloping. The planners got it all wrong, for sure.'

He frowned. 'No. You misunderstand. I not saying the developer's scum.' He smiled. 'I meant the druggies, burglars, thieves and TWOCers. Twocers, you know; the car thieves, twocers. That lot.' He nodded to the wrecks in the turning area. 'They were Twoc'd. Look at it. We all suffer for them. I know you people do what you can but your hands tied, aren't they?'

'Well, I suppose they are. Yeah, I know, Twocers; taking without consent. Doesn't sound as bad as stealing a vehicle but it is.' He stole a glance at his wristwatch. He saw the dog man notice and felt a little rude, a little guilty and insensitive. He felt embarrassed. He made up for it. 'So, so tell me, what happened to your wife? He could no longer resist. 'You say she was killed?' he said exploringly.

'Yes. Last April fourth, just carrying shopping home on bicycle. Stolen car came belting out of ten-foot alleyway.' His hands clutching four leads he chinned towards blackness forty yards away, 'She never had chance. Straight over her.' He wiped a tear with his shoulder. 'Four in the afternoon. All schoolchildren witness it on their way home. Terrible, terrible.' He shook his head in disbelief as he relived the event. 'They have many drugs in car.' His eyes streamed; his nose dripped.

There was a moment whilst he sorted it.

'Sorry to hear that. Sorry about your loss, sir.' He waited. 'Did we get them?' he asked gingerly, afraid he might get an answer he didn't want to hear.

He stared down at the ground, recalling the past. 'Yes.' He nodded. 'Your officers got them all, *five up,* as you say.' He looked up into the distance. 'Half a mile from here, they stop and *star-burst* out of car, you police say. Some, they got away. None would admit being driver, they say drugs not theirs; belongs owners of nicked car. Owner of car owned drugs, they say. They not admit to it, they admit nothing. They never go to court.' He looked back along the street to the place then settled on a house twenty yards from it.

Sarge's gaze went along with him.

'That was our home, my lovely Anna and me. We lived there one time. We were so happy. Now just me and children.' He paused. 'We all miss Anna. They miss their mutka - their mother as you say, their mamma.' He took a long sigh, 'I miss mutka, also.'

Angry, he chewed hard. 'I'm sorry,' he said.

'Don't be. Not your fault. I no want pity or to self-pity,' he snapped. 'Is not good. I just miss my Anna so much, life not same anymore.' He hoisted out a crucifix on a chain around his neck, kissed it hard and long before letting it go. Then sternly said, 'God rest her soul, she's with Him now, God. *God never pays his debts in money*; I think you say. They got what was coming to them.' He looked down, nodded thoughtfully to himself before looking into Sarge's eyes for his reaction.

He felt awkward and didn't want to ask but couldn't help himself, 'I don't know about the God thing.' He was hoping for good news, so asked, 'What happened to them, the crooks?'

It was painful, he was hesitant. 'Well, a few months after they killed my Anna, they drove another car, stolen, into bus. They always twoc cars. They doing fast speed over eighty on the west of city. Newspaper say it was eighty. Had four of your cars right behind them, blue lights, noisy sirens. Still, they ignore police and don't stop. They crash. Two got killed; thieves that is. I hate them twocers.'

He sniffed, said nothing and thought. *Wasn't expecting that! Thought they might have gone to prison. Ah well. Better them than some innocent person minding their own business. Good riddance.*

'Bus driver was my good friend, Klimek. And Anna's too. That's what I do also; I drive buses. Klimek, was good man. Police blamed him for accident. Said he should have seen stolen car coming, shouldn't have pulled out. He says he see them and didn't want them to hurt anyone else. He told them he do right thing. He stopped them. He now in prison for long time. Long time.' He shook his head, thought a moment. 'Funny really, name Klimek in my country means gentle and merciful. And he was that. Now he suffers with mind – cos what happened. And he misses family, they miss him.' He shrugged defeatedly.

It was the same old story Sarge had heard a thousand times; *bad guys do what they want; everyone else suffers. Good guys get hammered if he confronts or intervenes.* His spirit sank a little but his determination and righteous self-belief in the imminent Kairos moment he knew was coming; grew.

The man with his canine pack looked so sad; heartbroken.

Sarge chewed hard. He stared at him. He wished he could turn the clock back. He wanted to give him belief, some hope, faith. Faith in a system that failed those it was supposed to protect. A system that protected those it was designed to punish.

'Kairos!' Sarge suddenly proclaimed.

The dogs came to attention. Puppy gave a single bark, deep and guttural.

The old man snapped at his lead, frowned and thought a moment. 'Kairos? What is Kairos?'

Sarge was re-energized, enthusiastic. 'The Kairos clock! Well, Kairos time. A moment that's significant. A time.' He heard himself sounding staccato with a raised voice as though that would enable him to be understood better. 'The hands of the Kairos clock. They go from one significant event to another. Kairos!'

The man's expression didn't change.

Sarge checked himself, shook his head and calmed. 'She's got me at it now,' he thought out loud.

The man looked blank.

'Nothing. Never mind.' He chewed.

'I don't understand.'

'Ok. It's just something a friend told me. I thought you'd know, it being a Greek word and all. Kairos?'

The man remained blank.

'Never mind.' He smiled.

'Not Greek. I Polish. I a Pole.' His eyes lit up and narrowed with a smile. 'I remember, Kairos. In the bible, yes?'

He was mindful of the time. He wanted to check his watch but knew he shouldn't. He chewed. He needed to end the encounter not start a new conversation. Changing the subject, 'So where you heading now?'

'Just wandering. Looking around. Is that ok? Why you ask?'

'Just wondering. Ok, well go steady.' He backed towards the car boot, a hint that the conversation was over. 'Nice meeting you. Sorry about your Anna, your friend and your dog. Goodnight, sir. You take care.'

The hint was taken. 'Ok, officer. Goodnight. You take care also.' Looking at his dogs; 'Friend, friend. Ok.'

The pack ambled up the street, stopping occasionally for Pliny, Plutarch and the others to have a sniff and mark their territory. They faded into the blackness between rows of terraces.

He watched and waited until they were out of sight, then turned away.

The Pole and his pack did a U-turn a moment later and watched from the shadows. They all stood, unseen, like statues. He watched the police car. It was dark but could see a man there struggling into matt black coveralls. He was wearing a ski mask, thought the Pole. From that distance and in the poor light, he couldn't tell for sure. He noticed the persons shiny boots. He watched them as they were purposefully marched off towards the alleyways on the opposite side to the patrol car. They were on a mission. They were smart. They were soft-soled and made almost no noise. They kept a regular pace and vanished between two houses. They took a few turns and diagonals, tripped a security light on the edge of an inhabited block that was ignored, made some dogs bark, scattered some cats and gathered more ground dust and became less shiny as they made progress. A minute and a half in and another dog barely heard the boots going by. Unsure, it went to the gate, poked its nose out, sniffed hard in and sniffed hard out; boot polish, latex and gum. Not a threat to the animal, it remained silent. The sound and smell soon faded. The boots continued with purpose, steering a course north to south, through the rights and lefts of the alleyways and ten-foots. Three minutes gone, the pace and purpose remained.

Petty was heading in the opposite direction to the man wearing shiny boots. His routes were meandering and zigzagging, yet efficient and planned. He always knew exactly where he was. He knew the area intimately like the back of his hand. He'd been quick. All his customers had been served, just one to go. He collected the bag from his secondary dead drop containing the rest of the packs. The *Post It* read *188 Sue. 1173*. He'd marked it *10*. He had nine packets in the bag for her. *It would cost her the price of ten for the one he'd left uncollected.* He was no different to any other ruthless businessman. Money and profit were everything.

He made for the dead drop at the telegraph pole forty-five seconds from his home. It made sense to do his last drop near to it. It was a bad habit he'd gotten into. It had become predictable and not as random as it used to be. A lot of his clients had realized that he used the telegraph area as one of his last drops for the last one on his list. Some had even worked out his pattern of dead drop areas. His face glowed in the light of his mobile as he scrolled down his contact list whilst heading back. Stopping on 188 Sue, he pressed *connect*.

She answered after one ring. He never had chance to speak. 'Hi Mike. Really sorry. I'm on my way. You know how it is. Might need a bigger *Deal* later on. Bigger than I first said. Is that ok?' She never gave him a chance. 'I know it's always the other way around but can you give *me* five minutes this time, please? I'm sorry. Five minutes? It's usually you saying that to me'

He'd had a reasonable night and was feeling ok and a *ten deal* was worth it. 'Well, I'm not happy. But ok. The telegraph pole. In three.' He pressed, '*off*.'

He always kept his mobile on silent. It lit up and buzzed whilst it was still in his hand. If it was a druggie wanting to order a deal, he'd leave it. They'd have to wait until he was home and when *he* was ready to answer. They all knew his ways. He checked first; *188 Sue. 10.01pm*. He pressed *talk*. 'Sorry Mike. I'll call you in a bit. Problems. Why don't you go back home and I'll call you then? Sorry.' The line went dead.

Two right turns, a couple of left's passed the telegraph post, a right, across a road, fifty yards and he'd be at his rear gate. *Why not? He could take another half dozen calls and head out again.*

He was on autopilot; a left turn, *fifteen seconds to the next left. Twenty seconds to the next turn.* His mind was home ahead of him; *fifteen seconds to the turn right, thirty-eight steps later he was upon it; his familiar rear gate.* He'd be there in no time.

Half a second before the turn right his brain registered a whiff of gum on the fresh, night air. He ignored it as he rounded the corner of the garage block. He was suddenly confronted square-on and less than a yard away by a figure dressed all in black. He was standing in an unusual posture. Petty was alarmed, he'd seen that stance many years ago. It stopped him in his tracks, he stood to attention. He looked the stranger up and down in an instant. He was smaller than himself; black ski mask, coveralls, gloves and boots. He could see his right foot was slightly to the rear. Right fist tucked in midway down his side; thumb uppermost, elbow back. It was dark but he could make it out.

He'd walked the route many years and hundreds of times, he rarely encountered anyone. He was shocked to see the image before him. His brain was scrambled, assessing. His adrenal gland sprang into action - fight or flight, it told him. Flight had never been an option for Petty. Well-rehearsed, his hand dived into his jeans pocket and grabbed his razor-sharp flick-knife, thumb over the release button. At the same time his vision focused on the eye holes in the mask for something to recognize; a clue; to make sense; to give his brain an answer. He questioned; *Who was it who dared be on his territory and stand before him?* He was angry. *He would destroy the threat - regardless.*

The ski masked figure assessed back through the eye-holes. The figure before him was as large as ever and had put on about fifteen kilos since they'd last met years ago face to face, he thought. The distinctive blond hair hadn't changed much, neither had the face. The *jam-jar bottoms* reflected what little light there was. Even though the baseball cap was pulled low, he could see who it was. *It was his man. For sure.*

Outrage flashed through the big guy's every nerve. He tensed. *This was his territory and he would defend it. The man in front of him was a threat.* His brain sent a message to draw his knife and stick the object blocking his path. His eyes acquired a target in the area of the stomach. His brain visualized what he was to do next. He was quick; he'd been in these kinds of situations before. It meant nothing for him to stab. Many thought-processes were firing off much faster than his body could react. But he was well practiced, confident and care-less. He was quick.

But not quick enough. With no time to react, the stranger struck him in the side of his chest, midway, just left of his sternum and remained there momentarily. Both men rocked an inch or so on their heels upon impact. The attackers arm remained outstretched. Motionless. It caused Petty to be slightly off vertical.

The speed of the blacked-out stranger surprised him just as much as the way he had knocked the wind out of him. The pain was searing. He felt confused; *this little guy packs quite a punch!* He felt his left side deflate. His coordination was out of sync, his body tensed causing the thumb on his knife to press involuntarily. There was a metallic click as the catch released the spring that shot out the blade. It sliced cleanly through his pocket and the denim surrounding it. It remained there, rigid but impotent. He could do nothing.

His arm still outstretched, 'Lucy!' shouted the attacker, controlled and rehearsed. He knew that his seven inches of tempered steel would have severed Petty's external and internal intercostals; the muscles that help expand and retract the ribs for breathing. It would then have poked through the chest-cavity housing the body's vital organs. Then several inches later would have torn through the sack containing the pleural fluid surrounding the lung. It would then pierce the lobes and bronchioles of the organ and perhaps the larger bronchi higher up. Above was the heart, so to avoid it the target area had to be fairly low; ideally between the second and third rib up.

He knew lungs were complex and although he'd seen many at the mortuary, he knew he could not be precise in the situation he was operating in.

He knew that whilst the blade remained inside that it would restrict the free-flow of blood from the severed vessels. Equally, he knew that psychologically, from those who'd given accounts of being stabbed, said they felt greatly violated whilst the stabbing instrument was inside of them; they imagined, *like a rape victim would feel,* some described. Many had felt powerless to react or move; paralyzed.

The blade swiftly withdrew. There was a sucking noise as it exited his chest. Petty felt some relief, no longer violated. He rocked forward a touch, then corrected. Blood and pleural fluid escaped freely. He glared searchingly into the eyes of the masked-man for an explanation. *How come the man packed such a powerful punch?* he thought. He felt he knew nothing anymore.

The man stared out wide from within the eye holes. He knew lots.

He knew that with pleural fluid loss, each breath would burn like fire; like hell. Air would suck in through the puncture wound and less oxygen would get absorbed by the blood and circulated. The brain in particular would suffer greatly through oxygen decrease; it was a highly sensitive organ. It would already be in shock through the visual stimulus alone. It would become disorientated and confused. It would send messages to increase heart rate and breathing. It would demand more oxygen and in doing so would pump out more blood and so create more loss. Therefore, there would be less oxygen uptake. Blood pressure would also be dropping dramatically.

Petty felt dizzy. His mobile fell from his hand. He heard a plastic rattle as it hit the ground. He looked down to where it hit the ground, it was an effort. He saw the silhouette of his mobile against pale concrete at his feet. *He wanted to pick it up,* he thought, *but he couldn't.* Things weren't working as they should. Instead, his free hand went instinctively to the site of the strike. It felt strange; wet and warm. He felt more confused. He automatically looked to where his hand was; *blood,* he thought. In the darkness he saw it as black, not red. The warm sticky feeling of it told him it was red and that it was blood, that he was losing a lot of it and that he was in a bad way.

No time to react, a second strike hit him same place but on his right side. Again, both men rocked on their heels, Petty more so, this time.

'Carlos!' shouted the man. He waited a shorter moment then withdrew the knife.

Again, he rocked and corrected but it was more difficult, he had to take a short step forward. His legs felt shaky. He couldn't believe the power of the punches, *and how come he was bleeding? He needed answers.* He looked at the fist reloaded in its breach just under the masked man's arm pit, ready to strike again. He saw it wrapped around a dagger held parallel to the ground and pointing his way. It was matt black and not easy to see. Trembling, he wanted to pull out his own knife but his arm refused. He needed help, he needed his mobile. He knew it was near. He started to look towards the ground where he'd last seen it. His eyes never reached the floor; he saw more blood staining his Christian Audigier tee shirt. His knees went weak, his eyes unfocused. He tried to adjust his vision; he pushed his spectacles along his nose with his index finger and blinked hard. Nothing changed. His lungs burnt with every breath in and every breath out and every breath was taking more effort. He looked at the stranger in front and was unable to grasp the situation.

The stranger looked back, impassively. The eyes gave nothing away.

Disorientation was taking over. All he knew was that it hurt and it was serious. His strength drained. He landed heavily on his knees. The spectacles catapulted off but that didn't matter. He found himself knelt before the much smaller man dressed all in black. Feeling nauseous and confused, he looked up at him. Again, he searched the eyes behind the mask; *'Why? Who the hell...?'*

He looked down at the confused expression under the cap.

Petty's eyes searched desperately. The paleness of the lips in the ski mask slot contrasted against the black surround and moved slowly and deliberately, 'Lucy...... Carlos,' said the attacker dressed in black. 'Remember?'

His brain searched for meaning and recalled the name from all those years ago, *Lucy Carlos*. It had remained a fairly recent memory, they'd laughed about her from time to time; *the fun they'd had in the park*. He was back there, he smiled fondly to himself. The smile slowly faded, realization was kicking in. He knew he couldn't take on the threat and needed to get home to safety. More adrenalin flooded his system. With new found strength, he struggled back onto his size fourteens.

The man in black stepped back. He wasn't expecting him to get vertical. He knew his lungs would be around six or even seven litre capacity and they'd be filling fairly rapidly. He had not been able to calculate how long it would take him to drown in his own blood or become anoxic. That was an unknown. He'd known of accounts where it had taken quite some time. Some self-doubt crept in; he questioned his own ability to have accurately targeted the correct parts of the anatomy. He assessed the injured man before him. The punctures wounds were sucking in air, his throat gurgled. There was heavy loss of blood, yet he remained upright.

He considered inflicting further damage. He gripped the knife tight in preparation.

At that moment Petty coughed hard. Projectile vomit mixed with dark blood, sprayed everywhere. He wiped the back of his hand across his mouth to clean up when he'd thought he'd finished, like it mattered. It was ok for a second. He concentrated. He fought to take a deep breath. It didn't happen. He coughed violently. Frothy blood ran out from his mouth and bubbled from his nose.

The masked stranger did nothing.

Petty staggered forward and was greeted with a hand-off to the chest that easily sent his big frame stumbling backwards. Vulnerable; he could do nothing. He came to rest like a felled tree. He lay, motionless on his back.

The stranger clearly relieved, relaxed his knife-hand down his side. *It's over,* ran through his mind. *Though not quite as planned, it had ended more abruptly than anticipated.*

He suddenly sat up, both hands covering the black stains on the front of his tee shirt like some shy girl caught naked without a bra.

The masked man automatically stepped up to him, shouting, 'The Trok girl too!' Then, like a cop kicking in a door, he slammed his boot into his chest.

It knocked the wind out of him, what little there was. He rolled backwards and groaned hard. Star-fished, he stayed down. His chest heaved. The wounds sucked harder. For a short moment he did nothing else. Staring up at the empty night sky, he looked like he was wishing he was anywhere else, *anywhere but there*. Suddenly he writhed wildly like he was fighting off an invisible enemy. Gravity alone was pinning him down; he didn't have the strength to fight it. It beat him. His head thrashed one side to another. He gasped, 'It's, it's hard to breath. Please help me? Please mate.' He gurgled some more. Lines of dark blood traced the contours of his face in all directions. He almost sat up, half resting on his elbows a moment until they lost all strength and fell away from him. He fell backwards. His head smashed down on the unforgiving concrete.

The stranger stood to the side of him, then with his boot, rested more than forty kilos weight on his chest. It pinned him, though it wasn't really needed.

There was a moment of peace.

The scene looked like some great white hunter proudly posing for photographs with his foot on some poor unfortunate beast that he'd just slaughtered.

Petty's body struggled again but the weight only increased. He tried to breathe; the pressing foot made it worse. He could see wisps of clouds and the brightest stars and wished he could be up there amongst them. His mind flashed back to the time all the years ago when he observed Lucy Carlos in the same position, he was now in.

He pulled off a glove, exposing latex underneath that patted the beast's front pocket; *blade in that one*. Patted the other; *felt what he was after*. Fingers slid in then fingers slid out. Attached was a dog-poo bag and a small bunch of keys. He dropped the bag and held up the keys, selected one, snapped it off the clip, then carefully returned the remainder. The selected key found its way into the coveralls. The beast didn't move. The attacker checked for his vital signs. He was still alive. *What to do next?*

Barking interrupted the moment. It echoed from the end of the alleyway, thirty-odd yards away. It was some dogs with a man, watching. He held the animals back. They were well controlled.

The glove went back on. He stood back from the bloody mess. He considered his options. He watched the man with the dogs. *What to do?*

The beast groaned. It didn't move at first. The masked-man glanced down at him. *Hallow eyes, mind definitely elsewhere,* he thought. He watched on as he rolled over and up onto his hands and knees. Salivary blood spilt from his mouth. He struggled to raise his head enough to look up the alley towards the noise. 'Please, help me.' He pleaded. It wasn't loud but loud enough.

The dogs responded to the plea but were instantly quietened. They all looked on in silence.

He pleaded again but he was far too quiet to be heard clearly. He breathed in, hard. Thinking it could be his last, 'It's getting so hard to breath,' he gasped. He held out a grasping hand towards the dog man; a gesture for help. Again, he pleaded, 'Do something. I need an ambulance. Get the police. Don't leave me.'

The man turned away, he and his dogs ambled off. And they were gone.

His hope went with them. He returned his hand to the ground for support. He rolled over. Pushing up on his hands, semi press-ups position resting on his knees, he lowered his head. Jaw slack, long threads of thick stringy-blood formed, snapped and dripped.

The masked-man kept still. Options were being considered.

A moment passed before a boot silently crushed a hand that slowly reaching for a mobile that wasn't far away. Petty made no noise. He was powerless. He couldn't do anything but try to look up at the motionless, silent victor.

The masked man shouted, 'Anna!' The same boot slammed him hard in the ribs, a solid *Thud*.

His back arched in pain. He choked, dropped onto his elbows, his forehead smacked into rough concrete surface and rested there. More vomit swilled out, no longer explosive. He gagged and retched.

Another, *thud,* to his rib cage. Then another. Then another…
He arched each time.
'Debbie!' He shouted and kicked again. *Thud.* Again and again.
Further kicks were coming in, thick and fast. He groaned on each impact.
Then they stopped.
There was a moment.
Petty was hopeful. He slowly turned his head sideways to see the man in black crouching at his side. He saw him smiling at him from the opening in the mask. He returned to hanging his head low again. Another moment passed.
Growling angrily in frustration he gathered his strength. Every ounce of his evil got him back up on all fours.
The man in the mask sprang up, he needed to think fast. He always knew this part of his planning was impossible to predict. He was in unknown territory. More options were considered. He didn't want Mrs. Petty or some other innocent passer-by traumatizing if the body was found later or worse still, much later and in daylight. Besides, he'd planned to have an alibi - just in case.
It was time to act and almost time to go.
The mobile was picked up and had to be wiped before use. He did it with his gloves. He got much of the blood off. Much remained. The police emergency number was punched in. He held the mobile away from his ear. The call tone rang out. The caller looked attentively skywards and listened carefully whilst he waited fifteen long seconds. The operator picked up. A sterile, unattached voice asked how she could help the caller.
He disguised himself to sound foreign with a really bad accent and gave his location. 'You come quickly. Man, very sick. The man, very sick. He bleeds badly.'
Just then the noise of yapping dogs rolled down the alley. The caller looked towards them. They were back where they were before, at the end of the alley. He had to put his hand over one ear to mute them out. He raised his volume, 'Come quickly. Need ambulance, now. He dying.' He left the problem with the operator then hung up. The dogs and their walker ambled on passed the end of the alley and out of view.
He reassessed the situation; took it all into consideration. The bloody mess was now half crawling, half kneeling towards home, only meters away.
Decision time!
The mobile was deliberately dropped to the ground, the dog-poo bag picked up. His eyes darted. He nervously glanced up the alley and down the alley; the place where the dogs had stood, up at the sky, down at the ground, the dark pools of blood, bloody footprints and at Petty. Urgency prevailed but he needed to stay calm, logical, focused. He took out his Mag-lite and shone it around the scene. Everything turned from monochrome to vivid colour, and it was messy. He was a little shocked at the amount of blood and the area it covered. He continued to examine the scene. It was looking ok.
The dogs were back a moment later. The baying pack caught his attention. They now had a thirst for blood; they'd sensed it on the fresh night air. Their primeval urge was strong; they were hungry to tear through flesh. Frenzied, they strained on their leashes, front legs bouncing. The dog man did well to hold them. His words kept them in check - just.
The man in the mask started to flap. He breathed hard and sweated. He checked himself; breathed deep and slow. He was well-practiced at being in stressful situations.

He'd learned how to cope. He'd been in tight spots, many times. The scene seemed ok; he checked on Petty. He was strong, determined and fighting for his very life. It was painful to watch. Anyone seeing him that way would know that he'd be wishing he was somewhere else, anywhere but there. He stepped towards him. The contents of the dog-poo bag were tipped over him. Nine packets fell on him. Some stuck to the blood.

He hadn't planned on leaving him this way but to do anything else in the sight of the dog walker may just inspire him to let his best friends loose. And if he did, they would grip and tear at anything that moved. Or that smelled of fresh blood. Besides, he knew dogs would instinctively chase fleeing prey, so running away from them wasn't an option.

He needed to act - and quickly!

He considered the situation and options over and over, in mere seconds. He would be hearing, *Sarge,* over his radio any minute, he knew that. At the same time several units would be flooring it his way. India Delta would be already fired-up and ready to scramble; that's if it wasn't already floating around somewhere above.

He didn't have long to consider. *Skirting around the dogs on his escape route would take too long. But as he hadn't released the hounds so far, there was a good chance he wouldn't.* So, he decided on the quickest route out of there. He strode towards the man and his dogs still at the end of the alley.

They ambled off well before he reached them. He emerged from the darkness into the streetlight. He paused. They were nowhere to be seen. He looked back into the alley. It was dark alright but sufficiently bright enough for the dog man to have seen something going on. No time to waste, he carried on. Senses heightened, his hearing sharp, he hurriedly advanced north. His heart rate increasing each time a boy racer's exhaust note came into range. Thinking it could be India Delta heading his way, he'd look skywards. He passed an alley to his right and noticed a dark, thick-set figure looking back at him ten yards away. The figure had a familiarity about it. He chose to ignore it, he'd no choice. He had to put distance between himself and the scene. He carried on.

'*Sarge,*' came over the radio. He responded by picking up the pace, half jogging, half walking. There were a couple more, '*Sarge's,*' over the air, that went unanswered.

Other units were called. They acknowledged.

A few lefts and rights and he was in the deserted street and near to the vehicle wrecks. Slightly out of breath, he stood a moment. India Delta thundered south directly overhead at a hundred yards, full throttle, burning a full seventy gallons per hour. It was gone in a beat. *Hardly heard it coming, hardly saw it going.*

Mrs. Petty and the kids were expecting the door to bang open any time, announcing the return of Petty. It was a regular routine. But it was good that tonight was different. He was late and that wasn't like him. It had rarely happened before. She often hoped and sometimes prayed for such a moment. They heard the sound of the police helicopter, India Delta, growing louder. They were used to it; it was part of living on the estate.

Sarge sorted himself out near to his patrol car then climbed in. He felt somewhat anxious. He'd expected that. He popped in some gum, started the engine then reflected on matters a moment, checking things over in his mind. Everything was fine. He chewed a while then scanned the street before slowly setting off. Half a mile away he pulled over on the main drag next to a mail box. He felt a little ragged.

He sat a moment. Regained composure best he could.

He hurriedly read the note from the small Jiffy bag, though there was no need, he knew what it said, he was just double checking. That was him; always tried to be correct and thorough. Besides, there was no room for error. He wrapped a fancy, high security key in it before popping it back and sealing it. He took the larger bag and sealed that one too but not before carefully placing the sheathed item inside. Post in hand he watched in his rear-view mirror for a gap in the traffic before opening his door. He made a final check of the addresses, to be sure. He was that kind of guy. One was to a P.O box number, the other to an address on the estate. He sent them on their way, stepped onto the side of the road and waited to pull over the next boy racer – later to become his alibi. He didn't have long to wait.

He issued a producer; *timed 10pm* then replied to a voice in his earphone unheard by the boy racer, 'Ten four;   -   On my way.' He had a sudden urgency.

Before shoeing the boy racer away, he told him *he was lucky he wasn't going to court but he had to go to a more urgent job.* 'Make sure you bring your documents in. And I'll thank you the next time I see you to have lost the dustbin you have for an exhaust. Ok?' The boy racer was grateful and thanked him for only giving him a warning. He said he'd always remember him for that. That pleased Sarge more than the driver realized.

He sped off from the relieved driver, blue lights and two-tones. He slowed as he passed the street-end where he'd parked earlier. He glanced and saw nothing. Everything looked ok yet a small fire flickered in one of the wrecks. It went unnoticed, like the falling tree in a forest with no-one to hear and so makes no sound. It wouldn't take long before the sports bag, coveralls, ski mask and latex were reduced to little pile of ash and zip teeth. A scorched lighter fuel tin-can would also survive. It was a moment that would go unnoticed, as would the remains.

He focused back on getting to his latest call. He saw India Delta, fifty yards up, searching the labyrinth of alleyways. Its *night sun* beamed down like an X-Files UFO scene, then it'd go black again. Creeping elsewhere before sending down its *tractor beam;* searching, repositioning.

He was there in no time. A double-crewed unit was already at the scene. The sarge was the second unit there. *He'd had some difficulty finding it;* he told the officer who met him at the end of the alley.

'It's a mess, Sarge. Blood, snot and guts all over. He's covered in it. Dog attack, we think.'

The sarge looked at him sideways; said nothing.

'Like that one a couple of years ago. Half his neck's been ripped out by the look of it, Sarge.'

That; he was not expecting to hear. He chewed. 'Is he alive or dead?'

He didn't wait for an answer. He hurried into the darkness of the alley, his Mag-lite beam leading the way. It led him through patches of blood to a second officer kneeling at the body. It was right next to a gate. A second torch illuminated the scene. He was indeed covered in blood.

The cop got to his feet. 'Hi Sarge. Dead as a doornail.' He played his torch on the disassembled pallets reformed into a gate, now marked with blood. 'Looks like he tried to get into there, perhaps.'

'Maybe his home?' He suggested, as he pulled on his gloves, crouched and inspected. 'Any idea who he is, was?' He chewed.

'No.'

He rolled him over to see his face, pushing his torch beam into it then patting his pockets, 'Any ID on him?'

'No. No, ID, Sarge.'

'Knife. Pretty big one too. And open.'

'Careful Sarge, you'll get covered.'

He twisted around, held up his hands palms out, gloves blooded. 'Thanks, but too late.' He turned back to the body. 'Do you recognize him?'

'No. Not seen him around. Do you?'

'No.' He hesitated. 'No. No I don't.' He rolled the head to a side to examine the neck.

'Must have been a Dealer. Preliminary search found some wraps, big ones too. A cap too and some glasses - real jam-jar bottoms. Must have been half blind. Left everything in situ, Sarge.'

Sarge stood up with a sigh.

'Watch where you're stepping, Sarge. There's blood all over.'

No reply. He stood quietly looking down at the body, pondering.

'Sarge?'

He was deep in thought. A moment passed. 'Sorry. I hear you. The neck's a real mess.' He pondered some more. 'No. Can't say as I know him. I'm sure we'll get to know him better, down at the morgue.' He chuckled. 'Looks like another scumbag's been taken out. No great loss, eh?' He straightened up. 'Direct India Delta in, put some light down. We'll check at the house.' Sarge led. The cop got on the radio. They stepped over the body and pushed through the gate. He knocked on the door after nine short strides. It was opened immediately by an expectant Mrs. Petty. It led straight into the kitchen. Some kids were sat at the table watching a portable. She saw the sarge with his best sympathetic expression as the area behind him in the alley lit up with the *tractor beam*. It was like daylight. She squinted. The gate was ajar. She looked over his shoulder and saw everything. She gasped and put her hand over her mouth in shock. He did a one eighty. It was messy. He'd rather she hadn't seen. He couldn't do anything about that now. He turned back. He saw her injury. She noticed and touched it through embarrassment

He shouted over the noise of India Delta hovering close by, 'Sorry to bother you.'

Her eyes were drawn to his chevrons. She shouted back. 'Hello sergeant.' Their eyes locked a moment too long. 'What's happened to the arsehole?'

He was a little surprised; it wasn't exactly the response he'd anticipated. But it had been a night of some surprises. He had to be formal, 'Does a man live here, big guy, long blond hair, baseball cap, thick glasses.? Do you know him?'

She remained silent.

He turned back to the body and shouted above the noise of the twin engines and rotor blades. 'Well, that man laid there?'

She looked and nodded. Above the noise, 'My husband', she shouted, 'Mike.'

He frowned and chinned the air for her to repeat, just to make sure.

She shouted louder, 'Yes. Mike Petty, my husband! Yes, he lives here!'

He looked back at the injury to her face. It felt safe to shout; 'Not anymore he doesn't.' He looked over at the gate again. He shouted, 'I'm sorry.' He turned back to her, 'Stay inside. An officer will call to see you as soon as we get more up here. I'm sorry you had to see that.' He coughed with slight embarrassment. 'You, ok?'

A little stunned, she nodded and smiled politely.

He and the officer returned to the scene to become part of the *major incident carnival*.

She watched them leave the garden before closing the door. She leaned against it for a while; relieved.

She took a moment against the door. She'd known something was seriously wrong - or seriously right. It had just been confirmed. She stepped over to the kids, put her arms around them and told them uncle Mike wouldn't be coming home - ever. Her children didn't react, they weren't bothered. She couldn't contain her smile, which she hid from them.

Outside the home at the bottom of their garden a major incident response was swinging into action. There was frantic activity; stress levels were high.

Inside, it felt relaxed for Mrs. Petty and her children. They heard India Delta not far away. It was reassuring. They knew its name. They'd all grown up with it, everyone on the estate had. It's where it spent most of its time. They knew lots about it. They were used to it and ignored it. It lost novelty value many years ago. Its twin engines and its *Notor* system made it almost quieter than a boy racer, they knew that, though the noise could be annoying after a while. But tonight, it was a comforting sound as they all watched the fifty-incher together. They turned up the volume. Mrs. Petty broke out the biscuits and crisps and waited for the pizza delivery they'd just decided to order. The Pizza shop apologized when she'd called them; *they were going to have quite a wait, being Friday night and all.*

She told them *she didn't mind; they were in no rush; life had just become so much better.*

CHAPTER 3

DAYTIME.

It was after 4am before he'd managed to get home and crawl into his pit. Once the *Force carnival* was on the road, personal lives and home lives became irrelevant. Sleep, wives, families and prior arrangements just didn't factor into the equation. He'd organized, delegated, planned, considered, crossed the T's, dotted the I's and even knocked on several doors himself until 3am. Late Friday night with a major incident taking shape wasn't a time to leave the night-shift holding the baby. They had their own war to wage, especially late of a Friday night. He got as many of his staff off duty as soon as he could; back to waiting wives, partners and a life. For him he had little to get off for, his miniature Schnauzer and tabby would be waiting patiently as usual. He eventually headed home himself, to bed.

A ringing phone woke the sarge. Through tired, slitty eyes, he saw 8.07 on his digital bedside clock. He'd waited a dozen or so rings before he worked out what was happening and deciding whether to answer. He worked his mouth before picking up. Stale nightcap reminded him of the tipple he'd had to get him off to dreamland - a very large whisky - Famous Grouse; his favourite.

He groaned a rasping, *'Hello,'* into the phone.

The girl operator on the other end knew the sarge. She knew apologies and politeness wouldn't make a difference; he'd be grumpy anyhow. So, she came straight out with it, 'Morning Sarge.' she said cheerily, hoping it would help matters. 'The Detective Chief Inspector wants you down at the city morgue for nine.'

'Four hours sleep,' he moaned. 'Nine? I'm not due on until two.'

'I'll tell him you're on your way.' She was bright and cheerful. 'He said come in civvies. Thanks Sarge.' Then hung up.

One hour seventeen minutes later he was looking bright eyed and bushy tailed; inside he felt as rough as a badger's arse as he rushed up the steps and into the morgue's reception. In contrast to the fresh morning air a mix of disinfectant and the unique smell of death filled his lungs, instantly. They took exception to the noxious smell and spluttered.

The room was small; a row of six seats moulded from sheet plywood faced a teak counter with a sliding glass screen, like a doctor's surgery waiting room. And like a doctor in a white coat was the girl behind the counter. Slim, blonde hair tied back, heavy black rimmed designer glasses, aloof, looked like she'd just left university.

Her appearance was deceptive. She first met Sarge eight years ago. She was experienced, efficient, down to earth and good at her job. She was a qualified mortician, had a PHD in forensic sciences and a string of other qualifications. Sarge knew her well and had used here knowledge in the past. She was very intelligent.

'Morning, Sarge.' She held out a pair of blue plastic overshoes across the counter.

He was a little flustered. He coughed. 'Morning, Sal.' He tried to look pleasant and took them from her. He backed onto the moulded plywood, forced his shoes into the elastic openings then looked at his new blue shoes a second, like he was considering whether to buy them or not. He decided he was going to take them. He jumped up then fumbled with his tie.

'You ok, Sarge? You seem a little flustered.'

He nodded at the double doors marked *Strictly Private,* a word for each door, 'Flustered? Rush hour. So, what's going on in there?' 'Why do they want me?'

'No idea.' She paused a moment. 'They want me too.' She grinned.

Distracted, he said nothing. With puzzled expression, he chinned the air.

That was her cue to share her news. Excited, her face lit up, her grin turned into a broad smile. 'To use my expertise, as soon as they're ready for me. I'm on standby today…...'

He interrupted. 'Oh, so he's not been opened up yet, our friend from last night? I presume that's why I've been summonsed.'

She listened but never heard. 'Expertise with my *CRECON 2* computer.' She said proudly. She explained it. 'My new toy. Cost a hundred fifty thousand!'

He never registered her reply, never received her answer, only heard *new toy, cost hundred and fifty thousand.* 'You're a woman of many talents, Sal.' He said uncaringly.

He was a man who believed computers had a limited use for a police force and that they wouldn't catch on. How very wrong he was. All he saw since then was cops in offices playing with new technology instead of being out there on the beat where it mattered, doing what they were getting paid for. He resisted technology; he partly blamed it for the demise of the service that was once delivered second to none. Now all the cops, with their qualifications and degrees, preferred to stay in a warm, cozy office and tap away on keyboards watching computer screens, away from the public.

She knew he hadn't listened; she knew he had no time for modern technology or computers. 'CRECON.' She emphasized. 'You know, Crime RECONstruction. CRECON for short. We tried the prototype a couple of years ago. It's come a long way since then. Your Chief detective helped design it. He's a clever man.'

His mind remained elsewhere. He looked blankly at her, gave her a nod then turned away. He took a couple of steps towards the brass knob on the door marked *Private*. He went through, paced towards a double set just beyond. The air lacked oxygen, it was putrid, he took shallow breaths. It was an old building that had not been brought into the present century as it could be; no opening windows, no air conditioning. The horrible stink became stronger, almost choking. Eight more steps, he paused in front of the semi-glazed swing doors with frosted glass. He knew beyond them was the room used for slicing and dicing corpses. He'd visited there, numerous times over the years. He peered through the frosting; he couldn't make out any figures or movement.

He knew what he could expect to see when he went through the doors. He mentally prepared himself; the place would be covered in stainless-steel, bright lights, white ceramic tiles; floor to ceiling. Four paces in and in the centre of the room would be a stainless-steel table used for the post-mortems with drainage tray below. He'd expect to see it straight in front of him, probably empty. But there may already be a dead body laid on it beneath a khaki-green cloth, he considered. He was prepared for that.

Although he'd seen many corpses in his time, he still didn't like being there or seeing them. They looked grotesque once the mortician had gotten to work on them. To him it was always like some horror movie beyond any writer's imagination and descriptive ability. It was also a reminder of his own mortality.

He ran his tongue over his teeth, popped in some gum, took a deep breath then wished he hadn't; then chose the left-hand door to push through. It creaked open.

He stopped suddenly in the doorway.

The place was covered in white tiles, stainless-steel and bright lights, as he'd expected.

The post mortem table was four paces in front of him as he'd expected.

What he hadn't expected was to see Petty laid there on the table looking all sorry for himself. His head propped on a wooden block; chest opened up like some guy just decided to burst out like a hatching parasite. His front rib cage, attached to the sternum, was between his legs and his insides were missing. Missing too was the top of his skull. What remained of his head looked like a hardboiled egg with the top knocked off. His face was pulled forward and wrinkly like he was sulking about the guy who'd burst out of where his vital organs used to be.

On a positive, *At least he was all nice and cleaned up now,* thought, Sarge.

He stepped through and let the door swing shut behind him. To his left were the vital organs all lined up on a bench looking like a butcher's shop window. One guy wearing green waterproofs and green rubber booties was more interested in what the butcher had for sale. He took no notice of Sarge's entrance. The other guys lined up next to him in smart suits preferred an excuse to turn away from the display and see who just came in. Ten blue overshoes in a row seemed to take away some of their wearer's credibility.

One suit was pinstriped and belonged to a pale face topped with a shock of red hair. He was the tallest there. One had a small black padded bag over its shoulder and an expensive camera looped around its neck. The other three were nondescript. A double-take discovered that one was a woman, shorter haired than the others and certainly more masculine than some. Not that masculinity was an obvious overwhelming factor amongst the others. They all looked pale and queasy.

The one with the red hair sticking out was the Chief detective. He tapped his watch; sounding like a school teacher, 'You're late, sergeant. We started at nine. I said to be here for then.' He said sternly.

Sarge appeared unruffled, on the surface. 'Only got four hours sleep, sir.' He rubbed his stubbly chin. 'Didn't get the call till after eight. Came as fast as I could. I'm thirty-five minutes out the city. Traffic was bad; rush hour. But you know all that, sir.' Tongue in cheek, 'Thought you'd have worked that out, being a senior detective and all.' He flashed a smile. No-one else did. Sarge sometimes overcompensated inappropriately in awkward situations especially when he was put on the spot. This was one of those situations. He also wouldn't allow anyone to try and exercise control over him or belittle him.

There was a long moment.

He cleared his throat, reading the clock above the bench behind them he chewed. He needed to recover the situation, 'Nine twenty-six, sir. I reckon that's pretty good going.' Eyebrows raised he stepped forward a pace. 'So, what's the problem?'

He paused.

Everyone paused. The Chief's face turned more the colour of his red hair. The suits remained silent, some shot frightened glances, two turned away.

He continued. 'With you calling me down here, sir, that is.'

A chief, especially a high flyer, never wants to be belittled, ever, let alone in front of others, no boss does even if he is in the wrong. He was a high-flyer holding a First with Honours in Metaphysics; a philosophy including abstract concepts of the study of time and space. He was on the police accelerated promotion scheme. He'd worked hard to get where he was and demanded respect. It was never won through merit with those guys; two years at the sharp end and it was Administration or Personnel or anywhere for them for the rest of their careers as they climbed through the ranks. Anywhere but where times could be tough, that would be fine. Anywhere but on the streets doing grass-roots police work, anywhere but at the sharp end.

With so many high-flyers jockeying for position it had become more difficult to map out a career sat at some desk tucked away in some unimportant, unproductive, unheard-of department working office hours with weekends off and earning five times more than your average beat cop. So, the Chief found himself as an operational senior detective. Not what he'd planned. Things don't always go to plan.

Sarge was thinking precisely that; *things not going to plan.* He'd been planning on a lay-in, a walk with the dog and back on duty for early afternoon. The carnival would be over by then except for a few cops covering the scene and a few loose ends to be taken care of. The caravan of departments would be regrouped back at the headquarters major incident room where self-important officers would be bashing computer keyboards for all they're worth and talking about how they were going to spend their overtime pay.

'What d'ya mean, what's the problem!' The Chief growled. 'There are a few problems, sergeant. The first is the fact our friend here has two stab wounds that you missed last night.'

The sarge said nothing, he eyeballed with indifference the star attraction laid in the centre of the room ~ Petty.

The green waterproofs man spun round to Sarge. Tucking his chin in, his eyes peeped over thin silver rimmed spectacles framed inside a green cotton face mask with matching bandanna above. Sarge recognized him. He'd known him eight years but had rarely seen him without bandanna, mask and waterproofs.

He had a refined, educated accent, 'Hi Sarge. I'll show you.' He beckoned the sarge over as he stepped away from the bench.

They both headed over to the centre table, his rubber booties dragged on the tiles. The men met up at the side of the corpse. The suits stayed put and watched from a distance. The chest skin was already folded back like an unzipped quilted jacket. Pale yellow subcutaneous fat, white sinews and purplish muscle tissue made up the lining. He checked to make sure he had Sarge's attention then used his blooded latex to stretch out one side of the chest skin. He poked a finger through a slit from the quilted side and wiggled it. It was like a very large buttonhole. He looked at Sarge for a reaction.

There wasn't one. He kept his eyes on the waddling finger. He never made eye contact. He wore his best, *very interesting,* expression.

He leaned across and did the same with the other side. 'You see those, sergeant? Two of them. You know what they are?'

There was a short moment as Sarge sniffed. 'Puncture wounds.' Smiling, he looked up defiantly at the pathologist and chewed casually as he could. 'Them dogs were vicious.' He chewed some more, eyebrows raised. 'Big teeth.' He chuckled.

The pathologist glanced over at the detective chief then let go of the skin. He nodded back to the bench for him to follow.

He followed.

The suits were happy to step back as the man in green headed their way followed by Sarge. They remained silent. The only noise was the sound of booties and Sarge's rustling plastic over shoes. The group parted when they were near to reveal a pair of lungs laid between sliced brain-matter on one side and what looked like the remains of a dissected heart on the other. Further along was a stomach - no guts attached, then sliced liver and kidneys with a bucket full of other stuff at the end of the bench; spleen, pancreas, bowels, things like that. Sarge glanced over the gory mess and gave a short sniff.

'Here,' the man said, bringing the sarge's attention back to the lungs. He fingered them momentarily as though proudly adjusting them the same way a flower arranger would their display of flowers. He wanted them to be just right. Sarge stayed one pace back. It was clear he was feeling out of his comfort zone. All eyes were on him. He didn't look around him but he knew they were all staring at him. He fought his natural body language to react; instead, he sniffed and rubbed his nose. Chewed some more.

The lungs were like rubbery, pear-shaped sacks covered in veins and fine arteries.

They were displayed on apparatus to simulate how they would have been in the body. He placed a gadget over them which had extendible rods with protractor contraptions at the top marked off in degrees. He prodded the organs with the rods and pointed to the protractors. He swung around to Sarge. 'Look at the angles, Sarge. You've seen enough fatal stabbings. What do you think?'

There was a long pause as the sarge tried to figure out what it all meant. The suits looked on, grey and in silence. He resisted glancing at them.

He shrugged. 'Been stabbed twice, once in each lung?' He sniffed casually.

'That's right,' he said enthusiastically. 'What else?'

He looked over at the body and back. 'Got his neck chewed on.' He ran his tongue over his teeth and chewed faster.

'Look at the angles. Not your normal upward thrust or downward swing.'

The sarge chewed some more and kept his eyes on the centrepiece.

'It was a long, thin blade, around seven inches, near as damn it, according to my measurements. And CRECON's of course.' He added. 'One, maybe one and a half inches at its broadest. Went in all the way down to the stop end; the finger guard or handle, whatever you want to call it.' He turned from the display bench. 'Come on,' he beckoned. 'Sally's done a reconstruction for us on her computer using the CRECON 2 program.' He dragged his booties into a side room followed by a file of suits paddling in plastic overshoes. He sat at a computer desk made for two and was circled around by the onlookers. Except for Sarge and the chief, they all stared at a blank screen with their serious faces. Sarge and the chief were at either end of the circle and looked at one another with puzzled expressions; each one trying to read the thoughts of the other as though any moment one of them was going to say something profoundly important. The pathologist caught the men locked in their silent guessing game. He looked at one, then the other. He shrugged it off and buzzed Sally from an intercom on the desk. She was there immediately. She smelled strongly of perfume as she wafted passed the waiting audience. It was a welcome smell from the ambient odour of death that filled the building. She sat at the desk next to him and started tapping the keyboard.

The sarge leaned in. 'Thought you said you'd not started on him, Sal. Wasn't prepared to be greeted by him as soon as I walked in.' He chewed. 'By the way, you smell good, as always.' He smiled.

She looked at him puzzled. 'Thanks, Sarge. My fave, you should know it.' She smiled. 'Chanel number five. Remember?'

He gave her a knowing smile.

She turned away. 'And we've been here since seven, sergeant.' She tapped the keyboard a few more times.

The screen came to life and everyone leaned into it. A few more taps showed two colourful diagrammatic figures facing one another. One held a knife. They were semi translucent so their internal organs could be seen. Without being told, one repeatedly stabbed the other twice in the chest and kept on repeating the cycle like a stuck CD. It even showed the stabbed guy wearing a pained expression and dramatically throwing his arms up as he fell backwards. Then it would start over. It was overlaid with angles and degrees and calculation formulas and changing numbers that the sarge didn't understand but the Chief appeared to. The guy had been killed a half dozen times when she tapped another key that showed it in slo-mo and left a trail that tracked the knife. Another tap of a key and it showed the knife entering the body and the lungs filling with red. It even had graphic spurts of blood when the weapon was withdrawn.

'Even got the bad guy reaching for his stiletto just before he's out-drawn,' someone said, but no-one took notice of who said it. They kept their gaze on the screen.

'Clever stuff.' someone else remarked.

'So, what do think, Sarge?' The Chief tried to put him on the spot, 'Realistic? Is that how it happened?'

The sarge straightened up. He felt the question was personal - more like some kind of accusation. All eyes were on him again. It felt like a group confrontation. He felt uncomfortable and fiddled with his collar, like it was too tight. He gave a short sniff. 'Nice new computer.' He nodded at it, 'Very impressive. Hundred and fifty thou spent on a computer to show us a stabbing. So, what can it tell us we don't already know? A seven-inch blade to both lungs is pretty fatal.' He chewed. 'Is it not?' He looked around the room for agreement. There wasn't any; just blank faces.

Sally spoke up. 'Well, from the measurements taken and the angles the knife entered, we can tell lots of things. Estimated force, approximate height of the assailant, how each individual reacted. Which hand the knife was in and whether it was a frenzied attack.' She turned to the audience and with a smile said, 'We can discover things like that.'

'How did we ever get by without computers, Sal?' said Sarge, sarcastically. He looked around but was still on his own. 'And most of the population's right-handed.' Still on his own.

'In this case,' said Sal, 'we can see that the strikes were disciplined, not upward or downward, but parallel to the ground. Pretty accurate too, roughly the same place in each lung, about one third up and a few inches from the sternum. Either the attacker knew what he was doing or he was lucky or perhaps it was a mix of both. The left lung was punctured fairly square on. The attacker was right-handed. The right one was from an angle of twenty degrees from the left one. The attacker was tall, between six foot seven and six foot ten.' She took a moment to reflect on what she had just said before continuing, 'He stood directly in front of the victim when he attacked. He knew what he was doing, quite professional, disciplined, thought out, not frenzied and hurried like most normal knife attacks are. We think it was a premeditated stabbing done by a professional.'

End of commentary. Silence.

All eyes turned to Sarge. He coughed and fiddled with his collar again as though it was still too tight.

He felt uncomfortable and obliged to comment. 'So, we're looking for a right-handed, disciplined giant now.' He laughed, alone. He coughed nervously. 'How do you work that out? The height thing, I mean.'

'Research shows most level knife attacks come from below hip level and as the punctures are fairly parallel with the ground that would make him quite a tall guy in this case. They usually enter the stomach at an upward angle.' She never took her eyes of the animation. 'Lung punctures usually follow a downward strike like the shower scene in Psycho or if the victim drops to their knees submissively before an attack, as they often do, then it could still be an upwards thrust. Dropping down is a submissive gesture, the same way a dog rolls over to offer the more dominant dog its neck. It submits, hoping the attack will cease. There's nothing to suggest the victim was on his knees before being stabbed, according to CRECON.' She pointed to a screen display showing the predicted height range and lots of other data. She skirted over, 'Or it could have been a smaller guy who knew what he was doing.'

The chief turned. 'Someone like you, Sarge.'

Sarge coughed again, 'What do you mean, sir, someone like me? Sounds more like a rival dealer had the guy whacked if you ask me.' He glanced around looking for support.

'Well, you're our knife-fighting expert, aren't you?'

There was an anxious pause. 'I don't go around stabbing the bad guys, sir, even if the world's a better place without them.' He blinked twice and chewed, 'I'm certainly no expert. Is that why you've called me in?'

'Yes,' he said, hesitantly, 'And no. Well, partly. You have expertise in knife fighting and knowledge of techniques.' There was a moment. 'Well, the other problem I have is that we're belly to ground and my regular Detective Sergeant is up to his eyeballs in it. He already has a massive workload.' He turned to one of the nondescript suits, 'The acting DS (detective sergeant) here is on the accelerated promotion scheme doing his carrousel of departments and he's a little unfamiliar with major incidents. It's his first murder.'

One of the nondescripts leaned across two other nondescripts offering a limp-wristed handshake to Sarge. He carried a nice tan, slicked down hair, tortoiseshell glasses and an accent picked up from some university that charged maximum tuition fees. He smiled as he mumbled his name that Sarge never caught, 'Pleased to meet you, Sarge.'

There was instant friction. 'Yeah. Likewise,' said Sarge, dismissively.

The Chief intervened in a manner as though addressing school children. 'I want you to assist him best you can, sergeant. He'll be in overall charge and will be the official DS on the case. You'll play a supporting role. It'll be a good experience for him. It'll be good for his CV. I've told him to keep a close eye on you. Anyway, you know the area, he doesn't.' He changed up a gear, 'I see Petty's been off the radar a while, in terms of dealing, that is. Maybe he was going straight. We know he dobbed a girl in it recently. He has few friends. Well, few that will own up to it. His wife's uncooperative and I can't blame her. He's given her several stays in the local infirmary over the years. She was too scared to follow the complaints through, so withdrew. She also had her kids to think of. You've met her before haven't you, Sarge?'

'Err, yes. Yes sir, I have. But only last night.' He sniffed.

'I'm informed she liked you; you might get somewhere with her. You can be her liaison officer. Not only that, you've bags of experience and regardless of the DS's needs here, I want you on my team as of now sergeant.'

The last part of the speech was the motivator; *I'm picking you for my team.* It worked. The sarge knew it was bull but still felt good. But not for long.

'Anyway, how come you missed the stab wounds last night, Sarge?'

Again, Sarge felt pressured and scanned the faces around him before returning to the chief. 'Force policy and procedures, sir. You disturb the scene as little as possible; forensics, photographs, you know.' He gave one nod to the computer. 'Now CRECON's a consideration too it seems.'

'Forensics! There were footprints all over the place. Most of them probably yours, we thought. Roughish ground and no definite shoe pattern so we'll never know for sure, will we?'

He lifted his eyebrows. 'No sir. No, we won't.' He coughed, looked around then sniffed. 'Anyway, I could see his head was half chewed off. Arms were the same. He was dead forever and me raking around his body wasn't going to make a great deal of difference to the carnival coming to town. Besides if you'd seen his top, it was drenched in blood. Presumed it was from his neck. We had no reason to think he'd been stabbed.'

'Carnival?'

'Yes sir, carnival. You know, everyone and his *dog*, sir.' He waited and looked around. He laughed.

'Dog?'

'Sorry about the pun, sir.' The nondescripts and the photographer gave a token smirk, even the pathologist did, though eyes only.

The Chief wasn't amused. He looked puzzled and couldn't move on from Sarges flippant remarks.

'*Carnival.* Major incident procedure, sir. All the bosses and departments turning out.' He cleared his throat. 'Those that sit in offices, sir. Year in, year out.'

Sal kept facing the screen all the while.

'The program's good but what are your thoughts, sergeant.' The pathologist stood up and offered his chair. He took it. Lent into the screen and watched the stabbing for the umpteenth time, they all did.

He pondered; rubbed his stubbly chin. 'I reckon you've got someone who knows what they're doing. The estate's full of them. They all carry. They spend half their lives watching bloodthirsty gangster movies and playing violent computer games then get the idea they want to be part of one. But for real.'

'Surely it takes practice to knife someone that way?' said an unknown voice.

'Yes, but not so much. A knifes a basic weapon that requires basic skill so requires minimum practice. It takes gross motor skills; big, simple movements, you don't have to be a surgeon.' He glanced at the pathologist. 'Or a butcher.'

He frowned hard at the sarge for his comment about him.

An unknown said, 'I think the lungs were the target. I don't want to offend CRECON but there aren't too many men the height it suggests.'

The Chief was feeling left out and piped up, 'What do you think, sergeant?'

They all kept watching the repeats on the screen as they waited and listened, as though something more would happen or be revealed.

'Well, based on the studies I've read, and I'm no expert, it could be a shorter guy who held the weapon almost under his armpit, level with Petty's lungs. Rehearsed the strikes; snappy, straight out, fast and followed through.'

There was silence.

No-one responded so the Chief did, 'It's pretty obvious they targeted the lungs; seems like they wanted him to suffer instead of killing him straight away.'

Sarge responded. 'Possibly.' He said thoughtfully. 'Or maybe they didn't intend for him to die.'

They considered in silence but didn't come up with a result.

The virtual attack kept looping through on screen.

The green mask tried to move the huddle on from the lack of ideas. 'There are contusions on the torso as well; looks like he'd been given a good kicking. Fractured, or should I say cracked, a couple of ribs in fact.'

'Someone's been really pissed at him. I'd say.' He chewed hard. 'Relieved too, maybe.'

'Relieved? What do you mean?'

'I felt the flick-knife in his pocket. It was open, ready to go. Razor sharp: sliced clean through his pocket. Perhaps someone was quicker on the draw. The attacker or him. The killer got the first one in; a pre-emptive strike. Self-defence even.'

'Self-defence?'

'Yeah. What if the killer knew he carried a knife? He may have even known that he'd used it to kill before. These people often know much more than we do about who's done what or who killed who out there. He may have known that he too would be killed unless he defended himself. And maybe the only way he could save his own life was to kill him.' He chewed. 'The attacker, *or defender*, whichever way you want to see it, lives to fight another day. Maybe he knew what he was up against. And yes, maybe he wanted him to suffer. Slow and painful the same way he makes others suffer.'

They mood changed; the group looked on intently.

He sensed it. 'Just speculating, you know.' He laughed.

The Chief chipped back in. 'Do you mean that was the motive, self-defence? Is that your theory?'

He eyed the corpse sideways on, through the door-frame, 'I'm just a sergeant, not a clairvoyant.' He sighed. 'He was a bad man in his time. His record's bad. His whole life was bad. It's all on his records. He made other lives bad too; lots. He dealt in misery. It can be seen in the area he worked. So, he's just another less problem to clear up after.' He sniffed. 'So what? He won't be missed.' He brought his eyes back into the room. 'Sorry. Got carried away.' He coughed. 'Motive?' He thought a moment. 'Yes. I think he reached for his knife and if he'd been fast enough the other guy would be laid there now and not him. Good riddance, I say.'

No-one else remarked.

Sal nodded then tapped more keys. The screen gave out some pleasant musical charm noises that asked for attention and everyone looked. A display of graphics-created knives was now displayed on the screen.

The man in green touched one that was a dagger, 'We reckon that's the nearest one to what did it, a standard military-issue commando dagger. It fits with the dimensions perfectly. Even matches the hilt, or finger guard of two inches just as CRECON and I calculated.'

The sarge was more interested in the two animated flick-knives that were opening and closing, one from the side of the handle, the other from the end, 'So what's with the flick-knife display?'

'It was Petty's. We just fed that in for CRECON's database and for practice. It came up correct.'

'Talking of his knife, it's in the lab for DNA testing right now. Who knows, it might have the attacker's blood on it?' said the acting DS.

Sarge shook his head, 'Like Petty would put his knife back like that. Even CRECON worked it out.'

There was embarrassment all round.

The chief broke it, 'Right, Sarge, I'm going to make tracks; didn't sleep much last night. See me in the morning at nine, my office, with the daily M.I. sitrep. And don't be late.' He looked at the acting DS who appeared puzzled. 'M.I. sitrep - Major Incident situation, report. I'll see you in the morning too, detective sergeant.'

The DS fawned.

'This way, gentlemen,' instructed the green clad pathologist as he exited the room. 'We'll just finish off,'

His pair of booties were followed by five pairs of shuffling overshoes. The sarge watched them thread through the door. The booties made a last-minute decision to take a right instead of a left passed Petty's table. The overshoes followed like chicks being led by their mother. The red headed one peeled left through the swing doors. The acting DS had a change of mind, left the others and chased after the chief. A few others hesitated and weren't sure which way to go but instinctively knew to stay with mum and they all returned to the organ display.

Suddenly there was only Sal and the sarge remaining at the desk. They found themselves looking at one another.

'What do you think, Sarge?' whispered Sally.

'I think this job's going down the pan, Sal. That's what I think. A couple of years I'll be calling the acting new boy, sir, and he still won't have a clue.'

'I meant about the case, not the new boy acting DS what's his name.'

He threw his old gum in the basket next to the desk and ran his tongue over his teeth, took a deep breath. 'We'll have forty detectives working the case for a month then they'll wind it down as the overtime budget shrinks. Once that happens everyone loses interest and it'll fizzle out until it's forgotten about completely. The tax payer picks up the bill. In the meantime, the carnival's moved onto the next town to start all over again.' He shook his head and looked back at the screen. The flick-knife was in its loop and above it the men were still fighting, 'There'll be a thousand daggers out there, just like the one

CRECON here's come up with. With the new DNA testing we might get something but that's your department, you know more about that than me. I don't know about any of that. What I do know is a knife like that is easy to clean. Chances are the knife's probably long gone, along with any DNA.' He stood up and pulled his jacket to, eyebrows raised, 'You'll never get the killer.' He smirked.

She was still watching the screen. 'You know, he could have lived.'

He sniffed. 'What?' He slowly sat back down.

There was the sound of shuffling plastic overshoes and swinging doors then the man in green shuffled back in, 'That's right. It's the dogs that probably finished him off. There's wasn't that much fluid in his lungs. He lost most blood through his neck wounds. His carotid was torn wide open.'

More keys were tapped. CRECON showed the *virtual* victim on hands and knees. It was detailed. Virtual reality blood ran from his chest, mouth and nose and pooled on the virtual reality ground.

'We map the size and shape of the patches of blood at the scene and input them into CRECON.' She faced the sarge. 'From that it analyses the events based upon estimated quantities, splash patterns, distances, past recorded technical data and so forth.' She paused. 'When you arrived on scene, you said he was face-down.'

He nodded and continued to chew.

'The bite marks were consistent with him being on all fours or face down when the dog bit his neck. The biggest patch of blood was where he was found.' She swung back to the keyboard and tapped some more.

The sarge was expecting to see dogs attacking the guy next but the screen closed down.

The green masked man added in muffled voice from the adjoining room, 'My opinion is, because he spent much of his dying minutes face downward, his lungs drained through the puncture wounds so preventing them filling. Oh, he'll have been in difficulty but he was in the best position he could be to survive.'

Sarge again rubbed his hand across his stubble. And puzzled, 'Well seems like the attacker had figured out most things, but not that. Nor had he reckoned on your CRECON friend here giving you a helping hand.' He took a moment. 'So how long could he have lived for?' He hesitated. 'Without the dog attack, that is?'

'Perhaps ten or fifteen minutes. Maybe longer. Long enough to get medevac'd to the infirmary. He'd have had a fighting chance.'

The sarge thought a moment. He sniffed, 'Nah. India Delta's rotor span is ten yards. The nearest place it could have dropped into is the old disused school off the main drag. It's over a quarter mile away at least. They'd have had to find their way there on foot first then carrying a guy his size on a stretcher would take at least another ten minutes to run back and load him. More than twenty minutes, easily.' He paused, 'Nah. He was never going to make it.' He smiled.

The other two said nothing but watched, frowning.

The sarge caught their expressions, coughed and stood back up. He looked down at Sal. 'Come on, he's no great loss to society, or anyone for that matter. Well, excepting his drug dependent friends. And even they're better off without him. Anyhow, changing the subject, thought you said you were here at 7am. Thought you'd have had all this worked out.'

'I was. Me and CRECON 2 were in the alley from midnight. Digital and laser camera technology feed the scene data into the program. Back here, all done and dusted by eight. The Chief's already watched the reconstruction CRECON produced, well before you arrived.'

'Jesus! Really?' he paused. 'I mean, we'll be taken over by computers next. Let me have your report as soon as you can please, Doc……, I'll see ya.'

He walked towards the door and was met by the tall Chief with pasty-face and shock of red-hair.

'Ah, sarge, I forgot to mention to you earlier. That other unpleasant business you were *involved* with; the murder of Uncle Billy.'

It was clear Sarge instantly took exception to his terminology. '*Involved?*' He scowled. 'What d'ya mean, *involved?* The word, *involved,* implies I had something to do with his demise.'

The Chief, back-tracked. 'I'm sorry. But keep calm sergeant.' He corrected himself, 'Ok, I should have said, *the murder you were under investigation for.* There, does that sound better?' He asked, patronizingly.

Sarge, shrugged like he didn't care.

The Chief paused a long moment for effect and to enjoy the anguish he thought he was inflicting upon Sarge.

He chewed hard, whilst trying not to reveal his anxiety. 'And?' he asked casually, eyebrows raised.

There was a further moment. He let him sweat it a little longer. 'Well anyway, it's been finalized.' He let him sweat it a little more before continuing. 'I was asked to inform you of the result. Not the best place to tell you but I thought you should know soonest.'

Sarge smiled with relief. The fact he'd not been re-arrested for the death, told him he was in the clear. 'Uncle Billy.' He murmured, then took a moment to reflect.

'You're in the clear.'

'Great.' He chewed.

'What did you expect?'

He casually shrugged.

There was a moment.

The chief needed to reassert his authority; he needed to regain ground, 'On the subject of words, a small but important matter. I said, *murder,* of Uncle Billy just then but you say *demise*. Don't you accept it was murder, sergeant? It certainly seems that way from your choice of words.'

'Words.' He chinned the air. His eyes narrowed. 'Well sir, is it murder when a guilty individual escapes justice time and again then finally gets what's coming to them? When lives get wrecked and those responsible go unpunished? When the law fails to protect the innocent? Is the ending of that scum-bags life murder or just their deserved demise? Natural justice I'd call it. His natural demise. An eye for an eye and all that, just like the good book says.' He smiled.

'Is that how you really see things, Sarge?' He never waited for an answer. He walked on by and stood next to the corpse. With his back to Sarge, he looked the empty corpse up and down. '*Uncle Billy. Circumstantial evidence against you,* they said, *that's as much as it will ever be.*' His volume went up a notch. 'You need to be more careful in the future about letting your mouth and especially your temper, run away with you Sarge.'

'More careful? Oh, I will be, sir.' He paused. 'I will be, for sure.' He looked over at the other two in the room. 'Uncle Billy,' he laughed, eyebrows raised. 'Ran out of his Kairos time, you know.' He laughed again.

The Chief turned to face Sarge. 'Kairos time?'

'Err, yes sir. Kairos. Like a significant time, a moment. Something defining.' He chinned at the corpse. 'Like our friend there.' He chewed. 'Last night was a Kairos moment for him. He's having a Kairos moment right now. His next one will be at his funeral and his last one will be at the crematorium when he gets smoked and blown out the chimney.' He took out the gum from his mouth and threw it into Petty's torso cavity like it was a waste bin. He laughed.

'Really! Have you no respect for the dead, sergeant?' snapped the chief.

'I have, sir, lots. But none for the likes of him there. We're all better off without the Petty's of this world.'

The chief shrugged, turned and disappeared through the swing doors.

Sarge turned to see the green man and his assistant staring at him. 'What do they teach them these days? A degree in Metaphysics and he's never heard of Kairos time.' He laughed and chewed.

'I'm sure he has, Sarge. He's not as cabbage as he is looking. Don't underestimate him or his egghead friends. Don't be fooled.' She looked serious and winked.

He frowned, 'Ok Sal. Maybe he's not as carrot as he is looking, eh?' He sniffed, and then sniffed again. 'Must be allergic to this place, that or death.' He sniffed again to prove a point. 'Nose always runs here. See you later.' He turned to leave.

'Uncle Billy!' said the pathologist. 'I remember doing his post-mortem examination.'

Sarge stopped in his tracks and looked over his shoulder at him. He wondered where he was leading with it.

The pathologist continued, 'That job was a long time ago. I'll never forget it. Head looked like a melon dropped from ten floors up. It was an extremely violent trauma. Someone must have been most pissed at him, I would say.'

Sarge felt under pressure to say something, he turned fully around, 'Yes, it was some time ago. I got roped in, me and my big mouth. Just because I said someone should sort him out. Then that same day he goes and gets himself killed. Naturally, I get fingered for it.' He chewed. 'But they got nothing on me.' He sniffed. 'This new DNA testing; they're opening up old cases. *Cold case investigations,* they're calling it. Half a dozen graduates on the fast-track scheme are running it. Created a department just for them boffin types and threw in one or two like me. Well, they need someone to watch the store whilst they're all climbing the promotion ladder. Promotion fever I call it. Looking over their shoulders and backstabbing their rivals. They don't like rolling their sleeves up and getting their hands dirty. They're afraid to do anything, but want recognition when things go well. Good for their CV's. So, one of them bright sparks started on the undetected case of Uncle Billy. My scalp would have been a real prize if they'd have pinned the death on me. I came up as one of the suspects at the time but they're never going to find my DNA anywhere near him. They're never going to prove a link between me and Uncle Billy's demise.'

'You might want to rephrase that, Sarge.'

He nodded. 'Maybe a poor choice of words. But they aint ever going to convict me on words. They ought to go after some case that's worth investigating.' He chewed. He looked at Petty laid there with his open chest cavity, one last time. He chewed some more. 'Whenever I see a post-mortem corpse on the slab, it always looks like someone's just burst out of them.' He laughed.

He looked over at the pathologist and Sal. They were expressionless.

'One other thing, Sarge,' said Sally. 'No-one's mentioned it to you yet but we believe two people may have been involved in Petty's death.' She looked over at the pathologist for approval. He gave a slight nod.

Sarge looked uncomfortable. He pulled at the front of his shirt collar to loosen it. 'What are you saying? How do you make that out?'

'Footprints. We discounted all the paw prints of course.'

'Thought you said you didn't get any, 'cos of the dirt on the ground?'

'That's true, we didn't. We didn't get enough detail to make any matches sufficient enough to compare with someone's footwear. What CRECON obtained was the bloody tracks of where people had walked about at the scene. It showed tracks. Tracks coming in and tracks going out.'

'So, lots of tracks. Is that all?'

'Yes. The dog owner, the two officers initially attending the scene, Petty's and yours.'

Sarge took a moment. He coughed a little nervously. 'That's only five. What are you saying; that me and the dog man were the attackers? We were the two?'

'Oh, sorry. And tracks left by the two unknowns of course; presumably the attackers. We reckon there was seven different tracks at the scene,' she said with a smile.'

'But you've not enough to match up, right?'

'No.'

'Ah well, at least that's something to think about. Thanks for that.' He glanced at his watch. 'Got to dash. See you later.' He headed for the doors, binned the overshoes in the container placed in the corridor and exited the *Strictly Private* doors out into the reception area. The acting DS was sat next to another suit on the moulded chairs. It was the masculine one with shorter hair than most. They both sprung up when they saw, Sarge.

The DS, 'This is acting detective inspector. .....'

'Blades,' she finished off the introduction, 'Thank you but I can speak for myself, detective.' She smiled assertively and held out her hand to Sarge.

'It's my first suspicious death also. I'll need your assistance, Sarge. I'm pleased you're on my team.'

The sarge shook on it, said nothing. He wondered how *the team* would do without him and how many positions he was to play. *Her team!* he thought.

He led outside and down the steps.

They followed.

They walked slowly. He took in big lung-fulls of fresh morning air. It was the city but it was still fresh compared to the morgue. He sniffed at his sleeve and turned his nose up. 'Takes days to get rid of the stink of death. Have you noticed that? It clings to the inside of your nostrils. It clings to everything' He sniffed. 'I think I'm allergic to it; death.' He laughed.

The other two remained silent and serious.

'It's the first time for me,' said the DS eventually.

Sarge cocked his head in sarcastic surprise. He came to a halt. They all came to a halt. 'So, an acting DS and an acting, Inspector Blades.' He glanced at them with a disdain he couldn't hide. 'That's really appropriate,' He sneered.

Shoulders back, chest out, she came to attention. 'What do you mean sergeant?' She demanded.

The DS looked away.

Sarge was silent.

She bristled, 'What are you trying to say?'

Before replying, he popped in gum. He took his time. 'Blades. Your name, ma'am. A job like this. A murder with a knife. Blades? That's all.' He sniffed. 'You need to lighten up, keep a sense of humour, ma'am. You'll never get through the next ten years of this job let alone thirty, unless you learn to laugh through adversity. Some call it a cop's sense of humour; finding the funny side of the most serious of matters.'

Her eyes narrowed, 'I thought you meant because we're acting ranks! I thought you meant we were inexperienced, incompetent.'

He said nothing. Raised his eyebrows and shrugged. It said it all.

It was obvious she felt foolish for overreacting.

They carried on walking in silence, three a breast.

She was struggling with a stuffed brown leather brief case. Both hands were to one side, holding the handle. It was too heavy for her and banged against her thigh.

Sarge noticed. *It looked like the guy who'd burst out of Petty's chest cavity was hiding inside the case.* He chuckled to himself.

He let her struggle.

She stopped and placed it on the ground, flexed her aching fingers and huffed. She wanted help but was too proud to ask. The three of them stood there. She shot a glance at Sarge. He was gracious and too much of a gentleman, the standoff got the better of him. Besides, one day soon he knew he'd be calling her ma'am permanently and there was no point in making unnecessary enemies. She'd wind up OIC, (officer in charge) of personnel or some such administration department and his fate would be in her hands.

He bent down and took the handle. 'Here, let me carry that for you, ma'am.'

She quickly bent down and grabbed the handle too. 'No, I can manage thank you!'

He looked at her close up and raised an eyebrow. They both kept hold of the handle.

She wanted to refuse his offer but couldn't, she reluctantly let go and sprang back to attention.

The case was surprisingly heavy. He slowly straightened up. *'Why had she insisted on struggling with it?'* He thought. *'She must have been indoctrinated by the 'assertiveness for women course'. They always had to prove they were equal to any man, regardless of the truth.'* He deliberately tried to make it look lighter than it was. They moved on. He carried it one handed and did his best to make it look feather-light but he was convinced more than ever that Petty's escaped parasite was holed up in it. 'What you got in here, ma'am?' He groaned.

'Books. My law books of course.'

'Feels like a whole library.'

'Well, where do you keep your books, Sarge? She asked. 'Knowledge is power.'

'Me? Oh, I keep them in my head. You get to remember things when you've been around awhile and get stuck in.' Half a dozen steps later, 'And you're right, knowledge is indeed power.'

She said nothing. No one did.

The short walk to his car and the drive to the incident room were made longer by the silence. A busy, awkward day, passed.

CHAPTER 4

EARLY TIME.

The glowing red numbers on the screaming digital alarm read 07.30a.m as the sarge squinted at it from beneath his warm duvet. He felt exhausted, like he'd not slept. He'd had a lot on his mind. He hit the snooze button and closed his eyes again. *'I want you on my team!'* rattled around his head. The previous day hadn't been made easy, playing so many team positions and all. *'Damned buzzwords and phrases!'* He thought. He detested the buzzwords used by the next generation of senior officers, the transparent motivational psychology they used; that didn't work. *'Yesterday's team game had been tough. It hadn't felt like a team effort at all.'* He felt everyone had sat on the sidelines, especially the acting ranks, whilst he battled through. He looked at the time again then, with some difficulty, dragged himself from his pit. He struggled to get on with the new day but he soon found himself clean shaven, showered, suited and heading for the city.

He managed to be outside the Chief's half open office door 9am on the dot, major incident sitrep wedged under his arm. He waited in the corridor and listened. He heard him on the phone. He waited a moment longer before knocking and poking his head around. The chief saw him and dropped his feet off his impressive desk that could easily seat eight for dinner. He frowned at his wall clock then gave Sarge a surprised look and a smile as he waved him in.

He entered and helped himself to the water cooler that only senior officers were allowed to have in their offices, as though lesser ranks didn't require hydrating. He glanced around the spacious room pretending he wasn't listening to the phone conversation.

The Chief remained engrossed with whoever was on the other end of the phone. *Seemed like he was in no rush to end his conversation and get on with their meeting that he insisted started at 9am sharp,* thought Sarge. *'Privileges of rank! Hey ho.'* He stayed by the water station and helped himself to a second cup then headed towards the four low chairs placed in front of the table for eight. He chose one and slowly lowered himself onto it taking care not to spill his drink. He was almost sat at floor level. His eyes peeped over the acres of empty desk. It was highly polished and land marked with a couple of photo frames, some cheap golf trophies, a display of pens and an oblong of immaculately white blotting paper mounted in fine blue leather. There was an executive de-stress toy in the shape of a rubber ball next to a phone docking station to the extreme left. The Chief was observing him from his executive swivel chair way across the other side. Their eyes locked. Sarge gave him a stare that showed impatience. The Chief frowned before rotating away 180. All Sarge could see now was the back of the plush chair, all that could heard was the Chief's one-sided phone conversation.

Sarge sighed loudly for the Chief's benefit then looked around some more. On the wall was a collage of academic-type frames holding academic type certificates. They surrounded a portrait photo of the Chief wearing a smug grin and graduate gown. A *mortarboard* rested on his red hair. On the wall nearest was a large photo with a hundred or so other gowned individuals stacked in neat rows. Sarge spotted the Chief amongst them for something to do. He noticed others too who were now also police officers and climbing very nicely up the promotion ladder. He glanced around some more; until he'd checked everything out.

With nothing else to look at, he revised up on the report he'd carried in. He part listened to the phone arrangements being made about golf venues, excuses for a poor performance in a recent match and, *how the wife and kids were,*' *Forthcoming holidays and the date for the University re-union bash.* Social things like that.

Twelve minutes later, which felt like half an hour later, the chair swung back around. Without any apology the phone was cradled and eyes below the shock of red hair were peering down over the desk above folded arms in a gesture that said, *now I'm ready, tell me all about it.*

Sarge responded with a polite smile. 'Mornin,' sir,' He didn't wait for a return of pleasantries; he got straight down to business. 'Well sir, what we got is a start but I don't think we're going to get a finish.' He crossed his leg over his knee to support the file and cribbed down the sheet. He chewed. 'Ok. Here's a summary. The deceased, Petty, is in and out all evening. It's been his routine for as long as Mrs. Petty has known him. We know he's a dealer, a smart one too. The guy is lots of thing but what he isn't is gone for too long, ever. He had strict times and he made them jump to it, his clients that is, well his family too for that matter. She knew something was different that night7, him not getting back so soon.'

He was interrupted. The two acting ranks entered after a polite tap which was greeted with a friendly smile from the Chief and a not so friendly sideways look from Sarge. They filled the empty chairs and sat like timid mice peering over the desk at Sir.

'Ok sarge, cut to the chase.'

Clearing his throat with a cough, 'Well, sir, basically this fellow's dealing big style and has quite a regular customer base. Seems like he has a system to make sure he's not set-up, as he once was, according to his records. We worked out his system from books he kept. Simple but effective, but that's a side issue.' He skipped a couple of pages and looked up. 'Drugs never enter his home. The delivery is somewhere else and if it's not already *cut,* he goes away and does that some other place, possibly at friends. By the way, we may know who that is.' He looked around at the others to make sure they were following, then back at the chief. They were.

The Chief was squeezing his de-stress ball, 'I'm listening. Carry on, Sarge.' He sounded like a headmaster as he came from behind his desk and headed over to the water station. 'Detective Inspector, Sergeant, would you like some?'

'Thank you, sir.' In fawning harmony.

Sarge snorted at the situation. 'Anyway, he has a good system going and it works well. But as with any system, it was flawed. Seems like he collected the wraps hoarded somewhere close before dispatching the goods. He's not too concerned about being a target; he can handle himself, he knows that, they all know that. No, that's not his worry. It was so if *we* jumped him, he only possesses enough gear for a slap on the wrist. We only get him with a few packets rather than dealing big time.'

'He was smart,' said the inspector.

'He was smart alright, but as I was saying, there's always a flaw. He lived in the middle of a maze; ten-foots, alleys, cut-through's, pathways, unlit and unused. He used them. He had so many routes it would have been impossible to take him down. He knew that, pretty much.'

The D.S. 'So, what's the flaw?' He asked like an excited kid who can't wait to know the end of the story.

Sarges eyes rolled. He sighed. 'Well, like a rat coming and going from its nest, the options narrow the closer to home he is. Anyone knowing his home knows sooner or later he's going to appear close to it. There's an alleyway at the rear of his terrace about a hundred yards long with loads of alleys and accesses feeding off. One alley is less than fifteen yards from his gate. CRECON suggests from the blood splashes that he came out of the alley and was greeted by the guy who dispatched him.' He looked back at the Chief. 'He must have been ready for him as soon as he turned the corner. That's my idea by the way, not CRECON's.'

'But Sarge,' said the inspector, 'I know it's early day's but so far no-one admits to knowing where he lives, so who could have waited for him? Who knew? I say find out who knew and you'll find your murderer.' She was pleased with herself and looked towards the Chief for some recognition and was rewarded with encouraging smile.

Sarge responded. 'Well ma'am, no-one's going to admit knowing where he lives, are they?' Addressing the Chief, with smugness. 'Puts them right in the frame if they do.' He rolled his eyes in disbelief at her comment and shook his head.

D.S. 'Sir, we've spoken to a list of names from his mobile. We're half way through. We might get someone who helps.'

After a hard chewing; sarcastically, 'Yeah right.' He snorted. 'I'm sure they're all waiting for the call.'

The de-stress ball was getting worked hard. 'Carry on Sarge.'

He turned a few more sheets.

'Excuse me, sergeant,' said the woman inspector, rubbing her chin like a guy with stubble. 'Why would a fellow be waiting for him and how would he know where he was going to come from?'

'Well ma'am, as I said down at the morgue, I'm not a clairvoyant. But my guess is someone's been good at watching him, maybe. Perhaps he always gets sloppy when he's near home, you know, like a lot of drivers crashing within a mile of home; statistics, fact. They get sloppy, they think they're home safe and dry, they let their guard down. Maybe he always uses the same alley near his nest; his home run. Maybe they worked him out and waited. They may have just got lucky. Take your pick. I don't have all the answers.' He paused, 'You're the one with the brains and a degree.'

She didn't like his smart remark, she snapped, 'Well, what I really meant is the motive for the attacker waiting.'

He sniffed. 'Wasn't for drugs. His system didn't allow for it. They'd know that. Everyone knows how they deal these days. Besides, even if the guy was after that, several wraps were left at the scene. Any smack-head wouldn't have left them, they can't help themselves. You know what they're like.' He realized his wrong assumption and looked at the acting ranks, 'Well anyway, he was a big guy, violent and bad through and through.

Everyone knew he carried a blade. No-one was going to take him on. They were scared of him. The whole neighbourhood lived in fear of him, some decent families too. We were never going to put a stop to him.'

'Just an observation, sir.' She then turned to Sarge. 'You take it quite personally, don't you, sergeant?'

'The reason I joined up, ma'am. To fight the enemy, the bad men.' He nodded. 'Yeah. It's personal.' A moment passed. 'What were your reasons for joining?'

Her eyes narrowed contemptuously.

The Chief intervened, 'Anyway,' he cajoled. 'Moving on, Sergeant.'

'OK.' He quickly scanned the pages some more, though there was no need. He knew the details well. 'DNA tests on his blade showed three results, apart from his own. One sample unrecorded and two knowns. One of the, *Knowns*, didn't report being stuck by him and still refuses to talk. The other, *Known*, never got chance, he's lying in the Eastern cemetery six feet down - a druggie-thief, stabbed Christmas Eve two years ago. No great loss to the world but none-the-less, murdered. Never got the murderer but the knife matches Petty's blade. Draw your own conclusions. Incidentally we might be able to write that one off as a *detected crime,* sir.'

'I have to correct you there, sergeant. You say Petty was no great loss to the world. Well, he was someone's son and a father of five children.' She looked for a pat on the back from the Chief. It was a nice Political Correctness touch and good for gaining Brownie points.

She got one by a sly whiff of a smile from the Chief.

Sarge caught it. 'Are we here to point score or to get on with the job?' Eyebrow raised.

'I read the sitrep before you arrived, Sarge,' she said smugly.

'Well, did you ma'am? He said sarcastically.

'Yes. Imagine his poor family, Christmas day. It must have been dreadful.'

'You'll also have read he regularly beat-up his partner. Three of his kids are in care. He never worked a day in his life.' He flicked quickly through the file and refreshed, 'First time caught, he was thirteen. Since then, he racked up thirty-two TWOC's, about the same in burglaries and two armed robberies. And they're just the jobs we caught him for. Cautioned four times for social benefit's fraud. Spent six of his twenty-eight years on this Earth, behind bars.' He leaned forward and looked her in the eye. 'I reckon they had the best Christmas, in a long while.'

She made no reply.

'So, who we looking for, Sarge? a druggie, ex-military perhaps with a knife like that and knowing how to use it? Who?'

'Well, sir. My best guess is....' He sniffed. 'Anyone. We got no-one else's DNA or other forensics. We've got nothing but a list of phone numbers and books which add up to nothing. But finally, sir, the pathology report concludes that the cause of death would have been down to the dogs. He'd made his way nearly fifteen yards to his gate but the dogs finished him off. They were the final nail, or tooth, in his coffin'

Silence. Shock horror at the humour. No one responded to his quip. They were well conditioned.

The D.S broke the moment..., 'So the attacker had dogs with him and carried a dagger?'

The inspector joined in. 'He made him suffer or incapacitated him so the dogs could finish the job? Is that how it happened?' She turned to the Chief, 'I think it was.' She said proudly.

'Me too,' said the D.S., hoping for a pat on the back and a gold star.

The Chief nodded in agreement and looked at Sarge.

'Maybe. Maybe you're all right. It certainly looks that way.' He sniffed.

'We need to check all the dog owners in the area,' she said.

The D.S and Chief nodded in agreement.

'Well, why don't you get onto it, ma'am.' He sniffed. 'I'll help the D.S here with his list.' He stood up to leave and pulled to his jacket to. The other two did likewise.

'Sarge, could I have a word with you before you go?'

He paused, 'Sure, sir.'

The two mice squeaked then scuttled away quietly, closing the door behind them.

He sat back down and looked across the table. Chewed hard.

The Chief rocked back on his chair. He locked his fingers behind his head. He stared at the sarge. 'I'm impressed with your thoroughness and attention to detail, sergeant.' He smiled. 'You're known for it…...'

He nodded in humble acknowledgment. His eyes rolled. 'So, where's the, *but,* sir?'

'How far back did you go into Petty's history?'

'Initially?'

'Yes.'

'Five years, sir. Standard procedure.'

'You always go beyond procedure, Sarge. It's in your nature. I'm sure you looked right back to the beginning. You look for detail; the whole picture, you have to get results, you take it personally. You're good at what you do and you're good at remembering, recalling events, faces, names, times and places.'

'That's what they pay me for, sir.' He chewed, 'I'm still waiting for the, *but.*'

'Ok. Here's the, but. Had you ever come across Petty before?'

'Before all of this? He pondered a moment; shook his head. 'No sir.' He chewed hard.

'You sure?'

'Not that I recall.'

'I know you don't like us graduates and our ways or the accelerated promotion scheme but we are the future of the modern police service. In my opinion all officers should have degree qualifications. Well anyway, I pay attention to detail too.' He placed his hands palms down on the desk and leaned into them. He gave his hardest stare, which to the sarge was comparable with that of an angry sheep; just didn't work. 'You met him before,' he accused. 'Many years ago.'

'Really? Don't recall.' He chewed, 'What of it? Now unless there's anything else, sir, the day's passing I've got lots to do.' He looked at his watch, stood up and pulled his jacket to. He sniffed as he looked down at the Chief.

'You were one of his victims. A.- O.- B.- H.' He said, slowly and deliberately. 'Assault Occasioning actual Bodily Harm. A.O.B.H.'

'I'm familiar with the abbreviation, sir.' He sniffed. 'Well, it's a small world.' He took a long moment. 'So what? I've had a few take a pop at me over the years. Could have been one of many. Can't recall him.' He chewed impatiently. 'Is that it? Are you finished?' Eyebrows raised.

'You were his victim many years ago. You and a friend. You were off duty trying to protect a young lady who cried rape. That must ring some bells; looking at your police medical records; he beat you up quite badly.'

'Well firstly, sir, I'm no-one's victim, let alone one of some scumbags, like Petty. And secondly, you pulled my records over this? The bad guys, sir,' he looked out the window and nodded. 'They're out there. Not in here.'

'Not a common name, Petty. Sticks in the mind. Thought you'd have recognized it.'

'Didn't ring a bell. He didn't exactly introduce himself at the time, as I recall. It was a long time ago.' He chewed. 'Are you leading somewhere with this, sir?'

'No. Just an observation, Sarge. Just throwing it out there.'

'It was a very long time ago. Water under the bridge and all that. Forgot about it years ago.' He recalled the event, ran his tongue over his teeth.

'Ok, Sarge. You understand why I had to ask and why I pulled your records.'

'You do what you've got to do, sir. I do what I've got to do.'

'I mean, it's to protect you.'

'Yeah, right. Is that all sir?' He frowned.

'That's all, sergeant.' He worked the stress-ball.

He nodded at it, 'Is that any good for stress, sir?'

'Wouldn't know. I don't suffer with it. It's to build up my golfing grip. Do you play?'

'Me? No. No I don't.' He thought, *Wrong background, wrong social circle, wrong school tie and not a Lodge member.* Then headed for the door.

The mice were huddled outside the door. Right outside. They suddenly stepped back as the door was unexpectedly swung open by Sarge.

'Did you catch that?' he snapped.

She gave a half smile. 'We already knew.'

'Tell me, Ms. Blades. What was your degree in?'

'Sociology. Why?'

'Nothing.' He turned on the D.S. 'And you?'

'The same.'

He laughed, 'I might have guessed. Do you play golf?' He chewed.

'Just started,' came the reply in harmony.

He laughed, 'I might have guessed.' He took two steps past them then returned close up to the D.S. Serious face on. 'Show me your tongue, detective.'

He did so, like a good boy he stuck it out like a New Zealand Rugby player engaged in the Hakka.

He tutted. 'Nasty. Funny colour, brown. I wouldn't put it back in.' Then about-turned and walked off.

'Sergeant!' Shouted the more masculine of the two.

He turned. 'Yes ma'am.'

'I want you to assist the D.S. with the phone list.'

'Already said I would.'

The D.S. approached him and handed him a list of mobile numbers on A4 sheets. He kept some sheets himself. Some, but very few, had full names and addresses next to them but mostly they were just numbers followed by a name just like in Petty's books. There was a full sheet with about half having ticks next to them. The sarge familiarized himself with the sheets.

The DS waited. 'Those ticked off are the one's we've contacted but they don't want to know. None of the unregistered ones want to help, we did those first. As you can see, all the ones with names and addresses don't want to know, so far.'

'As I can see, no-one wants to know. That's why they go for the unregistered sim cards – burner phones. But I suppose we've got to show willing.' He scanned the sheets again. 'Here, let me have a look at the others.'

He gave them over and waited. 'Are you looking for anything in particular, Sarge?'

He chewed. 'No. Just looking. I'll take a couple of sheets and finish off. What we got here?' He looked up and down the lists. 'Maybe fifteen to twenty left to do. I'll take care of those. You finish off yours.'

Two coffees in the canteen and several phone calls later and more ticks added, the Sarge was heading out of the station. The DS watched him from a fourth-floor office window take a plain blue pool-car.

Four miles away a Yammy 350 power valve was pulling up to an address on the estate. The rider lived nine miles out of the city and had rode in specially. He had not been there for quite some time. He was expecting to rekindle some old times with a girl called Sue who'd invited him around. He was excited.

He leaned patiently on his machine after there was no response to his knocking on Sues door. He used his mobile but not for too long, the person expected on the other end didn't pick up.

A plain blue car with three aerials drove past. The driver appeared to take no notice of the biker and carried on by. The biker watched for signs to see if the driver had noticed him. He felt confident that he had not. He knew it was an unmarked police car. Although it was an unmarked car, everyone who needed to know, knew it was a police car. The fact it was a basic, impersonalized model, less than three years old and that it had three aerials, gave it away. Any car less than ten years old attracted attention on the estate. The suited driver wearing a tie was also a further clue if one was needed.

The biker watched as the car rounded a corner and went from view. He slipped his helmet and gloves back on to leave then started his machine. His mobile vibrated in his pocket so he reversed his actions. He answered the call. He looked disappointed but not too much so. He took a final look at the house, ground floor and bedroom windows, before preparing to leave again. It was a fine, dry, sunny day. He squinted into the sun through his visor and told himself what a great life he had as he mounted. Off he set for home.

A mile and a half away and he joined the main route towards his home town. He had ridden for several years. He was a careful rider, he had to be; his bike registration was cloned from an identical, legitimate one. He kept his real address and details secret. He had no credit cards or official documents except for some stolen identities and a Post Office box number. One of the few references to him that showed up was his criminal record but that was unlikely as he could always produce false identification. He'd made his living through his criminal activities and so he was another who kept below the radar – off grid. He knew he was wanted from many years ago but the cops were never going to catch him unless they got lucky or unless he became unlucky. He had been stopped and questioned routinely before but the cops never realized he wasn't the person he pretended to be.

He throttled up to the speed limit, always checking his mirrors. He'd outrun and out manoeuvred the police many times. The bike registration was ok, it tied in with a legitimate one, but for all that, he didn't want to be stopped more than he had to be.

The sun was fairly low and now behind him. There was very little traffic, the roads were almost deserted. He noticed a car silhouetted in his mirrors was too close for comfort. It had come upon him quickly then settled in to match his speed. He was wary; he checked his mirrors more regularly and more carefully looking for the tell-tail signs of it being more than just an ordinary car. He saw the three aerials that told him it was the police but didn't panic; another mile up was the turn-off to his town.

The road passed through his town with no other exits. Some other roads led off to nowhere, some circled back onto the main road after passing through some small homesteads and countryside. Once he was close to home there was only one way and that was straight into town. He knew he could outrun the car if he had to. He knew once he passed the last road that led off that he'd have fewer options. He slowed and took the left onto a minor road towards home.

The car followed, menacingly, he thought. He was soon up to the speed limit. He spent more time watching his mirrors. The car was still too close for his liking. He felt uneasy but he'd been in this situation many times before and was confident of his riding ability to keep him out of trouble.

The car pulled back; so, he felt more relaxed.

The last chance to turn off was fast approaching. He checked his mirrors; *false alarm,* he thought, the car was well back. He decided to carry on and head for home, besides he still had the option to outrun him through the town.

Half a mile ahead was a bus parked on his side of the road. A quarter mile away he noticed it indicating to the side it had pulled in to. Anticipating passing it, he throttled back a little. He looked in his mirrors to see the car closing fast, very fast, headlights flashing. He knew it meant trouble. He gave it full throttle and moved out to pass the bus which was now creeping forward. Suddenly the bus pulled hard over towards the opposite side of the road. Too late to react the bike glanced off the side of the bus; rider and machine parted company. The bike slid off grindingly into a shallow ditch, sparks flying. The rider did an out-of-control luge along the tarmac before rolling off like a limp rag- doll through roadside shrubs into a field.

The bus carried on. The car parked nearby. The driver sprung into action. He assessed the scene.

The rider lay lifeless on his back. His helmet was gone. The elbows on his leather jacket had given way to the road surface, blood seeped from the holes. A thigh bone protruded through his denims.

The minutes were ticking by. Several minutes had now passed. The car driver reassessed the scene.

The bike was a mess, it had been his pride and joy and was now embedded deep inside the ditch several yards away from him. The bike's toolkit was scattered, the cheap pliers from it were next to the rider's head. His mouth was bloodied, some teeth were missing, one was in the pliers' jaws, a few were scattered nearby.

He remained motionless. Then a boot repeatedly nudged him in his rib cage with an uncaring monotone, 'Come on Cross, wake up……, Come on Cross, wake up……'

His eyes were closed and in a darkened world his senses fought to assess as to where he was and why a boot kept kicking him in rhythm to an incessant voice that penetrated the blackness of his mind. His mind raced; *how had he become where he now was, laid on his back in the open air in a strange environment?* Confused, he flashed back to the bus swerving into his path, then nothing else. Senses returning, he could now hear birds singing and feel the warm air of what had been a pleasant day with promise. Yet now he could taste blood. His tongue felt gaps and splinters where teeth used to be.

He could hear a voice and feel his body being rocked by the nagging force of a boot in his ribs.

His eyes opened. It was blindingly light, everything overexposed. A figure was set against the bright sky, the sun behind him; it appeared just a dark form standing over him, kicking him.

Suddenly, searing pain from his thigh forced him to sit bolt upright and to grab the site of pain. Screaming, eyes wide open, he looked at the snapped thigh bone that had torn through his jeans. Disorientated, he pulled at it believing it to be a piece of wood or a twig that had stuck in him. The more he pulled on it the more pain it delivered. He was confused.

The figure looked on impassively. He knew it was the femoral bone, the longest bone in the body. He knew Cross was confused about the sight of it; he'd seen it before with crash victims. He observed him awhile then casually stepped onto the site of the fracture. Cross's senses heightened in the extremist. He screamed, writhed and vomited before closing down again and slipping back into painless unconsciousness.

All senses closed down.

When they returned, they told him he was on his back and the leg pain was still excruciating. That he was shaking and there was a cold boot on the side of his neck over his carotid artery. He attempted to sit up again to pull at the femoral bone he thought was jagged wood.

'It's your broken leg bone, dick-head. Leave it. Lay still!'

He screamed in pain, anger and frustration.

'Mr. Cross!'

He stopped screaming but made no reply. Teeth gritted; body ridged he squinted skywards at the stranger hovering above.

'I know who you really are and your time's running out, Mr. Cross. Your friend Petty's not here anymore to help you, but you already know that. You have just part paid for something you both did many years ago.' He snorted. 'But the debts not yet paid in full.'

Cross tried hard to see who the stranger was but could not move. He tried to grab hold of the boot that pressed on him. When he tried, the pain was too much.

'Let me up!' He growled; teeth gritted. 'Get off me!' he cursed. His hands and knees began to tremble. He was heading into a state of shock.

Nothing was said for a long moment.

'You're a bad man, Cross. Your days are numbered.'

'Who are you?' He groaned and cursed some more.

He said nothing.

'Finish me off now then, big man!' he growled as he spat blood. 'Do what you've got to do.'

He chuckled, 'No. I've got other plans for you, Cross.' He stooped over him. 'You are

Cross, aren't you?'

He cursed a muttered reply.

'You're hard work, Cross.' He laughed. 'It's like pulling teeth.'

The boot pressed harder onto his artery. The physiology and autonomic responses of Cross were studied like some scientist testing out a well-read theory. His eyes rolled and flickered, his trembling hands and knees turned into spasmodic twitching. His senses slowly faded. He felt no more pain, no more anger, no more anything.

An impression of Cross's door key was taken then he was left alone to be discovered whenever and by whoever. It was a quiet country road in a remote area; it could be quite a while.

He was found alone in a critical condition. His senses didn't return until he woke the following day to find himself in the infirmary.

CHAPTER 5

LATE.

    More time had passed and the carnival continued to wind down. Most loose ends had been tied off and a token number of staff were left to clear up. There was little else to be done. The Scientific Aids Team was sifting through a list of samples longer than the DS's list of phone *numbers* that would take months to complete and examine.

    The suggestion about the dog owner's inquiries was taken up; seemed like just about every other household on the estate had a Rottweiler, German Shepherd, Doberman, Bull Mastiff or some other equally purpose-bred four-legged potential killing machine.

    The longer the time went on, the less chance of a result. Sarge knew that, though it didn't concern him.

    The carnival rolled on to its next task. Sarge was returned to normal duties; he'd served his purpose. The acting ranks took the credit and meticulously added their endeavours to their developing CV's. The Chief praised them in their personal records. Sarge never got a mention anywhere nor did the many officers; the foot soldiers, who actually did the investigations; the real work. That's the way the system worked.

    Cross, still under a false identity, was to be released from hospital to his home address. He wore a pot cast on his leg. He would make use of the ambulance service; he had little choice. It would be a further eight weeks before he could have the pot removed.

    The police had attended his '*accident*' and impounded his smashed-up bike for safe custody. They were unable to trace the bus and its driver involved and there were no witnesses. According to all the local bus companies they didn't have a bus scheduled to be on that road that day. Cross declined to make an official report about it. The case was marked NFA and filed.

    It was known when Cross was to be released from the hospital. Information like that was easy and untraceable. The ambulance delivering him home wheel chaired him in. The house was situated fairly private; away from prying eyes. Fifty yards away stood a man unnoticed, who watched and who chewed hard.

Over two hundred miles away a new beginning started that same week in Kensington, London for a mother who wore a fancy five lever door key around her neck; the key to her new home, or Pad as it was called there and whose life was running out sooner than it ought. She and her much loved daughter were happy; life was good for them. It was a Kairos moment the day they took up residency in an expensive apartment; a world away from the housing estate they had come from. She wondered about her old home and if Cross would connect her with the day that he turned up on his 350 Yammy and waited outside her home expecting sex, and the 'accident' with a bus he was involved in on his way home. She laughed at how she'd set him up and didn't care whether he knew or not; after all, he would never find her. She was safe. She felt closer to God and thanked Him in prayers for her salvation. She felt a million glorious miles away from the council estate and her old life. She looked back over her years and saw it all as moments of Kairos time. It all made sense to her now. She knew her time was running out but it held little fear for her, she had repented her sins and knew where she was going. She realized how fleeting life could be and how everyone's just passing through. She realized it wasn't about the quantity of life but its quality. It was about leading a good honest and spiritual life and having the right priorities. Friends, family and happiness were what counted. She had realized that drugs, following the crowd and clamouring for material things could never bring true, long-lasting happiness. She had learned. She was happy.

A further week and the sarge was on a night shift. He patrolled his area. He saw that Petty's former home was now boarded up. A new life had also started somewhere else for Mrs Petty and her children. Victims of circumstance. She wouldn't miss her husband; her children wouldn't miss their step-father. They were all better off without him. Society was better off without him.

Mr. Petty's life was going nowhere anymore, he stayed in the morgue's refrigerator and that's where he'd remain for the foreseeable future. He was going nowhere, for a long time.

On foot patrol, the sarge paused a moment outside the Petty's old house. It stood quietly and soullessly in the darkness, no longer inhabited; a testament to how fleeting the dynamics of life can be. He danced his torch beam over it and reflected upon the recent events. He thought of Petty laid like a piece of meat in some butchers' refrigerator, still looking sorry for himself rather than sat in his armchair awaiting calls from desperate addicts.

He wondered about the dogs and their owner that helped put him there.

He took a moment.

He wondered too about the druggie clients who would have gone elsewhere for their *gear*. And who would have filled the void of one less and very dead, dealer.

His mind returned back to Petty laid out in the cold dark refrigerator down at the morgue. His chest laced up with big stitches, like those used on a potato sack, just to hold his rib cage and organs in place. And how his next Kairos moment in this world would be his funeral. Which got him to thinking of Sue; how she was doing and whether her God would forgive Petty's string of sins and allow him into the Kingdom of heaven. He wondered too, whether the person who was responsible for his death would be forgiven by her God. He liked to think they would. *Perhaps they'd even get a pat on the back from the big man himself,* he thought.

He wondered whether the killer was in fact an instrument of God's Will. He liked to think so. He hoped so, if there was a heaven. The thought gave him some comfort as did the thought that it was a pack of dogs that was actually the final instrument of death and not a knife. Though that would always be open to debate. Perhaps, he thought, it was a combination of all those who were involved, not just the dogs, their owner, or the one who stabbed him. He considered how Mrs. Petty and Sue fitted into it. Sue, with all her Kairos moments that had passed before along with the Kairos moments Petty had created himself, the ones which were part of his life's path. He thought of the influence where Heaven meets Earth, the coming together of the two that Sue believed in.

He shook himself out of the God stuff, replaced his torch and took a long sigh then walked on passed the sad looking house. Seconds later he saw a little man in the distance at the end of the street with his dogs. Four of them; Rottweiler.

He chewed, contently. *Life goes on,* he thought. He gave the dog-walking bus driver a wave and thumbs up. The man acknowledged with a nod before quietly disappearing into the maze of alleys with his pack.

It was to be Sarge's last set of nights. He was to start back in the vice squad for a short while only.

The week passed with all the usual dramas and in a typical week of events, most were Kairos moments of the negative sort. Perhaps those moments were a rolling procession of past events which brought about their current Kairos moments; ie. more negative events. It was the same criminal faces up to the same old criminal stuff.

9 a.m., Wednesday, Chronos time. In Kairos time it was a significant moment; the first day back in Vice for the sarge.

He looked around the office. It was a small room that comfortably fitted in a half dozen desks surrounded by notices; posters of missing and wanted persons and a duty roster board. There was a large white Nobo board with the names of mispers (missing persons) written in black, blue and red felt-tip. An old, battered TV sat on top of a large grey metal filing cabinet that was heavily padlocked. It held a store of seized porno material; mostly confiscated videos to be checked through before evidence submission or disposal. A video player and the latest consumer must-have, a DVD player, were wired to the TV from a makeshift shelf at the side.

Two plain-clothes officers were already there. 'Can't remember if you take sugar, Sarge.'

'Mornin' Mandy. No thanks, just milk.' He ran his tongue around his mouth. 'No sugar. Got to look after your teeth.' He asked how she was.

She replied positively and said how pleased she was that he'd returned as her sergeant. She was at the drinks area and was already in her loyalty mode. She'd worked with the sarge previously. She was a bright girl and often held her gaze at the sarge for a little too long at times for his liking.

She was a good athlete, lean, mid-twenties, olive skin, brown eyes, dark hair tied back in a tail. She was confident on the athletics track but lacked a little in the workplace. She more than made up for that with enthusiasm and loyalty.

The other officer, Roy, coolly swerved his way around a desk to shake hands with Sarge. He was laid-back, late thirties, an ex-paratrooper and was built wider than he was tall. It wouldn't be possible to be any wider without being relabelled as a barn door. His width made him look shorter than he was. He had no neck or waist. His arms were twice the thickness of most men's. He had cropped hair and a 70s Mexican moustache that suited him. His passion was pumping iron and it showed.

One word, 'Sarge.' Followed by a nod, said everything in Roy's language. His voice was deep yet as smooth as velvet. He was a man of few words; more a man of action.

'Roy.' The sarge reciprocated the greeting likewise as manly and as coolly as possible. And smiled.

Roy pulled him up close as they shook hands, put a hand around his back and hugged him. That was Roy. He patted him on his back like a long-lost friend, took a pace rearwards and came almost to attention. He looked him up and down like a drill sergeant, gripped both his shoulders and with a slight shake of reassurance said, 'You're looking good, Sergeant.'

Sarge felt comfortable with it but not so comfortable as to enjoy it too much.

'Thanks, Roy. So are you, but don't take that the wrong way.'

They laughed.

He saw a white opened-faced motorcycle helmet on a desk. 'That yours?' asked Sarge. 'You still got your Harley?'

He nodded, smiled proudly.

Mandy passed them their drinks and they gathered around one desk. They caught up on old news, a way of rekindling friendships, of re-establishing orientation.

The Vice office was on the top floor of six; the same floor as the canteen, the locker room, the offices of the Area Commander; Chief Lomax and his deputy, Chief Curry and that of the Top civilian support staff. All the other offices and officers were below them, in many ways.

The Area Commander was a graduate. He was a shy man who carved out his career through careful planning. Two years on the beat followed by many years dodging the *sharp end*; administration, planning, recruiting, research services, personnel, logistics, even Internal Affairs (I.A); the police's police. Office jobs like that.

It all culminated in his goal through accelerated promotion; the Area Commander, one of the top Chiefs. A highly paid job, far removed from the fast and tough life operational officers endure.

Although having little experience as a *'practical on the beat officer'*, he had determined other's careers, terminated some, fast forwarded others, wrote policy directives, changed the way the police functioned and dabbled blindly in all sorts of other ways with a belief that his ideas were the right ideas. Not based on experience but purely the belief that he was right. He was in a powerful position. He'd upset many people along the way. He'd made few true friends, if any.

He may have been blessed with more than his fair share of academic brains but not a great physique; years of inactivity sat pushing a pen at a desk had reduced his body to an atrophied form. He lacked muscle and form. His torso was small and undeveloped with narrow stooped shoulders which made his head look too big to belong to such a small body. He was less than five ten, had a hang-dog expression and wore a beard that would have suited a down-and-out more than it did him. It was sparse and ragged. A curly pipe was often stuffed in it. He wore the cheapest, ugliest health service spectacles. If his nose was to be included with his pipe, spectacles and beard the casual observer could be forgiven for thinking they came as a set from some joke shop and that they were all attached and removable from his face. But they weren't.

He was a late starter so was fairly old for a man of his rank on the *fast-track* scheme. He was a serious character who used his rank to compensate for his inadequacies both as a man and particularly so as someone whose role was to be a leader of men; an example; a decision maker, a man of character, charisma, someone dynamic. He lacked all such attributes. He was the opposite to all of that. He had no respect from any of his officers. He could walk into any office and his presence went unfelt. No-one showed him genuine respect and yet, through a system which catered for officers with impressive educational qualifications and CV's, he'd pretty much made it to the top. Once he'd reached that place in an ivory tower, he was untouchable and fairly unaccountable.

He had enough grovelling wannabes to delegate to. Their careers rested in his hands so it was in their best interests to look after him. Like the time he was chased by vice squad officers from a public toilet where gays hung out for *cottaging* purposes; soliciting for immoral purposes in a public place, a criminal offence in the interests of protecting public decency. It was his second time of him being caught breaking that law. The first time around, a senior officer of lower rank tried to help him by binning the evidence and it worked. But the second time; a plain brown envelope containing a report and photos of the incident was eventually passed anonymously to the Chief of police for his information and decision.

That matter too was swept under the carpet. The Force had had a tough time in those recent years back then. Of the twenty of so high-ranking officers in the force, one had been investigated for obtaining a Police Authority money loan at ridiculously low interest rates for the purpose of using it to buy a car for work purposes but instead used it to buy a mobile home and take his family on a luxury holiday. What he did was criminal. That was not in question. Due to his rank, it went no further. To prosecute *would not have been in the public interest*, it was declared. It was kept from the public domain. In the same year a low-ranking officer, a good street cop, was dismissed for claiming a few pence more than he was entitled to for his traveling expenses. Everyone compared the two and was outraged at the contrast in outcomes and sums involved. *But then that's the system we work in,* they thought, and so life moves on. The unfair system remained.

The senior officer, even though dishonest, was further promoted after the episode then retired soon after. He got a greater pension, in line with his promotion. He was headhunted to run a national security firm dealing in counter-fraud and the transportation of bank money. Ironic.

The dismissed low-ranking officer, full of remorse and anguish trying to deal with the error of his ways and guilt, disappeared into obscurity after spending bouts in and out of a mental hospital. The injustice of the system was the major factor in his decline. He knew his faux pas was nothing compared to that of the senior officer.

Another senior officer had hit the Nationals when he was arrested in another police area kerb-crawling the red-light district; home to prostitutes, brothels, pimps and drug dealers. He was a married man. Their vice squad caught him in his car dressed all in black leather, wearing a black leather gimp mask, even black leather underwear. He had with him an array of whips, coshes and other masochistic paraphernalia, even rectal beads. It was impossible to sweep it under the carpet as it was in the public domain before it could be stopped. He denied any offence. The Chief gave him a way-out through resignation. He got his lucrative pension. He never went to court – *deemed not in the public interest to prosecute.* NFA.

Another senior male officer had been moved to a different station for indecent assault and sexual harassment of some of his staff, including some women!

Another high flier had been chased through the city driving his Ferrari at high speed and ran into his home after abandoning his vehicle on his lawn. He was drunk and asked his partner to lie to the police and tell them she was the driver so that he would avoid being arrested for driving whilst over the permitted drinks limit. Unfortunately for him she'd had enough of his abusive ways, especially the beatings he gave her. So, when the police knocked, she told them the truth. He was shocked. He was arrested and was over the alcohol limit. He denied driving. The case never went to court. He was given the option to resign. He resigned and collected his generous pension.

All those incidents. That was just the tip of the iceberg. It had not been a good couple of years for the Force's reputation and credibility. But it stumbled on from crisis to crisis. And so, it went. Kairos moments in their lives, determining future events, directions in time.

Mandy gathered the empty mugs and went over to the drinks area to refill them. Sarge and Roy carried on chatting. She turned around and made an obvious question about Sarge's sugar again. She'd not already forgotten; it was done to attract the attention of her colleagues. She pointed to the door, put her finger to her lips in a *shush* fashion then pinched her nose, indicating a smell.

The insipid Area Commander had a nasty habit of prowling the corridors and listening outside of offices; Paranoia. It was clear he'd never been in the Criminal Investigation Department as he smoked a pipe and the smoke was often detected long before he was, though he never realized that. It always gave him away.

At that moment Roy and the sarge smelled pipe smoke. Roy knew what Mandy meant and what the smell meant, the sarge wasn't sure. He was aware that something was different, even more so when Roy changed the subject.

'So, Sarge, tell us about that Uncle Billy killing.' He winked. 'They suspect you were involved. Were you?' asked Roy. He winked and nodded over to the open door. The police were famous for their sense of humour and the *winding-up* of colleagues; it was the establishment's culture. It was seen as a way of coping with the day-to-day stress and horrors which life threw at them by the very nature of their work. Police humour.

The sarge interpreted this as one of those moments, so he obliged. A wry smile came to his face. 'Well ok, this doesn't go out the office.' He said seriously. He coughed. 'It's between the three of us. Ok?'

Roy chewed, smiling, nodding encouragingly.

Sarge carried on. 'How can I put it?' He glanced over to the open doorway. 'I have to be careful what I say.' He paused. 'If I tell you that fat perverted Uncle Billy went down faster than a whore going down for a fifty note, perhaps you'll have your answer.'

They all laughed.

'So, you were involved?' asked Mandy, winking as she brought the drinks over.

'Well believe what you like. All I know is it's one less for the system to chase around after. And where he is, he aint going to hurt anymore little girls. Ever.' He laughed.

Roy grinned. 'We guessed it was you. But seriously, you have quite a lot of kudos around here, Sarge.'

It was a conversation stopper, Sarge was modest; didn't like praise. They knew that. An embarrassing moment descended... they sipped their drinks...

Mandy mimed to Sarge and pointed to the door, 'It's the Area Commander.'

Sarge broke the silence as though raising a new subject. 'So, what's the new commander like, Mandy? Who is he?'

'You tell him, Roy.' She found it hard to keep a straight face. 'About Lomax......' She bit her lips to stop herself laughing. Her eyes were wide, she pointed again at the doorway.

'Lomax Climax.' said Roy, in all seriousness.

'Who the hell's that?' He chewed.

Roy was a veteran of active service with the Paras (Parachute Regiment) and Special Forces. He was good at his job and as tough as they came. He feared no-one and nothing and although he enjoyed his current work, he was a free spirit and if he lost his job tomorrow he would still be a happy-go-lucky individual. He wasn't interested in promotion so it didn't matter who he upset, he was never going to suck up to anyone to further his career and no-one could put in an adverse report that would upset him or his plans. That was Roy; a free spirit. So, any chinless senior officer was never going to make him miss a beat. Respect had to be earned and some scrambled-egg on a senior officers' shoulders was never going to do it for him. Especially one who had been chased from public toilets on more than one occasion. Roy had his own set of rules and standards.

Roy explained, 'Lomax Climax.' He laughed. 'Well, Mayhew Lomax, you might know him as. Everyone calls him Lomax Climax.' He paused. 'Do you get it?'

It was childish but they all laughed.

The sarge thought a moment. 'Lomax. That one that got chased from the gents' toilets for *cottaging,* or should I say, loitering for immoral purposes?' He recalled him from many years ago. 'Well, well. So now he's climbed all the way up the ladder. Who'd have thought it?' He shook his head and looked over at the door. 'Well, they need chasing off.' He looked back. 'When my son was a young boy, he went into the gents on his own and came out petrified. He'd heard two of them going at it in a cubical. He didn't understand, he was only nine. Frightened him to go in alone for a while.' He hesitated.

Roy whispered, 'It's ok, Sarge.' He winked. 'I know what you're going to say next. Tell us your favourite joke.' He smiled.

Sarge was never comfortable telling jokes but he made the effort and stuck to the same old ones he could remember and knew worked. He never dealt with failure or ineffectiveness very well so fretted unnecessarily even over the poor delivery of a joke. It was in his makeup not to be in the spotlight for appearing foolish.

'Ok. Well, I came across some gays one dark night when I was on uniform foot patrol. There was a load of them hanging around the toilets.' He chewed. 'They saw me and ran; did a star-burst. I chased two of them down an alley. I grabbed one, the other disappeared. I said, *if I knew where your mate was, I'd shove this torch right up his arse.* Just then I heard a wimpish voice from farther down the alley shout, *'I'm in the bin......'*

They all laughed.

Roy said forthrightly, 'We can't stand them lot that pretend to be hetero and are really gay. Or the bisexual lot.' He directed his voice over to the door. 'Especially them that are married and hang around toilets waiting for a cheap thrill.'

Mayhew Lomax then walked past the doorway, eyes like poached eggs, puffing hard on his pipe and leaving angry clouds of smoke behind him.

They smiled then sipped their drinks.

'Anyway, Roy, by the look of it you still don't mind that joke, do ya?'

'Not at all. I remember it as being one of your favourites. It's only a joke. No different than if it was a joke about hetero's. If jokes were banned for fear of upsetting anyone, it'd be a pretty sad and serious world. If that was about hetero's no-one would bat an eyelid. You don't need to start worrying about offending me, Sarge. Sometimes that PC brigade make things a lot worse for us, for everyone. A joke's a joke. Just humour. Doesn't mean you're a homophobe or evil, Sarge.'

'You got that right, matey. You're the one they should be asking what's right or what's wrong.' He sipped. 'You still with the same guy, what's his name, Dave...., Darren...Dan...?'

'Yeah, Dave. We've been together getting on for five years now. He moved in with me a couple or three years ago. But yeah, we're very happy thanks.'

'Well, I'm pleased for you, pleased for you both, matey.'

'Well two great looking blokes and both gay. Typical!' Said Mandy, laughingly.

Two more officers entered the office. Sorry we're late, Sarge. Didn't get off until three this morning.'

'No problem,' he said. They shook hands and all agreed it would be good to work as a team again.

'By the way, Climax was ear-wigging outside the door just then,' said one of the latecomers. 'He moved off when he saw us coming along the corridor. Don't know what you guys were talking about but he didn't look very happy.'

'Yes, we knew he had been there but we thought he'd gone. It's unfortunate that he's my next chain of command. I didn't realize that's who was hiding in the corridor and eavesdropping at first. Ah well, there's no love lost between us. I remember him in his early days as a scruffy rural cop. I ought to go introduce myself sometime soon.' He ran his tongue over his teeth.

The day moved on, the sarge came up to speed. The team were doing drugs busts almost every other day. Drugs raids were the flavour of the month. The Area Commander's deputy, Chief Curry, regularly appeared in the local newspapers where the team had raided yet another house for drugs. He didn't get involved himself but he enjoyed the publicity and seeing his photo in the newspaper. It was good for his CV. He'd even gotten the TV cameras to join them on some of the raids, the ones he went along on. He had initiated the pro-active drug searches at the expense of all other areas of police work. He was riding high on the publicity. He was another graduate entrant but his promotion had hit a brick wall when he was accused of sexual harassment by several staff. He was trying to regain his place in the hierarchy. He was doing a lot of brown-tonguing.

Sarge was sorting his desk out when came across a drugs raid warrant that had almost expired. It had seven of its twenty-eight days left before a new one would have to be applied for. It related to a particularly nasty piece of work, Adam Buck. Even though he was of slight build and only five foot seven, he was a violent man and had numerous previous convictions. The Intel (intelligence) stated he was running around the estate with a handgun and had threatened some individuals with a sawn-off twelve-bore. There were several reliable informants to the man's criminal escapades.

He chewed. 'Hey Roy, this warrant here, how come it's not been acted upon?' He slid the file across the desk.

He scanned over it. 'Didn't know about it. The sarge we had before you kept things close to his chest. He was only passing through on his carousel of departments, newly promoted and all that. You know how it is. It was probably in his, *too difficult to do,* tray. Guns involved and all, a little too different for him to get his head around maybe. Bit risky, could spoil a career if it all went wrong and tits up.' He slid the papers back.

Sarge took them then headed to the Area Commander's office.

The commander boasted he had *an open-door policy.* By that, he meant anyone could pop in to see him anytime; no appointment necessary. Which was a little odd as his door was always kept closed and more often than not, he could not be located.

The sarge rapped urgently on the hollow plywood door. Whatever the occupant would have been doing, it would have gotten his instant attention.

There was a long pause.

The door next to the one knocked upon was opened by a thin, weaselled faced man whose skin was so pale it was clear it had not seen the light of day for many years; too long inside offices. It was Chief Curry, the Commander's right-hand man. He was *the troll* at the bridge. Anyone wanting an audience with the Chief had to get past him first.

'Yes sergeant. What's the problem?'

'Hello, sir. Need to see the Chief, pretty urgently.'

Chief Curry sported a beard similar to the Commander's. He had been an officer in the navy until he crashed his fifteen thousand ton, high-tech, state-of-the-art warship into the quayside after only its third time out. He lost his officer Commission and was busted to the rank of able seaman so opted for another career rather than be a mere low rank rating.

He knew of the sarge's arrival into the department and so *welcomed him aboard.* He finished by adding, 'The Commander doesn't want disturbing today. Can I help you?'

'No. Not really, sir. I need the Commanders authority for a firearms job. It has to be the Area Commander.' He paused and looked Chief Curry up and down as though he was an inferior being. 'I need to see Lomax sooner rather than later. Besides, I can only approach him regarding Vice squad matters, as you know, him being my next in the chain of command and all.' Eyebrows raised.

'Or if I'm deputizing for him, sergeant.'

'Which, you're not, sir. I'm told he's used his fifty-two days of leave entitlement and more when he stayed over in Thailand after getting caught up in some scandal. Young Thai boys and girls involved; I'm told.' He laughed.

The chief said nothing; did nothing. He knew what Sarge was inferring but high ranks close ranks.

He chewed and nodded at the unanswered door. 'So, what's he get up to in there, were he can't see anyone? There'll never be any paperwork on his desk, he's a Chief. It's not like he's exactly busy, is it?' He glanced over Chief Curry's shoulder at his empty desk.

The chief glanced over too and knew what he was getting at. He coughed nervously but made no comment. Not only that, it would be like the pot calling the kettle black to agree or laugh with him. Instead loathing swept across his face. His jaw tightened. 'Or if you are in dispute with him and it cannot be resolved, then I can assist.'

The sarge was dismissive. 'Well, it's not that either, sir. But I'll remember that. Thank you anyway.'

The chief retreated backwards into his office like a hermit crab retreating back into its shell and closed the door.

The sarge waited five then returned to the Commanders office door. He banged twice and walked straight in carrying an A4 manila envelope. He gave a false look of surprise when he saw the commander sat at his desk.

The Commander didn't know how to react.

'Oh. Sorry sir. I was told you weren't in today so was just going to leave this envelope for your attention.'

He was not pleased.

'As you may know, sir, I've been posted into Vice as of this a.m.'

He was further displeased. He said nothing.

'Well seeing as I'm here now and so are you, sir, perhaps we can sort it.' He scanned the empty desk. Eyebrows raised; eyes wide open. 'Unless you're busy, sir.' He smiled.

He helped himself to a chair, dragged it to the executive-style desk then slid the envelope to sir's reluctant hands.

He made no reply. He opened the envelope then studied the sarge a moment. 'Have we met before?' He asked.

There was a hesitation. Sarge knew exactly where their paths had crossed. He recalled it the moment he saw him. It was many years ago, around the same time he met Cross and Petty for the first time, along with officer braces down. 'No.' He shook his head. 'No sir. I don't think we have, sir.'

'Ah well. You look vaguely familiar. We must have crossed paths sometime in the past. I'm good with faces. It'll come to me.'

He abruptly changed the subject. 'Here's the problem, sir. We've got a *dealer* running around the estate with shooters. Even had a report that one was discharged, so they're the real thing. We've known about it sometime. There's a warrant to enter and turn his place over. We got less than seven days to execute it or it runs out. If we do nothing the courts have to be informed and aren't likely to issue another. They'll need to be told why we did nothing. Worse still, if someone gets blown away in the meantime it could look embarrassing for those in charge.' He popped in some gum, 'If you get my drift, sir.'

'Well, sarge, it's not good enough.' He made his best effort to appear stern. 'I want a report submitting as to why nothing has been actioned. Who's the incompetent who left it gathering dust?' He said enthusiastically.

He waited a moment. 'My predecessor, sir.' He chewed as he revelled in the situation. 'I'm told it was that guy you recommended to run Vice for the last six months.' He paused. 'And some of your other key departments. Left quite a trail of disaster I'm told,' he said smugly. 'Accelerated promotion scheme; degree in Biology the team tells me.' He chewed with satisfaction.

'I still want a report about it,' he said, with less enthusiasm.

'Do you want me to let him know, sir?' He smiled.

'No. I'll do it.' Which meant it would be forgotten about and swept under the carpet. 'We need to get on with the job. I'll let you deal with it.'

'Ok, sir. I'll need your authority for the firearms team to assist in the raid, they'll do their own reconnaissance. The target, Buck, rarely comes out of the house. Seems like he sleeps with the twelve-bore, according to the intelligence department. I'm thinking of a dawn knock. I'll get back to you when we're ready.' He stood up, pulled his jacket to, leaned over and gathered the loose leaf's of the file and left.

The target house backed onto other houses at the rear so that the gardens butted up to one another. There were easier houses to carry out reconnaissance on but the armed response team snuck into the rear gardens in the dead of night. The plans of the internal layout were studied and orders were drafted for the operation to enter aggressively with force and without warning. Insofar as tasks went it was a straight forward matter and they would be upon the dealer before he had chance to react. They'd done it countless times. All that was required was the final authorization from the Area Commander.

With three days left of the warrant, Sarge sought authorization. He'd made several attempts to have an audience with the Commander but he was always too busy to be seen or no-one knew where he was, including Chief Curry.

It was late afternoon the day before the planned raid when Sarge caught the smell of pipe tobacco drifting along the corridor. He headed towards its origin; the canteen, where he found him sat in a soft chair reading a file over a coffee. The TV on the wall in front of him was showing his favourite sport; cricket. His eyes were on the TV more than the file.

He looked up. 'Not now, Sarge,' the Commander pre-empted, 'I'm busy.'

'Not a problem, sir.' He smiled and thrust a folder with the firearms authorization form on top with a pen tucked under his thumb. 'Just needs your signature. It's for the raid. You know, the one we spoke about the other day, the dealer with the guns. Adam Buck. Planned for four in the morning.' He gave a second thrust.

He sighed. 'I don't have time right now.' He jumped up and headed out of the canteen and down the corridor to his office.

Sarge followed like a sheepdog after a scared sheep. 'Sir, it's planned to take place less than twelve hours from now,' he shouted after him. 'You'll be home in an hour and if I don't catch you before you go the twenty guys already gearing up to make the raid will not be happy.'

Area Commander, Mayhew Lomax stopped and turned.

The sarge walked up to him in eight steps, 'Even less so the Chief of Police if the bad man shoots someone sooner or later and we didn't act. There'll be some awkward questions coming your way. Worse still, Buck gets to keep his guns. He'll always be a bad day waiting to happen. Is that what you want?' He sniffed then poked the folder at him once more. Raised his brows.

He sighed defeatedly, 'Very well.' He took the folder from him. 'Come into my office, sergeant.'

The head of the civilian support staff intercepted before they got there. It was some question about a meaningless administration issue but the commander seized upon it as a possible means of escape. It was clear to the sarge that he was looking for a way out so he was reminded of the importance of his signature for the raid to go ahead.

He delayed several times and explored ways of breaking away from the Sarge rounding him up. He ran out of options and they moved along. Another officer was waiting for him outside his office door with a bunch of papers. The sarge corralled him past and into his seat behind his desk. He returned to shut the door then stood over his shoulder whilst he sat quietly inspecting the file and plans for the raid. It made the Commander feel uneasy having Sarge watching over him; he invited him to take a seat. So, he did. He dragged it in front of the desk and peeped over it.

He took his time reading the file. He raised several *ifs* and *buts* but was met each time with a suitable answer from the sarge.

Finally, he submitted. 'Well, Sarge, I'm not happy.' He said cautiously. 'There are two children involved. They will be at risk if the firearms team is deployed.'

'True, sir, there is a risk.' He chewed. 'But they're at risk anyway. He's got at least one handgun and a shotgun in the place. Intel suggests the kids sleep in the bedrooms at the rear. We've got that covered. They're too old to be sleeping with mum and dad. It says it in the operational report, sir. It's all there. Very comprehensive, as you'd expect.'

There was a long moment as he searched the file for more reasons to duck out of authorizing it.

'Well, I think we should wait until he comes out. Take him on the street.'

'He rarely ventures out, sir. Besides, it becomes an uncontrolled situation once he's not contained. Too fluid. Best at four in the morning like the firearms team advise, sir.'

Another long moment.

'What about appointments? Is he due at court or can we arrange him a meeting with his probation officer or social worker, away from the house?'

'No, we can't, sir. We considered that. He never keeps any appointments, never did, so the system gave up on him years ago. He won that one. The neighbourhood doesn't lend itself to covert surveillances either. There's nowhere to watch his front door for when he comes out. It's a none-starter. It would be impossible to wait for him.' He sniffed. 'Everything's in place, ready to go. Just like it says in the armed response team's operational briefing, there. It's a routine raid for the firearms team at HQ.'

There was a long, agonizing moment as the commander's mind went into overdrive.

Sarge chewed impatiently and noisily. 'So?'

Another long moment passed.

The commander looked up. He was edgy. 'No. No we can't do it. I can't give the go ahead.' He slid the file towards the sarge.

'And why's that, sir?'

'Too risky. It outweighs the purpose and importance of the task.'

'And letting some psycho drug dealer run loose around the estate like John Wayne, isn't a risk?'

'There are children at the address.'

'On that estate there's children in every street and at nearly every address and usually more than two.' He chewed fast. 'Does that mean anyone in your area with kids at home has a license to hold illegal firearms? Surely you don't mean that, sir.'

'That's my decision, sergeant.' He glanced at his clock, ten minutes fast. He stood up and donned a grubby beige raincoat that had been hanging on the back of the door.

The sarge remained seated.

He opened the door and waited. 'Is there anything else, Sarge?'

'I think you're wrong, sir. I know you're not too bothered about those people who live on the estate but what if some unsuspecting cop comes across him in the street or goes to the guy's home for some reason and doesn't make it home at the end of his shift to his wife and kids? What are you going to tell them?'

He fastened his coat as he walked to his window. He looked out and pondered. Most of his police area could be viewed from there. He surveyed it. 'It's a risk I'll have to take. That's what I'm paid for.' He turned around. 'The same as those officers down there on the street, they know the risks they take.'

'Well perhaps you'd like to change places with them and take the risks they take, sir.'

'That's what they get paid for.'

'They don't get paid to take unnecessary risks.' He chewed. 'You're pretty bullet proof up here, sir.'

There was a long silence whilst he pulled a pipe and tobacco pouch from his raincoat pocket. He went through the ritual of preparing it, ready for lighting.

The sarge watched on. 'You've authorized other firearms jobs, why not this one?'

'It doesn't warrant it.' He bit onto the pipe and spoke through gritted teeth. 'If you insist on executing the warrant it will have to be without the armed response team. That's all I'm going to say on it.'

There was much angry chewing. 'Ok. You've put it back on me. You know that I won't go ahead without the firearms team, so it's not going to happen. I won't risk my men unnecessarily.'

'That's your decision, sergeant. Is there anything else?'

'Well, you've forgotten to sign the form and give the reasons for your refusal, sir. I just hope no-one gets shot 'cos this will come bouncing back your way.' He chewed.

He stood and signed the form after writing a few remarks then handed it back to Sarge.

He checked the form. 'You just put *unsafe, force not justified* as a reason not to proceed, sir. In that case every such raid could be marked up as that. Why is this one so different?'

'They're my reasons, sergeant. Now I'd like you to leave my office.'

There was more hard chewing and glaring as the sarge left and waited outside his door whilst the commander locked it. He watched him amble along the corridor leaving a trail of smoke then get into the elevator.

Deputy Chief Curry's office door next to the Commander's, was closed. He chewed hard. He was annoyed. He knocked and walked in without hesitation. Sat at the chiefs' desk was the head of the civilian support staff. He was alone. He was like a child that had been caught in the act of doing something naughty. In front of him were several piles of papers. He gathered them up, roughly.

'Oh. Hello,' He focused on Sarge's ID tag, 'sergeant. Can I help you?' He tried to sneakily slide some of the documents back into a top drawer to his right. But it didn't work. He'd been caught.

The sarge looked at him knowingly. 'Where's the deputy chief?'

He looked at the wall clock which was thirteen minutes fast, before answering. 'The chief? He's just left for home.' He slyly placed his hand over a bunch of keys in front of him.

Sarge noticed. He looked at the clock then his own wristwatch. 'He's got a going home clock too, eh? A little fast, isn't it?' He laughed.

He said nothing.

'Does Curry know you're in here when he isn't? You're a civilian, should you be going through things?'

He laughed, nervously. 'Surely you must have gone through a boss's desk in your time to see what's going on. That's how you find things out. Anyway, I'm the senior civilian officer. I'm equivalent rank to the chief.'

He made no reply. He stepped over to the desk and spun some of the documents around to read, raised his brows at the frightened man sitting there then spun them back.

'I know who you are. Stop fooling yourself, you're a civilian. You've no rank within the police. And I'm sure the boss wouldn't be too happy about you using your master keys to rifle his confidential stuff, would he? You should know better, being a senior support staff employee.'

The man was ashen. 'Is he going to find out?'

He let him sweat it a moment.

He grinned. 'No. It's our secret.' He waited. 'But you owe me one.' He said in a serious tone.

'One what?'

'A favour. You owe me a favour for keeping my mouth shut.'

'Thank you, sergeant.' He relaxed. 'What is it you were after? Can I help you?' He grovelled.

'Well, I know you like to think you're equal rank to a police boss, like Chief Curry, but unless you can resolve a dispute between me and Commander Lomax over a firearms job, then no.' He sniffed. 'You can't.'

'Well, how does that work? Surely the chief will always side with the Commander. It's in his best interests not to go against him, him being the superior rank and all.'

'Exactly. That's why the system made it that way. Two against one. Two noes are better than one.' He chewed. 'Just wanted to drag him in too, that's all.' He turned to leave. 'Make sure you put everything back the way you found it, mister.'

He headed straight for the Vice office and was immediately greeted by Roy in there. 'Sarge, whilst you've been away, we got a call from HQ.'

'About the job planned for the morning? It's off.'

'Really? Ok. The call was about something else. They've got a paedophile works in their area that lives in ours. He's a university lecturer who's been using their computers to look at child porn sites. Some really bad disgusted stuff of the worst order, apparently. They suspected him for quite a while and so monitored his use. Sounds serious.' He paused. 'So, what's happened about the morning raid? Did you say it was off?'

'It's off. I've just seen Lomax. He let us mess about and waste time only to say he won't authorize the firearms boys to assist us. He said we could do it without them if I wanted to go ahead.'

'Well, that's just like him. Anyway, HQ, they're asking if we can assist them first thing in the morning, so maybe it's worked out ok. They want us to put the paedo's door in at first light.'

'First light? Ok. Can you call the firearms team and cancel everyone ASAP? Tell them the boss's too windy to authorize now. He's gone back on his word...... Strange. I think there's more to it than I know.'

Roy chewed. 'Roger that.'

'You still can't lose your military jargon, can you?' He laughed. 'Rustle up the rest of our team for a briefing, would you?'

'Roger. By the way, can you ring their Area Commander, they asked. Not their Vice sergeant, she's away on holiday.'

He agreed. A quarter of an hour later the sarge came off the phone with a sheet of notes.

Roy, Mandy and the rest of the squad were standing-by.

'Well, here's the good news. We don't have to be back here quite so early in the morning. Instead of 3 a.m. it's now 6 a.m. Instead of a dealer with shooters, it's a thirty-four-year-old paedo lecturer who lives at home with his eighty-year-old mum. We're going to give him a knock and raid his home first thing. But let's hope the boss's we have don't hear of it or they'll say it's too risky.' He laughed.

Those around did likewise; in sympathy and understanding.

The pre-operational briefing was given.

It was soon 6 a.m. in the Vice squad office the following day. The plans were finalized over tea and coffee. The intention was to enter quickly, control any computers on the premises so that data could not be destroyed and then seize all relevant material and remove it to the police station. They knew the target was not due back at work for several weeks so he should be home with his mum.

A couple of *uniformed officers* were drafted in to assist.

Kevin Smith Bibby was in on it too. He was the regular postman for the area and also everyone's friend. He was retired SAS; he'd retired 20 years previously; he rarely spoke of his past. He was well into his 50s, a modest man with a great sense of humour. Only his closest friends knew his background history.

He'd chosen to opt out of *the system*; *the establishment,* no longer wanting to carry out the dirty work of Politicians. Physically, you'd be forgiven in thinking he was just a regular bloke; just a posty, but he wasn't. Personality-wise; one of the nicest, gentlest fellas you could wish to meet. And he was. With several confirmed combat kills to his name, he did them without hesitation. He was a loving husband and the father of Poppy Beau Bibby. He taught her from an early age all he could in order for her to survive the harshness of the rapidly changing world and so avoid becoming a victim to anyone. She could take care of herself, in every way.

Kevin Smith Bibby was now not only a postman but also part of an unofficial, secretive, national network of right-mind civilians and veterans wishing to help out society, protect it, keep it safe and do good - especially when the law or its law enforcers, failed the people. The police force had for decades recruited poor quality individuals not up to the task and so the organisation had become not fit for purpose. They had become part of the Woke Marxist movement where pronouns and hurty words on social media, virtue signalling and rainbows were now their remit and priority. Traditional crime was generally ignored. The police became a politicised entity, controlled by politicians. Totally against the values of the police affirmation to be none political and carry out their duties without fear or favour. The affirmation was now worthless.

Kevin helped out when he could. Someone had to do it. Afterall, politicians had stopped serving its electorate and keeping society safe many years ago. They were too wrapped up in hairy fairy ideological agendas, making themselves and their cronies very rich at tax payers' expense whilst at the same time keeping the tax-payer poor and State dependent. Government was bowing more to big corporations who gave them lobbying cash for being their puppet masters. The puppet Government had become sponsored and owned by the rich elite. The two-party political system had become different cheeks of the same arse. There was no balance, no opposition, no accountability. It had become a uni-party sharing the same ideology and doing a smoke and mirrors show to fool the public. It worked on many but there was a growing awakening.

Kevin supplied postman's uniforms to police and others, at times intercepted mail for the greater cause, gave information/intel and stood aside when required. He once intervened in a house burglary he stumbled upon whilst doing his postal round. The prolific burglar happened to be a particularly violent thug; a career criminal. He was young, well built and strong. He unleashed his violence upon the apparently harmless and unassuming postman just doing his deliveries. The fight was vicious, it ended quickly. Amongst other injuries; he sustained a broken arm, broken nose and seven broken fingers in resisting, Kevin Smith Bibby, detaining him. The burglar had picked the wrong man to tangle with for sure. No doubt Kevins physical appearance perceived by the burglar, had betrayed Kevins physical ability, unarmed combat skills and most of all, his mind-set. His mind-set that no scum bag was ever going to get the better of him.

One officer was dressed in postman's garb complete with postbag. They had a two and half hour wait as that's the earliest time the postman ever called in the street they were bound for. A couple of plain clothes were deployed to keep covert obs on the target house.

It was a semi in a small quiet cul-du-sac on the edge of the estate. From the outside it appeared well-kept and respectable. The white Ford surveillance van with tinted rear windows parked farther down the street, went unnoticed.

A little after 8 a.m. and it was joined by a similar van which parked nearer to the target address. A postman rounded the corner holding a handful of envelopes. At the same time four men in casuals, lined up alongside the house.

The front garden was short. The postman was soon knocking on the door.

It was opened by the man fitting the description of the lecturer. He was small; about five foot seven and stout. Pale faced with black greasy hair. He wore trousers but wasn't wearing socks, shoes or a top. He was spotty faced and flabby.

The postie stepped back a pace. 'Signed for mail,' he said. That was the signal to say, *it was their man.*

The sarge was first to appear from around the side of the house. He took hold of the paedo's wrists then introduced himself. He told him the reason for the surprise visit and that he was under arrest. He was told his rights.

He was calm, polite and well-spoken and asked that his elderly mother, sitting in the living room, not be informed of the purpose of the visit.

Two officers were immediately deployed to the bedrooms.

He also wanted to go to his room to finish dressing. As he went up the stairs it was noticed that black lacy underwear was peeping over his waistband from behind. The sarge kept a hold of his wrist. They entered his bedroom. It was stacked high with computers, printers, screens, DVDs, Cd's, porn magazines, photographs, letters, sex toys and sample bottles containing various bodily fluids, mainly urine.

The legislation covering the offence of child pornography was fairly new as was that kind of porn on the Internet. Seeing such a bizarre room was also new to the officers. It was a room that screamed; *the occupant of this room is a sick individual, a sex maniac and a perverted one at that*. It was someone whose existence was purely for sex. It was the first such offence in the county.

It took hours to collect, bag and record the items seized in the house.

His mother was very defensive of her son who had never been married and had always lived with her. She denied all knowledge of his criminal behaviour and the contents of his bedroom.

He'd looked after her and was very close to her.

She was proud that he was a lecturer. She gave the Vice team a hard time and told them they were making a big mistake; *he was a good boy and wouldn't do anything wrong*.

She made several phone calls. It wasn't long before a well-respected, retired high ranking senior police officer arrived upon her request. His home phone number was in the prisoners' address book along with some other serving police officers' names and numbers. They all belonged to a religious sect and knew one another very well. The retired officer was also of a high rank within their church. He gave some kind of forgiveness words to the detainee along with a loving embrace. He did not judge him; there was no hint of prejudice or bias. He seemed to be a man who practiced what he preached. He had to be admired for that. On the down side he tried to find out how strong the evidence was. Being an ex-officer, he should have known better than to ask such questions. It was disconcerting that he wanted to know. The sarge would not divulge the information, he told him *he should know better than to ask*. The ex-cop hung around and comforted the prisoner until he was picked up to be taken to the station.

Many sex offenders have a tendency to self-harm or attempt suicide for lots of reasons. One being the shame and public disdain for the perversion; the humiliation. Another, the realization they were no longer in control. Sex offenders are particularly at risk. Prisoners are thoroughly searched for anything they may use to injure themselves especially in cases where it is believed there may be potential for the prisoner to self-harm.

And so, he was strip-searched in the police charge room. He was found to be wearing a woman's suspender belt and black frilly panties. He had no shame in admitting that he was due to get the train at 10a.m that day to travel to a nearby city to have sex with a man and woman whom he had never met before. It was clear he saw nothing wrong or unusual in that. To him, that was normal. He had intended to be back in time to have afternoon tea with his mum. He felt a little bit put out that the police raid had messed up his day and that he'd had to cancel his plans.

Both waiting vans were filled to capacity with all the material taken from the bedroom. It was secured in a small storeroom near to the Vice office. There were only two keys to the store and the sarge held both of them, not only for the purposes of evidence security but just as importantly for the integrity of it. It would take days to sort through and itemize it all in detail.

It was only a matter of hours before the sarge's next-in-line, the Area Commander, Mayhew Lomax, summonsed him to his office. It was a rare event for the commander to take an interest in any operational police work but for some reason he was showing an interest in this matter. A great deal of interest.

He was straight to the point with the sarge and wanted to know what porn material had been seized.

He was told in broad terms how it was mainly child porn.

But the Commander wanted the finer detail.

Sarge kept it as broad as possible. He saw no point in being explicit. He felt a little uncomfortable at the intense interest and curiosity Lomax was showing.

But he persisted and wanted to know what kind of pictures there were and whether any of the videos and DVDs had been watched.

He was informed that there had been little opportunity to view much of the material and that they still had to log all the items. It all had to be catalogued.

The Commander was aware of the retired senior officer's connection with the prisoner. He insisted that the names of the officers who appeared to be personal friends of the prisoner were not disclosed; the ones listed in the seized address book. He knew of their photos too. He admitted the retired senior officer had already been in touch with him. He reiterated that the officers' names and the connection with the retired senior officer, in particular, should be kept strictly within the Vice squad. He emphasized that he wanted to be kept updated about the case.

It was an odd conversation that seemed to dance around the real reason the Commander was interested. He never showed an interest in anything. Towards the end of the conversation, it became clearer as to why he was showing an interest. He asked for a key to the store.

'But sir, you know it's policy that only the Vice sergeant has a key; that being me. Security and integrity.' He chewed.

'Never the less, sergeant, I'm your commanding officer and I'm telling you that I want a key. The policy you mention isn't written; it's only been accepted practice all these years. So, I'll thank you to give me a key,' he demanded.

'You'll be compromising the integrity of the evidence. Besides if anything goes missing then you'll be in the frame, along with me. I can't see why you need a key.'

'Sergeant, what are you suggesting? Anyway, I don't have to explain myself to you or give you reasons for anything but on this occasion I will.' He paused as he fumbled for his pipe. 'I've been thinking of replacing you, so if anything happens suddenly, I'll be a source of reference to provide a key to your successor.'

'Replacing me, sir? That sounds like a veiled threat. Why are you thinking of replacing me?'

'Take it how you want.' He paused whilst he stuffed his pipe into his beard. 'And here's another one you might want to think about. I eavesdropped on the conversation you had with your staff the other day, you know, the one about me and the joke about the gays. You could get into serious trouble over issues like that. Not Politically Correct, definitely not PC. You know that. We've sent you on enough courses to make sure there's no doubt that you know what you should and shouldn't say. Isn't that so?'

'It is, sir. I've been on more of those courses than law courses. Diversity, eh?' He shook his head. 'It's a good thing we have such intensive training on correctness,' he said, sarcastically. 'And also, to be P.C.'

'I'm glad you agree, Sarge.'

'Brain-washing.' He said quietly but loudly enough to be heard.

'Say again?'

'Yes, there's a whole Empire sprung out of it and half the officers who should be out there on the streets are now safely lodged in the training department preaching Political Correctness. And how many of them will see their careers out there too?'

'You are a very bitter and cynical man, Sarge.'

'Well yes, I am, sir. If being honest and saying it the way it is, is classed as cynical and bitter, then that's me. Most of them in there are your graduate-types, the ones without backbone, sir.'

'Well anyway, a warning, be careful what you're saying. You never know who is listening. Next time you may find yourself in real trouble.'

'Sounds like another threat, sir.'

He said nothing.

He chewed hard. 'Well, you're known for your knowledge, sir. Where would you stand in eavesdropping on employees? Is that lawful?'

'How do you mean, sergeant?'

'Well, you listening in on private conversations between colleagues. We have rights. It's only recently that one of your slightly lesser ranks hid a voice recorder in the locker room because they thought they were being talked about.' Eyebrows raised. 'It was a real, no, no.' He leaned forward. 'Caused lots of problems for the officer.' Eyes wide open. 'Hit the headlines of the tabloids. Think on that one. Sir.'

'Is that a threat?'

'You have far more to lose than I do, sir.' He smiled, stood up and pulled his jacket to. 'If there's nothing else, sir?'

'I want that key. That's a direct order, sergeant. I want the key.' He held out his hand palm up ready to receive one.

He shrugged. 'Ok. I'll bring you one before I go off duty today, sir.'

He left and headed to the evidence store via the *technical support* office. That was the department that installed electronic gadgetry such as hidden listening devices and video cameras, stuff like that. He was there some time and chatted to his equal. They'd worked together on many occasions. They agreed on a secret mission to be done before the end of the day and that definitely, *no-one else was to know.*

They slipped unnoticed into the store room. Shelves, floor to ceiling, were crammed. They quietly closed the door behind them. They were automatically sombre; respectful, as though in the presence of some great loss; like when someone's died too young; which is what it was like. It was the same in many ways. The evidence stacked around them was like a young corpse, it shouldn't have been laid there as it was. The great loss was the death of their innocence; of all the abused children it represented.

There was a difficult moment.

'As death takes life forever; abuse takes innocence the same way,' said Sarge.

The *Tech support* guy said nothing. He felt a little uneasy being amongst such taboo material. He thought about his own children, their friends, his young nieces and nephews. He felt distressed. He felt somewhat paralyzed. He was amazed at the amount Sarge and his officers had seized from the suspect's home. He felt uneasy; odd.

He snapped himself from his strange feelings. He got to work. He scanned the room, seeing where he could plant his gear out of sight. His eyes kept drifting back to the evidence. He was curious; like when a parent tells a child not to look and so the need to look becomes far greater. The Tech guy was curious, not because of any perversion or that he wanted to see any disturbing images, no, it was because he couldn't believe how one man could be so wrapped up in a life centred around sex. *It must have been his very reason for being,* he thought. But he was curious. Being a right-minded individual, he tried to ignore it. He didn't really want to see *that* kind of stuff. He was decent and a professional, he focused. He checked where he could put his covert equipment. He went about his task.

He eventually glanced at Sarge for approval before gingerly pushing aside a few things here and there, like they were sacred or dangerous to even disturb or touch.

He checked the light; natural and artificial, distances and angles. He visualized where his hidden gear would fit and where it wouldn't be detected. His body language said, *reluctant and unsure.*

Sarge could see the awkwardness of the man, how uncomfortable he felt. He knew how he was feeling. He helped him; he spoke-up to break the ice and passed comment on the sick mind that had created this world since in his teens. How he was a very intelligent person; a lecturer, and yet he was driven to immerse himself into a way of life that was far from normal and beyond any normal person's imagination. A way of life society abhorred.

Tech-guy theorized, he said, *it was almost an animal-like existence. Driven by an autonomic force that could not be resisted. A force that overruled the natural instinct of any living thing to protect the young of its species.*

Sarge agreed, said *it was pure evil.*

Their spoken thoughts and acknowledgment of their distain somehow helped. Both were more relaxed. They were joined together in their disapproval, like old men who complain about anything and everything. Their eyes become more and more taken up on the room's contents but not in detail, whilst they grumbled. They were still complaining as they fleetingly looked through some of it. It was clear this was a seriously affected individual. Hundreds of CDs, photographs, porn mags, contact mags, sex aids, computers, papers and address books.

Diaries, letters and postcards going back years.

Containers filled with urine and other bodily fluids; some his, some not. Some were packaged-up and addressed, ready to go. Some of the destinations were grand-sounding places with high-class addresses dotted all over the country. Some were addressed to well-known celebrities, journalists and some working in Main Stream Media. Letters were enclosed, they were sleazy, child-like and disturbingly sick; *seems like they drink a stranger's urine or pour it over themselves or their partners,* Sarge said. *There were so many uses for such an innocuous waste product from a human body.*

Sarge didn't know it back then but his path would cross with some of those celebrities and other recipients in the future.

There were piles of sexually explicit photos showing naked children in various sexual poses; poses with other children, with adults and no doubt in some, with their own parents.

Piles of A4 sheets apparently listing some sort of codes such as; F: D7BJS: followed by a longer number. Many thousands of them.

Scores of contact magazines offering phone numbers and locations for *stranger sex; twosomes, threesomes* and more; with animals, reptiles and more. *Swingers' venues* and *deviant services; SM services, bestiality. Heterosexual, gay* and *mixed*. It was all there, a whole world of abnormal, perverted sex.

'There were four names of serving officers with phone numbers written in his most recent address book.' The Sarge told the Tech guy. 'There were large portrait photos of the officers too. They're all based at different precinct stations. I don't know what that or any of it means. Maybe it means nothing, except sometimes I look too deep into things.' He told him. He knew he could trust him.

The Tech guy didn't have an answer. They continued with their task.

The computers had been securely bagged, ready to be taken to a newly set up central location to be forensically examined. As much information as possible would be elicited from the stored data. Every scrap of information on the hard drives, even deleted data, would be extracted and sifted through. It would take years to check out all the information but it would be done.

All the data, written addresses and phone numbers would be fed into the intelligence system. Discreet and covert enquiries made into all those who had showed up on the radar. There was a network of like-minded individuals. It would need a dedicated, proactive team to carry out a thorough job. Many of the enquiries would involve other police forces.

It was a newly discovered crime that the police had every intention of cracking down on. To date, it had been rare. The Internet was relatively new. It lacked skilled people, especially police officers, with the know-how to access and analyse stored data held within a computer.

It wasn't known back then but the scale of Internet paedophilia on the World Wide Web was just about to be realized, it was waiting around the corner and this case was just a very small snowflake on the tip of a very gigantic iceberg.

The two men alone in the secure store room surrounded by all the material evidence; a testament to countless abused and unheard children, were quietly drawn into a world they had never imagined before. Not from any illicit gratification but sadness that such a world even existed out there. The sickness of those who actively sought out such perverse pleasure in child sex abuse and any other form of immoral sex that was available, to them, was shocking.

There were detailed diaries going back to when he was aged thirteen. He described in them his experience of puberty; how he masturbated several times a day, every day. How he couldn't help it. How he had sex with his aunty, she thirty-nine years old and he just fourteen years of age. How he tried to have sex with the family dog but it turned around and bit him so it was destroyed and how he had anal sex a year later with his father. Most day-to-day entries made reference to a sexual experience or sexual thoughts. There were few other entries relating to any other topic. More than twenty years of diaries showed that his daily life consisted of living from one sexual moment to the next. It was as though it was his *driving force; the very reason for his existence.* He described how he'd indecently assaulted nieces and nephews and their young friends. How he'd *groomed* them, how it was *their secret* and *their fault.* How he covered his tracks. How their parents refused to believe their accounts, against his. *Afterall, he was such a nice, polite, well-behaved person,* they thought. *He would never do such a thing.*

How most of them kept *their secrets.*

There were newspaper cuttings of rapes, indecent assaults and flashings. Some of the descriptions of the offender were not unlike that of his own. One cutting related to two men on the estate who received prison sentences for assaulting the detainee lecturer five years earlier. He needed hospital treatment when he was found unconscious. In their defence the men said that they had caught him masturbating in the park in front of some very young girls so punished him. He denied it and gave the excuse he was urinating in the bushes at the time. The court believed him. After all, he was well educated, spoke with a refined accent and was a respectable lecturer from a respectable background at a respectable university.

He had clearly been abused himself as a child and believed that the way of the world revolved around sex with no barriers to age, gender, deviancy or even species. Many abusers are themselves victims of abuse. Many go on to abuse but thankfully many do not and so lead an ordinary life.

Time quickly slipped by as the sarge and the Tech guy sifted through some of the stuff. There was only so much that could be said about the whole sorry affair. And so, the Tech guy had played his part, the hidden surveillance gear was set up. Sarge gave a final check around, they left, closed the door and locked it. Both were pale and felt in a strange place, mentally. They agreed on a coffee and a change of topic for conversation. Tech guy passed him a small device for future use. They headed to the canteen.

They shared a quiet coffee break together. It took a while to shake off their morose feeling but it eventually faded. Yet they still parted with an uneasy feeling.

Sarge and a colleague took the lecturer from his detention cell and led him along a series of corridors towards an interview room just off the main Cell complex. No-one spoke on the way there. They kept serious expressions. A heavy, plain door opened into a small room without a window. The walls, ceiling and door were covered in soundproofing tiles painted an indescribable drab colour. A thin slab of veneered board fixed to the wall and resting on a chrome pedestal formed a table; enough room for two simple chairs each side the same colour as the rest of the room. The floor covering was black rubber matting. Sound was absorbed in an instant. A hushed silence was present. The door sounded airtight as it was closed with a *whoosh* behind the detainee. He was told *to sit on a chair farthest from the door so he couldn't escape. He would have to get passed the officer first, to do so. And that was never going to happen.*

He didn't know if they were serious, he did as he was told. He went around the table and dragged the chair out over the matting, silently, and sat.

Sarge sat across the table to him, eye to eye, much less than a yard away. He gave him a very long moment of a very cold stare until the man broke eye contact. He diverted his eyes down to his hands on his lap half under the table and fiddled.

There was a bulky, purely functional-looking tape recorder mounted on the wall above the table.

Sarge chewed as he tore off the cellophane wrapper on a pack of two tapes before popping them into the tape deck with well-practiced efficiency. He looked like he meant business.

That got the lecturer's attention. He studied every move like a patient watching a dentist.

Sarge ignored him. He laid out some forms, papers and notes and placed his pen precisely next to them. He slipped off his jacket, loosened his tie and rolled up his sleeves.

The prisoner avoided eye contact. He nervously glanced over his shoulder at Sarge's colleague positioned a little to a side and almost behind him. He felt intimidated so smiled at him. He sought reassurance in return. He never got it.

Instead, the colleague's blank face stared back coldly. He leaned against the wall just a short pace away and slightly out of his line of vision. It was an interview tactic to make the interviewee feel psychologically off-balance; to put instil subtle pressure upon the interviewee. For most people, having someone out of view and knowing they are observing, can have a psychological effect. It had been part of police interview training and practice, it was effective.

Effective, until the smart lawyers labelled it unfair and oppressive for their clients. It was banned by the courts. The police appealed, they argued *if someone has nothing to hide, why should they feel oppressed*? The argument was dismissed. The ban remained. Numerous past interviews were held unreliable. Many prisoners of such interviews were released; their convictions overturned and many were handsomely compensated.

The lecturer shuffled nervously or excitedly; it was difficult to tell. He was a weak-character driven by sex. No doubt that would have been his strong area as would his intelligence. He was indeed very intelligent and although there were lots of offences against him that were easily provable, there were lots that would need to be proved. They would need some admissions. Equally important, was to get his co-operation so that contacts of his could also be rounded up and dealt with.

Child porn is big business with a massive demand. It's a business that is fed by misery, abuse and young minds affected for a lifetime.

The main driving force for the lecturer was sex. He clearly had great enthusiasm for the subject; he couldn't help himself. In his mind his way of life was normal and the rest of society were lacking. He was enthusiastic about his lifestyle. He embraced it with vigour. As with any enthusiast if you share their enthusiasm, they enthuse. The sarge needed to tap into the interviewee's enthusiasm, though it wasn't easy to face a man across a desk knowing that he was indirectly responsible for the adversely affected lives of thousands of young children. He was directly responsible for the effects upon his own family; the young relatives and others referred to in his diaries. But the end game was to gain his trust and therefore obtain more damning evidence against him; to gather intelligence, to spread the net over the whole wicked network.

The procedures and legalities before interview were carried out. He declined the offer of a solicitor. It was followed by some small-talk to put the interviewee at ease, to know a little about the person, a sound check too. Sarge flattered him on his academic achievements, the fact he had a degree, was a lecturer and had exceptional computer skill prowess.

He liked that.

The sarge admitted to his own failings and lack of knowledge on the subject.

He liked that.

Sarge was softly spoken, none threatening, casual; like two good friends having a regular chat over a small difficulty that Sarge would help him with.

He liked that.

Unbeknown to the detainee, he underplayed his knowledge of technology and the subject of paedophiles. He asked him for his help.

He liked that, after all, he was a teacher by trade. It was one of his stronger points.

He tapped into that strong point. He wanted to turn that strength into a weakness. He wanted it be part of his downfall; his own self-destruction. Truth was; he needed his help. Truth was; he knew relatively little of computers or the workings of a highly intelligent, lifelong paedophiles brain. So, he shared a contrived common ground of the excitement of sex and how it's a basic driving function of the human trait; no big deal, as basic as eating, sleeping and surviving, as basic as the drive to reproduce, as basic as any bodily function.

He agreed, although he partly knew the reason for Sarge's behaviour and that by cooperating, he would ultimately be helping with his own incarceration. His enthusiasm, self-esteem and ego would not allow him to do what was best for his own good and so he went headlong into helping Sarge with his questions.

Sarge was surprised how easy it was. He'd been expecting clever replies and resistance; avoidance. The questions and answers rolled back and forth. Lots of ground was covered. There was a good rapport.

The tape deck buzzed a warning, an hour had passed. The tapes were full, they needed changing. The lecturer was happy to continue without a break, so was Sarge, though things had started to become a little repetitive and stale.

The interruption was a good thing; a fresh start. Sarge changed tack slightly. He never asked him outright but he acknowledged that the man had probably been abused from an early age and that he needed help, that he was a victim and that it wasn't too late.

He liked that and agreed.

How he was turning other young children into victims by subscribing to the child-porn sites. How he was feeding the need for child porn.

He agreed.

Sarge asked for his help in sorting the matter out and putting a stop to the sickness of child porn and his unhealthy, obsessive way of life.

He agreed.

Sarge knew it was never going to happen, well not long-term anyway. He was particularly interested in the sheets of codes they had recovered. There were hundreds in a pile sat on the table between the two men. They could have been placed on the floor or a spare chair, but they weren't. They were put right there on the table deliberately, listing tens of thousands of short, simple codes. Tens of thousands of little children's lives ruined forever. A serious crime with serious consequences. A particularly repugnant crime to the rest of society. The lecturer knew it full-well. His eyes snuck a glance now and then. It made him gulp and blink long and hard in denial as though the pile would have disappeared when he opened his eyes again. But it didn't. It seemed bigger and more menacing each time. A silent, innocuous pile of paper put there deliberately. But it was like a screaming claxton in the mind of the lecturer. He tried his damnedest not to listen, not to hear it.

The colleague shuffled noisily or coughed at times. A reminder that he was still there, still present, still just out of view, still observing.

Sarge laid several code sheets in front of the man. He spun them one eighty so he could read them. And said nothing.

A long silent moment passed as the three men stared at the sheets.

The tape was running.

The man shook his head. He glanced up at Sarge.

He stared back.

He looked sideways over his shoulder. The colleague stared back, expectantly. He turned back and stared down at the sheets, his jaw set. 'I want a solicitor; I want my *brief.* Now!' He panicked. 'Stop the tape!'

His solicitor, also known as a *brief*, was there in no time; or rather a solicitor's rep. arrived. Crooks usually believe they're the real thing. Mostly they aren't. They're *solicitor's runners, reps: representatives*. Errand boys who know the basics.

His *brief* was overweight, scruffy, cheap suit, balding, grey pallor. Briefcase, worn and battered, just like its owner. Slimy, sycophantic, self-important, no-conscience, money's king. A chameleon; everyone's friend. Poor diet, uncertainty, long hectic stressful hours; heart attack waiting to happen. Your typical rep., thought Sarge.

Just the rep and his client had a private conversation alone in the interview room, they took what seemed a long time.

Sarge and his colleague waited impatiently outside the door.

He told his *brief* of his wrongdoings and that he had been assisting the officers. He was advised to make no comment and not to assist the police in any way.

Time passed; the door opened.

'Ok, Sarge.' The *brief* smiled, 'We're ready for you.'

'You had time to concoct your story or sort your strategy?' Sarge asked.

The brief made no comment and gave a look of contempt as he stepped farther back and pulled the door wider after him. The officers entered. They all took up the same positions again except now the client had his *brief* sat next to him.

The tapes were set in motion. The reason why and present time recorded; the questioning commenced where they'd left off.

The lecturer wanted to help, he really wanted to help. He said so.

The brief advised him to say nothing except, *No Comment to all questions*.

He agreed.

For twenty-three more minutes Sarge's questions went unanswered. *'No comment.' 'No comment,'* is all he got.

The brief sat smugly staring at Sarge.

He was getting nowhere fast. He felt he was being taunted by the two sat across the table to him. That, he did not like. He paused a moment. He looked deep and hard at the lecturer. He leaned in over the table towards him. He frowned his hardest most serious frown. 'Is your mother involved in any of this? Does she know anything?' he asked sternly.

A look of horror flashed across the lecturers' face. Like a frightened child he turned to his brief for help.

'Now stop there, sergeant. What is this?' The brief asked.

He chewed; looked at the brief a moment. 'Well, I'm just wondering whether we got everyone involved in this case.' He chewed. 'That's all.'

Wide eyed and looking at his brief. 'What does he mean?' panicked the lecturer.

He ignored his client. 'Sergeant, you're not seriously thinking about arresting his mother, are you? She's an old lady, she's not involved. You know that.'

'No. I don't know that. I'm starting to think our friend here has something to hide and perhaps mother knows something that your client here isn't telling us.'

The briefs' tone mellowed. 'The days of *hostage taking* are gone, Sarge. Come on, you've no evidence against her.'

'She lives at the same address, it's her home. She must have known about all this. Reasonable grounds for arrest, I would say.' He chewed.

'What does he mean?' The prisoner asked his brief.

Sarge leaned back and chewed. He addressed the brief. 'Why don't you tell him? Or do you want me to?'

'It means they'll arrest your mother to put pressure on you to assist them. In return they'll let her go.'

'Is that right, sergeant?' asked the lecturer.

Sarge chewed, said nothing and flashed a quick smile. It said it all.

The lecturer dismissed the *brief* there and then. They had a short argument. He left in a noisy protest and slammed the door behind him.

'For the benefit of the tape recording,' Sarge said, 'The solicitor has left the room. I'm now showing the defendant several sheets of paper with what appears to be codes. I'm pointing to one code; F: D7:BJS followed by several numbers. Firstly, are the sheets yours?'

The lecturer looked at them. Relieved his mother wasn't to be arrested, 'Yes. Yes, they are.'

'And what do the sheets refer to?'

'They are my codes for photographs.'

'Photographs, where are they?'

'Stored in my computers or on discs.'

'What are the photographs of?'

'Mainly pictures of children having sex or just posing sexually, naked. Child-porn, basically.'

'Ok. So, explain the code. This one for example, F: D7:BJ?'

'It's a simple code really, so I know what I'm looking at. The F stands for father, the D is for daughter. 7 is her age and the BJ is…....,' He hesitated. The numbers are listed in my computers so I can type that number in and that's the photo that'll come up. Simple.'

The sarge stared hard into his eyes and chewed just as hard. He tried to contain his emotions. It was a long moment. 'Ok. Thank you for explaining that to us. So, what would that picture show, exactly?'

'It'll show the girl's father with his daughter in an act of sex.'

'BJ?'

'You know, oral sex.'

There was a long moment and more hard chewing.

'Do you not see how wrong that is? How very criminally wrong it is?'

He made no reply.

The sarge ran his finger down the list and stopped randomly. 'For the purposes of the tape there's another code here; F: S9: A. Explain that, would you?'

'Well, F, again, father. S is son then 9, his age and A; anal. See? It's simple.'

There was another long moment and more chewing.

The sarge took a deep breath and thanked him for his co-operation. He selected another from the list; M: S13: F. He read it out to the prisoner.

'M is mother, S means son and the numbers mean he's thirteen and you can probably work out F.'

'No. I'd like you to tell us if you would, what's F?'

'F.' He smiled. 'Full sex.'

'Full sex with his mother?' He chewed; eyebrows raised in astonishment.

'Correct, sergeant, full sex. There are lots of other permutations if you want to go through them.'

'Ok. Enough of that! We get the picture. Don't want you getting yourself all excited.' He paused and scanned the pages. 'So, you're telling us that all these thousands of codes are all meaning similar to what you've told us and you can access the photos relating to them on your computer?'

'That's right.'

'How many stored photos or images or whatever you want to call them, do you have?'

'No idea.'

'You must have a rough idea.'

There was a pause.

'Over a quarter of a million,' he shrugged casually, 'perhaps more. I don't know.'

'More than two hundred and fifty thousand? So, for every one of those photos, some child is being abused. You do realize that?

'Yes.' He paused, 'And no. Some say its abuse but it's only the law that has labelled it that. It's perfectly natural to me. And others like me. But I understand what you're saying, sergeant.'

'Are they all different children?'

'Mostly.'

'How do you know?'

'Because I've seen them.'

'You've seen all the photos? Surely not!'

'Yes, probably many times over.'

There was a stack of A4 photographs showing child pornography like the ones described. They were spread out on the table.

'We took these from your room. Are all of them yours?'

He looked at them and for a moment seemed to be getting some pleasure from them. It was noticed. They were removed.

'Yes. Yes, they are,' he said, matter-of-factly.

'Are the computer images you described to us, similar to these?'

'Yes.'

'What about video recordings, the DVDs and Cd's we took from you? There are thousands of them.'

'Same. DVDs of sex videos and Cd's with images on.'
'What kind of sex and images?'
'Children, mainly. Kids having sex or posing naked.'
The sarge stood up, slipped his jacket on, pulled it to and chewed fast.

He looked down at the detainee. 'Just take a while to think of all those children who will have been badly affected by doing all this stuff.' He chewed. 'Have a good, long think. We need a break but we'll be back to see you. One thing before we break, does everything we took from your room, belong to you.'

'Yes,' he said.

The interview was concluded, the prisoner was returned to his cell.

After two days and several interviews he was charged with offences under the Sexual Offences laws and released on bail. He had built up quite a trust with Sarge who frequently called him to assist him with his inquiries and to clarify matters. He would sometimes call in on him and his elderly mum. She remained in denial about her son. The sarge had read some of the lecturer's diary entries relating to her; they were most disturbing and unnatural. But what had taken place between her and son happened many years ago. There would be little point in pursuing those past events. She was now a very old lady and there had been an unspoken agreement between her son and Sarge regarding the matter. Sarge honoured that agreement. It was of significant value to him. Besides, he had other plans for the lecturer.

Six months later he appeared before the courts and was given a two-year prison sentence. That's all.

Everyone was shocked at the light sentence. Sarge wasn't. He knew why. Many lines of enquiry and information had come from the assistance he had given the police in return for a light sentence. Thats how the system works. Many right-minded people are often shocked by light sentences but it's often in exchange for informing the police about other criminals' activities.

His incarceration almost over, he enjoyed weekend release to his home from an open prison where of course he was given free internet use. He was completely free within the year. He kept contact with Sarge and gave him lots more information about his seedy network of similar inclined individuals. As a result, other sexual deviants up and down the country continued to be arrested for similar offences as those committed by the lecturer. Some influential and powerful people too; Judges, Magistrates, doctors, paediatricians, social workers, teachers, police and politicians. There was a total cross section of society all getting off on the child porn, stranger sex and stranger's bodily fluids thing.

The great, the good and the influential who were arrested because of the lecturers help, took exception to conforming to morality and the laws of the land. After all, they were pillars of society, they had their reputations to protect. Many lost their livelihoods and public office. They were discredited and reviled. Relationships were ended and their own families disowned them. Quite a hornet's nest had been stirred up. The lecturer was aware of the anger and resentment that had been created through him assisting the police. He feared that some of them may somehow find out that he had given them up to the police. He had good reason to be concerned. Indeed, he had several death threats made against him.

He was found hanged from a bridge just months later but the coroner could not determine a verdict. There was evidence of suicide but there was also substantial evidence to suggest that it may not have been. There were too many questions that went unanswered. The coroner seemed uneasy over the case and appeared biased, without justification, in ruling out the evidence contrary to suicide. The verdict was left open. Evidence of foul play was strong. Sarge wondered if the so-called elite were being protected. He had, *'seen it all before; times over,'* he told people.

The mother accused Sarge of giving information to others about her son. She said she'd heard him subtly threatening him; that her son told her that he knew the sarge had anonymously informed some of those involved that he had been the informant. People had told him so directly, he'd claimed. It was never proved. She alleged Sarge used to talk of *Kairos moments* to her son and how a really big one was coming her son's way. That her son would never be cured and that he would abuse and feed his need for child porn until the day he died. She accused the sarge of being directly or indirectly responsible for her son's death. None of it was proven.

More had come of the raid and the incident than just a criminal conviction and a man going to prison who was later found hanged. There was more, much more. Scores of others up and down the land were kept under surveillance, investigated, computers hacked, homes raided, people arrested, children taken into care. Careers destroyed; families split. There was shock-horror everywhere. It had been a very effective and successful operation to round up those linked with the lecturer. That's the way the Chief took the credit and the limelight when he presented a summary of the case to the TV cameras.

But there was much more. It was to turn into a Kairos moment at a later date for someone with a connection to the matter. Secret video recordings were made of a man with pipe and beard entering the Vice-squad evidence store containing the child porn material on the same day it was seized and secured there. He was seen to rifle through the photos, DVDs, Cd's, code sheets and in fact almost everything relating to the job involving the lecturer. It was after office hours and the man left with a wedge of material under his arm. There were only two people with keys to the store; one being Sarge, the other being the man recorded on the hidden video.

A DVD of the incident was prepared and handed over to Sarge. He knew he couldn't deal with the matter on his own. He knew that even the Chief of police swept indiscretions under the carpet where senior officers were involved. He had *previous form* for it. He would especially protect his own as all the recent bad publicity reflected upon the man at the very top; him.

Sarge knew that for having the secret video equipment installed by his trusted colleague in *technical support* that he'd be threatened with breaching employment laws and rights and there'd be a big legal wrangle over the lawfulness of the recordings obtained. He would probably get suspended whilst the senior officer on the DVD would be posted elsewhere and the matter would drag on for years. In the meantime, everyone's life carries on as normal, except for Sarge's.

He took the DVD of the incident to a trusted higher-ranking officer than himself, Gerry Smithson. The officer had an axe to grind with the Commander. He'd been one of those who had chased him from public toilets years earlier but was discredited; his loyalty questioned. The word of Commander Lomax was preferred over that of the officer. It was that simple. He was wrongly labelled a liar and posted to places no-one wanted to be. Not only that, Smithson had morals and integrity. His hopes of further advancement within the service were halted. He was hurting, he'd hurt for a long time.

Smithson accepted the DVD and told Sarge that he would raise the matter with a more senior officer in another police area whom he trusted and who, for personal reasons, also disliked Lomax.

The weeks passed. Life carried on as normal.

Monday 10.30am was the weekly meeting in Chief Curry's office. Commander Lomax was usually absent and the minutes of the meeting usually reflected his apology for his none attendance. This week was no different.

Around the room was the heads of departments; the detective's squad; Uniform, community policing; crime prevention; child protection; domestic violence, dispatch, traffic department; Intel and miscellaneous others and of course, Sarge from Vice. Senior officers were also invited. It was a packed office. Tea, coffee and biscuits flowed freely.

Once the pleasantries were out of the way it was the usual meeting of hot-air; individuals setting out their stalls to impress. Most craved a pat on the back from Chief Curry. They wanted to be noticed. To do that, they bigged up their own departments and slyly criticized others in a none-personal or threatening way. All very gentlemanly.

Personality-clashes and past vendettas were woven in there too. None the less it was a carefully crafted war of words by those who were ambitious; those with promotion fever. It was dynamic and the topics flitted from one to another.

Sarge generally remained fairly quiet.

About thirty minutes was allocated for the session. Each Head knew this was a time when they could point score, grab some recognition or defend their failings.

Sarge had little to say; he always said there was a lot spoken in those meetings but nothing said.

Chief Curry rounded off the weekly event and made a point of asking Sarge to remain; *he needed to speak to him.* The rest of the meeting filed out, some reluctantly; Sarge remained seated.

He walked over to the coffee-maker and poured himself another. Never offered Sarge one. He carefully sipped as he looked down at Sarge sitting low, nearby.

'Close the door, Sarge.' He ordered. 'Thank you.' He sipped again.

He was as close to the door as the sarge.

He shot a glance at Curry that let him know, *why the hell couldn't he close it himself? Management psychology games,* he thought.

He jumped to his feet. 'No problem, sir.' Popped in some gum, took the four steps over to the door then turned. 'Just got to pay a call of nature, sir. Two minutes.' He could play the *games* as good as the next. He left the room.

He stood in the stall; thinking. He didn't know what he wanted to talk to him about but with Curry it was never good; *he was a slimy snake.* He puzzled over what it could be and prepared himself. A quick five minutes passed. He needed to gain some ground, throw him off balance, so he waited some more.

He returned a full ten minutes later and closed the door behind him.

Curry looked up from some papers on his desk. A fresh brew was steaming from his mug in front of him.

He stood. 'Sorry about that, sir.' He patted his stomach and frowned. 'Must have been something I ate.' Eyebrows raised.

He sat down on the nearest seat.

'We have a problem, sergeant.' He reached for a biscuit, carefully chose one then nibbled the same way a rabbit nibbles.

Sarge was impatient. He was aware of the games Curry played *but it didn't work on him,* he told himself.

'And what's *your* problem, Mr. Curry?'

He continued to delay momentarily. 'Some of the yearly reports you wrote on some of your officers before you left for Vice. That's the problem. Some have come bouncing back.' He gulped his drink.

'And? Is that all?' He glanced at his wrist watch to let him know he wasn't bothered. He knew what was coming.

'And it's not looking good for you. Not looking good for you, at all.' He delighted.

He paused for thought. 'For me?' He chewed. He was rattled. He got on his soap box. 'I know the reports you're talking about but I'm not the one who screwed up or will never make a cop so long as I got a hole in my arse.' He chewed. 'I'm not the one who'll be drawing the tax payer's money for the next twenty years and giving poor service in return. They're not up to the mark. Once those officers are out of their probation, we're stuck with them. They've got a job for life and we all end up carrying them, clearing up after their mess. Incompetents. The job's full of incompetents.' He chewed and nodded at Curry, accusingly, 'You of all people know that, sir.' He took a moment to revel in the subtle innuendo.

The chief sipped, irritated.

'It's an insipid rot, sir, that's set-in because everyone's scared of tribunals and accusations of bias, sexism, racism, bullying, harassment or any other excuse they can trump up to justify why they shouldn't be dismissed.' He chewed, took a deep breath. 'So, what get-out card's being used this time?'

The chief placed his mug on his desk and leaned over to a side drawer. He took out three manila folders one at a time and neatly spread them in a line in front of him. Each had a yellow *Post It* on top with a list. He placed his hand on the file furthest to his right.

'Young Ryan here. Four years' service at the sharp end yet he's a bright young man. I was his mentor. He objects to your criticism that he's lazy, a loner, doesn't get along with his peers, has poor leadership skills and has a chip on his shoulder.' He smiled. 'You know he was expecting to have been promoted a year ago?'

'I'm aware of that, sir. You may also be aware that my comments were evidenced and also supported by other supervisory officers too. He is what he is and a cop going places, isn't one of them.' He paused. 'You missed out that *he's not a team player* either and is disliked by all his colleagues.'

'Yes, sergeant but he's a graduate entry, he's on the accelerated promotion scheme.'

'Well, he's failed then, hasn't he? He smiled and chewed.

'He's done some good work during the year.'

'That's what he gets paid for. He's not the best officer out there.'

'Your report will delay his promotion by years.'

'That's life. Promote him and it'll be the blind leading the blind. He's a problem-child that's going to become an even greater problem. He thinks the world, and in particular the police service, owes him a living. Give him rank and you'll have a tiger by its tail.'

The Chief sighed. 'I suggest we change the report.'

'Really?' he chewed hard and looked away. 'I don't.'

'I'm not asking you, sergeant.'

There was a long moment of eye contact. The Chief lost.

'Ok.' He chewed. 'You tell me!'

'Change it. That's an order.' He placed his hand on the middle file. 'Jackie Prince here. Nice girl.' He smiled. 'Struggled for eighteen months but she's a real trier. Well-liked by her colleagues. A team player. Your report could mean she gets dismissed before her two years trial probation ends.'

'That's why we report on them.' He nodded. 'Sorting the wheat from the chaff.'

'Yes, but she's claiming it's sexist. And because she's small in stature.'

'She can claim what she wants. It's all documented.'

There was a long silence.

Back on his soap box, 'In the weeks leading up to the report she lied that she'd followed up on a crime report. A guy that had been arrested told her in interview that the leather jacket and Rolex he was wearing was from the burglary and that he'd return them. She let him walk out with the evidence; basics! The evidence was never seen again; he couldn't be charged; no evidence; the victim doesn't get their things back.' He shook his head. 'One night she was shouted at by some *scrote* in the reception area, she came in crying her eyeballs out. She was in bits for the rest of the shift. She went on sick leave a few days later with stress. She was often late for duty too. Do you want me to go on?'

'Well, the recruiting chief is backing her claim. Perhaps you'd like to amend your report on her. The force doesn't like tribunals hanging over it. It costs between twenty thousand and one million just for going there. So, we usually pay out twenty thousand out-of-court settlements to lessen expense and the embuggerance, regardless of who's right or wrong. You know that. She's Romanian too, so she may allege racism against you.'

'The racist card too, huh?'

'Yep. The recruiting department needs her to stay. Good for the stats. DEI – Diversity, Equity and Inclusion. We're low on ethnics compared to the national average. We need all the ethnics we can get. We have to have a fair proportion. It's only fair.' He paused. 'And as I say, the recruiting chief's supporting her.'

There was a moment.

'Yeah, well here's the truth. The recruitment chief supports her now just the way he did after he watched her run around the track on her physical when she applied for the job. He couldn't take his eyes off her thirty-eight double D's bouncing up and down under her tight Tee shirt for a mile and a half. She failed the test but the chief over-ruled it. She was allowed in. Everyone knows he later got his hands on her. I heard other senior officers have too, these last eighteen months.' He raised his eyebrows accusingly at the Chief.

He reddened and banged his hand on top of the file to the left. 'Ok. Moving on. Angela Waltowski. Not long out of her probation. What about her?'

'You tell me, sir.'

'She's claiming harassment against you.'

Sarge laughed and shook his head.

'She claims you told her to go to a call even though she was busy. Says you've been abrupt with her. Found it upsetting, she said.'

He chewed. 'Are we talking about adults here, police officers, or sensitive little children in a Kinder Garden? So how many examples would you like? They're all there in my report.'

He said nothing.

'Well, here's an example.' He chewed. 'One night I'm parked-up on the estate. She pulls alongside, passes the time of day; small talk. Then she tells me she'd seen two guys a few minutes ago unloading a van into another one down a dark side-street, looking all suspicious. I asked what happened. She says, *nothing, she drove on by.* I asked why she didn't call it in and investigate. She had no explanation. She looked scared. So, we go take a look and the van is in the same place but now in flames. Turns out it was a stolen vehicle and had been spotted at a major robbery on an electrical appliance store.' He chewed. 'Yeah, I was abrupt with her. Perhaps I should have put her on a charge of neglect to duty?' His eyebrows raised at the chief.

'None of us get it right all the time, Sarge.'

'That's true, sir. But we're talking of basics here. Gross negligence; incompetence. Scared. She'll never make an officer then we're stuck with her for years.'

'I was referring to the notebook incident.'

Sarge laughed. 'That? Ok. One morning, half an hour into the shift, an urgent call comes in for her area. She's sat in the station. I give her the details and tell her to go immediately; *it's urgent.* I leave it with her. Twenty minutes later she's still sat there in the briefing room. She's chatting and drinking coffee. I ask her why she hasn't attended the task. She says she was writing up her notebook for the previous day. She was indignant that I dare question her. Yeah, I was abrupt.' He sniffed. 'And I've done nothing wrong.'

There was a long moment.

He eyed the files. 'What else you got?'

'She says she's got a witness who heard you talk about her.'

'Oh yeah? And what did I say, sir?'

'Says you called her a poisoned dwarf. She being less than four feet ten inches and all.'

Sarge frowned and chewed.

He lifted up the file, opened it and read. 'Said she made it known she wanted to join traffic patrol and you'd said she'd have to have them big patrol cars adapted so she could reach the pedals. Is that true?'

He laughed. 'The pedals stuff is true, and its fact. She's too short to reach the controls of those vehicles. The dwarf thing is bull.' He chewed. 'You need to ask her colleagues what they call her.' He chewed some more. 'That's where she got the poison dwarf thing from. She's a small cute looking package but she's a nasty piece of work underneath. I overheard her pin her colours to the mast one day. Said that if her application was refused to join the traffic patrol, she'd cry sexism or even heightism; whatever argument that is. Seems like there's an *ism* for everything these days.'

'As I say, sergeant, it's not looking good for you.' He stacked the files and pulled out a few more from his desk and added to them. 'I know you believe in having a certain type of officer but times have changed. We need all diversity of the local population now, good or bad. We're under pressure from the Government to reach goals in ethnicity and gender. Hell, we even have to scout for gays to represent their section of society; one in ten apparently. Anyway, the latest instruction is to get some transvestites and transgender types. And why not! You need to get up to date, Sarge.'

He raised his eyebrows and cocked his head. 'I've no problem with any of them, so long as they can do the job well. It doesn't matter what or who they are. And what's your problem with gays, sir? You need to be careful how you speak about them. That was a negative inflection in your voice when you mentioned them. Sounded really biased. I might have to report your behaviour.' He smiled and chewed. 'Just my interpretation.'

'Please, don't get smart, Sarge. People have different strengths and weaknesses.'

'Agreed. But aren't we supposed to be a police force and not some all-embracing employer that's here just to represent a cross section of society in statistics? I thought we were here to catch the bad guys; the burglars, robbers, druggies and thieves. Hell, we'll be recruiting them next so they're fairly represented as part of the society. It's ridiculous.'

'As I say, you need to get up to date.' He tapped the stack. 'We still have a problem. I want you to rewrite all the reports so they're not contentious. Can you do that for me?'

He stood up and pulled his jacket to. Adjusted his tie, stepped over to the desk.

'Yes sir, I can.' He sniffed.

The Chief smiled.

'But I aint!' Eyebrows raised.

The smile was lost. 'Well, if you won't do it, I will. And you'll go down with your dogged refusal.'

'You do what you have to, sir. I'll do what I have to. I'll keep my honesty, values and integrity. The courage of my convictions and doing the right thing by the tax payer is what's at stake here.' He cocked his head, turned and made for the door.

'Video recordings! Secret video recordings,' said the Chief.

Sarge stopped at the door and turned. He cleared his throat. 'Video recordings?'

'Yes, sergeant.' There was a moment. 'Nothing's confidential.' He looked smug. 'Of all people, you should know that.'

He stepped back towards the desk, stuck his chest out and turned his head slightly. 'Meaning?'

'Meaning, if you want to reflect on your decision, you have until five this afternoon.'

'Sounds like some kind of veiled threat to me, sir. And what's that about video recordings?' He glowered.

'Let's just say it's open to interpretation, Sarge,' he paused, 'as you say.'

Sarge nodded in contemplation then turned and left the office. He got straight on the phone to his ally, senior officer, Gerry Smithson. It rang twelve long times before being answered.

'Hello. Smithson. Can I help you?' He said efficiently.

'Gerry. What's happened?' He spoke quietly as he slowly walked along the corridor. 'Sounds like the cat's out of the bag.' He looked over his shoulder. 'Curry hinted that he knew of the sensitive matter regarding Lomax, the DVD.' He sniffed. 'We've known each other a long time, Gerry.' He hesitated. 'Tell me I'm wrong.'

There was a long moment.

'Ah yes, the video recording. Sorry, Sarge. I didn't know how to tell you.' He paused. 'I trusted the chief I went to with it. Told him all about it. Never thought of checking him out about where he stands with anyone else in the organization. I thought he was squeaky clean. Of all the cops, I thought no-one had the black on him. As soon as I told him what we had he seemed interested but strangely quiet, moody. I even asked him what was wrong. He said, *nothing*.'

He paused.

'And?'

'And so, I left the DVD with him. He called me a few days later and gave me the bad news; some split-arse recruit had gone to Curry saying I'd used my position to have sex with her in return for helping her career.' He coughed nervously. 'Perhaps not so much as helping her career, it was more like keeping her in the job....'

'Did you?' he interrupted.

There was an awkward pause.

'What; have sex with her? I'll *no comment* that question, Sarge.' He laughed, nervously. His tone turned more serious. 'Curry called me the other day saying this girl can prove it. He's after me.'

There was another long moment.

'Not only that Sarge, I've known George in recruiting nearly twenty years. I know his wife and kids. He's a year off retirement. Internal Affairs are after his balls for the same thing. He could lose everything.' He paused, 'Bloody split-arses!' He said, angrily. 'It's worse 'cos she's married to a cop. Besides, if it got out about Lomax, it would be another scandal. The Force can't take another one.'

Sarge took a long sigh, 'So, the point being?'

'The point being, there's been a trade-off. Curry had the black on the boss I went to. Simple as that. Some indiscretion. He needed to be able to give Curry something and what you gave me was enough to sweep everything under the carpet for him, George and…,' He paused.

'Yeah. And you.'

'Yes. He'd gone straight to Curry to get him and me off the hook. He hadn't even told me when I went to see him with the DVD that Curry was after me. I had no idea, I didn't know. He thought he was doing me a favour,' He paused, 'which he was. I got twenty-three years of my life invested in this job. I can get my full pension in less than seven.'

'Yes, I know. You've just got your long service and good conduct medal. And that's a joke. They give 'em out like toys in packets of breakfast cereals.' He chewed. 'So why Curry, how come he's such a key player?'

'Strictly between me and you?' There was a moment. 'It's about you. The job's out to get you. You've ruffled a lot of feathers over the years, especially recently. You're a none-conformist; you know that. You always have been.' He paused. 'Why can't you play the game; toe the party line?'

'But why him? He's not even in our policing area.'

'It's not just him. It's all of them. It's the Establishment. By the way, I heard your name came up at a chief officer's meeting. As I say, they're out to get you and whoever does it will get a feather in their cap. The dirt's still stuck on you from the murder too.'

'So, it's someone pretty high up who's after my scalp?' He chewed.

He didn't answer.

There was a long moment.

'It's ok, Gerry, I don't expect you to tell me. It's perhaps best I don't know. You did what you thought you had to.' He chewed. 'Does Lomax know we got him on the video?'

'Knowing Curry, he'll have gone snivelling to him. He'll have made use of the *info* in return for looking the other way. He's desperate for promotion. He sees himself as Commander, one day. Commander Curry; it'll happen.'

There was an awkward pause.

'Sorry I gave up your DVD, Sarge.'

He took a deep breath. 'Ok, Gerry. No probs.' He said disappointedly. He sniffed. 'I got a copy anyway. Perhaps the *Kairos time* isn't right just now. Maybe it's not time.'

'Kairos?'

'Nothing. See you around, Gerry. Take care.' He cut him off. He had now arrived outside the Vice office. He went in. He closed the door behind him and leaned against it, mobile still in hand. No-one else was there but Roy sat at his desk. He looked up from his paperwork.

'You alright, Sarge?'

'Yeah.' He was distracted. 'Yeah. I'm fine thanks, matey.' Just then, his mobile jingled. *Gerry Smithson* lit up the screen. He walked over towards his desk. At the same time Mandy came in and headed straight to her desk after giving Sarge a warm smile. He acknowledged then pressed *talk*. 'Yes, Gerry.' He snapped coldly.

'I feel bad about what happened, Sarge.'

'Forget it. It happens.' He chewed, hard. 'What is it? What else you got?'

There was a moment, just the low hiss of empty airwaves.

It was broken by a heavy sigh, like it was a great effort. 'Strictly between me and you. Rumour is you're up to some strange stuff, serious stuff. Possibly with another officer. Extra curriculum stuff.' He paused. 'Not with a split-arse either, not that kind of stuff.'

'Hold it there, Gerry. What are you saying? There's no-one straighter than me. I'm one of the last true hetero's left on this planet. Although with some of the experiences I've had with the women in my life, I've considered going over to the other side. You know, becoming a shirt-tail lifter.' He laughed. 'No, joking, never. Not in a million years.'

It caught Roy's attention. He looked up at Sarge.

He noticed and cringed. '*Sorry,*' *Roy,* he mouthed.

Roy shrugged and smiled, forgivingly.

'Not that there's anything wrong with *batting for the other side*, Gerry. I don't have a problem with it, so long as *they* leave me alone.'

Roy shrugged again and shook his head.

'No. Not like that, Sarge. Other stuff. Serious stuff.'

'Like?' He chewed, hard.

'I don't know. I don't know the details. Be careful, that's all. Sorry, got to go. Catch you later.' He cut off.

Sarge pondered.

'Everything ok?' Roy asked.

'Fine. Yeah, fine.' He said hesitantly.

'Was that Gerry Smithson?'

He was distant. He chewed, slowly. 'Yes. He said thoughtfully. 'Why do you ask? Do you know him?'

'Kind of.'

'Oh yeah. How?'

'Don't ask.'

There was a moment.

'Is he gay too? Does he bat for both sides? Tell me he doesn't.'

Roy ignored him and got on with his paperwork.

Sarge looked on. He waited a moment. 'There's lots of Gerry's. What made you think it was Smithson?'

Roy shrugged, raised his eyebrows and carried on working.

Sarge went over to the drinks area, still concerned over the phone call. He waited for the kettle. Roy and Mandy were heads down in their work. 'I wonder why he called back then had to get off so quickly,' he said quietly, thinking aloud.

No-one took any notice.

'Maybe I'm becoming paranoid,' he said, at normal volume.

Nothing. No response.

Kettle boiled; he made a brew and took it over to his desk.

Roy sat up, indignant. 'Don't ask me if I want one, will you?'

'Sorry, Roy. Wasn't thinking, matey,' he paused. 'Sorry for earlier on as well, you know, about the gay thing with Smithson. Came out all wrong.'

Roy shrugged. 'One thing though, Sarge. You said you'd considered becoming gay. Well, it's not an option. You don't just choose to be. You either are or you are not. It's not a conscious decision just 'cos some women have cheated on you and screwed you're head up.'

'Sorry, matey, I didn't mean it. I was joking.'

'Gays don't have a lot of time for the guys who just decide to be gay nor the ones that don't come out of the closet or the ones that hang around public toilets for sex with other guys.'

'Ok, Roy.' He said humbly. 'I get your point, my mistake.'

There was a short, tense, silent moment.

'You're forgiven.' He sighed. 'It's not your fault.' He stood up.

Sarge smiled and gave a slight nod.

Roy nodded in acknowledgment then left the office. Mandy glanced over, made sure he'd gone. She glanced several times at Sarge, checking, building up courage. Two minutes passed.

'Heard you need to watch your back,' she said cautiously.

'What? We still on the gay thing here? Don't worry. I'll be careful where I bend down.' Sarge laughed.

She shook her head disapprovingly; said nothing.

Sarge lost his smile.

Roy walked back in.

'I'll tell you later,' she said with a glare.

Sarge got the message, frowned and nodded.

Roy sat at his desk. He sensed an atmosphere, looked left at Sarge then right at Mandy then set about his work again. He glanced over at Sarge a couple of more times, unsure. Roy's eyes settled on him. 'Heard a rumour, Sarge. You need to watch your back.'

'Oh yeah? You too?' He looked over at Mandy then back at Roy. She kept her head down as though she'd not heard or wasn't interested. He sniffed. 'About what?'

'There's a couple of uniform sergeants after promotion and after your job in here. This role in Vice, apart from it being one of the best jobs in the Force, would look good on their CV's. They're looking at trying to drop you in it, to get you out of here.'

'Is that all?' He seemed relieved. 'I didn't know I'd upset any of them so much that they'd stoop to that.' He went over to the drinks area. 'Do you want a brew, Roy?'

He nodded. 'Thanks. You don't have to.'

He made the drink and walked over to him, passed him his mug.

'Cheers, Sarge.'

'You're welcome, matey.' He went over to the door, opened it, looked along the corridor, left then right then closed it again.

'You getting paranoid, Sarge?'

He said nothing, gave him a sideways look as he returned to his desk. 'Ok. So, who are they? I can guess one of them.' Eyebrows raised. 'Frosty?'

He nodded. 'And his oppo.'

'Who? Melton? That dick-head sergeant on Delta relief who hardly got through as a basic cop?' He shook his head in disbelief. 'Didn't think he had the balls.'

'You know what it's like, Sarge, with those chinless wonders once they get promotion fever. They've back-stabbed and grovelled all their careers to get where they are. They could never have done it on merit.' He paused. 'Different world to my old job. They wouldn't have lasted five minutes in the Para's.'

'Yeah. Shame this job doesn't have the camaraderie it used to.' He sniffed. 'Do you miss the old days, Roy? I know I do.''

He nodded. 'Yes. Me too.'

'If only we could turn the clock back. The good old days, eh?'

'They're gone forever. One time, your back was always covered. Now you have to cover your own back from your own kind. One thing's for sure though, Sarge.' He paused and took a long sip.

'What's that?' He asked, impatiently.

'If ever you need an alibi, just say.' He nodded once and winked.

The sarge mirrored him, 'Likewise.'

There were no more words, but there was an understanding. Both understood what was meant.

There was a long moment whilst they drank, wrapped up in their own thoughts.

'Well, they won't get anything on me.' He laughed. 'Besides, those two wouldn't be able to detect my arse after six pints of beer and a hot Indian curry from the night before.'

They both laughed.

'Well, be careful, Sarge.'

'Always am. But what are they up to?'

'One of the girls in the *crime records office* tells me they've been in there pulling reports with your name on and then copying them,' He reached into his desk tray and held out a bundle of photocopied reports towards the sarge.

He took them. He studied them as he finished his drink.

'Nothing unusual here.' He popped in some gum. 'I wonder what those idiots are planning.' He stood up and pulled his jacket to. Straightened his tie.

'Remember, Sarge, you've always got me to back you up.'
'Yeah. Yes, thanks. Appreciate that.' He nodded, 'We're a dying breed.'
'*An endangered species*, our graduate colleagues would say.'
They laughed.
'Yeah. And without cops like you and me, they'd be extinct.' He chewed.
He re-opened the door. The strong smell of pipe smoke wafted in. He stuck his head into the corridor to see Lomax a few steps away, heading off.
In a loud voice, Sarge said, 'Think I just disturbed something that doesn't smell too good, Roy.'
A large cloud of smoke trailed Lomax, who clearly heard the words, sucked angrily.
He turned back to Roy. 'Going over to see Frosty,' he said, quietly, 'if anyone wants to know where I am.'
'Best form of defence is attack, Sarge.'
'You got that right. *Get the first one in*, as my old mentor used to tell me when he showed me around the beat. God rest his soul.'
'I know you so well.'
'Maybe you do, Roy. Maybe you do. You're one of the chosen few.'
'Likewise, Sarge.'

Within minutes the sarge was outside the patrol sergeants' office. Sergeant Frost was sat inside shuffling papers at his desk. Sarge entered and closed the door purposefully behind him. His posture erect; chest out, mouth firm.
He looked up at Sarge.
He nodded a business-like greeting, 'Frosty.'
'Sarge. How are you?'
Sarge was stood right up against the front of his desk and was scowling down at him. 'Not happy!'
Frost leaned back in his chair, looking somewhat anxious. 'Oh really, why's that?' He said in his refined, educated voice.
'You tell me.'
Frost shrugged.
There was a moment.
'I hear you been trying to rake up some dirt on me.'
He swallowed hard. 'Me? Not me.'
'Not what I heard. What you trying to do, score more Brownie points?' Mouth tense he chewed hard. 'You ought to try getting out there on patrol, support your officers instead of hiding in here your entire shift.'
He made no reply.
He leaned forward and rested his palms on the desk, closing the space between them. 'The bad guys are out there, Frosty.' He chewed. 'Apply for Internal Affairs if you want to chase cops. Anyway, me and you will be having more than words if you're not careful.' He sniffed. 'And you wouldn't like that.' He stared and chewed.
Frost found it almost impossible to keep eye contact. 'Is that a veiled threat, Sarge? If it is, don't make them to me or.....'
'Or what?' he laughed.
He made no reply.

Sarge straightened up, popped in some more gum, chewed hard, stared him out, turned, then left.

He returned to the Vice office.

'The Commander's just been on the phone, Sarge. Wants to see you in his office, now.'

'Ok. Thanks Roy. I'm just in the mood for him.' He did an about-turn, paced towards the door then stopped in his tracks. *'I wonder?'* He thought out aloud.

'Wonder what?' asked Roy.

There was no reply. He went over to his desk, reached underneath and pulled out his briefcase. 'Won't be long, Roy.' Then marched out with his case.

He burst open the Commanders door, the same time he thumped on it.

He was startled by the abrupt entry.

'Yes, sir. You wanted to see me.'

He quickly tried to compose himself and regain some authority. 'Yes, sergeant. Close the door. Have a seat.'

He took the nearest one, the farthest from Lomax and waited as Lomax pulled a pile of papers towards himself that were sat on his desk. He peeled through them, briefly studying them one at a time.

Sarge knew the game and tried to conceal his anxiety and impatience.

'Here sergeant, look at these.' He said in his best, stern voice. He kept his eyes on the wad of papers as he held them out for Sarge to take. No eye contact.

Sarge stood up in no hurry and took a few steps to collect them. He remained in front of the desk and flicked through them, glancing down at the Commander from time to time.

He was uncomfortable with the situation of Sarge being so close and looking down on him, after all, the chairs in his room were deliberately low so that the he had a psychological advantage of those sitting on them.

'Sit down, Sarge!' he snapped.

There was a long defiant moment as Sarge looked down at him with disdain. He chewed as he observed the senior officer then returned to his seat farthest away.

'So, sarge, explain why you did nothing with the report of the young girl who broke her arm at school when she was pushed on some steps. A very serious assault.'

Sarge looked at him a long moment then chewed before reading the paperwork. 'These are from when I was in uniform, sir. What would you like me to say?' He chewed. 'What would you like to hear?'

'An explanation.'

'Ok. Well, it's the system we have. Been like it for years, you should know that.'

'Where's the quality of service? It was nearly a week before we got to see the girl. It's not acceptable, is it?'

There was a moment.

'No sir. No, it isn't.'

'So, you admit it's not acceptable?' he said enthusiastically.

'I do.' Sarge, chewed.

The Commander flushed with success.

Sarge flicked through the wad. 'Along with all the other crimes and victims that get stacked until we can get around to dealing with them, sir. It took its place with the rest of the reports. We've not had the manpower for years to deal quickly with anything anymore.'

'Well, why didn't you use other resources and departments? The detective's department, community police, child protection. Those kinds of people.'

Eyebrows raised in astonishment. 'Because they're all busy and can't deal with their own workload let alone someone else's. They all have their own priorities. I could have passed them over but it wouldn't have made any difference. Besides, they wouldn't have taken them. They're overwhelmed too.'

'There are about twenty reports like that one. What about the quality of service we promise the public?'

'With respect, sir, the rest are relatively minor stuff. None urgent.'

'Well, that's not the point. It's not acceptable. You admit that.'

'I do but I'm not the one in charge of this divisional police area who can change things.' He raised his eyebrows putting the onus back on the Commander.

He faltered. 'In future, deal with matters, don't pass them on.'

'If you'd read the reports, sir, you'd see that they were passed on to me and my men by Delta section, in fact sergeant Frost's name's all over these. And Melton's. They're known for passing work over to others and doing nothing themselves.' He looked over the reports again. 'I passed these back to sergeant Frost.' He paused. 'It's him who brought it to your attention, isn't it sir?'

He made no reply.

'Isn't he a graduate entrant waiting for promotion? Chewed Sarge.

He made no reply.

'Do you really know your own system here at Division, sir?'

Lost for words. Realising he had no argument. 'Get out sergeant!' Demanded Lomax.

'I brought my own reports to show you what goes on. How reports for investigation are passed on all the time.' He opened his brief case, stepped over to the desk and handed them over. He waited a moment before returning to his seat.

The Commander quickly scanned them. 'I've nothing more to say. I'd like you to leave.'

'You'll notice, sir, the number of reports Mr. Frost passes on without doing anything. I don't see him trying to give them to other departments. You'll see too that other supervisors do the same. It's the system, your system at your division.'

'Leave now, sergeant.' He again demanded.

'No sir, I won't.'

He lost his temper and threw the papers at Sarge. They fell short and scattered over the floor. Sarge took a long look at the papers then back at the Commander. He shook his head in disgust.

'Get out of my office,' he yelled.

'No sir, I won't. I came here for some progress about quality of service; you asked me here and I aren't leaving until we sort it.'

'Chief Curry!' he shouted. 'Mr. Curry! Get the sergeant out of my office.'

Both men looked towards the door. A long moment passed.

Nothing happened.

Sarge looked back over at Lomax then slowly stood up. He pulled his jacket to and chewed hard. Eyebrows raised. 'Losing your temper and throwing papers at me shows you lost the argument, sir. You haven't a clue about what's going on in your own police area.' He snorted, 'Quality of service.' He sneered. 'You talk a good job but that's all.' He shook his head. 'Just hallow words, sir. That's all you've got.'

There was a light tap on the door. Curry appeared as it opened. He was ashen and quiet.

Sarge looked him up and down. 'It's ok Chief Curry, I'm just leaving.' He stepped aside as Sarge headed out along the corridor. He whistled happily as he made his way to his office. He seemed unaffected. Inside; he was burning with rage.

Roy heard him coming and was ready for him, 'Coffee, Sarge?'

'Please, Roy.'

Sarge got on the phone to the Union. There was a heated conversation for five minutes that resulted in him slamming the phone down. 'I don't believe this job. It's all one-way traffic at times. The bosses in their ivory towers and cushy offices pass down instructions, policies and mantras for us to follow but they all do what they want. Double standards!'

Roy interrupted, 'Just like our politicians.' He handed him his drink. Sarge took it. 'They're a law unto themselves. Do as I say, not as I do, eh Sarge?'

'The Union rep tells me to calm down, *the Commander isn't the type of fellow to bear a grudge,* he says. But it's him that's in the wrong and should be apologizing to me, senior officer or not.' He sipped. 'The idiot lost the argument and threw the papers at me. What sort of leadership skills does that show?'

'Well, we know what they are. The days of a boss making it on merit rather than some university qualification and who they know, seem to be long gone. A degree in nuclear physics or zoology seems to be what the police want these days, not common-sense, practical police officers.'

He laughed. 'Yer, you got that right.' He took a deep breath and sipped. 'So, what we got on today?'

Roy handed over a document. 'Warrant for arrest, you might be interested.'

Sarge scanned it.

'Amos Gull, eh? He never learns. He's used the same M.O all his life. He must know we're going to come looking for him.'

Just then a young, fresh faced uniformed officer politely knocked on the open door. Sarge and Roy swung around. 'Excuse me,' she said nervously. 'I'm on my fact-finding week as a recruit.' She stepped into the office and helped herself to a seat. She was under five foot tall with a petite frame, long blonde hair and heavy make-up. Attractive.

'Fact finding, eh?' He chewed and looked over at Roy. 'Things in this job are changing.' Eyebrows raised. 'Well, this officer is detective Roy Lee and I'm Sarge. So, what facts do you want to know?'

'I overheard you mention, M.O. What is that?'

'You were listening in to our conversation? You a relative of the Commander's?' he asked sarcastically.

The recruit looked puzzled.

Sarge and Roy laughed.

'Ignore the sarge,' said Roy, with a smile. 'M.O. Latin, meaning Modus Operandi; method of operating. M.O, as in this case, how or what the criminal did. In this case the bad guy drilled through the window frame, lifted the sneck and climbed into a house not belonging to him. Now he's Billy burglar. The old couple asleep in bed in their own home woke to find our man standing over them with a stick. He terrorizes them for their valuables then leaves.'

Sarge chewed. 'But not before he takes a dump on the old lady's face as she's laid there next to her husband. Naturally, the old guy's too scared and too frail to do anything.'

'Charming,' she said. 'So, you know who it is just from that.'

'It's recorded that way so we can match other similar jobs up to it that have a similar M.O. We recorded over twenty the same in the last six months.'

'What if it's a copycat?'

Sarge and Roy looked at one another.

Sarge chewed some more. 'Do you watch a lot of TV, Miss?'

She looked blank. 'TV?'

'As in those cop story's where there's a copycat nut-job messing up their inquiries.'

She remained blank.

'Never mind. If it's not TV, then you must have a degree in something or other?'

'Yes, I have. With honours.' She smiled.

He glanced over at Roy. 'That figures.'

'Biology.' she said proudly. 'So how can you be certain it's the same man?'

Sarge chewed. 'You heard of DNA? A fairly recent discovery.'

'Ah.' The recruit blushed. 'I should have known.' She hesitated. 'About the DNA but especially about M.O. I took Latin as one of my languages. Anyway, thanks.'

She stood up to leave.

Sarge chewed. 'You're very welcome. Remember, M.O; modus operandi. You'll come across it a lot.' He smiled. 'That was a short and sweet visit, for sure. Hope you weren't offended. Take care.'

She headed for the door then turned around. 'But where does the DNA come into it?'

'The DNA? You must be joking me.'

'No. I'm serious. Really.'

'The guy's faeces.'

'Ah. Never knew that. I'll remember that.' She headed back towards the door.

'Hey!' said Sarge.

She spun around.

'Here's another one to remember when you're a senior officer, a chief or whatever, A*cta non Verba,* you knowing Latin and all.' He chewed.

She smiled, said nothing, then puzzled. She shook her head slightly.

'Acta non Verba; *Action not Words.'* Said Roy. 'I know that one, Sarge. He looked back at the recruit. 'I'm Sarge trained.' He smiled.

She laughed politely. 'I'll remember your phrase, sergeant.'

Eyebrows raised. 'Well, try remembering it when you're some high-ranking officer, eh?'

She smiled then left. Roy and Sarge shrugged at one another in agreement.

Sarge sniffed. 'Ok, Roy, I'll go see our friend Gull sometime during the evening. You've got enough to do. I'll be ok alone with him.' He winked.

'Ok, Sarge. Be careful. Last time he was locked up it took four uniforms, one ended up in casualty. He can be a violent bastard.'

'I remember it well, broke a policewoman's nose, really bad.' He sniffed. 'I'll catch up with you later.'

The evening passed. It was a typical shift; the radio traffic was constant. Sarge called in that he was at an address to make an arrest of Amos Gull. The dispatcher noted the address and acknowledged Sarge's message.

Gull was over six feet three inches, heavily built, a violent man. Although only in his late twenties, he'd already spent almost eight years of his life in prison.

Thirty seconds later a fairly calm, unconvincing message crackled over the airwaves from Sarge. 'Sarge to control. Urgent assistance, Code ten nine.'

Other units were immediately dispatched to the address but were cancelled twenty seconds later when Sarge radioed another message. 'Cancel all units. No further assistance needed but the guy here requires an ambulance. One man arrested for assault upon a police officer.' Shouts of protest in the background of Sarge's transmission could be heard. The dispatcher called off the other units then confirmed an ambulance was required.

Half an hour later, Sarge used Gull to burst through the door of the charge room. He was his angry self and *cuffed* behind his back. They were greeted by the detention staff. The Commander was also present. That was unusual.

Gull's hair was blood-soaked. His shirt looked as though he had showered in a bottle of thick claret. His nose was spread across his face, definitely broken. He screamed about making a complaint about Sarge for assault. He found the receptive ear of the Commander. That was unusual. He alleged that as soon as he offered some verbal resistance to Sarge that he'd drawn his baton and struck him on the centre of his head without warning then across his nose. The Commander was interested in Gull's version of events. He instructed that a formal complaint be taken from Gull as soon as possible. Sarge remarked that Gull had taken a swing at him first so had to strike him with his baton. No-one was interested. He headed up to the Vice office where Roy and Mandy were waiting.

Mandy offered him a coffee as soon as he sat down. She took a moment too long staring at him, long enough to make him feel it was a longing stare.

He broke the moment. 'Well, let's hope Gull won't be so keen on burglaring the old folk after today, eh? Or taking a swing at a cop.'

Roy laughed. 'Sarge, it was pretty obvious what happened out there. I heard it over the radio, we all did.' He chewed.

'Oh yeah? And what's that?'

'You're losing your touch.'

'You think so? I got him dead centre, made him a new parting in his hair.' He laughed; eyebrows raised. 'He went straight down. Eight stitches later and he's sat in the cells feeling all sorry for himself but not before Lomax listens to his side of the story. Used to be a time when a chief would have chinned him too for accusing one of his officers of wrong-doings.'

'Didn't mean that, I'm sure you struck him good. No, I meant the way you sounded over the air, like you'd hit him first then called for assistance then cancelled it for an ambulance.'

'Really!' he laughed. 'Justified assault, Roy. Took a swing at me. I had to hit him. Self-defence.'

'Yeah, right,' he said sarcastically. 'Stick to your story,' he laughed.

'You ok, Sarge?' Asked Mandy. 'You've got a small bruise under your eye.'

'Yeah. I'm fine thanks.' He looked over at Roy. 'Well, I got to have some injury to justify pegging Gull, haven't I?' He winked.

'So, it happened how Roy said?'

'Yes, of course.' He paused. 'Mandy, never admit to anything. You should know that, you're Sarge trained.'

They laughed.

Lomax was standing at the door. He puffed hard on his pipe, turned and walked off.

'Do you think he heard all that, Sarge?' whispered Mandy.

'I don't know.' He shrugged. 'I don't care. They'll never prove anything. Gull's word against mine. Besides, the Establishment sticks together, unless they're after you.'

Roy and Mandy glanced at each other.

Sarge noticed. 'What? He asked. 'Do you two know something I don't?' He chewed hard. 'What now?'

Mandy ignored his question and moved closer to Sarge. She examined his bruise.

He automatically offered up the injury to her. 'Well?'

She never replied.

Roy looked at his watch. 'I've got to go, Sarge. Work to do.' He gathered his stuff and left, fairly unnoticed.

The remaining couple were wrapped up in their moment.

Another long quiet time, passed.

'You sure you're ok, Sarge?' She gently asked.

'A little bruise like this? Of course. Why shouldn't I be?'

'No. Not that. You've been under a lot of pressure lately.'

He sniffed. His eyes rolled. 'Pressure?' He knew it was no good denying it. 'Truth is, it's a rough time right now. I feel like a plate juggler with a whole stack wobbling and ready to come down.' He glanced for her reaction.

There was none.

He feared he'd let her in by admitting too much. He laughed to break the moment.

She cupped his hand in both of hers and squeezed gently. 'Well, you know where I am. I'm always here for you.'

Her big brown eyes locked with his for a long moment.

Sarge coughed to break the awkwardness. 'I'm ok. Well, ok for me on my scale. On someone else's it would rank somewhere around ready to reach for the hotline to the Samaritans and ready to jump off a bridge.'

She didn't react, kept hold and blinked her long lashes sympathetically, sweetly. She knew him better than he realized.

He placed his hand on hers and smiled.

'Do you remember when, Sarge…?'

He coughed. 'Let's not go down memory lane, Mandy.'

There was an awkward silence.

He interrupted with a smile. 'Come on, we got work to do.' He patted her hands and withdrew.

'It just seems like there's lots of people out to get you. You're too hard on yourself. You can't save the world single-handedly.'

He laughed. 'Story of my life, sweetie.' He leaned forward and kissed her forehead like a father would his daughter. 'Anyway, *illegitimi non carborundum*. Right?'

She smiled. '*Don't let the bastards grind you down*. I know, one of your favourite sayings.'

He stood up and pulled his jacket to. 'Say, you heard of Kairos?'

She thought a short while. 'Actually, I have.'

Surprised, he frowned. 'Oh yeah? You have? Where from?'

'Someone said you'd mentioned it recently.'

'Really? I need to be more careful about what I'm saying.'

'Why?'

He shook his head. Said nothing.

'It's a word for fate or moments in time or something, isn't it? It's not something which can be changed or altered.'

He sniffed. 'Yes.' He hesitated. 'Yes, that's right. Fate and what is to be and has already been, I think? I have my own interpretation.'

She frowned. 'Que sera, sera.'

'What will be, will be.' they said in harmony. Then laughed.

'That Latin too or you being Doris Day now?' He smiled. 'Come on, let's go get some bad guys.'

Their evening shift passed. It was late when they returned to the office before going off duty. A yellow Post It note was left on Sarge's desk. It was from Gerry asking him to call him first thing in the morning. Sarge puzzled over it.

Mandy noticed; she asked if everything was ok.

Sarge snapped out of his thoughts and nodded.

'Come on Sarge. You need a beer.' She cocked her head to a side and smiled sweetly. 'My treat.'

'Well actually…...'

'No excuses,' she said firmly. 'Let's go. My car.'

They smiled at one another for a long silent moment that said many things. His peripheral vision caught her erect nipples poking through her top. A Kairos moment of the not-too-distant future crossed his mind. 'Do you think it's possible to see into the future, Mandy? You know, a moment that's going to happen? Or has it happened and we already know it, or if we visualize something who's to say it didn't happen for real? Maybe everything around us is all imagined, an illusion.'

'Deep, Sarge. Deep.' They both laughed. 'I think you're losing it, Sarge. Come on, let's go.'

A couple of drinks and twenty minutes' drive later, they were at Mandy's home. It was cheaply furnished, basic, practical but feminine. It was well kept, smelled fresh and clean.

She went through the ritual of asking if he wanted coffee. He responded by saying a casual, *yes. Though it was filled with hoped for expectation.* He sat on the cozy sofa whilst she was in the kitchen. He glanced around like any cop would. He tried to assess her from the items she surrounded herself with. It was minimalist. There were no ornaments or things that were of no use, just a handful of books piled on the floor and a few framed photos here and there; too small to make out. A media centre seemed to be the main focus of the room. A pedal cycle rested nearby. It looked like the occupant had a lonely existence which was work orientated, self-disciplined, self-centred but chosen. It reminded Sarge of his own home.

He homed-in on a bible laid on an occasional table. It was open at Romans. He leaned forward and looked closer and read; *Kairos time is here. It calls for action, conversion and transformation - a change of life.*

She popped her head around the door with a smile. She broke his moment. 'How do you like it?'

He said nothing, raised his eyebrows and smiled knowingly. She did likewise. They stared briefly at each other. He stood up, slid his jacket off and laid it on the sofa. She stepped towards him until they were toe to toe.

Within seconds their breathing became noticeably deep. He trembled as she hugged him and pulled herself in close. He held her tightly in return as he let out a sigh of relief. He calmed. They nestled into each other's neck and pressed their bodies together. They both felt the hot breath and the pounding heartbeats of one another.

'I'm nearly old enough to be your father.' His voice was deep and husky.

She looked him in the eyes before lightly pressing her lips against his. At first it was unsure, careful, almost controlled. He remained passive. Then it became hard, passionate and excited. He held her head gently in his hands. She kneaded his waist and pressed her body closer. He felt unsure. His eyes were open, watching her. Hers were closed. She was lost in the moment. Then the feeling changed for him too, it washed through him. He closed his eyes. He could feel her firm breasts against his chest. He hugged her tightly and pressed himself against her. She could feel him, he was firm. She liked what she felt, her anticipation built. She took the lead and stroked him a couple of times; hard, looked at his reaction then kneaded him again. Encouraged, his hand slowly found its way to her thigh then slid between her legs and upwards. She adjusted her stance to accommodate him. He rubbed her over her pants. He looked for her reaction; he was reassured. She gasped and tilted her hips forward. It felt good.

She ran her other hand from his waist around to the front, grabbed his shirt and yanked it out from his trousers. She went for his tie, pulled at the knot but it tightened and stuck. He tried; it was too tight so he left it. He popped the top buttons of his shirt and turned his collar up before trying to slide the noose of the tie over his head. He couldn't, the loop was too small. He returned to his shirt and popped a few more buttons. She eagerly rived it down over his shoulders and sensually kissed his bare chest making her way down as far as his waist band. Crouched in front of him she teasingly ran her tongue around the area a while. That pleased him; he thought it was a sign of things to come. He stroked her hair and allowed himself to enjoy the moment. She worked her way back up to his lips then slipped off her shoes. He followed her lead; he bent down, got one sock off then trying to keep his balance he briefly hopped about struggling to get the other one off. Meanwhile she pulled her top over her head. He fought with his tie again. He lost and gave up. 'Amateur hour!' he blurted, to cover his embarrassment. They both took a moment and laughed. He looked at her standing there half naked, she looked beautiful. Their laughter faded. She looked even more beautiful in her lacy white bra. He took a moment to admire her and then caressed her breasts with his hand whilst kissing her hard on the lips. He popped the button of her pants and slowly unzipped her. He struggled to gently push the tight waistband down over her curvy hips. She helped him, they dropped to her ankles. She stepped out of them and kicked them to one side. Wearing only her bra and panties; the girl knew what she wanted. Her chest heaved as she waited. They hugged and kissed some more. Hot, soft skin pressed against hot soft skin. He worked her bra fastener, one-handed. The clasps parted easily, she stepped back rounded her shoulders, dropped her arms and let the bra fall away. Her breasts spilled out. She was proud of what she had. She pushed her chest out. Her nipples erect, he teased and tongued them a moment. She ran her fingers through his hair and held his head whilst he did so. They hugged and kissed. Both were more than ready. Only a few more minutes passed until she could wait no longer. She pulled him into her bedroom by his waistband and placed him with his back against her bed. She pushed him backwards onto it. He lay passively as she straddled him, frantically unfastening his belt and zipper. Before he knew it, he was naked, all but for his tie. She took him straight into her hot mouth. He let out a satisfied groan. She was good. She kept him on the edge and drove him wild. She glanced up at him occasionally with puppy-dog eyes. She looked so beautiful, he thought. He felt honoured to be in such a situation.

 He played with her nipples and rubbed her between her legs but it wasn't easy in that position. As much as he was enjoying things, he could contain himself no longer. He sat up, rolled her over onto her back and knelt beside her. In awe of her youth and beauty, he took a moment to enjoy the sight laid before him. Her cheeks were rosy, her eyes dark, her lips full. His eyes moved down her body. Her perfect breasts defied gravity. Her stomach was toned and flat, it accentuated her wide hips. Her thighs were inviting, her skin smooth and fresh. She held him in her left hand and tugged him gently whilst he gazed upon her. It all got too much. He pulled at her panties; she helped by arching her back so lifting her buttocks. He slid the panties all the way down her long legs until they were off. She parted her knees slightly, ready to take him. He positioned between her legs. He looked on. He felt overwhelmed and had another moment; everything about her was indeed beautiful. He touched her sensitively. She loved his touch. Her body reacted; it was clear she was desperate for him to enter her. She noticed how serious he had become so broke the moment by laughing loudly. He lightened up. She grabbed his tie and threaded it under her inner thigh then pulled it through from the other side. Sarge's head followed; he didn't resist. She knew what she wanted; he knew what she wanted. He explored her with his tongue and found what took her to that special place. His tongue danced lightly and slowly over her. He waited for her reaction; he listened to her breathing and groaning and noted the way she moved her hips. He played her; he'd build up to being harder and faster, then he'd slow again at that crucial moment. He teased and teased until she could stand it no longer. She held his head tightly and writhed until she got the release she needed. He helped all he could. She groaned noisily at first but slowly quietened and stilled. She sounded wonderful, he thought. It was a sound he wanted to hear over again, it showed him he had pleased her too. He gave her a moment before gently kissing her inner thighs and delicately flitting around with his tongue. She was sensitive and flinched when he touched *the spot*. Slowly and ever so delicately, he started over. She loved it. Her need for release was building once more. He kept her there a long while without bringing her to climax.

 Now it was his turn, he was soon between her young thighs and entering her, gently at first. Performing with all the experience of a man of his years, she loved every second. She loved him. She showed it in what she did for him.

 She felt safe, uninhibited. She played out many of the fantasies she had imagined for so long. She more than pleased him.

He used his experience to the full. He delighted her beyond her wildest expectations. He was far sexier than any younger man she had known.

She was pleasantly surprised at his energy, stamina and youthful enthusiasm. She realized he was a guy who knew his way around. She told him so.

Afterwards, they cuddled, happy; exhausted. They chatted awhile but not so much.

They had only just drifted to sleep when the gentle music from her alarm woke them to find his arm around her and she lay across his chest. Their warm bodies felt right, together.

'Kairos,' said Mandy, softly.

Sarge nodded. 'Kairos.' And smiled.

They were quiet, content and sleepy.

They had breakfast and shared a shower before heading back to the station for their day shift. She dropped him a few blocks away so that he could walk in. She would get there ahead of him. The organization would frown upon their behaviour if it were to find out.

Her and Roy were already in the office when Sarge walked in. He sensed an atmosphere but tried to act normal. It was strained. The couple snatched glances at one another like children that shared a naughty secret. Roy was suspicious but never said anything. He sensed something. He was a sensitive guy, but he never said anything.

With a glowing smile she passed Sarge his coffee.

He over-reacted; he was more serious than usual. Roy noticed.

Mandy was still glowing. 'Don't forget your phone call, Sarge.'

'Huh?'

'Your *Post it*.'

'Oh yes.' He hesitated. 'Yeah, thanks Mandy. I'll do it.'

Just then Lomax appeared at the doorway in a cloud of pipe smoke, wearing his usual hang-dog expression.

'Sarge, there's a meeting in half an hour in the conference room but I'd like to see you in my office first. Now!' He puffed and turned.

Sarge raised his brows to his colleagues then followed in the wake of the smoke trail and took a low seat in Lomax's office.

Lomax looked down at him from behind his desk. 'Not looking good for you Sarge, this latest assault.'

'The one upon Gull? It was reasonable force to affect an arrest, sir. Justifiable.'

'I.A says this latest one could be your down-fall.'

Sarge sniffed. 'Internal affairs,' he muttered dismissively and shook his head.

'There are too many complaints against you. They're starting to stick. They'll get you one day. It's a matter of time.'

Flippantly; he quietly asked, 'Time? What sort of time?'

'Sorry?'

'Oh, nothing.' He coughed. 'Shows I'm getting stuck in and doing my job, sir. I can't please everyone.'

'Well, I may be able to help you. My opinion counts when I.A are after one of my officers. I can either support them or …...'

'Yeah.' He interrupted, 'I get the picture. Anything else, sir?' He stood up, pulled his jacket to then ran his finger round his shirt collar loosening it as he chinned the air. He adjusted his tie and had an unexpected flash back to last night at Mandy's. He coughed, nodded at the Commander, turned then stepped towards the door. *If only he knew.* He thought.

'You're not chewing this morning, Sarge. How come?' He paused. 'It's not a good image. I hope you've given up the habit.'

Sarge turned. 'No. No I'll never do that. Got to look after what pearly whites I have left.' He ran his tongue over his teeth. 'Can't afford to lose anymore. Gum keeps them clean; you know.' His memory involuntarily flashed him last night's events again. 'Didn't have time to get any this morning, sir. Usually pick it up on the way in.' He smiled before turning. 'I was busy last night.' His smile soon disappeared when he saw Gerry Smithson hovering around the doorway. They *played the game* and ignored each other. Lomax read it as though they were relative strangers.

'Sir.' He nodded as he passed.

'Sergeant…...'

Smithson went into the office as Sarge left. The door was closed.

Sarge returned to his office. Half an hour passed; it was time for the meeting. Sarge entered the conference room. He was the last one there. Sat around the table was a sea of faces all looking his way. Chief Curry was next to the Commander at the head of the table. Then there were several uniform sergeants and other bosses all facing each other. At the other end were senior officers from neighbouring police Divisions including Gerry Smithson. He was the only face avoiding eye contact with Sarge.

It was quite a select group, Sarge thought, *they all looked very serious*

The Commander looked at his watch. 'Ok. Now you're here, Sarge, we can start properly. Shut the door,' he said officiously; it was his way of trying to assert some authority.

Sarge chewed exaggeratedly at the Commander a moment, closed the door then took his seat next to a young upcoming officer, Stevie; a newly promoted sergeant. He had lots of Sarge's own traits when it came to police work; he was Sarge trained. They smiled and nodded at one another.

Curry outlined the reason for the meeting but made the unusual comment that anything said was not to leave the room, it was strictly confidential. He spoke of the recent months where two criminal brothers, the Lord's and their associates, had waged war upon the police in several Divisions. Their main crimes included terrorizing a young officer's family at their home by breaking their windows and throwing paint at it during the night. They had to be re-housed at a secret address on the other side of the city with all the upheaval that comes with such a move. No good for the cop or any of his family.

They also rammed a stolen car into the foyer of a police station, firebombed a ground floor office in another and set fire to unattended police vehicles. They had followed officers own personal vehicles when they'd left the station at the end of duty when heading home. Their most recent antics were to box in lone policewomen in their patrol cars at night. That was all just the tip of the iceberg.

They were active criminals that hated the police and authority. They believed the law didn't apply to them. They were taking the fight to the Establishment. They had good lawyers at public expense and never admitted to anything when caught. They had contacts and informants within the police civilian staff too. They had police radio scanners and monitored the air waves. They were always one step ahead and making a mockery of the city's police.

Everyone seemed to know it was the Lord's but nothing was stopping them.

Sarge asked for sure how they knew it was the Lord's gang. The Divisional field intelligence officer spoke up. He hinted that one of the gang members was an informant for a hundred notes a time. Everyone in the room read that as pretty good evidence.

Lomax was clearly anxious; a very worried man, he moved the meeting along. He emphasized the embarrassment of the articles published in the local newspaper and how impotent and ineffective the police were appearing to the citizens. 'The Force's mantra and slogan on the patrol vehicles; Reassure, Help and Protect, was looking pretty lame.' He added, *the chief of police had been on his back about it.*

Until the mention of the Chief of police on his back, Sarge actually thought that Lomax cared about affected officers and the damage to police property. He subconsciously shook his head in disappointment and disgust when he realized what he really meant. The message picked up from Lomax was his concern over the adverse publicity. It wasn't about the welfare of his officers so much but more of how it was looking bad for him. Bad publicity for a chief could affect a promising career up the promotion ladder. He may even get ousted from his cushy number.

Curry picked up on the Chief's none-verbal's. He said, 'The Lords' have to be stopped. Some way. The ways by lawful means, isn't working. We need to come up with a different strategy.' He asked for suggestions. Some in the room couldn't believe what they were hearing.

Stevie, the Sarge-trained sergeant, spoke up. What he said was radical, aggressive and unlawful in so many ways.

Sarge kept his own counsel. He glanced at Smithson several times and pondered the recent events between them. He glanced back; didn't respond – gave nothing away.

Lomax and Curry frequently looked to Sarge for answers. He was aware of it but remained quiet. He had some answers but kept them to himself.

Some others threw in a few comments but radical thoughts were mostly kept private. There was an air of mistrust; after all, several senior officers were present and they were of the generation where they went by the book. If something went wrong, they'd be like rats deserting a sinking ship. They'd throw their own grannies under the bus to save themselves. They were career men on the ladder to promotion and generous pensions, actual police work, results, effective policing, upholding the law, protecting the citizens; came a poor second. But there was a mood for action. Even Lomax stirred occasionally and hinted at ideas outside of the normal practice of law keeping and doing things by the book. He accepted that the normal methods of policing and upholding the law weren't working when it came to this particular problem. He'd put some of his cards on the table. A little trust was building amongst the group.

In return, some of the methods used on the Lord's to stop them was shared with those present in the room. They had been pulled over whenever seen, their vehicles and documents examined. They'd been threatened, humiliated, poked, prodded and provoked but it hadn't been effective.

In return they and their associates had complained about the harassment from the police. Internal Affairs had put out instructions to beat officers not to arbitrarily stop or otherwise interfere with the Lord's or their associates. Officers had no choice than to comply or risk disciplinary action. The Lord's had used I.A; the police system of checks, to prevent them doing their jobs.

It became obvious to all present at the meeting that the kind of policing used so far with the Lords, had not worked and was never going to. Yet they still had a problem. It had become personal. All those in the room knew the Lord's could never be allowed to beat them; the Establishment.

A loose plan was muted; to set them up one night then ambush them. Sarge could not believe he was at such a meeting, especially where senior officers were present. But then he recalled his early days within the force where his sergeant told him many times *that the Establishment looks after its own when the chips are down*. Here was one such moment. *A Kairos moment was about to happen,* he thought. It was like going back to the old days. He felt nostalgic, he was starting to enjoy the moment.

He eventually spoke up. He was still wary about the trust thing, he was careful. He trusted no-one. He reminisced about the good old days, as anecdotes; he told of a time when, for example, they placed a uniformed officer as bait for when the bars and clubs emptied. 'The usual criminal, bad-guy element would see the lone fresh-faced officer and call abuse.' He told them. 'The officer would remain impassive. They would walk on by, becoming braver and surer and more abusive when the officer failed to respond. Several yards further along the street three of the biggest, meanest officers would suddenly appear from an alley, drag them in and dish out instant summary justice without the need for a law court. The unruly got a few bruises and learned a lesson in life and new found respect for the police. They understood pain. There were no complaints in those days; just an understanding.' Rather than make suggestions which could come back and bite him, he gave other examples of policing the good old-fashioned way. Events now assigned to the past.

Heads nodded and faces lit up at Sarge's stories. Even the senior officers liked what they heard. Sarge trained, sergeant Stevie, kept the momentum going, he told of other underhanded deeds which kept the criminal element in their place. They were stories similar to Sarge's except they were of more recent times. Sarge's pride swelled for his prodigy; he was surprised at all the underhanded tactics he'd used. He was proud of him.

The atmosphere became more relaxed and trusting. Things were happening but everything was worded very carefully, very diplomatically, so as not to be accused of any conspiracy. It was clear what the senior officers wanted, there was no other way. The Establishment had to win, at all costs.

The meeting was lengthy. Sarge reminisced some more about a time he and his men ambushed a gang of prolific night-time store raiders. They set them up and waited in position to pounce, and pounce hard. They were a professional gang who scanned the police airwaves so they'd know if their activities were mentioned. Sarge got around that by giving out a password known only to his units. When the observer at the target location radioed the agreed password, it meant that particular store was being attacked. The password was broadcast. The officers pounced, caught them in the act and arrested them. They made sure most of the gang required hospitalization. Many in the meeting liked that plan, it was met with smiles and nods. It was a framework for what could be implemented upon the Lords and their gang

The meeting dragged out, painfully. Nothing was set in concrete and any outsider listening-in would think that only ideas had been floated. There were many suggestions and no firm plans, just nods and winks and un-responded to remarks often greeted with approving smiles and noises expressing approval.

The meeting was concluded when Lomax summarized the difficulties; the need to act within the law and that any action taken would be supported by him and other senior officers. That was his get-out card if it all went wrong; he would quote his statement and others would confirm it. He told Sarge and his Sarge-trained oppo that, *he'd leave it with them*. Everyone knew what he meant but it was always open to interpretation one way or the other. Sarge and the others were in no doubt what he meant.

Finally, Lomax changed the subject to a new proposal to have civilian police officers with few powers but whose job it would be to interact with the public and to be the eyes and ears of the police. To gather intelligence to feed back to the Regulars. 'The police Union opposed it, labelling it as, - *policing on the cheap that would be ineffective and detrimental to the service. Unprofessional; inefficient - a waste of public money.*' Lomax said. 'They would be known as Community Support Officers who would be there to support the regular cops.' He toed the party-line and said, *he was all for it. It would be a great benefit to the police service.* He went on to say that, *if anyone wanted to know what the meeting had been about, that it was a discussion on the proposal of these new-style civilian community police officers.*

The meeting dismissed, Sarge and his oppo headed for the canteen where they grabbed a coffee and found a quiet corner to discuss the real issues of the meeting. They were joined by Gerry Smithson who wanted a private word with Sarge. He took him to one side. He told him that Lomax had contacted him about the problem with the Lord Brothers, that's why he had the meeting with him earlier that morning. He said *he had hoped to have spoken with him before the general meeting and that's what the Post It was about. He said Lomax was going to support Sarge with the pending I.A matter involving Gull being given 'a new hair parting,' in return for sorting the Lord problem. Lomax couldn't tell him directly, he needed to keep some distance in case it went wrong,* he told him. *He was just his messenger boy,* he added. He said it would be a win-win situation all round, for all of them; Lomax gets his problem cleared up, in return he gets I.A off both his and Sarge's back's. He reassured Sarge that he'd be given a free rein as no-one else seemed to be getting a grip of the Lord's issue. He encouraged him to sort the problem immediately. He finished by adding, *the Establishment would support him*. He then left the sergeants to sort out the detail.

Sarge returned to his oppo and sat next to him.

He looked up at Sarge, expectantly. 'Game on?' He grinned and wrung his hands in anticipation.

Sarge chewed a moment. His face set. 'We need to be careful here. If this all goes belly up, it'll be down to us. Lomax and company will be back-peddling for all they're worth, that's for sure.'

He lost his smile and enthusiasm. 'They sounded like they'll be right behind us, whatever we do.'

He looked at him sideways a moment. 'Oh, they will be.' He said with sarcasm, 'Along with I.A shoving the devils fork right up your arse towards losing your job, even going to jail. Me too.'

'Christ, what you got planned?'

'Who knows what Christ has planned? Anyway, less of the *Christ*.'

'What?'

'You heard of Kairos?'

'Kairos?'

'The bible? Nothing. Forget it.' He chewed hard.

There was a pause. He studied Sarge to see if it was safe to ask. 'Heard you'd gone religious.' There was a cautious moment. 'Is it true?'

Sarge looked straight ahead. He chewed. Said nothing.

'Didn't believe it.'

'Not religious.' He said firmly, 'Just opened my mind to certain things, that's all. You ought to try it. It's quite enlightening, empowering.'

There was an awkward moment.

'Sorry.' He paused. 'Are we planning a 'Kairos' moment for the Lord's and their associates, Sarge?'

There was a short moment.

'You heard too, huh? Well, it doesn't mean that but, in a way, yes, I suppose we may be.' He chewed. 'But actually, it's of their own doing. They'll get what's coming to them.'

'So, what is it?'

'Kairos?' He sniffed. 'In this case and for right now, it says in Romans thirteen; *Kairos time is here. It calls for action, conversion and transformation - a change of life.*'

'Wow. Really? I like the sound of it. You have been bashing the bible.'

'No. Not really.' He snapped. 'I happened to read it last night, by chance.' He flashed back to last night at Mandy's. He smiled to himself.

'By chance? Or was it a Kairos moment?'

Sarge frowned at him and pondered.

'Only joking, Sarge,' he laughed.

Sarge didn't.

They got down to business and talked tactics. They made their plans then went their separate ways.

Sarge returned to the office. No-one was there except for Lomax. He was browsing Roy's desk and had his back to him.

'Can I help you, sir?'

Lomax swung around quickly and puffed hard on his pipe when he saw Sarge.

There was a moment.

He coughed anxiously and pulled his pipe from his beard. He leaned over to a metal waste paper bin and loudly banged his ash into it. He straightened up. 'Close the door, Sarge.'

Sarge looked at Lomax warily as he sluggishly carried out his request.

'Have you made plans to sort the problem?'

'The Lord's?' He flashed a smile, 'As good as done, sir.'

'Well, you are known for your ability in planning.' He pushed his empty pipe back into the side of his mouth. Gripping it with his teeth as he spoke, 'Talking of which, do you ever think of Petty?'

He sniffed. Eyebrows raised, 'No sir.' He paused. 'And what has my ability in planning to do with Petty?'

'Oh, nothing. I just wondered if you ever gave him a thought.'

He smiled. 'Only when I want cheering up, then I imagine that night's events.' He got serious. 'I don't like the way you linked my planning abilities with what took place that night. Petty got what was coming to him.'

There was an awkward moment.

'Perhaps I'm just getting a little paranoid, sir.' He coughed.

'Perhaps. Well anyway, I'd like to support you on the Gull case. I.A wants to know why you cracked him over the head. You of all people know you should aim for the fleshy parts, not the head.'

'That's what I was aiming for but he moved and got his head in the way.' He chuckled.

'They're not happy, Sarge, you being a baton instructor and all. They said you should have gone for his arms or legs.'

'The hallway we were in was way too narrow. I told them that. There wasn't room to swing a cat, let alone my baton. Aimed for his shoulder but I'm not that accurate. If I.A had more operational experience, they'd have understood.'

'What about his broken nose?'

'What about it?'

There was a brief moment.

He smiled. 'Stick to your story, Sarge.'

'Oh, I will, sir.' He paused. 'I definitely will.'

'What, that you'll stick to your story?'

Sarge made no reply and remained blank.

'Try not to be so stick-happy in future, Sarge.'

'I'll try.' He thought a moment. 'We'll make sure we cover our backs if that's what you mean, sir.' Eyebrows raised.

There was a long moment.

Sarge chewed. 'Anything else, sir? You look like you want to say something.'

'You scratch my back, Sarge, I'll scratch yours. I could do a lot for your career, you know that. You can't always be a one-man band.' He patted him on his upper arm.

Sarge nodded and chewed.

'We stay within the law with the Lord's, Sarge.' He ordered, not meaning it.

'I'll remember that, sir.' He chewed. 'Now if you'll excuse me, I got a list of stuff to do.'

'One other thing, Sarge,' he paused. 'You know, you can trust me. Well, what I'd like to know is what really happened between you and Gull? I've never been in that situation. I'd love to hear it from the horse's mouth.'

Sarge stared at him, said nothing.

Lomax got the message, nodded and left.

Several nights passed without incident from the Lord's.

Then a little after 2 a.m. on a particularly dark night Mandy drove a plain car out of the station parking lot.

It was like any other night, except that night a full team of nineteen officers remained on duty to cover the night shift. They had something that needed attending to.

Just down the road was a couple of boy-racer's cars parked up, tinted windows, big-bore exhausts, boom boxes; the Lord's and friends.

They *clocked* her leaving the parking lot. She drove slowly by and did her best to look nervous. They took the bait. Two cars followed her; two more joined the convoy in front. All full of angry young men, they repeatedly flashed their lights, speeded up then suddenly braked. They blew their horns, hung from the windows, screamed and hollered. One of the rear cars pulled level with her and swerved towards her. She kept her position.

They came to a long stretch of out-of-the-way road. She'd led them there. The cars in front slowed, the ones behind closed in. She allowed it.

She held her nerve and forced the front cars to keep her pace until she approached a disused filling station just off the main drag. She knew they wouldn't want to damage their precious cars, they meant everything to them. They boxed her in. She slowed to a halt.

One of the Lords' swaggered over to her door and opened it. He stuck his head in. Mandy remained calm and impassive. His associate, holding a baseball bat, opened the passenger door.

He was instantly greeted by a man who sprang out of the rear of her vehicle wearing a scary latex horror mask of a wrinkly ugly old guy with big crooked teeth, maniacal smile and wispy hair. The baton he was holding went unnoticed.

He was shocked and instantly stepped back. He took up a stance to swing his baseball bat at the scary-masked man.

Unsure of the surreal sight before him, he hesitated. He was stunned by the appearance of the masked-man then further stunned as a baton crashed down upon his skull. He fell to the floor semiconscious, covered in blood.

Lord straightened up in disbelief as a hulk of a guy wearing a pink sequined ballerina's dress, Doc Marten boots, Mini Mouse mask and boxing gloves, exited the other rear door. He was as wide as he was tall and took one pace towards him. Lord froze in disbelief until a swift right-hook sent him spinning to the floor. He landed in a crumpled heap, motionless. The big guy took a few more steps to land another punch to make sure. But it wasn't necessary, he was out cold. 'Nice one Roy.' Shouted the man in the old man's mask.

The other four cars started to unload as eight men in balaclavas ran screaming from behind the station. They carried baseball bats and commanded the disembarking occupants get back into their vehicles. Most complied. Those that didn't and made the choice to stand and fight were struck; arms, legs and ribs. They put up strong resistance but were soon overcome. Then they laid into the cars, a bat wheedling man either side, the windshields and side windows were furiously smashed. The noise was deafening. The occupants inside adapted the foetal position covering their heads as the glass imploded in on them. It was over in seconds.

Police vehicles, lights and sirens wailing, converged front and rear.

The police cars screeched to a halt. The scary masked-man, ballerina and balaclava men disappeared into the night.

A sergeant and the cop who had been forced to move to a secret address, were first out, followed by other uniformed officers. The gang were rounded up and thrown into the detention cells. Some required a hospital visit first. *They'd brought it upon themselves,* they were told.

Early next morning, Sarge paid a call on the two Lord brothers who were sharing a cell. They didn't look good, bruises, swellings and dried blood was everywhere.

Roy joined him.

They took them into an interview room. It was small with a fixed table and four loose chairs; the lightweight kind with moulded plastic seats and metal tubular legs.

They all remained standing, across the table, facing each other.

He chewed awhile as he scanned over their injuries. He snorted a laugh at them then chewed some more. Roy was quiet.

He chinned the air, 'Ok you two, it ends here.' He chewed angrily. 'You got that?'

They made no reply.

'We are the law; the Establishment. Scum like you and your friends are never going to win,' he growled. 'Sooner or later you'll always lose.'

They made no reply.

'Is that clear?' he boomed.

Still no reply.

'Arson - damaging police vehicles and property, terrorizing police families and policewomen is only going to get you more of what you got last night.'

No reply.

'So, you'd better pray that everyone behaves themselves from now on.'

There was a silent moment.

'So, what's going to happen to us?' asked one of the Lord's. 'You going to let us walk out of here?'

'No. You're going to get charged, you're going to court. That's what's happening. You're never going to be law-abiding citizens but from now on you're going to be on your best behaviour.'

He looked away from Sarge and over at Roy, he pointed, 'I was attacked by that big bastard. He was in that ballerina costume. We know it was him.' he shouted angrily.

His brother joined in. 'Everyone knows him around here. Look at him, look at him, he's a freak. He's as wide as a barn door.' He looked him up and down and sneered. 'We knew it was him last night. And those other idiots in balaclavas, they were all you lot!'

The officers remained impassive.

The other Lord looked at Sarge then spoke up. 'And him with the mask on. I bet that was you. We want to complain. Officially.'

Sarge took two deliberate steps around the table and went nose to nose with Lord. His brother made an aggressive move. Roy instantly stepped forward and slammed him hard against the wall, pinning him there one handed.

Sarge chewed. 'What mind-warping substances you been on Lord?' He sneered then looked over at Roy. 'You know of anyone on our patch matching those descriptions officer?' He chuckled. 'A ballerina with boxing gloves and a masked-man.'

Roy shook his head. 'Did he look like a fairy? I know a few of them, Sarge.' He laughed.

The Lord's scowled.

The one not held by Roy muttered, 'We heard you were gay.'

Roy turned his full attention to him. 'What of it?' He barked.

He froze.

Sarge chewed and broke the moment, 'You got anything else to say, Lord?'

'About what?'

'Maybe about the colour of his skin. 'Cos if you have, I'm sure the officer would like to hear it?'

There was a moment.

'No,' he said quietly then looked downwards, submissively.

'We were off duty last night. I've no idea what this officer was doing but I was tucked-up safely in my bed.' He chuckled then seriously said, 'Well you tell those descriptions to whoever you want.' He chewed.

'We have. No-one believes us.'

The officers laughed.

'I don't expect you to change your criminal ways of thieving, Twoc'ing and assaulting. You are who you are. But always remember, we are who we are.' He paused. 'But on the other matters, have we an understanding?' He sniffed.

They made no reply.

Roy released his hold and stepped over to Sarge. Sarge stepped backwards.

Lord with indignation, adjusted his clothing where he'd been held. He was red-faced, he was angry.

There was a short moment.

Without warning, Roy took a long step forward and bitch-slapped both Lord's, who were standing next to one another, with speed and force; palm of the hand to one then a backhander to the other, like swatting flies, one after another in quick succession.

They had no time to react, they went over like skittles. Dazed, they hit the walls then landed on the deck, noisily. They became verbal as they tried to re-orientate themselves. Roy growled and flung a couple of the chairs in the air, they bounced and clattered around. The Lord's curled up, covering their heads; afraid, intimidated. They were both over six foot but looked small and insignificant as they cowered.

Sarge felt overwhelming pride at Roy's performance, he half expected him to roar and beat his chest like King Kong.

A voice from the other side of the door asked if everything was ok.

'Fine, officer,' shouted Sarge. 'We're just getting control of the situation in here.' He laughed.

The brothers quickly got to their feet with the help of Roy who held them both up against the wall by their throats. He made them be quiet.

They were angry but knew they were outmatched. They reluctantly complied.

'Either of you heard of Kairos?' asked Sarge.

Roy looked over in surprise at Sarge. 'Sarge!' He cringed.

Sarge ignored him.

He released his grip and took a step back.

'Kairos?' asked one of the Lord's. He massaged the side of his face where Roy had given him a slap. 'Who the hell's Kairos. I don't know him.'

'It's not a, *who*.' He chewed. 'I discovered it recently. It's been around forever. It's a time.' He sounded as though he was giving a sermon. 'It can be a dangerous time.' He chewed some more as he chose his words. 'It is critical to recognize it, for if you allow it to pass, the loss will be immeasurable. There is a burden of responsibility tied up in the recognition of the Kairos,' He chewed. 'That's from Luke.' He nodded and smiled.

There was silence.

Roy frowned.

'Luke who?' asked one of the Lord's.

'The bible,' he chewed. 'It's from the bible, you moron.'

More silence.

The Lord's looked at Roy. 'What the hell is he on about?' asked one.

'Well.' He hesitated. 'You think about what the sarge just told you. Think about it.' said Roy.

'I may be older and smaller than you two but when push comes to shove, I can shove better than most, as you've discovered.' He chewed. 'Just you remember that.'

'So, it was you in the mask last night!'

He stepped forward. 'I've been fighting scum-bags like you all my life. Remember that too.'

There was a moment.

Sarge stepped back and rapped on the door.

The brothers were led back to their cell.

   The weeks turned into months and there were no more attacks on the police by the Lord's or their gang. They still drove their, now battered, beloved boy-racer cars and continued their criminal activities. That was never going to change. But the Establishment had reasserted itself, chief Lomax was a much happier individual.

For so many years the Lord's had hidden behind their *rights* and used the law to protect themselves from being prosecuted for their wrong-doings. It was an overburdened judicial system that was lenient beyond reason and effectiveness. The Lord's had come to believe that they were uncontrollable and immune to the law. The S*ystem* had encouraged them in that belief.

They knew the System and had made a mockery of it. But they had crossed the borders of an unwritten law that had mutual respect woven into it. A respect shown to the police by the criminal and in return a respect shown to the criminal by the police. Mutual. Without that time-honoured respect, matters become personal. And it had become personal. They were out of control.

Respect is often given and acknowledged as a *right; expected, the norm,* it's part of the fabric which holds a society together. It is essential.

Sometimes when it's not given; it *has* to be won.

CHAPTER 6

GOOD TIMES.

The weeks rolled into more months; everyone living their Kairos time; getting on with life, living their moments and storing up future events in time. Some moments were predictable, like Sarge and Mandy's. They had rekindled old feelings but fought to keep them under control. Relationships had hurt both of them in the past. They had an unspoken understanding that they would reach a certain level of emotions and honesty in their friendship and no more. One that could be ended as quickly as it had started so neither of them got hurt. It wasn't going to be forever. They'd learned that nothing lasts forever. But this way, they would be forever friends. No loyalties, no expectations, no control, arguments, hidden agenda, rights or love. That should equate to no jealousy, were freedom reigns supreme. Which seems fine; ideal - except the human trait rears its complex human head from time to time.

The only accepted rule in their case being an unspoken constitution that neither one sleeps with anyone else in the meantime; forbidden are any restrictions placed upon each other and jealousy was a no no. Freedom was all.

The couple had their needs, not only sexually but also in terms of companionship, the interaction between two people and the sense of not being isolated. The warmth of a hug, another human-being pressed against another. The affection and want felt by both in a simple embrace. The physical act of release and intimacy, a powerful part of mankind's evolution - just as strong as the need to eat, sleep, survive and reproduce - basic elements that few can resist. Mandy and Sarge were no different. They had strong instincts in many ways. They kept in check their desire for anyone else and so sex without strings was liberating for them; passion without the emotion, a relationship without ties. Neither one wanted to feel they needed anyone. They wanted it to remain a choice. Through painful experience they wouldn't allow anyone to become so close where an attachment was formed.

Yet secretly, both craved normality; to be able to let down their barriers. To expose their emotions and so reveal their vulnerabilities and risk becoming dependent upon another person. To loosen the control and hold over their own lives, plans and destiny. Their future Kairos times ahead, mundanely predictable. To express their feelings freely and safely. To be part of someone else. Both closed their eyes to what they really wanted.

But the overwhelming power of love raised its powerful head. It was almost 3 a.m. Sarge rolled onto his back; spent, exhausted, content. She lay, glowing and quiet on his outstretched arm. Her breathing was rapid, her heart pounded. She tingled. They slowly calmed.

She gently stroked his chest affectionately. He succumbed, faced her and caressed her face. Their eyes met; they said everything.

There was a long moment.

They both knew what the other was thinking, or thought they did. She had let down her resistance. Him too.

Although he was much older than her, she didn't care. She loved him all the more for that except she knew love was outside the terms of their relationship and her own self-imposed rules, though he was the one who stringently enforced the conditions. She knew that. She went along with him believing one day that he may weaken. She lived in hope. She knew she wasn't as self-controlled as he was.

He saw a young, beautiful woman beside him; lean, her skin taught, soft and smooth, her eyes bright, her lips full. Her breasts; perfect. For a moment he wanted to believe. He wanted to believe that they'd always be together, no cheating, no lies, deceits or arguments, no controlling or jealousy. He wanted to be who he really was and to show it there and then. He wanted to show her love; to be vulnerable. He wanted to kiss her and tell her how he really felt.

His hand affectionately ran down over her breasts and stomach then tantalizingly found her crotch; her hips moved welcomingly with pleasure as it did so. Her breathing increased as did the feeling of love she had for him. He too felt love.

Her legs relaxed open for him as he slid his fingers slowly, gently, back and forth over her plump *quim*.

Emotions fired up, both were soon short of breath and pleasing one another until he could resist no more. She too was desperate to feel him fully inside of her.

Passion intense; their feelings vented through their actions. He pumped her hard as she writhed and made sounds that he had to shut from his mind; he wanted it to last.

It felt like love. She whimpered from time to time as he banged hard to give her greater pleasure, though it was also an expression of his passionate love for her. They kissed between gasps for breath.

Panting, he mouthed her nipples, kissed her shoulders and neck. He wanted desperately to please her to her absolute limit.

She could resist no more. 'I love you!' She blurted.

Caught up in the moment, he banged her harder and he too cried out that he loved her. His voice was loud and emotional like someone finally confessing and the relief of the admission. Relief.

She gave an excited shrill of satisfaction. Not only through pleasurable stimulation by sex but from his words; the achievement that she had got what she really wanted; to hear the man tell her how he felt. She always thought he loved her but longed to hear it.

She cried. Tears of joy. The sex was now secondary. She loved more, clung tighter and kissed harder. She felt him quicken then tense as a hot fountain exploded inside of her.

He slowed until he became still. His head was buried in her neck. Heart pounding, hot and breathless, she waited.

She waited motionless all but for a slight roll of her hips occasionally, in response to him.

His breathing returned to normal.

She was patient.
She wanted so much to see his face and tell him how she felt; love.
He took his weight on his elbows and raised himself to look into her eyes. He saw that they were tearful, happy, dilated and beautiful.
A boundary had been crossed. She was delighted.
The realization began to dawn on him.
She was smiling.
He smiled in return, blinked a couple of times in thought, then frowned.
She told him once again, *she loved him.*
There was a long moment.
His feelings were waning. He couldn't allow himself to lose control; to be vulnerable and dependent on another. The risk of hurt. A predictable future, the complications of a relationship; he couldn't do it. He wanted to, but he couldn't.
His expression and loving feelings faded.
She detected it.
They both knew.
She lost her smile.
They said nothing.
He carefully withdrew and rolled off.
It was silent and awkward.
He looked back over at her and raised a smile.
She smiled back, her eyes searching his face.
He pulled her in close. Nothing was said. They were tired and still....

  It wasn't too long before her alarm was waking them.
They had their morning ritual and headed for work. She dropped him away from the station. That's how he wanted it.
Sarge entered the office a few seconds before Mandy. Roy was already at his desk. He sensed Sarge was not his usual self and a little prickly in the *good morning pleasantries.*
Sarge made a brew and avoided eye contact with Mandy as he passed her a tea. He did the same with Roy before sitting at his desk and reading through the *sitrep.*
Roy felt some tension in the air. He looked for reasons; his eyes covertly darted between Mandy and Sarge. He knew they were different. He tried to pick up on what was going on. He'd suspected there was something between them for a while. It was clear there was something different. He finished his drink and found an excuse to leave the room.
Mandy couldn't help glancing over at Sarge.
He was aware, but ignored her. He got on with his work. Time slipped by.
She went to make another drink. 'Do you want one?'
He shot her a look. 'No thanks,' he replied awkwardly before returning to reading.
There was a moment.
Smiling apprehensively, 'What's wrong?' she asked.
He looked up coldly and shrugged. He knew the answer.
Distressed, the corners of her mouth sagged. 'What's going on?'
He looked up at her then glanced away. 'We're in works time now. I've got things to do,' he said coldly.

'No, there's something else. Come on, what is it?'

He nervously coughed. 'Ok. Truth is, we shouldn't have done what we did last night. We've both been down that road before. It's no good for either of us.'

Her face reddened. 'You were all over me like a rash last night; telling me how you felt. Now this.' Her eyes flooded. 'You're like all the rest.'

He coughed. Shot her a fleeting glance. 'Sorry.' Clearly troubled, he looked down and shook his head slightly.

She fixed her stare on him and bit her lip so as not to cry.

He looked stern. He didn't look up. 'We shouldn't see one another for a while.'

There was a long moment.

He nervously patted his pockets, looking for gum; he was out.

A tear rolled down her face. 'Commitment-phobe!' she snapped.

He felt embarrassed. He coughed to clear his tense throat.

She stormed towards the door as Lomax strolled in. She brushed by him, head down to hide her face.

He frowned. 'Problem, Sarge?' He glanced to where Mandy had just left.

He stood up and sniffed. 'Er, PMT, sir.' He tried to laugh. It didn't work. He hadn't noticed her in the doorway until after his remark. She'd clearly heard him. Her face crumpled into hurt and tears, she turned and left. It made him frown.

Lomax swivelled to see what Sarge had seen but she had gone.

He puffed thoughtfully on his pipe; he did that when he couldn't strike up conversation or when his devious mind was working overtime. He did a lot of pipe-puffing.

Sarge wasn't in the mood to make conversation.

The difficult moment was broken when Roy walked back in. He acknowledged chief Lomax then Sarge. Lomax turned and wandered out, leaving a trail of smoke.

Roy looked at Sarge, rolled his eyes about Lomax's odd behaviour and laughed. Sarge would normally have joined in but remained stony-faced. He picked up the *sitrep* again; flicked over to the second page.

'I see a Yammy 350 power valve got stolen. Second one in a month.'

Roy said nothing. He chewed.

'I have an idea who might have them but I'd need someone to call in with information.' He looked at Roy, eyebrows raised. 'If you get my drift.'

'Why you bothered about motorcycles, Sarge? It's not what we do in this department'

'Best you don't know.' He winked. 'A means to an end.'

Roy remained blank.

He looked back over the sitrep. 'I've been waiting for this to happen.' He smiled. 'There's more than one way to skin a cat, as they say.'

Roy nodded in puzzlement. His mind was elsewhere.

It told sarge everything. 'Ok. What's on your mind matey?'

'You and Mandy ok, Sarge?'

He sighed and deflected by searching himself for gum.

Roy threw him his packet.

'She thinks the world of you. You could do worse you know.'

He popped in some gum and chewed fast. 'Cheers, Roy. I didn't want to hear that.'

More awkward days passed. Sarge was troubled. Mandy took some leave. His troubles didn't go away.

A new recruit was assigned to Vice; *Exploration week,* they called it. Sarge had his own terms for it.

During that same week Roy had a meeting with an informant who'd reported in about the possible whereabouts of the stolen 350 Power Valves. He'd been reliable in the past and had secretly *grassed up* criminal associates, many times. Some did long prison stretches for some very serious stuff. If ever they found out he'd grassed them up, they'd kill him. He knew that. Criminals hated *grasses*. He took the recruit along for the ride. They met up with him at an out the way location. He gave him and the recruit the information they were looking for, an address just out of town. He got paid some on account and the rest was to follow if his information was correct. He was to firm up the facts and report back.

Roy was experienced at handling informants, he cultivated lots of them. He had a good working relationship with this particular one, even though he was scumbag of the worst kind. He would do anything for money. *He'd shop his own mother*, as they say; anything for money. Roy had used him on many occasions. He'd been a useful tool.

The recruit witnessed the transaction but felt she was missing something. She told Roy that she didn't believe the *grass*. She said she thought he was fabricating it; *as though he'd been told what to say.*

Roy was surprised at her powers of perception. He didn't tell her that, instead he told her to keep her inexperienced opinions to herself. He softened his remark by adding that he thought the *Grass* (informant) had taken a liking to her, and who knows, he may even want to give his information to her in future rather than him. None of it was true but he said it to make her feel better. He was that kind of guy.

She was flattered by the remark. She believed it because she wanted to believe it.

A few days later she got a message to contact the *Grass,* he had what they wanted. She was proud and excited that she'd made such an impression that he wanted to give *her* the information rather than Roy.

They met up. He claimed he'd seen the stolen motorcycles for himself; they were inside the thief's house. *He was assembling one decent machine from two donor one's. He doesn't open his door to anyone he doesn't know.* He told her. He said the thief's real name was Cross.

She reported back to Roy. A warrant to search the place was taken out.

Early the following morning two plain vans were parked. One was in Cross's Street with Roy and the recruit inside; the other was just around the corner.

The morning wore on. There was no sign of movement from Cross's house. The hours passed; the day was becoming unproductive.

A decision was made. As a result, shortly afterwards, a postman was delivering along the street, he wasn't the regular one. He called at Cross's with a large jiffy bag in hand and knocked.

Nothing happened.

He ran his tongue over his teeth. He kept his head down and knocked harder and louder.

Still nothing happened.

He waited.

The living room blinds twitched.

The Jiffy bag was obvious.

He chewed as he stared down at his feet. His tongue checked his teeth again. He waited.

The door opened cautiously, part way.

The Postie partly glanced up from underneath his cap.

The occupant wore coveralls and a black baseball cap.

'Signature please, sir.' Is all that was said. He turned away, stalled and fumbled in his sack. He kept his head down. He chewed.

The occupant waited in the half-open doorway. He nervously tugged on his peak.

The white van from farther along the street pulled up nearby.

It went almost unnoticed; the occupant was focused on the Postie.

He sniffed and chewed then pulled out a receipt book.

Cross impatiently tugged at his peak again then waited some more.

Roy and the recruit climbed out of the van and headed their way unnoticed.

He chewed, fumbled open a page and handed the book over.

He took it.

The Postie padded his pockets for his pen. Found it, dropped it, then picked it up. He apologized and passed him it. He kept his head down.

Roy and the recruit were closing in fast.

Cross signed his false name and handed back the book. He looked up and saw the two heading his way. His instincts told him something wasn't right and that he should shut his door. But he wasn't sure. Confused, he hesitated.

'Mr. Cross,' said Roy, as he walked up the garden path.

Cross nervously pulled at his peak again, he dithered.

The Postie turned and walked away, almost unnoticed.

'Mr. Cross,' he said again. 'That is your name, isn't it?' as he jammed his foot in the door.

Cross made no reply. He guessed who the callers were. He was shocked and annoyed that he'd not listened to his instincts. He knew he should have slammed the door and done a *runner*.

He was handed the warrant.

He took it.

He was told they had court authority to search his home for the stolen motorcycles.

He read the warrant for himself.

They waited patiently.

He finished reading.

Roy stepped in.

Cross, though small, was defiant.

He was asked to step aside and allow access.

He remained.

Without any warning, Roy suddenly palmed him in the chest with no great effort. Cross flew backwards. He was angry but powerless to do anything about it. All he could do was shout and curse.

They entered and quickly found the dismantled parts of two Power Valves in his kitchen and the incomplete construction to make just one good machine from the two.

Roy took out his cuffs and gestured to Cross to hold out his wrists by showing how.

Protesting his innocence all the while, he reluctantly limped a few steps over to him and complied.

He told him of his rights *not to saying anything unless he wished to do so.*

He made no reply.

'How come you have a limp, Mr. Cross?' asked Roy, knowingly.

He scowled, 'An accident, officer.' he said facetiously. 'Leave it at that.'

'Ok, will do.' Smiling. He nodded over at the motorcycles. 'You have quite a weakness for your Power Valves, haven't you Cross?'

Wrists held out as instructed, the ratchets clicked as the cuffs tightened.

Just around the corner the 'Postie' threw his uniform and gear into the back of the van. He climbed in, sat, waited and chewed.

The recruit set about searching drawers and cupboards. Roy poked around too. Cross looked on.

Roy noticed substantial security locks on all the window fastenings The rear door had heavy bolts. 'You afraid of getting burgled, Cross?' He chinned at the security.

Cross's eyes followed. 'Don't want any thieving bastard breaking into here, or pigs like you.'

'Yeah. You're all the same, your type's, Cross. You spend your life in crime and making countless victims but you're the worst kind when it's you that becomes the victim. You all feel so badly done to.'

'That's right officer. And I'll be officially complaining about you referring to me as a *type*. I'm supposed to be treated like anyone else. I know my rights.'

'You ever been a victim, Cross?'

He said nothing.

'You ever been burgled?'

'Never. Why?'

'Oh, nothing. Just curious.'

'That's a strange thing to ask, Mr. Police Officer.'

Roy shrugged. Said nothing.

Cross pondered a moment. 'Here, what you up to, asking me that sort of question?'

'You sure you've never been a victim?'

'Positive. Your records would show if I had. No-one could break into here.'

Roy turned to the recruit. 'You hear what the man said? *Never been burgled.* He's a lucky man don't you think?'

She smiled and shrugged.

'Have you ever been violated, Cross?'

'Never. Well, what do you mean? Why?'

'Oh nothing.' He smiled. 'Heard someone knocked you off your motorcycle recently. But I'm sure that was just an accident.' He smiled.

Cross glared and reddened. He focused back on the recruit now poking around. She felt uncomfortable from his attention.

'The warrant is to search only for the bikes or their parts, nothing else. You have two complete bikes there so that's the end of it, Mrs. Policewoman.' Cross sneered.

The recruit stopped in her tracks. She agreed with his remark and told Roy they should stop their search.

Cross added, 'You search for anything else and whatever else you find will be outside the warrant. An illegal search. Not admissible in court.' He smiled smugly, then looked at Roy.

He shrugged. 'The man's right. We can't search anywhere else. The rest of the house is off limits. That's it. Just check the frame and engine numbers.' He paused. 'You do know your rights, don't you, Cross.'

He smiled confidently. 'Yeah, I know my rights.' He taunted them. 'You won't find any ID anywhere either, no frame or engine numbers, no registration numbers. Nothing. You'll never prove the bikes don't belong to me.'

'Why, you filed off the numbers already?' asked Roy.

'No comment, officer.'

They loaded the parts into their van and called for a patrol to collect their prisoner. When they arrived, he was allowed to witness the door being locked before leaving. Roy made a point of proving to him it was secure. They headed for the station in convoy. They passed the parked van with the single occupant. Only Roy noticed it. He chose to ignore it. He chewed.

The van's occupant climbed out as soon as they passed and went out of sight. He walked to Cross's house and casually bent down to pick up a small lump of Plasticine laid on the grass. It had a key impression in it. He put it in his pocket.

Down at the station Cross was being searched. His pockets were emptied and his personal possessions; a door key, a comb, packet of gum, a packet of condoms, a block of blue pool-cue chalk, a wallet containing a few notes, loose coins and a laminated solicitors business card were placed on the charge-room counter. One woman police officer picked up the condoms and pool-cue chalk and examined them.

Cross watched on.

'What are the condoms for, Mr. Cross?' asked policewoman, Poppy Beau Bibby; part of the detention-cell staff. She held up the packet in front of him, finger and thumb only, like it was disgustingly dirty.

He went all shy and coy and was surprised at her question. Then grinned. 'You know…...'

She smiled in a warm, flirting kind of way. 'No. You tell me.'

Still coy: 'They're for, you know…... for………' He hesitated.

'I know,' she interrupted, 'I bet you wear them and look at yourself in the mirror. You do, don't you? I bet you walk up and down in front of the mirror looking at yourself with one on.' She laughed tauntingly.

His face altered. He was clearly angered. 'No, I don't!' He cursed indignantly. 'You stupid slag.'

She said calmly, like a parent to a child, 'Don't be getting all angry in here, Mr. Cross. You're in the wrong place and speaking to the wrong person for that?' It only served to anger him more, she knew it would.

'You're going to get a slap. If you weren't in uniform, I'd give you a slap.' He cursed.

She continued to smile and ignored his threat. She placed the condoms down on the counter. She ran her finger over the block of blue chalk so there was some on her finger. She held it in front of his face. 'And what's this? Eye liner? What are you doing with eye liner?'

He shook his head. 'It's not eye liner,' he cursed. 'It's chalk for the end of a pool cue.'

'Eye liner. We'll record it with your belongings as, Eye Liner,' declared policewoman, Poppy Beau Bibby.

Cross immediately snatched her chalked finger in temper. In a flash she simultaneously struck him hard under his chin with the palm of her free hand; it was an instinctive reaction for her. His face jolted upwards. He reeled backwards and hit the deck. She took two long paces forward so she was standing over him. He didn't know what had hit him as he laid there. His eyes rolled. Shocked he looked up at her with a confused expression. She stared down at him whilst in some kind of subtle Martial Arts stance she'd adopted just in case he wanted some more of the same. Her hands were in a ready to strike position. He considered his options; he decided he didn't want to fight. He remained still. She slowly stepped back. Other officers helped him to his feet and advised him that she was definitely the wrong woman to mess with. He remained quiet and subdued as he was led to a detention cell. His possessions were logged then security sealed in a secure bag.

Meanwhile elsewhere, a key was being cut. The customer, who chewed and sniffed occasionally, told him *the spare had been lost, the only existing one was in use and couldn't be brought in*. The locksmith didn't question or doubt the reason why he had to work from an impression. He had done this kind of thing several times before for this customer. He knew he was a cop but they both played the game of covering their backs like everything was genuine and innocent. It was soon done.

The customer headed for Cross's home with the shiny new key.

It was getting on towards dusk when he arrived; the time just before everyone was returning home from work. He eased into a pair of black leather gloves, donned a black baseball cap, pulled it low and turned up his collar. He sat quietly in his van. He chewed. He bided his time.

Home lights were lit, blinds and curtains were drawn. No-one was around to see him. He climbed out. He knew exactly what he was to do. He was soon walking up the garden path where he'd called earlier dressed as a postman.

The key could have been more precisely cut; it had to be coaxed into turning the five-lever door lock. The passing twenty-five seconds at the door seemed more like long minutes. Then there was a satisfying metallic *clunk* as the lock gave way and the key turned fully. It was followed by immediate entry without looking back. To glance over his shoulder to see if he'd been seen would have only looked furtive and maybe drawn suspicion by any casual observer. He hoped anyone seeing him in the poor light would have thought he was the owner of the house. Besides, realizing he'd been seen would have made no difference, he wouldn't have been able to change that, he was committed to his plan.

Once inside, he remained in the entrance for a moment; still. It was silent and fairly dark. He didn't switch on the lights. The stale scent of cannabis hung in the air. He lifted his left elbow away from his body where a Jiffy bag had been wedged. It broke the silence as it fell from under his jacket. He caught it one handed as it slid down. He pressed the switch on his small flashlight, it gave out a dim red beam which was just bright enough to be useful. Dim enough not to be noticed by anyone outside. He ran it over label on the bag. It was franked with an old date and addressed to a Post Office Box.

He took a moment to reflect on some past events then made his way passed a hall-table. On it he noticed an unopened Jiffy bag, the one delivered and signed for hours earlier. He laughed to himself then carried on up the stairs into the bathroom.

A few minutes later he was without the Jiffy bag he had taken in and was back on the ground floor. He peered out from behind the very same blinds Cross had done not so long ago. He glanced up and down the street. It was clear. Just glowing curtains and slivers of lights in blinds. Behind them, the residents getting on with their evening, oblivious to events nearby.

He grabbed the Jiffy bag from the table as he headed for the door. He exited and locked the door behind him. Once again, the key was difficult and the ticking seconds felt far longer.

The low sun had dropped well below the roof lines. Darkness had replaced it as he made his way back to his van. He pocketed his gloves and cap. He thought of Cross locked up at the station. He glanced at his watch; worked out that he would have been interviewed by now. He would have had his Brief present who would have continually advised him to make *no comment* to the questions asked by the interviewing officers. The police would then be given the option dictated by the law to either charge him with theft of the vehicles, or release him on bail or release him without bail. *As all identifying marks had been erased; the frame and engine numbers were gone. With no positive evidence as to who were the lawful owners of the vehicles, Cross would be getting released any time soon; without charge. Because he knows the system, he would demand the police provide him transport home.* He thought. But that didn't really bother him unduly on this occasion. He had something far greater planned than pinning the theft of two motorcycles on Cross. That was a means to an end. Contented thoughts filled his mind as he drove the police station in the van no one paid attention to. The journey passed quickly; he was soon there. He entered through the main doors.

Cross and his brief were sat next to one another in the station foyer, smiling and chatting. The contented thoughts melted away quickly for Sarge as he deliberately fumbled and delayed in entering the secure door that led from the foyer into the rest of the building. He tried to pick up on their conversation. He heard snippets. It was the same chat he'd heard countless times; talk of victory, beating the system; using the very guidelines woven into the law to minimize miscarriages of justice and the premise that a person is innocent until proven guilty. But it was geared up to encompass and protect the guilty too; the new law made in the 80s, dealing with police and criminal evidence procedure. It was a turning point in the fight against crime. But no so much in a good way. It put in place many obstacles for the police when carrying out an investigation. It was an advancement in defining how things should be done; procedures; it laid out the powers of the police and the rights of the suspect. It was fair to say that the police had been given some clearer powers and extra powers but it was also clear that the criminals were now given extra rights and greater rights. It was almost mandatory for a suspect to have a public funded lawyer. So, lawyers thrived as more state funding was poured into representing suspects.

Lawyers; part of the judicial system, is part of the Establishment. Therefore, it was well funded by the public purse; the tax payer. For decades the majority of politicians were qualified lawyers and many were still concerned in legal practice businesses even whilst in government. So naturally they looked after their own interests. They made the law and the rules; bias human nature. The new law was a booming business, criminal lawyers' offices sprung up all over the place, almost overnight. The gravy train was rich and delicious and they all jumped on board. In the meantime, those criminals who were honest enough to own up to their misdoings before the new law, were now supported and advised by their Briefs to make *no comment* and to *let the police prove the case if they can*, even if it was obvious their client was as guilty as sin. And everyone knew it. The criminal, the lawyers and the police labelled the new law *a Criminal's Charter*. And so, it was.

A wise old inspector of many years' experiences often told Sarge that the judicial system is a system set up to control the masses. And it went back hundreds of years. It wasn't for the upper echelons of society. It wasn't made to apply to them. The old inspector often remarked that the rich, the elite and politicians were rarely held accountable for their corruption, their illegal activities and their dodgy dealings where billions of taxpayer's cash would be diverted to their friends, families and cronies in the name of commerce or expediency. Time and again this was proven. It was the masses that were controlled by laws and got hammered for their wrongdoings.

Cross and his Brief became aware of Sarge's presence. He'd delayed a little too long. They became aware and stopped talking. They looked over to him. He got the message. He avoided eye contact with Cross.

Sarges contented mind changed to anger; he chewed hard and went on through the door. He reflected upon matters as he made his way to the Vice office. Although he'd known in his heart of hearts that Cross would be released and the case wouldn't be proved, it still hurt him to think that once again justice would not be done. And that the owners of the motorcycles would never have their treasured machines returned to them. They would eventually be returned to Cross due to lack of evidence proving they had been stolen and he was under no obligation to prove where he got the bikes from. He would then legitimately be able to build one machine from them and register it with the authorities. *Sure enough, he had his rights protected by the law. But what about the victims' rights?* He pondered. *It was like a game where justice wasn't the issue but how much public money the lawyers could take and who could win in the law courts; the defence or the prosecution, regardless of the truth. As though the system with its rules and the clever lawyers with their clever words is what it was really all about. The lawyers always won; they got handsomely paid in any case; win or lose.* They had nothing to lose.

He was at the office in no time.

Roy was sat at his desk. He didn't look happy.

'Alright, Roy?'

He looked up at Sarge.

'Yeah.' He paused. He put his index finger to his pursed lips and then pointed to Sarge's desk. He carried on. 'Well, no, not really. This bloody system, it's all geared up in favour of the crooks. Cross has been released. He, *no commented,* all the way through interview. His Brief kept putting in his two-penneth.'

Sarge bent over and looked at the underside of his desk where Roy had been pointing. He saw something taped underneath. He straightened back up then nodded at Roy, knowingly. 'I know what you mean.' Agitated, he shook his head. 'I just saw them in the foyer revelling in their triumph.'

'Yeah, they're waiting for a patrol car to give him a lift home. It's a joke. Some days I feel like doing a different line of work. This job's starting to get to me. There's no justice.'

He thought a long moment.

'Well, as an old cop told me when he showed me around as a fresh-faced recruit, *if you wait long enough, you get your own back*. Try and remember that. It always helps me.' He chewed.

'I'm not so sure, Sarge.'

'Keep believing.' He paused. 'Do you know, the older I get and the more I see, the more I believe in the wisdom that old cop used to share with me.'

Roy got up and walked over to the drinks area.

Sarge sat at his desk, ran his eyes over a few *Post It* notes, shuffled his mail then studied the Intel report.

The kettle clicked off. He made them coffee, passed Sarge his, then sat down.

'Do you ever feel like changing things, Sarge?'

He slowly lifted his head from concentrating on the report. He frowned. Focused on Roy's words and said nothing.

'You know,' he nodded to a side, 'like the Lord Brothers incident.'

Sarge remained quiet.

'Why don't we do more stuff like that?'

'Bending the rules?'

'Yes. A means to an end; make the system work. We're supposed to be in charge, not the shits out there on the streets making life hard for everyone. The system's gone soft on the criminal. The victim loses out all the time. We all live in fear and pick up the tab for the thieving bastards.'

Sarge walked over to the door, peeped down the corridor, then closed it. He went back to his desk, threw his chewed gum into a basket and replaced it with a fresh piece. 'You've got to be careful what you say, Roy.' He looked over at the closed door and nodded. 'You never know who is listening.' He laughed. 'I know how you feel. When I joined up, there was a lot of that stuff went on. We made the system work. We were supported by the organization and the Establishment. We had our own set of rules. The criminals did too. It worked. All that's changed. These days you've got to be a one-man band. You can't trust anyone. You have to keep looking over your shoulder these days. In the old days you knew your back was covered. Even our bosses were on our side. Then it all changed. They stopped recruiting your practical ex-armed forces guys and took on more of your academic types, your liberalists; university kids with grand ideas and some radical ideologists who live in fantasy land. They were all promised promotion and that's what it was all about for them, not catching criminals at the sharp end. They headed for the safety of some office in some out of the way department. Well, those very same cops are now the ones who are our senior officers sat in their Ivory Towers dictating policy and how we should run the Force.'

'Force? You mean, *police service*, sergeant. I am under a duty to correct you.' He said sarcastically then laughed.

He ranted, 'Exactly! That kind of stuff. I'm sure it'll be a matter of time before the military will be calling the Royal Air Force and the United States Air Force, the Royal Air Service and the United States Air Service for fear of offending the enemy. The word Force sounding too aggressive, they'd argue. Anyway, thanks for correcting me, officer.' He said sarcastically in return. 'That's what it's come to. It's all political correctness; garnish; bollocks! Undermining everyone and everything we have ever stood for. Centuries of culture, sanity and civilisation being diluted and flushed down the pan. Why? What's their agenda? As an organisation, we've lost sight as to why we come to work. I joined up to get out there and catch the bad guys: protect society, catch the burglars, the assault merchants, your sex offenders, your robbers; not to be brainwashed with the latest trends and buzzwords and to sit around in a classroom and talk about it. Being asked about feelings and how do you feel about this or that BS? Action is what's needed.' He checked his enthusiasm, took a deep breath, slowed and chewed. Calmer; 'Acta non verba - deeds not words.'

Resigned, he said. 'You got that right. I prefer action not words.'

Sarge picked up the Intel report from his desk.

'You see this?' He held up the report. 'Same every day. We have a whole department working nine to five, Monday to Friday, gathering intelligence and churning out figures and statistics. They circulate it to everyone then they all go home and couldn't give a rat's arse. None of them do. And it's what you've got to work at doing or you'll find yourself in a strange place. Don't let it get to you Roy, is what I'm saying. If you care like we do, it can warp your mind. You need to pace yourself if you want to make it to the end and collect your pension for thirty years of your life dealing with all the scumbags and shit that society throws at you.'

'So how do you deal with it, Sarge?'

There was a long moment whilst he stared at him, hard. He sniffed. 'Me? Well, I got my own way of dealing with things. Let's just leave it at that.'

'You mean like your jogging routine?'

'Yeah, well not exactly, but it helps in a different way.'

'What then?'

'You really don't want to know. Leave it at that.'

'Roger that. So why aren't we pro-active anymore, like back in your day? We should be out there taking the battle to the enemy.'

'Cos that's not important anymore. Times have changed. The Force is too accountable to the public and a bunch of individuals who enjoy feeling important and so volunteer to be on the police committee. They tell us what to do now. What other job has unqualified individuals directing and shaping their organization? We have weak management too that never had time to learn how to be good cops or what policing is all about. It used to be an art, a craft. They're out of their depth these days. They don't have the strength of character.' He paused. 'Even if they knew what they were doing, they're not leaders. Their direction is poor, it's based on guess-work and what they've read-up on. They're afraid to disagree with those who want to control the Force. Even if they had the balls and belief to carry out what they're paid for, they'd still put their own career ladders first before doing the right thing and what's best for the job and society. They're all self-centred and putting themselves first. It's just another job to those in charge these days.'

There was long moment.

Wow. They're not all like that, Sarge.'

'No, Roy, they're not. But you know what I mean.'

'Oh, I do. Instead of trying to be progressive and treating the service like a corporation, they should look back at what used to work. It's not a corporation or a business it's a police force and they can't be compared. Even the standard of recruit and the background they're from doesn't seem important anymore.' He paused. 'The Para's Regiment select the right man for the job. At least that's still a good outfit to be part of.' He lowered his tone. 'God help the Regiment if the PC brigade gets their way.'

'You're right in what you say. This job's had it until someone wakes up, sees it for what it is and turns it around. The police Force was a big and important part of society.' He sniffed. 'It was independent of everyone who wanted to meddle; the Chief of police more or less ran things as to how he thought would best serve the public. Now it's all changed. It used to be written in the constitution that the police service had to be none-political. Politicians have changed that. Now we have an unqualified Political Commissioner in every force running the job. They have no police background or experience of running such an organisation yet he tells the Chief and the rest of the Force what to do, what direction to go, what the priorities are. The politicians have won. They have control now. Politicians want to able to say, *due to their meddling, things have improved, that crime figures have gone down, that the public feels safer.* It's a good vote winner. They don't really care about crime. They don't care if you as an individual gets burgled or mugged once a year or three times a year, they live in a different world to us, they aren't affected. We fight and squabble amongst ourselves whilst they live a wonderful life in a nice area surrounded by nice people and get well paid for it too. We're employed just to keep the lid on it so they can have their wonderful lives. There's the privileged and the rich, then there's the less fortunate; the not-so rich; us and the majority of the rest of the population.' He sniffed.

There was a stunned moment.

'Wow, Sarge. You really do feel passionate about law and justice, don't you?'

He nodded thoughtfully. 'Guess I do. I wish I didn't care so much but the truth is, I do. I can't help it.'

Deep in their own thoughts, there was a quiet moment of reflection, sipping of coffee and no eye contact.

He looked back down at the Intel report. 'Take this here. An ex-SAS officer is going around burgling pharmacy's, surgeries and dentists, for drugs. They know his name, what he looks like. Even that he carries a knife - it says here. And he's used it. He does the jobs in the early hours and always goes in through the back way. They say he's in our area and it's known through anonymous information that he's going to do a job on the High Street in the next couple of nights. Says he's known to use accomplices as they've caught a few in recent months.' He laid the sheets back on his desk. 'And what are we as an organization going to do about it?' He slammed his hand on top of the report. 'Nothing. Sweet F.A, that's what.' He looked up at Roy.

'Why aren't we there, staked out, waiting for him?'

'Because it's not a priority. Those who make decisions are sat with their thumbs up their arses not knowing what to do. They're not cops in the same sense we are.' He paused. 'Besides, with the health and safety lot preaching, saying what can and can't be done and the way litigation and suing is so popular lately; no-one wants to get involved. They're all afraid of winding up in court if our ex-SAS man decides *not to come quietly and has to be taken down.'*

'Be nice for a change if some boss had the balls to take a risk and do something pro-active, like in this case.'

'Well, it would be a feather in their cap if they did. I mean, there are only a couple of premises on the high street with rear access so the rest could more or less be eliminated. A couple of cops on overtime, staked out around the back with night vision would get our man, even if he is ex-SAS.'

'Yeah.' He said thoughtfully. 'With the new stab jackets and batons, we got, be a piece-of-piss. Me and you could cover it, easily.'

Sarge leaned over the edge of his desk, there hidden just under the rim was taped a mini-audio recorder. He straightened up and smiled at Roy.

He smiled back, gave a thumbs up. They both grinned and nodded.

Sarge coughed. 'Well, we'll see if any of them have the balls. I can bet you they haven't. In fact, I'm so certain nothing will be done that if I'm wrong, I'll confess to those things the job accused me of.'

'You mean, Petty?'

'Petty? No. I meant Uncle Billy.'

'Sorry. I heard you were in the frame for Petty too and some other stuff.'

He laughed. 'Steady, Roy. Careless talk costs careers. And freedom.' He sniffed. 'But I could tell you a few things I heard about Chief Lomax recently.'

'Oh yeah?'

'If it's true he could be up to his neck in it. He may need to have a feather or two in his cap in the near future if he wants to stay in this job.' He sniffed again and tapped the side of his nose.'

'Tell me more.'

'I will. Grab your coat, I'll tell you over a beer.'

Just then the door opened. It was Lomax, pipe in mouth. He stood insignificantly in the doorway.

A slightly uncomfortable moment past.

'Can I help you, sir?' Sarge chewed, 'Unusual to see you here this late of an evening, sir.'

He sucked clouds of smoke into the air before speaking through the gritted teeth clamped around his pipe, 'Had a few things to take care of, Sarge.' He sucked some more. His eyes involuntarily darted to Sarge's desk, right where the recorder was; a real giveaway.

Sarge noticed, said nothing.

'Wondered if you could help-out, actually.' He stepped into the room. 'The patrols are really busy. I'm trying to avoid using them. The city's opposition politician has got a flat tyre a few miles out of town. He called on the emergency number requesting we assist him. Sounded desperate, apparently. He and his wife were heading home from a civic function and it'll be an hour before the breakdown vehicle will be with them.'

'And the emergency is?' He chewed, hard.

'Well, they want to get home, sergeant. His Jaguar will be recovered later by a tow truck.'

'A Jag, eh? Well sir, if my vehicle breaks down, I wouldn't be calling the police. I wouldn't expect preferential treatment just because I'm a cop. I'm just a nobody as is the fellow with the flat tyre. He's not even a cop.' He shook his head. 'I have better things to do. Besides, why can't he change his own wheel?'

'Why can't you ever just conform, sergeant? He said, exasperated. 'Life could be so much easier for you. For all of us.'

'I'm not employed to be a taxi for some jumped-up individual who thinks he's so important he can use cops to deliver him home. He's not even in Government, he's in opposition, there's no security risk. Tell him to call a taxi, sir. Stand up to him.'

'Well, I'd like you to pick them up. Dispatch has the details.' He sucked hard, his pipe crackled and glowed.

Sarge stood up, glared at Lomax and chewed quickly. He turned to Roy. 'See what I mean? Exactly what we've just been talking about.'

Roy nodded in agreement.

'And what have you just been talking about, sergeant?'

He turned back to Lomax. 'Private conversation, sir. Between me and the officer here. And I'm not picking them up.' Eyebrows raised; eyes wide in defiance.

Lomax puffed hard. 'I'm not asking you, sergeant, I'm ordering you.'

'I'm not doing it, sir.' He paused for thought, 'Unless you're paying overtime. And if you do, try explaining that expense to those in accounting.' He smiled. 'Me and the officer here are now at the end of our shift and we're leaving. Unless there's anything else, sir.' Eyebrows raised.

Sarge pulled his jacket to and sniffed. 'By the way, sir,' he paused, 'I'd be careful about your decision to help out. It would look bad if it was leaked to the newspapers that police patrols were diverted and misused over a flat tyre. A nobody's, flat tyre.

Lomax turned to Roy and smiled, 'How about you officer? I'd appreciate it if you could help me out.'

'Come on, Roy,' said Sarge. 'Home time.'

Roy said nothing, grabbed his helmet off his desk and threaded an arm through his backpack. He clearly felt a little awkward.

Sarge led; Roy followed. They squeezed passed out the door, leaving Lomax looking furious. They walked along the corridor heading for the elevator.

Roy whispered. 'Do you really fancy a pint, Sarge, or did you just say that?'

'Both. I fancied a drink but it was also for effect.' They stopped at the elevator. He pressed the *down* button. The doors whooshed opened immediately. They stepped in together. The *Ground* button pressed; there was a *whoosh* and a *clunk* as the doors closed. He waited for the floor to drop beneath him before continuing. 'Make him fret about what I had on him; what I was going to tell you. Get him worried.'

Roy said nothing. He preened himself in the elevator wall mirror. Flicking his hair, glancing this way and that.

'Listen, how did you know we were bugged? I presume it was Lomax? His eyes gave him away, I saw him glance towards it.'

'It was just by chance. I came in early….'

'As you do.' Sarge interrupted.

The elevator car jerked to a halt. The doors whooshed open. Two senior officers from I.A were standing there waiting to get in. They couldn't hide their surprise to see who the occupants of the elevator were. It was an awkward moment. They all recognized one another and nodded with a polite half smile.

The I.A guys stepped aside. Sarge and Roy stepped out. The I.A guys stepped in. The doors whooshed shut.

Sarge and Roy looked at each other and walked on quietly, in deep thought. Ten steps and they were through the exit and into the car park. The background noise of the city filled their senses. They continued walking, both remained quiet.

'Yeah,' Roy eventually said, 'Where were we? Oh yes, I opened the office door to see Lomax near your desk looking like he'd been caught out. He made some lame conversation before leaving. He's a sneaky bastard so I searched around and there it was taped under your desk.'

It took a moment for Sarge to come up to speed. 'Nice one, matey. But why? What's he up to?' still distracted.

'Could it be for I.A or for himself? You know how paranoid he is.'

They stopped at Sarge's car. He leaned against it. 'I don't know, Roy.' He said thoughtfully. 'I wonder how long he's been doing this kind of thing.' He paused. 'What other conversations does he know about?'

Roy shrugged.

Sarge looked troubled.

'What's wrong?' asked Roy.

'Not quite sure. Perhaps we need to take out a little more insurance.'

Roy frowned, said nothing.

'You know, against certain officers in case they try to rubber-heel us.'

'You think they're after us? For what?'

He looked up at the sixth floor; said nothing.

There was a long moment.

'Sarge?'

'Look, can we pass on the drink tonight? I've got something else I need to do.'

'Ok. Sure.' Roy stalled. 'What's wrong, Sarge?' He asked again. 'Can I help?'

'Those I.A guys' He chinned over at the station. 'Did you see the look on their faces when they saw us? Or am I getting paranoid?'

'I noticed it too. Like they'd have preferred us not to have seen them.'

'Just watch your back, matey.'

'And you. I've told you before; if ever you need an alibi, just say the word.'

Sarge said nothing. He looked at him thoughtfully.

They nodded and parted company.

Roy headed over to his Harley.

Sarge headed into the dispatch office, took a photocopy, then drove to a location a few miles out of town.

Nine fifteen the following morning saw Sarge back at his desk. Thinking of the events of the previous day, he checked for the mini recorder. He thought long and hard as he subconsciously ran his fingers over where it had been. It had gone, someone had recovered it. An invisible sticky patch from the tape is all that remained. He'd accidentally discovered it. He felt around some more. There were other patches. He checked under Roy's desk; the same there. He made a quick search of other likely places around the office. It seemed clear. He wondered for how long his office had been bugged. His mind raced over the private conversations that had taken place that may not have been so private after all. He decided it was pointless worrying about it so made himself a brew, sat at his desk and got on with the day, best he could. A note had been left for him to go see Lomax as soon as he was on duty. He made another coffee then headed to his office.

His open-door policy was working well; the door was shut.

He knocked and opened it. He remained in the doorway. 'Morning, sir. You wanted to see me.'

'You're late. You should have been on at nine.' He spun his chair round one eighty from gazing out of the window, to face him.

'Busy?' He chinned at the windows behind Lomax. 'Good view out there this morning, sir?'

Lomax fumed, said nothing.

'Oh, by the way, I was on time. Just been reading up on the occurrence sheets in Dispatch.' He paused. 'For last night.' He smiled.

Lomax reached for his pipe.

'Read an interesting entry about a broken-down Jag, sir. I hope the papers don't get wind of it, especially the tabloids.' Eyebrows raised, expectantly.

He snorted. There was a long moment whilst he fumbled for his Ready Rub. 'Sergeant,' he said patronizingly, 'there's nothing on those sheets to show there was any misuse of police vehicles or time.'

'You're right, sir. There isn't.'

Lomax was smug. He invited Sarge in and to take a seat.

Sarge took up his offer.

He filled his pipe.

Sarge waited patiently.

He lit up and puffed with relieved satisfaction.

'So, what is it, sir?'

A cloud of smoke hung above him. He picked up the previous day's Intel report off his desk and told him of the information about the ex-SAS burglar. He droned on for some time.

Sarge listened carefully.

Lomax had to re-light more than once. He asked him to narrow down the likely premises on the High Street and carry out observations upon them overnight in an attempt to catch the drug-stealing offender. He authorized him to cover it all week.

Sarge acted like it was breaking news. He complimented him on seeing an opportunity to be pro-active, how refreshing it was and how uncanny it was that only last night he and his officer had been discussing the matter in the office.

Lomax was feeling good about himself; assertive; in charge. He wanted Sarge to change his duty roster to a night shift to do the obs.

'I'd rather do it on paid overtime, sir. On overtime if that's possible?' Sarge suggested politely with a slight grin.

He thought a moment then reluctantly agreed. He brought the meeting to a close and asked Sarge to close the door on his way out. He looked down as if to read other papers on his desk.

He stood up. 'Of course. Your open-door policy.' Sarge quipped.

Lomax glanced up at the remark before looking down again. He couldn't say anything.

He sucked, hard.

Sarge pulled his jacket to and adjusted his tie. He waited a moment.

He looked up, 'Anything else, Sergeant?' then looked down dismissively.

He shook his head and headed for the door, then paused and turned. 'Well sir, there is one other thing.'

Lomax looked up clearly annoyed but trying to disguise it, put on a smile.

'I heard a rumour that a couple of patrol officers were dispatched to pick up our stranded Jag-man and his wife last night after all.'

Lomax said nothing. He puffed hard.

Sarge laughed and chewed with satisfaction. 'Yes. I heard someone covertly used a video camera to record the event. Got the whole thing on tape.' Eyebrows raised with pleasure. 'Even followed them for twenty-seven minutes to their home. All on video, apparently.' He chewed. 'You heard about that, sir?'

He frowned, said nothing.

'Yes, story is, the two officers weren't available for over an hour. In the meantime, there were urgent jobs swinging with no-one to attend.' He chewed. 'Just a rumour, sir.' He smiled then left, leaving the door wide open.

Mandy and Roy were sat talking in the office and on their second brew by the time Sarge returned.

'Everything ok, Sarge?' asked Roy.

He gave him a nod, a crooked smile and a thumbs up. 'The job's on. Overtime too.'

Roy nodded. 'The place you suggested?'

'Yes, Wilson's surgery but there's not enough money in the pot for two, sorry. I'll have to do it alone.'

Roy shrugged. 'No probs.'

'One other thing. Check with our lawyers on the latest regarding admissibility of secretly recorded conversations and video in the work place. You know the things I'm referring to.'

'Roger that.'

'Let me know as soon as you can, I need to move fast.'

'Roger.'

Sarge let Roy know he had a busy day and would catch up later. He left the office whilst Roy got on to the lawyers down at HQ. In the meantime, Sarge met up with the man who informed on Cross. They had a short chat. He was thanked for his assistance and handed him a little more cash. The man was happy and thanked him. Before leaving he laughed and affectionately accused Sarge of being a *devious bastard,* in his words, *'but if ever he needed anyone else fitting up, to call.'* In return Sarge told him that only the two of them should ever know that it was Sarge's idea to set Roy and the *new recruit* up with the fabricated information so they had *Just-cause* to swear out a search warrant. It also meant it looked like he wasn't part of it. They parted company. Sarge headed back to the station.

He called at the office of the senior civilian staff, the one he'd caught rifling through the Chief's office when he had no right to. He knocked first before entering. He asked if the Chief was in.

He was told he wasn't.

'In that case,' he said, 'it's time to pay me the favour you owe. You know, the one so as I keep my mouth shut.'

He frowned.

Sarge held out his palm. 'The keys to Lomax's office; give them to me, now.'

He hesitated before pulling them from his draw then reluctantly handed them over.

'Thanks.' He smiled. 'With all that spare time he has in there, there must be something he gets up to, to pass the time.' He headed into the Chief's office. He locked the door behind him.

He went through the place. He was there quite a while before returning with the borrowed keys. He walked straight in without knocking. He was angry and marched up close to the desk.

He chewed. 'Last drawer on the left, down at the bottom.'

'What of it?'

'What of it? You know what's in there. I'm sure you've been in there enough times.'

'Don't know what you're talking about, sergeant.'

Not convinced. 'Oh yeah? So, I won't find your prints all over the child porn photos that are in there then?'

There was a moment.

'Ok. I've seen them. But I swear it's not something I'm into. I only looked at them out of curiosity.'

'Try telling that to a court. Curiosity! That's the usual excuse but it's not a defence.'

He looked worried.

Sarge let him sweat a moment. 'Ok. Here's what we do. We pretend none of this happened. You got that? It stays between me and you.'

Red faced, he nodded.

Sarge tossed the keys to him and left.

Roy was in the Vice office when he got there. He greeted him with the news that the lawyers had told him it was a none-starter; that secret, covert recordings were most unlikely to be allowed as evidence. It could infringe upon human rights in the work place and the person responsible for recording could probably be sued, even imprisoned.

Sarge thanked him and acknowledged it was pretty much what he'd expected. He lowered his voice almost to a whisper; he told him what he'd discovered in the Chief's draw and how there was nothing they could do about it as he'd searched without the support of any law authorizing it; how he'd been in there without any authority or reasonable excuse. 'But I'll change that.' He chewed. 'The Chief has a big Kairos moment heading his way. I'll see to that.' He slid out an A4 envelope from under his jacket and placed it on a nearby desk. 'This is a small sample.' Roy looked on as he emptied the contents. Large photos of child porn spilled out. 'He had a whole drawer full.' He chewed.

Roy casually scanned them. 'What's he doing with them? I reckon they're from the raid on the lecturer, the way he wanted a key to the store and all.'

'I thought the same at first. I even considered if he had a lawful excuse to be in possession of them but I don't see how, we deal with all this kind of material. Then I looked closer.' He sorted through some and pulled a few out. 'See who that is?' He pointed out a man in the pictures.

Roy looked closely. 'Well, well. Adam Buck. Well, it figures, him being a dealer.

He'll be into anything and everything.'

'Yes, probably his own kids he's with too.'

'How's he come into possession of them? Do you think the Chief got them directly from him?'

'I asked myself the same questions. We may never know but it could explain why he wouldn't authorize the raid on his house. A lot of these child porn sex-rings are all connected. Could be the Chief is part of a network. By protecting Buck, he protects himself, who knows? What I do know is we have something very powerful right here, it's working out how we can use it.'

'It's hard to believe, Sarge, him being a Chief and a family man with his own kids.'

'Well, we know that counts for nothing, it doesn't stop their thirst for this sick, perverted filth.' He paused and thought about what Roy had said. 'Buck. His own kids, eh? How old are they?'

'Teenagers, I think. Do you think they're at risk?'

'Lots are, as we know, but they often don't come forward about it until they're much older.' He sniffed. 'We don't have that much time; we need to speed things up.' He slipped the photos away. 'I'll think of a way where it'll be lawful to expose him for what he is. Knowing he has kids gives me a few ideas. I'll think of something.'

Roy smiled. 'I'm sure you will, Sarge, I'm sure you will. Remember, as always, you know where I am if you need me.'

The following night, Sarge, found himself secreted amongst the bins at the rear of a dental surgery. He was there for 10pm. It was pitch black. He had night vision and baton at the ready. He'd asked for the loan of one of the city's stab-proof jackets and got one. It was a cumbersome item to wear. He left it in his vehicle. He didn't believe he'd need it anyway. Nothing happened there that night.

Four more nights passed. He worked the same shift, same location. All he saw was the darkness of the night once the dental surgeon had finished his night-time routine. He lived on his premises and was oblivious to Sarge's presence nearby; following instructions, quietly watching, patiently waiting in case the ex-SAS man comes to burgle and steal.

He watched the dentist's and kept a written log, a record of any event. He had to under the rules governing surveillance. The dental surgeon was regular as clockwork, same every night, always recorded: -

10.00pm, bedroom light goes on, curtains drawn by a woman.

10.10pm, bedroom light goes out.

10.20pm, rear door opens, cat trots out.

10.40pm, rear door opens, cat trots in.

11.05pm, rear door opens, dentist steps out, has a smoke.

11.10pm, stubs cigarette on wall, goes back inside.

11.20pm, a different bedroom light goes on. Goes off after thirty seconds.

04.00am, stood down.

Nothing else gets recorded for the rest of the night. It's the same each time give or take a minute or two.

The M.O shows the ex-SAS man never does a burglary after 4am so there's no point in using up the overtime or being there when chances are nothing's going to happen.

Sarge is home in bed by five; he's thankful the guy didn't show up; *to take on a man like that who carries a knife, would be a worrying scenario. A scenario that would be best not taking place for real,* he thought. He recalled the Chief seeming a little surprised when he took on the task, it being so risky and him asking only for a stab-proof vest.

Sarge watches and waits in the silent darkness on the final night. He's left alone. Few people know where he is. He records the log the same as the previous night, he notes nothing different. Meanwhile the rest of the city life goes by.

Across the other side of the city, Adam Buck went to meet someone who'd called his wife. According to her, *the caller said he had some photos her husband may be interested in and that if he wasn't, the police would be.* That's what she told the officers when they called at her home to say he'd been found, *blasted with his own shotgun,* they believed.

Sarge recorded the log the same as always and stands down from his obs. at the usual time, 4am. He heads home and is in bed by 5 a.m.

At 10.32 a.m. he's woken by a phone call after a disturbed sleep. It's the red-haired Chief detective asking if he carried out the obs. on the dentist last night.

He tells him he did and asks, *why?*

The chief says the dentist is in a bad way, down at the Infirmary. 'His wife found him strapped in his chair not long ago. Lots of his teeth had been pulled.' he says. 'No anaesthetic.'

Sarge ran his tongue over his teeth. He asks how he can help.

The chief tells him he wants to see the log when he comes on duty later that day.

2 p.m. soon came around for Sarge. He went to his office first rather than to the Chief detective's. Roy and Mandy are already there. They all pass the usual pleasantries. Sarge sat at his desk, the overnight *sitrep* was laid on it. He picked it up and looked over at Roy. They gave one another a hint of secretive nod. He read the sitrep. He glanced over the usual stuff until he reached the dentist incident.

'You read this about the dentist, Roy?'

Mandy and Roy looked over. He ran his tongue over his teeth. 'Yes, yes, I have. Didn't want to mention it, you being there last night. Seems like your man must have showed up. You must have just missed each other. Sounds like a nasty job.'

Mandy glanced over at Roy; something didn't seem quite right the way he replied to Sarge. She couldn't put her finger on it so carried on with her paperwork.

'Says here, *he was bundled into his chair after a knock on the door.* Must have been soon after I left……. huh…. Why did he answer the knock, that time of night?'

'Don't know yet, they say. But apparently, it's not the first time he's let someone in for emergency treatment, middle of the night. Seems like he's a man who likes to earn money, no matter what. Greedy, I'd say.'

'Yeah, you got that right, Roy.'

'Perhaps he just cares if people are in pain,' said Mandy, without looking up.

He chewed. 'Yeah, right. Those types do nothing for anyone. It's all about them and their love of money. That's what drives them.' He then jumped up and headed for the Chief detective's office.

He wasn't there, only his secretary. She told him he was at the crime scene over at the dentist's and that he wanted to see him there as soon as possible. Sarge, drove over.

He approached the front of the surgery; it had a large note; *Closed until further notice.* All the blinds were drawn. He went around to the rear. A crime scenes investigator's vehicle was there along with a couple of plain cars, other than that, there was no sign of life. He walked straight into the rear entrance. It had that distinct smell of a dental surgery, that smell that causes anxiety and raises the heart rate. Memories flooded back; he ran his tongue over his teeth. He took a moment then called out. A voice responded from somewhere deeper inside the building. He made his way to where it had come from. A frightened cat shot passed him on the way, it looked familiar. The carpet, furnishings and décor were expensive, it was clear he was in the residential part of the premises. There were several doors to choose from. He chose the one that looked more solid; he presumed it led into the surgery. He was correct. He'd entered a small room. It was a typical dental surgery that was made smaller by having a half dozen police specialists poking around in it. Watching over them was the detective Chief. He spotted his red-head immediately and headed towards him. He met Sarge midway and led him back out.

They took seats in the residential part. *It was ok as the dentist's wife was also in hospital suffering with acute shock,* the chief told him. He asked for the log.

Sarge handed it over and told him where he was staked-out and that nothing happened on his watch.

The chief quizzed him about the time he stood down, what time he got home. He was eventually satisfied with his answers. Then he continued to bring him up to speed; he told him, *the dentist recalls going through his usual bedtime routine, smoking, putting the cat out etcetera. He said he remembers going to bed and quickly falling asleep. He woke when he heard knocking. He'd no idea what time it was and thinks it could be an emergency call so he answers the door, the rear one. Two men were there, one was a really big guy, as in broad. It's too dark to see their faces. Before he knows it, a hood is over his head and he's bundled backwards into his surgery. They tape him into his chair and tape over his eyes. They give him a little gas, just enough where he knows what's happening but he can't do anything about it. Nothing much was said. He recalls them saying that they can't save his teeth, they need to come out. He pleaded with them even though he could hardly speak. The men insist they have to come out. They yanked most of his teeth out. He's a real mess, lost a lot of blood.'*

'Yes, sounds really bad, sir.' He paused. 'Quite a Kairos moment.' He muttered.

'What's that you say, sergeant?'

'Oh, nothing, sir. Thinking out aloud. So, how's Mrs. Wilson? How come she's in shock, did she witness anything?'

'No. Slept right through it. They sleep separately, separate bedrooms. In a big old place like this he was too far away for her to hear a thing. Besides they never gave him chance.'

'Good. You got anything to go on, sir?'

'No. It's looking unlikely. Whoever did it knew how not to leave a trace, no prints and no forensics. They used his disinfectant to clean up, put him out-cold whilst they did it. They trashed the drugs cabinet, took a load of stuff with them. But it's odd. It doesn't add up.'

'What's odd about that? Sounds like our Ex-SAS man has an oppo and he's turning even stranger. It's not just drugs now.'

'No, I don't believe it was our man, sergeant. It was after 4am.'

He left a long moment.

He tried not to ask but couldn't help himself. 'Why's that, sir?'

'They could have taken more but didn't. They left a load behind. And why torture and maim the poor man? Whatever has he done to them to deserve that?'

Sarge shrugged, ran his tongue over his teeth and said nothing.

The Chief stood up, thanked him for his time and said he would get to the bottom of it. He asked Sarge and his team to assist; he wanted some background information on the dentist; *check to see if he was squeaky clean, see if he's upset anyone or had any disgruntled patients. Things like that. Check out his wife too. See if there are any skeletons in their cupboards, them sleeping apart and all.* He went back into the dental surgery. Sarge headed back to the station.

He updated Roy over a brew then set about gathering any information on the dentist job as requested by the chief detective.

The chief called to see Sarge a few hours later, he asked him what he'd found out.

Sarge was reluctant to help the graduate-entry boss. He resented how he got to where he was but he had no choice than to assist. He knew if he told him there was nothing of significance that he could be caught out. One thing he hated; was being caught out. And one thing he knew about the graduate-types is how much they enjoyed spending their time poking around on computers. And how much they enjoyed displaying their mental and research prowess.

'Well sir,' he said, 'not a lot really. Early days. So far, no signs of either one having a lover, no affairs. Nothing on her at all. He, on the other hand, was convicted for malpractice many years ago. He got suspended. Seems like he wrecked countless individual's teeth for the sake of being paid more from the health service and private insurance companies. Made a small fortune, apparently. Did work that wasn't needed. Not only that, prior to his scam of wrecking teeth for cash, he got away with allegations that he'd sexually interfered with several women patients whilst anesthetized in his chair. He got off with it, there wasn't enough evidence. The women knew things weren't right in the bra and panties department when they woke, along with other things, but that's all they had to go on. The lawyers said it wasn't enough, they wanted firm evidence. There were some others with stronger evidence that came out the woodwork when it hit the papers but by then he skipped over to Canada. He practiced there for some years until his suspension in this country expired and the sexual allegations ran out of steam. He slipped back over here unnoticed once things had sufficiently quietened down. He was having a quiet and lucrative life until this happened. Seems like he was up to his old tricks, he is shown to be one of the highest earners in his field. Semi-retired too.'

'Interesting, sergeant. Sound like he's still carrying out work that's not required, perhaps.' He paused. 'So, nothing more than I already knew. Anyway, I went through the records back at his office, they go back decades. I read the Medical Council's report. It was quite shocking. Seems like he got very wealthy from drilling, filling, pulling teeth and fitting dentures, when it was unnecessary. He was a corrupt and dishonest individual, that's for sure. He got away with lots for a very long time. In my opinion, the Establishment covered it all up. So perhaps he got what was coming to him, Sarge. Karma.' He smiled.

'Maybe so, sir. Karma?' He shrugged. 'Perhaps it was a Kairos moment.' He suggested.

'Yes, Sarge. Maybe it was.'

The chief turned to leave then turned back. 'Oh, one other thing. The dentist now thinks the bigger guy of the two may have been black.'

There was moment.

'Black. Ah well, it's not only me that doesn't like the dentist then.'

He puzzled a moment. 'Quite, sergeant. I'll leave it with you.' He turned and left.

Sarge returned to his desk. Within a few minutes his phone rang. It was Chief Lomax. He told him he'd called as he was reading the sitrep report from the precinct covering the other side of the city. He thought Sarge may be interested. He went on to say that Buck had been found behind a pharmacy early morning and that he's in a stable condition down at the infirmary. He told him Buck had never been known to assist the police but on this occasion he had. He'd made a statement saying he'd got a call to meet someone. When he got there, he was ambushed by a guy with a knife. He put up a fight and got his own sawn-off turned on him…...'

Sarge interrupted. 'Well, that's what he gets for being at the rear of a pharmacy in the middle of the night carrying an illegal firearm, sir. No sympathy. If you recall, I did try to tell you no good would come of letting him run around with his illegal weapons.'

The Chief continued. 'As I was saying; the guy who ambushed him made a real mess; he won't be having sex anymore.'

He laughed. 'I know. Blew away his reproductive parts, hardly anything left, they say. From now on he'll be sitting down to pee.'

There was a moment.

'How did you know that, Sarge? I've only just had their sitrep delivered.'

'How did I know? Oh, well.' He hesitated. 'Well, I keep my ear to the ground. You know that, sir. The jungle telegraph is faster than the sitrep.'

'Mmnn…. Anyway, it's an odd case in many ways. You're across one side of the city and all this is taking place elsewhere. There are some things that don't add up. I thought perhaps you'd be able to clear up one or two things for me.'

'I was across the other side of the city, for sure, doing surveillance. I've got a log to prove it. That's my alibi.'

'Sergeant, calm. Am I accusing you of being involved?'

He thought a beat. 'No. No sir, you're not.' He sniffed. 'Perhaps I'm a little paranoid. You know, past events and all. Me and him having recent history.'

'Mmmn…. Moving on. Some child porn photos were also found at the scene. What do you know about them?'

'Me? Why ask me, sir?'

'Well, there's no detail of them in the sitrep, it's a very brief summary. I wondered if you could update me, you seem to know a lot about the case.'

'Fair enough.' He coughed nervously. 'Ok. Only what I heard, sir. Buck was certainly playing a starring role in the photos, it seems. Perhaps with his own kids too. A real sicko, if you ask me. You know what I mean, sir?'

There was a strained moment.

He chewed 'At first it was thought he'd done a raid on those particular premises, perhaps he was even involved with our ex-SAS man but Buck says not. He reckons he'd got a call to meet someone there, is all. His wife backs him on that story. The pharmacy was turned over and it all fitted with the ex-SAS man's M.O; time, method. Maybe he was involved, we'll probably never know.'

'Seems like you miscalculated and chose the wrong premises to watch last night, sergeant.'

'Me?' He laughed. 'No. I didn't choose the wrong place, sir. Things worked out fine.' There was a moment.

'Besides, it was *we* who chose the wrong premises, sir.' He emphasized. 'Remember?' You were party to that decision. But don't feel too bad about it, sir, it was a good outcome. We got one less phyco-drug-dealer running around. Making more child porn - he won't be. That's for sure. As for the dentist, well I settle it in my mind by thinking of it as a Kairos moment for him. Might help you too, sir, if you think of it that way.'

The Chief thanked him for his help and said he'd only called him as he saw the connection with the stake-out he'd done.

Sarge responded by saying he was welcome and thought it was because he was interested in what the child porn photos showed.

There was an awkward moment before the Chief abruptly hung up.

Roy came into the office. He had a brew with Sarge whilst he told him that his informant, the one who'd previously *grassed- up* Cross, had been in touch with the recruit. He'd told her that Cross had drugs at his home and they had already obtained a warrant to search the place.

Sarge was pleased. 'This time you can search everywhere. Make sure you check it out thoroughly,' he said with a knowing nod.

'Roger. Will do.' He paused. 'Strange thing, my informant wanting to spill all to the recruit. He's been a good source of information for years. Now he suddenly wants to drop me and use her.'

'Don't worry about it, Roy. Perhaps he fancies her.'

'No. No I don't think so. He's also gay.'

Sarge shrugged; popped in some fresh gum.

Roy left and rounded up the recruit and a few others then headed out with the search warrant.

Meanwhile, Sarge paid the Top civilian support man another visit. He reminded him how his fingerprints would be all over the child porn photos in the Chief's desk and how it would look bad for him if it went to court.

The Top man said he'd tell the truth; that he only glanced through them to see what they were.

Sarge pointed out to him that his prints would be on every photo he'd touched. He said how the prosecutor would ask why he had gone through them all and had not reported the matter. It would be suggested to the courts that he was as bad as the Chief. Perhaps they got off on it together, he suggested.

The Top man was speechless.

Sarge told him that another sergeant would pay him a call when the Chief wasn't there and that he'd need a file from his office, urgently. He told him how he could use his spare keys for such emergencies and they'd both discover the child porn photos in his drawer. That it would be the first time he knew of the photos and so that's how come his prints came to be all over them. That's the story he would stick to, he told him.

The Top man reluctantly agreed.

Sarge patted him on his upper arm and left. His next stop was to see Stevie, *the sergeant who was Sarge trained.* They spoke in private awhile. When they parted, Sarge headed back to his office whilst Stevie took a thick file to the Chief's office. It was a file that required leaving with the Chief.

Meanwhile, Roy and search-party were at Cross's. He was his usual angry self and confident they'd find no illegal substances in his home. It was a thorough search for drugs; small items, unlike the search for stolen motorcycle parts done previously. This time drawers and other places could be searched.

They'd been through all the ground floor and most of the bedrooms. Nothing had been found. Roy sent the recruit to search the bathroom along with a more experienced officer to help her. Within seconds they emerged. She was carrying a Jiffy bag. She proudly handed it to Roy and said she'd found it behind the basin pedestal. He opened it. Inside was a dagger, the type used by Marines. He avoided touching it - fingerprints. He saw what he suspected to be dried blood on the weapon. He took it, along with the recruit, downstairs to Cross and showed him what they'd found.

He confidently denied all knowledge of it, said he'd never seen it before in his life. He protested that it wasn't his and that he was being framed. He was believable.

Roy inspected the packaging closer. It was addressed to a P.O Box. He showed it to Cross and asked him whether or not that was one of his PO Box addresses.

He said, *maybe.* He knew it was, he recognized it. But he didn't recognize the envelope and contents.

He then read him the date stamp. It was a date near to one Cross could never forget, the day after he lost his best mate, Petty. He waited for a reaction.

Cross couldn't help but say what the relevance of the date was.

He was arrested on suspicion of murdering Petty, cuffed and taken to the station.

The knife was tested for traces of DNA. It was no surprise to some officer's that it proved to be that of Petty's.

Cross was charged the following day with the murder of Michael James Petty. Alternatively charged with being involved with the retention or withholding of material-evidence of a serious crime, thereby obstructing the police and justice. He continued to deny all knowledge of the find.

Sarge was present when Cross was charged with the crimes. It had been a satisfying time for him, there had been lots of Kairos moments. It had been a good day indeed.

That same day, the Commander left early as usual. Stevie called at his office but he was too late. He asked the Top senior support man to assist as he urgently needed a file he'd left in the Chief's office. He wasn't too happy to help but he obliged and used his spare keys. They searched for the file and discovered the child porn before finding the file they were looking for. That made the search and *accidental* discovery, legal. What was found would be admissible as court evidence.

Stevie, with other officers, attended the Chief Lomax's home early the next morning. He was arrested in front of his whole family for possessing the child pornography. He wasn't happy, denied any wrong doing and objected in the strongest terms at being arrested. He was outraged and indignant. His teenage daughter and young son watched on, impassively.

Within hours of the arrest their mother attended the station with her children. They had something they wanted to tell the police.

Seeing him arrested gave them the strength to act and not to be afraid. They made lengthy statements about Lomax. As a result, he was charged with assaults upon his wife, he'd regularly beaten her over the last twenty years. Not only that, he was charged with raping his daughter from aged twelve and indecently assaulting his son.

Another day at the office and another sitrep. Sarge read it aloud. Roy and Mandy listened in as they drank their brew. He skipped over most of the usual stuff. He told them of Lomax's arrest and how Cross had tried to commit suicide. He laughed. 'Kairos moments. That's what they are.'

Roy and Mandy's smiles were soon lost.

Sarge noticed.

There was a moment.

'Sarge. Don't you ever worry about your own Kairos time or moment, whatever you call it?'

He chewed. 'Me? No, not me. I've got God on my side. That's for sure.' He paused. 'Besides, what will be has already happened, you can't change the future. The future's already been and gone, don't you see? Everything is history. All of us, this very moment, it's all history. We are just segments of it in time. It's never ending. You, me, the world and the whole universe; they've all gone and are dead already. We know the future and that future's been and gone. Kairos time, that's how things are really measured, events in segments. History captured in moments. Chronos time, as in the ticking of a clock, is all it is; man-made. Kairos is God made. That's the true measure.'

Roy and Mandy cautiously glanced at each other with a frown, said nothing.

The detective Chief with his shock of red hair was standing in the doorway, listening. 'There's a theory,' he said. The three of them looked towards him. 'That history is already written; we are all just here for this nanosecond. History is written, the global finances have collapsed and money is worthless. The world's resources are scarce. There's no more oil. Billions have starved, billions more were killed in the third world war. Buddhists' have been reborn many times over. Ice ages have come and gone. The sun died, all life on earth died millions of years before then. You see, history has already happened. It's just that we don't know it. Yet we do. It's something we struggle to comprehend. The seven billion people currently on earth are already dead. I could go on.'

There was a moment.

'Thank you, sir. The second coming is history. The Day of Rapture was quite a day,' said Sarge, a little uncomfortably.

'Yes, Sarge, you're right.'

'Well, you should know, sir, being up on Metaphysics and all.'

'Interesting conversation you were having, Sarge, hope you don't mind me interrupting. I've just come back from talking with Buck.' He paused. 'What I said just then were not my own words. It's what the guy told Buck after getting his weapon off him before blasting him with his own sawn-off.'

There was a long moment.

'You'll be pleased to know I told him it was a Kairos moment. Seems there's a lot of it about. Just thought you should know.' He paused. 'Oh, by the way, I'm to be the new commander. I'm making a few changes. There's a graduate entry starting in here, Monday. She's taking over from you, Sarge. You've done a good job but it's time you went back outside in uniform. You're needed out there. They need someone like you.' He turned and left.

CHAPTER 7.

WAITING TIME.

Monday morning, several weeks since the detective Chief interrupted and Sarge found himself back on uniform beat patrol. With him was Roy. He'd transferred out same time as Sarge. They soon got into their new role.

The never-ending criminal activities of crooks and dealers rolled on. The police and all the other social services went around cleaning up after them. Nothing changes.

The ex-SAS man was still raiding premises, allegedly, where drugs were held. It was an odd case, noted the new Chief.

One night, Sarge and Roy attended a burglar alarm at a pharmacy. They arrived in separate vehicles. Roy got there a few seconds before Sarge. A lean man carrying a knife ran out from the rear alley. Roy jumped out and blocked his path. The man, seeing the enormous frame of the officer between him and his freedom, suddenly stopped. Not for any physical reason, he had the edge on Roy. He could have used the knife to affect his escape but chose not to.

Sarge was twenty yards away when he pulled up. He watched the two men and their stand-off. The scene didn't look quite right, he thought. The body language didn't add up. He saw them exchanging a few words as he cautiously made his way towards them. Roy glanced over at him and shouted for him to stay put then stepped aside as the raider walked past. He put his knife away and nonchalantly headed in Sarge's direction. As he approached, he called. 'Acta non verba, Sarge,' Then glanced over his shoulder at Roy who was shadowing him a few yards behind.

'Yeah, action not words, my friend,' said Sarge, puzzled.

He walked on by; Sarge allowed him to.

'Deeds not words - to be correct, Sarge,' he said, as he walked away, not looking back.

Sarge nodded, to himself.

Roy joined Sarge. They watched him stroll along the street like any other regular person.

'Ok. What was that about?' He chewed.

There was a moment; they kept eye contact on the man heading away.

'The truth?' asked Roy.

'Give me what you've got.'

'It was our man, the ex-SAS one of course. I'm sure you guessed.'

'I guessed.' He paused. 'Well, it was more than a guess. You knew him, served in Iraq together, special ops. I knew.'

'Yeah? How? The military wouldn't give you that kind of information so how did you know?'

Tapping the side of his nose, 'I know many things. Besides, it's my job to know.'

'Ok.' He hesitated. 'Well anyway, don't judge him, Sarge. He's a good man at heart. He was a good Para, disciplined through and through. Served his country well. Hard as nails but a nicer guy you couldn't wish to meet. I was on the phone to him only a few years ago, he seemed ok then. Anyway, I owed him one.' He hesitated some more. 'I owe him my life.'

'Yeah, I know. So, why's he gone off the rails?'

'He lost his little girl to drugs. That, along with what he's had to do defending his country, I guess. He joined up aged sixteen, did nearly twenty years in the thick of it. Doesn't matter who you are, active service affects everyone. Those who say it doesn't are only fooling themselves. Things happen that no-one can imagine.'

'How do you deal with it, Roy?'

'Me? Best not to dwell on the past because you can't change it. That's how I deal with it. That's how he deals with it.'

They watched him cross over the road.

'Tell me he's on our side.' He chewed.

There was a moment.

'You should know.'

Sarge shot him a glance.

'Is he on our side? Yes, he's on our side. He's doing his part in the fight against drugs, believe me.' He paused. 'Perhaps he's one of God's instruments against evil. Try and think of it that way, Sarge.'

'Ok. That helps. I trust your judgment but I could do with a little more.'

'He said we'd find another burgling dealer around at the rear. He sets them up, lets them break-in then ambushes them. Leaves them in a bad way for us to find. Yeah, I'd say he's on our side. He's probably getting more dealers off the streets than we are.'

'Was that a commando dagger I saw him with?'

'It was. You still got the one your father left you?'

'Oh, yes. Could never part with that. You know that. It's a one-off; special.' He waited a moment, 'A powerful instrument of Kairos time.' he smiled.

Roy laughed. 'You know, at one point I thought the one we recovered from Cross's home, was yours.'

'It was,' he laughed.

Roy laughed, with uncertainty.

'I got a half dozen of them back home.' He popped in some fresh gum.

A moment later their man turned a corner and he was gone into the night.

'Sarge, can I ask you something?'

'Sure, go ahead, though I might not give you a truthful answer.'

'Did he say the, *acta non verba,* thing, to you?'

He sniffed. 'No, you must have misheard him, officer. Come on, we best go check out around the rear, find this guy he told you about.'

The officers found him, surrounded by drugs from the raid. He was in a bad way. They called it in. He survived and did his time. He was released after only eight months and looked at other ways to make a living. His thieving, drug dealing days were over, that was for sure. He was a reformed character.

In the meantime, Roy was no longer officially a cop. He never resigned from the Force, he simply drifted away to take on another role somewhere else in the country. He'd been head-hunted and signed up to some Government department involved in special projects; highly secretive. It wasn't Special Forces, MI6 or the CIA, it was beyond that. But no-one knew. He was no longer a cop, ex-Para or recognized Government official. He operated somewhere in a grey area doing grey tasks that were kept from the public domain. They were the kind of tasks, where if discovered, any official body would deny their involvement. He became a mysterious man doing mysterious things. He could never tell his closest friends, not even Sarge, of the things he was tasked to do. To do so would endanger himself and the person he disclosed to. The system he worked under was such that safeguards were in place that ensured no-one would find out the truth of any of the special projects. He had to become a lone wolf and so could not keep in touch with anyone. He fell off the radar. Before he did so he told those he was close to that if ever they bumped into him, they had to make out they didn't know him. It was as serious as that.

Mandy remained in Vice. Sarge plodded on as a street cop and found himself a new colleague to work closely with, Poppy Beau Bibby. She was ex-military with an impressive curriculum vitae and an even more impressive service record. She'd seen action in Bosnia, Northern Ireland and the Middle East. She had a flare to be ruthless; with medals and citations to prove it. There was more than a dozen confirmed kills to her name.

For all that she'd lived in a tough world and a man's world for so many years, she had retained her dignity, self-respect and femininity. She was a single mum who'd worked hard and carved out a life in spite of all the challenges that had been thrown her way. She could easily have given up when she was younger and let her life become one of self-pity, of hardship, dependency, victimhood and living on hand-outs. But she didn't. She was a survivor. She was more than merely a survivor.

Her appearance was fairly average; short mousy hair, almost five foot seven inches tall. Her build was muscular, a little on the heavy side. She was happy with that. She was generally a pleasant character but her attitude could be seriously scary when called for. Sarge felt very much at home with her, she was as good as any man, in his opinion and better than many. Through Poppy, he changed his outlook not only on women cops but women as a whole. They went through some tight scrapes together. Sarge trusted her in most things but there were times he needed to operate alone…….

It was a little after 11pm on a warm summers evening. A patrol car pulled slowly into disused school grounds. It had served the estate well but was now due for demolition. Some time ago it got a reprieve and was turned into a community centre. For a while it was popular with the locals, especially the kids. It was somewhere for them to hang out, it was great for the community. Then the drug pushers moved in, so caring parents stopped their children going to it. The police tried lots of ways to reverse the situation but the dealers won every time. So, there was no other choice than to close it. The police were turning timid and weak and instead went after people using the internet causing offence with hurty words rather than the real crime out on the streets and in the communities. Box ticking for recruits had become the norm rather than selecting the best people for the job.

That said, a handful of police officers made real efforts to beat the dealers They arrested many of them but the rules of law and smart lawyers put paid to a successful outcome. And so, the building, now derelict and boarded over, stood as a monument to the failure of the police; the Establishment and to society.

The patrol car stopped; the driver sat awhile. He chewed.

He scanned the area. It was a mix of new-builds and abandoned Local Authority (L.A) housing. There were well defined boundaries for each type. The new builds were large, privately owned with most having at least two vehicles on the drive. Much thought had been given to the design and layout of the new homes; crime prevention was key. They were securely encircled with high walls, one way in, one way out. On the other hand, the L.A homes were everything the new homes weren't.

He quietly got out of his vehicle and listened. Silence; except for the sound of dogs occasionally barking in the distance. He looked up to the sky; clear. He did a 360: clear. He reached into the vehicle and pulled out a hold-all then slipped into black coveralls before padding his pocket; checking something was there. He knew it was but it was just a reassurance, a comfort. He glanced at his wristwatch then gently and quietly pushed the door shut. He locked it and looked down at his boots whilst doing so. They were a little dusty so rubbed them on the back of his trousers. He had a final look around. It was clear, he saw no-one. He believed no-one would have noticed his presence.

A dark figure, motionless in the shadows not far away, watched on.

He chewed some-more as he set off purposefully into the labyrinth of passages and alleys created by the L.A properties.

Less than a thousand yards away was a man who had just left home, it was his third time that evening. He was as regular as clockwork and carrying drugs towards the new-builds. He had a lucrative business going on there; he'd managed to get lots of individuals hooked on what he had to offer. He was indeed a bad man. Tucked down the front of his pants was a fully loaded East European 9mm pistol, safety catch off. He used to carry only a knife, same as other dealers, but recent events showed that knives were no longer enough. Some of his peers had succumbed to someone else's knife over recent times. Dealing drugs had become a far more dangerous occupation, some had gotten out of the business altogether. He wasn't taking any chances. Most dealers now carried firearms. But for all that, some had been outmatched by a simple knife.

The man with the shiny boots heading his way carried something he believed was far more powerful than any firearm. His faith in his belief was incredible. He knew it would protect him. In fact, he thought it was far more powerful than anything on Earth. He marched purposefully on.

The dealer walked with equal purpose and headed his way, though he didn't know that. Neither did he know that he was also heading towards a significant moment in Kairos time. It would be one of very few left in the short time he had left upon Earth.

The man dressed in black wearing shiny boots and closing in, pulled out the gold chain he wore and kissed the cross attached to it. He muttered a short prayer.

India Delta hovered unnoticed, five hundred yards away and three hundred yards up in the night sky. It was one of the usual pilots but not the usual operators who were sat in the back seats. They had been replaced by strangers, without any explanation. The orders for the change had come from someone higher than the Chief of Police. No-one knew who it was, it was all very secretive. The operators had American accents but were not American. They'd attached some of their own equipment to the aircraft; cameras, sensors and other hi-tech gear. They had spent a fruitless week so far. They watched their thermal imaging monitor showing a particular part of the estate below. Suddenly it showed two ghostly-white figures closing in on each other with four hundred yards to go as they weaved through the alleyways. One appeared to have yanked something from around their neck and put it to their lips. As it was only a shade of varying grey thermal imagery, the definition was poor; the finer detail could not be seen.

They watched and waited.

At two hundred yards to go, they noticed one figure stop. The other figure carried on.

A moment later, as if from nowhere, another ghostly figure appeared only yards from the stationary one. It showed up feint on the screen, emitting little heat; at times almost invisible. They were shocked to see its sudden appearance. They zoomed in. They couldn't see where it had appeared from. It was as though it materialized from nowhere. It was a human form but not quite so at times. It seemed parts of it disappeared in a random sort of way and other bits came and went. It was an odd shape here and there and moved as though floating, as opposed to walking. They were baffled by the figure even though they'd witnessed similar events before. They knew they needed to focus on the whole scene rather than one area. And so, they did. *They were anticipating an MSE, a major specific event.* They told the pilot.

They watched and waited.

One hundred yards to go, the operators checked the camera was recording.

Still at three hundred yards altitude and now only fifty yards to go.

They watched and waited.

With yards to go, India Delta's fault systems erupted showing major mechanical failures. Warning instrument lights flashed; alarms buzzed. The whole display panel lit up like a Christmas tree that was about to explode any time. The pilot responded instinctively banking hard right and dropped altitude. The pilot knew to land immediately. The camera operators cursed in fear and then in frustration as the camera scanned the skies instead of the ground as the aircraft rolled. The pilot got onto his radio and calmly told Control that an emergency landing was being affected. There was no response. The operators adopted the crash position. Ninety seconds later and the machine made a perfect landing in a field on the edge of the city. The panel returned to normal as quickly as it had lit up. The engine was closed down, the quills slowed. Silence eventually replaced the roar of the engines and the *whoop, whoop* of the quills as they slowed to nothing. The three people on board gathered themselves; the two in the rear were ashen.

The pilot was the first to show his composure and broke the silence. He *was puzzled by what had taken place,* he told the others onboard. 'I've never known anything like it. Everything is showing *normal,* now.' he said.

'Good. Can we get back up there right now, this minute?' asked one operator, hopefully. He was clearly a dedicated individual who had no regard for his own safety.

The pilot turned around and looked at the operator in disbelief. 'No. Not until we're checked out. And that won't be tonight. Sorry.'

'But we've got to get back up there, now,' he pleaded. 'You don't know how important this is to us.'

He shook his head. 'You may want to meet your maker sooner rather than later, but I don't. The only place this chopper's going tonight is on the back of a low-loader to its hangar.' He got onto his radio to give a status report and to arrange recovery.

One of the operators turned to the other, said, through gritted teeth, 'A few more seconds and we'd have witnessed something remarkable back there. Now we may never know. Luck was on their side tonight.'

The other replied, 'Luck? Maybe. Or is it that God shines on the righteous?'

'Maybe so,' he nodded, 'God's Will, perhaps.'

The pilot removed his headset and helmet. 'Kairos?' he said with a smile.

The operators looked at one another and nodded in agreement. 'Kairos,' said one.

'Kairos.' Echoed the other.

More weeks slipped by. The guy found behind the pharmacy, in a bad way, needed hospitalization from time to time but was feeling much better. He was now a re-educated individual who was taking a serious look at his wrong-doings and lifestyle. He felt he'd been given a second chance to mend his ways. He promised himself that it was to be a new life for him and that he would never return to his old ways. The lost sight in one eye; the ugly scar across his cheek, a ruptured spleen and missing finger would always be a reminder that he had a near miss. And that out there on the streets there was a wind of change where he and his kind were no longer safe as King of the Pile. He realized that some seriously dangerous individuals were operating outside of the law that made him and his criminal fraternity look like a bunch of boy scouts. He'd lost his confidence. He never wanted to encounter such an attack again. He knew that many of his peers had succumbed to similar ambushes. Psychologically, he wasn't strong enough to shrug off his recent brush with death.

A man who had a habit of chewing and sniffing, visited him late one night and told him how things were changing. How he was to be part of that change and how he would help. He was offered help in return for spreading the word and becoming an informant, a Grass. He was given a choice; a new life with possibilities or the old life with more of the same. He made the right decision.

India Delta would be back, up and running, after a few weeks of being grounded for inspection.

No faults were found. The aircraft was stripped down and rebuilt to be sure. It was a mystery to the experts. *They* delayed its use. *They* questioned the pilot and asked him if he'd accidentally flicked the switch that tested the warning lights and alarms.

He insisted he hadn't.

Then they accused him of flicking the test switch, deliberately.

He angrily denied the accusation.

They asked him why he hadn't used the second dual-instrument panel that the aircraft was equipped with to check against the panel that was showing faults.

He told them it was his decision alone and his choice alone to react the way he did that night.

They couldn't argue with that, it was his prerogative.

The outcome showed nothing conclusive. No faults were detected. One aircraft technician quipped, *'it must have been an act of God.'* No-one took him seriously.

In the meantime, Sarge took a vacation the same time India Delta was being given a thorough check over so it could take to the skies again. He visited sunnier climes, took walks along the beach, sat by the pool and tried to get into a novel he'd been promising himself to read. He wasn't too keen on fiction, he preferred fact. But he tried to get into it. He found it difficult to chill-out and do little or nothing. He didn't like being out of touch with current affairs either. It made him feel isolated; not in control. So, he read the newspapers from back home; seems like there was a movement of like-minded people who were labelled as vigilantes, for a better word. Not the sort who get reported upon now and again; the stories where *locals* sorted out a local problem, a one-off. No, these were different. A smart freelance journalist, Ms. Bibby, had noticed crime was in fast decline, especially in Sarge's own city. It showed the first noticeable decline radiated out from his own police area to the rest of the city and then to neighbouring cities. It appeared to be sweeping the country. The reporter looked into why this was. She reported that individuals and small pockets of the public who had reached the end of their tether, were targeting criminal activity themselves, she suggested. She noticed that drug dealing had dropped dramatically and as a consequence other crime such as burglary, robberies, muggings and thefts had also fallen. She wrote that the public had finally lost trust and belief in the Government, Police and the judicial system to make and keep their world a good and safe place to live. And so, the public had taken matters into their own hands, like never before. The government, police and mainstream media tried their damnedest to demonise the caring, upstanding citizens. That's what they do. But many caved to the change. Main stream media had no choice than to report more facts – the truth, rather than the narrative the government preferred them to push.

Sarge, like the millions of others in the country, felt a radical change had been coming for quite some time. He read on with interest. It was in all of the papers, every day for a week. It listed incidents and gave short accounts of how society was regaining the streets and neighbourhoods, yet no-one really knew who was doing it; who was behind it. No-one had given themselves a collective name or took credit for the massive wind of change. The reporter likened the changed neighbourhoods to being like the times up until the 1940s but without the gloom of the World Wars hanging over it; a simpler, more pleasant time, where morals and the rights and wrongs of others were of importance.

Graphic maps of areas changed for the better were published. It showed incidents, crime trends and numbers of criminals targeted. There was terrific enthusiasm; the change was on everyone's lips. The comments of politicians and liberalists were dismissed when they tried to jump on the bandwagon for publicity and decry the events which were leading to a better place for all. The greater public didn't care about the local drug dealers who had been ambushed or the burglars who were laid in the hospital intensive care units. '*It was time for their very own human rights, not the criminals,*' they said, when they spoke to the newspapers. They had decided that the *system* was far too broken to be mended and besides it had fallen into such deep disarray, it was no longer fit for purpose. It had become almost meaningless, a charter for criminals and a way for smart lawyers to get rich at everyone else's expense.

Sarge was intrigued with what had suddenly been noticed back home. He had been aware of a change for some time but now it had gone public. *That can only be a good thing,* he thought. *Others around the country may follow suit even more so.*

One newspaper editor responded to the remarks of yet another politician in the clamour for publicity regardless, who supported the rights of the criminals. The editor replied by saying, 'The criminal gave up their rights the moment they abused the rights of another law-abiding citizen. The meek shall inherit the earth.' He went onto say that no-one should be excluded from retribution, including politicians, especially those who steal from the public purse under the guise they'd made an 'accounting error' or believed that buying something like a duck shelter with public money costing more than most people earn from a month's hard work, was reasonable expenses claim under the Expenses Rules. The corrupted had been going on decades.

The following days showed reports that the Government were doing their best to censor the newspapers from the kind of reporting they were publishing, just the same way they had done in the 1980s when cities up and down the country were hit with rioting from a dissatisfied and frustrated public. Politicians were not representing the people, only themselves and the real masters of government that hid in the background; big corporations, the ultra-rich elite – bankers too.

But there had been a change, the papers with a sense of morals continued to report the facts. In consequence the rate of change heightened and intensified. A theme that ran through the vigilante attacks was that they were clear and certain upon who was targeted and that *the Attackers*, or as some corrected, *the Defenders*, were anonymous or the one or two who had been apprehended were the most unlikely of people to be expected as a vigilante or Defender. They were ordinary everyday folk. The papers didn't know what name to give them. Normally they would have tried to demonise them with the label 'far-right.' They were not. They were ordinary hard-working people. They were supportive in what they did and, in that support, it was impossible to label them with a name that may detract from what they were doing. They weren't terrorists, though some likened them to urban mercenaries. When a criminal was attacked the papers referred to it as a 'sanction.' There were hundreds of sanctions every week, it was reported.

No-one professed to acting alone or as a group, it was a secret underground movement that had spontaneously evolved, reported one newspaper. *To give it a name could identify then castigate it. And no-one wanted that. 'Besides,'* said the paper, *'if it were given a name the Government would quickly outlaw it and its members in order to suppress it, as it did with the IRA.'* That was a contentious comment linking the IRA and with many it was becoming a hot potato. What was not in contention was that the country was slowly being reclaimed by right-thinking individuals who were good and had courage and belief.

The police and Government were concerned by the number of 'sanctions' and struggled to convince the media and the public that the very same people carrying out the sanctions were in fact breaking the law of the land and were no better than those they were attacking. The Government, although elected to represent its voters, were now a lone and selfish voice and not representative of their electorate. They had been given their chance to do what the public wanted but had failed, decade after decade, to deliver.

Sarge likened the change to the downfall of the great Roman Empire. Corruption, greed, self-interest and disregard to another's plight, was rife amongst the society of the 21st century. *Perhaps,* he thought, *the day of Rapture is what was happing right now.*

He knew he needed to get back but with just a few days of his vacation remaining he made best use of his time, given the current situation back home. He kept in regular contact with Poppy Beau Bibby. They had become more than just work colleagues.

He found himself making a call to Sterling Lines, Herefordshire, England, the home of Special Air Services and other special forces. The conversation was carefully worded even though it was a secure line and electronically encrypted. He knew *'big brother'* was everywhere and trusted nothing and no-one. He knew that over at British GCHQ that phone calls were monitored and recorded based upon specific voice recognition patterns, certain words and phone numbers. He arranged to meet the man on the other end of the line, *'in the usual place.'* They agreed on a time and date.

His vacation over, within a week he met with a lean man whose face was etched with the experience of an extraordinary life. He was sat at a table in the corner of an out of the way bar, his back to the wall. He faced the door so he could see all those entering and exiting. He subconsciously scanned everyone, analysed them and made a decision. It's what he'd learned to do most of his life; a habit. It had kept him alive on occasions. He was aware of the big guy mostly hidden almost out of sight behind a low partition casually watching him from the other side of the room, but chose to ignore him.

He clocked Sarge as soon as he entered. The men gave one another the slightest of nods as Sarge headed towards the crowded bar. He spotted the man behind the partition but chose to ignore him. He bought two beers and joined the man in the corner. He placed the drinks on the table along with a folded newspaper which he pulled from inside his jacket. They shook hands firmly without introduction and with just a low key, 'How you doing?' without waiting for a reply. There was an air of seriousness mixed with friendship and common purpose. Sarge sat facing him so his back was to the rest of the bar.

'Acta non verba,' said the man.

Yeah, acta non verba,' said Sarge, a little awkwardly.

The man detected it. 'You still enjoy being a sarge?' he asked, for the want of something better to say.

'Yeah, being a sarge is a good rank.' He sniffed, 'All the fun without the paperwork, matey.' He paused. 'So, how's life in Sterling lines? What you been up to?'

'It's still ok, not what it used to be. Up to? This and that. You know how it is.' The man diverted his eyes and sipped his drink a long while before placing his glass back on the table. 'Cheers, Sarge,' he said.

He nodded in acknowledgment.

Both men were a little on edge. They were aware of it and made small talk to calm things. They caught up on old times and had a few more drinks.

Once they'd caught up to speed they got down to business. 'You're doing a great job out there, matey.'

The man, somewhat embarrassed, took another long sip. 'Me?' He patted the folded newspaper. 'I thought you were responsible for all this. Seems like it's spread like wildfire.'

Sarge coughed nervously quickly glanced over his shoulder to make sure no one else was listening then leaned in. 'Well, I put all this down to you. Or down to you and your kind,' he said quietly.

The man shook his head. 'No. We do lots of things behind the scene, as you know, but this is nothing to do with us.'

'Are you sure, because they're so secretive they don't even have a name?'

'I'm sure. I'd have heard something. Besides, I've heard some of these vigilantes labelled with names like Repatriation, Avengers, Crime Slayers, Patriots even The Rapture and REVELATION. And that's not us,' he laughed. 'But what doesn't add up is for all that's going on, no-one actually knows who's doing it. Not even us. Some of your more extreme God botherers are claiming it's Divine intervention.'

'I don't know about any of that. But it does seem to have taken on a life of its own. It's getting out of hand. I don't know where it's going, with or without names? What I do know is that few are getting caught, coming forward with information or seeing anything. No-one seems to trust anyone anymore. Not only that, we had a couple of mystery guys use the Force chopper to try and catch one of these people or groups. It had to be grounded in an emergency, right at a crucial moment.' He sniffed. 'Wondered what you knew about it?' He looked for a reaction.

There wasn't one.

'You tell me, 'Said the man.

'You know something. We need to share here. Pool our knowledge.'

There was a short moment.

'Ok. It seems like *they* had a theory there was far more going on that could be explained. That's all I can say.'

'More going on? In what way? And who's, *They?*'

He took a long drink. It bought him some thinking time. He carefully put the glass back on the table. 'No. Sorry. Can't help you, Sarge. I don't know any more.'

'That won't work on me, you know that. How about Special Projects and supernatural stuff then?'

'Supernatural stuff?' The man pondered a moment. 'Ok,' he said. 'You obviously know more than you're letting on.' He nodded thoughtfully. 'Strictly between us. The mystery guys with the American accents and all the high-tech gear that went up in the chopper, they were Italians. I know that much.'

'Italians?'

'Nothing. Forget it. I shouldn't have said anything. It was just something I heard.'

'Are they part of your organization? Give me the whole story.'

'I heard they came over on behalf of The Vatican. That's all. Leave it at that.'

Sarge sniffed. 'That makes sense. I'd heard they spoke with American accents.' He thought awhile. 'You've got to give me more.' He demanded.

There was a moment.

The man sighed in resignation. 'Ok. I suppose I owe you. It seems like they investigate incidents that may have a supernatural origin or explanation. That's all I know.'

There was a long moment.

Sarge chewed. 'Sounds like the kind of smoke screen your lot would set up to cover things over.'

'Hysteria,' said the man. 'It's mass hysteria. That's what hysteria does.' He placed his hand on the newspaper. 'That's what's happening around the country right now.'

'Exactly the sort of thing the Organization has done in the past. I never know whether to believe anything these days, even you. Sometimes I think you're just yanking my chain.'

The man looked at Sarge, impassively and said nothing.

'I've got to say, there are some things about these so-called sanctions that puzzle me.' He sniffed.

'Oh Yeah?' he said, a little too eagerly.

Sarge noticed. He thought a moment. 'Yeah. Theres some elements of the events, *these sanctions*, that I can't explain.'

'Tell me more.'

Sarge leaned back, folded his arms and stared warily at him. 'No. No, I'll keep it to myself.'

The man smiled. 'Ok. I'll help you with it.' He leaned in. 'There are times when things happen and you can't find an explanation for it. Crucial, important moments which leave unanswered questions. Is that it?'

Sarge took a moment, then nodded cautiously.

'It's ok, you're not alone. There're others like you.'

He nodded again.

'You thought it was me or my kind right there with you in the shadows or just around the corner. Am I right?'

'Yeah,' He nodded. 'How come you know so much?'

He hesitated. 'As you used to say, Sarge, *it's my job to know*.'

Sarge laughed. 'You've kind of given the game away there, you knowing and all.'

'Yes. With your reply, so too have you. But no, it wasn't me or my team.'

Sarge sniffed. 'You'd deny it anyway.'

'Of course, the same way you would. But seriously, it's nothing to do with us. We're working loosely with the boys from The Vatican. And frankly, we're getting nowhere.'

Sarge frowned. 'Well, you would say that.'

'True. But you're not the only one out there that it's happened to, Sarge,' he said compassionately.

He looked uncomfortable and frowned some more. 'What are you talking about?'

The man took a long sigh. 'That feeling you get that you're not alone. That on certain occasions someone's walking with you, on your side, helping you; guiding you. Like an omnipresence.' he smiled, 'We've known each other a long time. You can talk to me about it.'

'Yeah. Sure,' he laughed. 'And the next thing is I'll be waking up in some asylum.'

At that moment a couple of guys entered the bar through the main entrance. One carried a small dark backpack over his shoulder. They were smart and had an unusual presence. As much as they tried to blend in, they appeared a little *out of place* in such surroundings.

The big guy behind the partition noticed immediately and sat to attention as though he'd been switched from standby mode to ON. The lean man sat across the table to Sarge clocked them but gave little away in body language that indicated he'd spotted them. Only a slight flicker of his eyes gave him away; had anyone been quick enough or near enough to catch it.

They briefly glanced around as they went over to the bar. They ordered drinks, stood and chatted; American accents with a slight foreign twang.

They seemed normal enough and not an immediate threat. The big guy slipped back into standby mode. It was impossible to tell whether the lean man did. He was difficult to read.

The man changed the subject slightly. 'The other thing about all this, Sarge, is this Ms. Bibby woman. She's your typical journalist-type. Much of what she's written is fiction, based on some embellished truths. The facts don't support all her claims. Sure, there's been a few copy-cat vigilantes perhaps, but not on the scale she's reported. That said, it's had a dramatic effect on crime, for sure. So that part's fairly true. Some other journalists have jumped on the bandwagon with her.'

'Yes, they're all the same these journalists and newspapers. You never know what to believe. Mostly they push the government narrative.'

Conversation between Sarge and the lean man drifted onto other matters, a change of subject; the more regular stuff.

The night past, it was soon time to leave. Sarge glanced at his wristwatch, quickly drained the contents of his glass, stood up and pulled his jacket to. Popped in some fresh gum. 'I've got to go.' He chewed. 'Nice meeting up with you, matey. Go careful out there and keep in touch.' He winked.

The lean man wasn't surprised by the suddenness of him needing to leave. 'Will do, Sarge. Look after yourself,' he said casually, 'Happy days.'

'Yeah. You too. And don't forget, by next week there'll be an eye in the sky again.' He chewed.

The man frowned. 'Roger that.'

Sarge turned and headed for the door. On the way out he passed the big guy sat partly behind the partition. They made eye contact. Sarge raised his eyebrows, is all. Any casual observer would not have noticed. The other guy made no response, he popped in some gum.

A few seconds later and the lean man headed for the exit. He looked around outside for Sarge, but he'd gone. The man set off with purpose in his stride. The big guy saw him pass the bar's windows. He headed outside too. He followed the man some distance behind, just enough to keep him in view. It led him to an alley at the rear of the bar.

A moment later, the *out of place guys with American accents,* left via the rear door. A large figure, hidden in the shadows, watched as one of the guys pulled out a sophisticated looking piece of equipment similar to a camera, from his backpack. The other got onto his cell phone and spoke hushed and urgently. At the same time a grey unmarked helicopter four miles away received instructions to scramble. It took to the skies and headed in. The guys took a brief moment to speak in Latin, crossed themselves then set off with purposeful pace into the passages and alleyways. Ahead of them was Sarge. A moment later and they'd lost sight of him. They weren't too concerned. They upped their pace and soon regained sight of the lone figure.

The big guy in the shadows chewed slowly and waited a moment before setting off in the opposite direction. He was joined by a much smaller man; lean They walked briskly as though on a mission.

Three minutes later and the helicopter was in position not far from the bar. It hovered, unseen; unnoticed in the night sky. Its thermal imaging and night vision cameras scanning every detail below. Suddenly, a figure weaving its way through the alleyways was picked up on its screens. Closely behind were two other figures, one carried a small object. The cameras zoomed in. They'd found what they were looking for; the *record* button was pressed. Less than a minute later the lone figure, ahead of the other two, emerged into a parking lot then stopped. It waited a moment before climbing over a fence then crouched, as though hiding. The operator monitoring the screen relayed the information via a cell phone to one of the two men on the ground nearby.

The two figures increased their pace immediately. The chopper operatives continually updated the men on the ground. Within seconds they were just around the corner to the crouching figure. They waited.

A long two and a half minutes passed.

The eye in the sky held position. They watched the screen. The lone figure behaved as though checking his wristwatch and looking back in the direction he had just come from.

More information was relayed to the two men nearby. One circled around stealthily towards the crouching figure then stopped only yards away.

Four more minutes passed without change.

The lone figure stood up and started towards some parked vehicles, glancing around as it went. It got into one of the vehicles and drove off. The helicopter followed, its cameras recording every second of the journey. They zoomed in on the illuminated registration plate. They knew within seconds who the vehicle was registered to. It headed over to the other side of the city. The aircraft covertly followed. Those on board believed the driver would have been oblivious to their presence.

Eight minutes later, emergency vehicles with flashing lights, sirens wailing, were converging on a location not far from the bar. The helicopter received a call, banked hard over, dropped altitude to head that way, full throttle.

Almost twelve minutes later and Sarge was at Poppy's apartment. She wasn't home. He knew that. He had his own key so let himself in. A log fire was burning. He threw on a few more sticks that were laid on the hearth. He watched it and waited a moment. It blazed. He looked at his watch then went into the kitchen and prepared a couple of drinks. He took them over to the sofa and sat down. He was anxious and chewed hard. His eyes flitted between his wristwatch and the door. It seemed an age. Suddenly the door swung open. In walked Poppy carrying a bulging refuse bag containing some garments. She placed it on the fire then joined him on the sofa. He passed her a drink.

She sipped, 'How did it go?' She asked.

He looked serious; concerned. 'Not sure. He's hard to read.' His expression morphed into a smile 'I think they all swallowed it, hook, line and sinker.'

'Really?'

'Really!'

They couldn't contain their relief, they burst into laughter.

After a while she said, 'So we've pulled it off?' looking for reassurance.

He nodded, 'Seems that way. We've fooled them all.' They hugged. 'You're a good cop and an even better journalist, Ms. Bibby.'

'So too are you, Sarge.'

They both sat back. 'Just goes to show, the power of the pen is mightier than the sword.'

'Well, just as mighty as the sword, perhaps.' She smiled. 'We both have our gifts in equal measures. I think we're quite blessed.'

'Perhaps we are, perhaps we are.' He became solemn, 'One thing that bothers me.'

'Oh, yes? What's that? Who's the pen and who's the sword?' She laughed.

'No. The supernatural element to all this. He knew something about it, yet that was never reported. So where did he get that from? I thought that was between you and me. And The Vatican guys, who called them in?'

She kept a blank face, made no reply.

He cupped his drink with both hands and stared into it a moment. She looked on. 'Weird stuff happens out there that I can't explain,' he said. 'I'm not quite sure what that's about. I used to think it was coincidence.' He paused, 'Or someone covering my back, such as you or Roy.' He took a moment. 'Sometimes I have my own belief of what it is.' He glanced at her for a reaction.

There wasn't one.

'Some really strange things happen out there,' he said, becoming more upbeat. 'Maybe I'm just losing my mind. What do you make of it? What do you think?'

She thought a moment. 'Perhaps not coincidence but Godincidence, perhaps?' She suggested, with a half-smile.

He stared thoughtfully at her. 'Yes, perhaps? Perhaps it is.'

She saw his worried expression and took his hands in both of hers. She smiled at him like a mother would a child.

He looked deep into her eyes a long moment. 'You know I have difficulty trusting anyone, Poppy B. Don't ever let me down; that's all.'

She lost her smile and found it difficult to keep eye contact. 'Don't worry, Sarge. I haven't so far, have I?'

He shrugged.

She glanced away towards the fire.

He noticed. The bag and contents were well ablaze. 'I know the answer but I've got to ask, how did your side of things go tonight?'

She jumped up, stepped over to the fire and stoked it. 'It was ok.' Her voice was shaky.

He detected it. 'Are you ok?'

She kept her focus on the fire. 'You know me, Sarge. I do what I have to do, same as you.' She paused. 'Tonight, was for Sue and all the others. That's what I tell myself. That's how I deal with it.'

'Well at least your sister had some quality time down in London, living the high-life with her daughter right until the very end. And you were pretty instrumental in helping her with that. It was a good thing you did. Always remember that.'

She turned to face him. A tear rolled down her cheek. She quickly wiped it away with the back of her hand. She didn't want him to see it.

He went over to her and held her tight.

'Someone told me the way they deal with bad things from the past, trauma and the like, is not to dwell on it,' he said softly, 'Because you can't change it. You can't change what's already happed.'

'I know that. But how do you stop missing someone?

'You don't, you learn to live with it. Where she is, she's found peace and that's what you've got to do, here amongst the living. You have to do whatever it takes.'

'How can I?' She broke away and stepped backwards a pace. 'Look, truth is, I don't know if I can do this anymore.'

'You need to keep strong, keep your faith. What about all that stuff you used to bash on about, *an eye for an eye,* and all that?'

'I know. And *a tooth for a tooth*. But it doesn't make it right, does it?' She was shaking.

'I don't know what's right or wrong anymore, Poppy. But I do know that there are people out there who need protecting.' He chewed. 'Ok, what about, *the meek shall inherit the earth*, then?'

'And what about, *vengeance is mine, says the Lord?*'

'Vengeance?' he asked. 'His and not ours, you mean? Well, vengeance is one thing. Maybe we're His instruments?'

'What about, *thou shalt not kill?*'

He paused. 'I don't know about any of that. And maybe you're right. You're the one who knows all about this stuff. Me, I just do what I believe in, what I believe is the right thing to do.'

'Some say, forgiveness is greater.'

There was a moment.

He nodded thoughtfully. 'Perhaps it's time for you to forgive and get on with your own life.'

'I want to, but I have so much hate inside.'

'Now hate is something I do know about. I carried hate in my heart a lot of years. One day I woke up and realized that my hate was only hurting me, every day. The person I hated wasn't affected by how I felt, so I let it go. Just like that. Since then, it's not within me to hate these days. I can't do it.'

Softly she said. 'Perhaps you get rid of your hate in other ways.'

'Perhaps I do Poppy B. Perhaps I do.'

Across the other side of the city the Police carnival was about to roll into town; fifteen detectives, uniforms, scenes of crime with Crecon 2 and a dozen vehicles. The *star attraction* topping the bill was one less drug dealer now devoid of life, laid face down in a dark alleyway. Two figures had been seen running away but no-one came forward to report in writing. '*They didn't want to get involved.*'

Sarge's phone rang as the carnival gathered momentum. It was *the job. They* briefed him about the incident and called him out to assist. He told them he'd be there within thirty minutes then hung up.

He prepared to leave her place. Poppy told him to take care.

He told her he would and that *the star attraction would be a mess*, then added, *he imagined*. He went on, *but he'd be having a terrific Kairos moment*. He laughed to himself.

She looked serious and frowned. 'I'm concerned for you. I think it's time to end it.'

He chinned the air. 'End what? Us?'

'No, silly. It. Or at least think about winding it down for a while.'

'Look, I've got to go. We'll talk about it another time.' He looked over at the fire. 'Make sure it's all burnt without a trace. Then get rid of the ashes, away from here.'

She told him she knew what she was doing. They said their goodbyes and he was gone.

Less than 30 minutes later, he was on the latest case. It was another long shift, full of miscommunications, false leads and individuals who couldn't care less. Chaos and inefficiency reigned but no-one would ever admit to that.

Meanwhile, down at the morgue with the pathologist, another corpse was being sliced and diced; looking for clues. And a whole team was imputing data into computers in the hope they would spit out some answers. Crecon2 was part of that, it was on overload. The basic street cop using his grey-matter was fast becoming a thing of the past but no-one noticed and no-one cared. They only cared about not being sued or criticized at some later date for negligence or errors in the investigation. Many reputations and promising careers had been wrecked by Official Inquiries and lawyers using *hindsight* and *the power of suggestion* many years after cases were closed. Partly because of that the emphasis had switched from catching the real villains; murderers, robbers and rapists, to covering the backs of the Force and those individuals within it. Partly because of that, the reliance on the use of computers to come up with the answers was preferable to it being a human responsibility. That way, when the huge finger of blame was to be pointed, it was pointed at *the system*; the technology, computers; Crecon and its cousins. It was a win - win situation for the Establishment and those incompetents with a severe case of Promotion Fever.

The following night, four Italians were suddenly recalled to Rome along with their equipment and recordings; Police attending the scene of the deceased dealer had discovered who two of them were. They were instructed to tell no-one. They used an unusual, sophisticated-looking camera apparatus soon after the police attended the scene. Someone from high-up had authorized them to be there, to be given free access.

Somehow the local TV media also found out and broadcast the information. *A spokesperson for The Vatican denied all knowledge of the men,* it was reported. *They said they were nothing to do with them.* The police and the Government followed suit in their denials. They were concerned that stories of the supernatural and The Vatican becoming involved would only fan the winds of change.

The denials served to fuel the speculation further. It strengthened the hysteria. This angered some officials. It pleased others.

A week later, the carnival wound down. As usual there were no identifiable suspects even though no-one was discounted, not even Sarge. He was put under the spot-light. *They* questioned him and suggested he was somehow linked to the incident involving the dead dealer.

They knew he was in *the area* that night, they said. *They* didn't say how they knew.

He used his *rights* and refused to comment.

They never told him so, but the camera footage from a helicopter *that night* gave him an airtight alibi. *They* knew that.

Sarge knew that. He never told them so.

It was a short interview but *they* had to show willing; *for the record.* They, *covered their backs.*

Sarge believed that merely, *covering their back's,* was never going to catch anyone. He believed that no-one would ever be caught.......

'All I have is a voice
To undo the folded lie,
The romantic lie in the brain
Of the sensual man-in-the-street
And the lie of Authority
Whose buildings grope the sky;
There is no such thing as the State
And no one exists alone;
Hunger allows no choice
To the citizen or the police;
We must love one another,
or die.'

W. H. Auden.
September 1, 1939.

ARNIE EXEL

FOR THE LOVE OF MIKE

You may identify with some of the things within the following pages.
You may even relate to some of the story.
You might find some comfort and strength from what you read or you may know someone else who might. If you do, or even if just one person finds some solace, then it was all worthwhile.

For many, Christmas can be a magical, happy and joyous time.
A time to remember the religious account from two thousand years ago; of Wise men, Angels and a guiding star, foretold events that led to an extraordinary birth.
For many it's an occasion for family and friends to come together, to show love and affection; to celebrate.
It's often a time to reflect upon the past where emotions can be heightened.
For some it can be lonely, sad, depressing and even fatal…..

#Love.

Quote by Pierre Chardin 1881-1955……..

'Love is the most powerful and still most unknown energy in the world.'

------   ------   ------

'Never forget that the most powerful force on Earth is love.'

…...quote by Nelson Rockefeller.

Dedicated to the memory, principles and faith of:

Shahbaz Bhatti.

Born: Lahore, Punjab, 9th September 1968.
Federal Minister for Minorities.
Pakistan.

Assassinated: 2nd March 2011.

And

to all those who seek to make the world a safer, more harmonious place where freedom, rights and justice are the foundations of their ambitions.

Also

to the people who fight on the side of righteousness

And

for all those who have been scarred, maimed or who have lost their lives in the struggle and for all their loved ones left behind.

Along with and particularly for: -

all of the 'Andy's' of this world.

#The phrase: -

'For the love of Mike.'

In word study this kind of phrase is called a minced oath.
To mince your words means **'to choose words so as not to offend anyone.'**
This particular expression began as a substitute for an outcry of surprise or anger, namely**, "for the love of God!"** But the speaker decided that using God's name in this way was blasphemous and therefore decided to substitute something else for the word God. In this case, **St. Michael.**

St. Michael is the patron saint of warriors and soldiers and he looks after them on the battlefield.

And so the phrase began, **"for the love of Michael."**
It was a **soldier's** mild curse.

St. Michael the Archangel is the chief of the heavenly host, the celestial army that defends the Church. He fights the rebel angels and the dragon of Revelations.
He is patron saint of knights and of all trades allied to the production of weapons.

Indeed, the word archangel in its original Greek means literally 'chief' (Greek, arkhos) + 'angel' (Greek, aggelos literally 'messenger' of God). In later ecclesiastical Greek the two roots meld to form arkhaggelos 'angel of the highest order.'
(Bill Castleman)

God.

If God does not exist, everything is permissible:
(Fyodor Dostoevsky).

THINK ABOUT THAT.

Introduction.

What is love? We all have it in our lives, whether it's from or for another person or even a creature like a cat or a dog.
Intangible things such as an experience, a memory, a song, scenery and so-on, are all capable of being loved.
Love is such a powerful word; it is said that it's easier to have sex with someone than tell them you love them, if in fact you don't.
It's such a powerful emotion. We're surrounded by it. We see it all the time.
We take it for granted; we cherish it. We want it; we reject it. We need it; we don't. We love it; we hate it.
It affects all of us daily. Its capabilities and effects are endless. It can be the most wonderful thing that brings extreme happiness and joy. It can dispel loneliness and it can bring loneliness. It can seem clear; confusing, dull or bright.
There's good love and bad love, proper love and wrong love. It can be toxic, nourishing, controlling, liberating, disappointing, exciting, boring, scary, safe, dangerous, thrilling; it can be all these things at once and more.
It can be the best and the most inspiring feeling in the world; it's equally capable of being the darkest and the most destructive of things. It can bring pain, heartache, sadness and despair. It can break hearts; it can mend hearts. It can save lives but it can also lead to suicide and even murder.

Being in love can be truly wonderful. Life its self can seem more wonderful when we're in love. When we're not in love or when we lose it, life may not seem so wonderful at all.

Love can be the catalyst for the creation of a new life but it can also be responsible for the taking of a life. And that can happen in a split second.

Love is always just round the corner. It's strong; it's fickle; it's rare; it's common; it's fleeting, long-lasting, it's perennial.

We all think we know what it is, but do we? Can we really recognize it? Is it learned? Where does it come from? Is it the same for everyone?

Love is not essential for life; though some believe it is. Indeed, love can be overwhelming and fill us with all we desire.

When feeling unloved, perhaps the mere hope of it sometime in the future is what is sustaining.
The idea of being loved and giving love at some point is perhaps what gives us strength and drives us on. But when that idea is no longer with us then the world can seem a cold, dark, hostile and empty place.
Yet those with a belief in God may be comforted through their times of anguish to

know that they are forever loved by Him just as a father loves his child. And that His love is eternal and unconditional.

Ah, the love for another person, a lover, can be most joyous and so beautiful. But is that love something worth losing something precious for, such as family and friends, your mind or even your life when that person takes their love away or betrays the love you shared? It's a very sad fact that some do end their lives; a last, desperate, final act that is so futile, and well, so final. If only they knew that it only hurts those who truly loved them and that love springs eternal.

Some people who've had near death experiences say that 'they've seen their lives flash before them.' They say that 'the things that stood out in those moments, was the people they loved and events connected with love and that their life seemed all about love.' They saw their lives as 'laced with love; love and life intertwined.'
    Love and life; perhaps some feel one cannot exist without the other.

One thing for sure is although we may not know it and sometimes, we may forget it; we all have love within us and we are all loved, yes everyone single one of us.

    What is life?
    What is love?

#Bibliography.

New Testament.: The Gideons International.

Wikipedia: World Wide Web

Kairos Time: Donna J Kazenske.

THE TRILOGY

Book One -   THE KAIROS CLOCK.

Book two -   FORTHE LOVE OF MIKE.

Book three -   REVELATION.

Printed in Great Britain
by Amazon